Strawberry Fields

Maxwell Kite

Contents

To the family and friends who helped me get here.

For the musically-inclined

If you'd like to enjoy Blake's classical playlist alongside the book, you can follow this QR code:

Blake's Super Awesome Classical Playlist

Chapter One

Mendelssohn's "Rondo Capriccioso"

The things that impress Blake Fields can be listed as the following:

1. An expert pianist performing Chopin,

2. His mother's home cooking, and

3. A werewolf who can actually keep their damn nose out of his business.

In no conceivable way could he include his current situation on that list. See, that's the thing about werewolves. Even the ones with the most diluted bloodlines can't resist taking a whiff when an omega strolls by. And Blake—twenties, blond, and with that desperate look in his eyes that only comes from a life lived hand to mouth—happens to be a prime target. That's the other thing about werewolves, particularly alphas: in Blake's estimation, it's always dick first, brain cells later, and it's exactly what he doesn't need today.

'Today' being late morning at The Wagging Tail, a café on the outskirts of downtown with two specialties: lattes and skimpy server outfits. He hadn't planned to take a job three-quarters of the way to stripping, but life has a way of leading you down a path paved with broken promises, and sometimes when you open the fridge to make yourself dinner, all you come up with is stale orange juice and week-old instant mashed potatoes, and you know what? That's as good as gold when you have no higher education and your mom's practically on life support.

Whew. A mouthful, which is more than he ate for breakfast.

No, this situation does not rank on Blake's Wishlist For Success, trademark pending; in fact, you could say it belongs in the dumpster with expired mayonnaise, the last season of that show based on that book you liked—you know the one—and Blake's dignity.

Ten minutes ago, an alpha broad-shouldered enough to take up the entire half of one of Blake's booths sidled in and ordered a black coffee, eyes the color of rusted cast iron and nose as flat as if he'd broken it in three places at once and it just gave up and stopped putting itself out there. Then he proceeded to stare so openly and sourly at Blake without blinking that Blake was pretty sure his coffee would curdle.

Then, as Blake is passing the receipt over (probably not getting tipped on this one), the alpha snatches his tight shirt and jerks him so hard that he careens over the table and nearly sends the sugar flying.

Fight-or-flight mode engaged.

"Who knows you're here?" hisses Flat Nose in a thick accent as his other hand encircles Blake's wrist and squeezes. Blake barely hears him over the roar of panic in his skull as he twists to get away, but the alpha's grip is uncompromising.

"Sir—" he starts to say, attempting to maintain a level of professionalism that, frankly, this place doesn't deserve, but the man pulls him closer, and their noses would be touching, if the alpha's wasn't so flat.

At this distance, Blake gets a faceful of the man's personal aroma, a wilting bouquet of cigarettes and acetone. He nearly gags but manages to control himself enough to pull that little tug of instinct in his mind that controls his pheromones. *Calm,* he pushes out around himself. *Stand down.*

It's almost always enough to get people to do what he wants. He's an omega, after all, and he's spent his adult life dodging alphas and betas tripping over themselves to get to him. Plus, it comes with the territory when you're—

The man twists his wrist so hard that Blake yipes.

"Hey!" A baritone voice calls from behind Blake. Someone at the counter. Another alpha. A tall shadow falls over them both, but Blake can barely get a look at the guy from this angle. Not that he wants someone to step in; the last thing he needs is for two alphas to draw blood on his behalf.

This stupid café really needs bouncers.

"It's fine," Blake grinds out between his teeth, releasing another wave of pheromones. "Please, just go—"

"It's not fine," the new alpha snaps. "He's hurting you." Then, to Flat Nose: "Let him go."

"Stay out of this, you—"

Blake snatches the half-empty coffee cup from the table and flings it into his aggressor's face. The man howls and rears back, dropping his hold and clawing at his eyes. Blake dodges back and puts the newcomer between the two of them, clutching his wrist to his pounding chest.

The new alpha—taller than them both by at least a head—grabs the other and yanks him from the booth.

"Get your hands off me, you filthy *nevolk*!"

Blake doesn't know what the word means, but the tone says it all. To punctuate the statement, Flat Nose cocks his arm back and hooks a punch straight for new guy's face. Blake flinches, expecting the crunch of bones—not a lovely thing at 11 a.m.—but tall alpha blocks with a forearm and throws a retaliation jab. Now something does crunch, and the odds don't look great for Flat Nose and his sinuses.

Blood in the air. Not the best with werewolves around. The other customers are practically salivating at the display. *God, don't let them be fullbloods*, Blake thinks. If somebody shifts right here and now and sends fur flying, he may as well get a head start on the unemployment line.

"What's going on?" A sharp voice calls from the doorway to the back office.

Ack. Mr. Garcia, proprietor and shorter-than-average alpha with an inferiority complex as obvious as his hair plugs, stands glaring at the scene.

"It's nothing," Blake insists, waving his hands as though he might magic it all away. "They were just leaving." He shoots a look at them both, and tall alpha takes the hint. He shoves Flat Nose toward the door.

"Fields. Office." Mr. Garcia snaps it like a trainer to a dog, and every fiber of Blake's being bristles with the urge to spit on the man's shoes and storm out. But then he remembers his mom, the promise he made to her, and the fire dies before it can kindle. He slinks toward the door, head down.

As he steps into the cramped office and the door swings shut, he hears a scuffle and shouts, followed by Garcia roaring, "Out! Out, both of you!" He lingers, standing in the middle of the room while the commotion dies down, and stares blankly at a photograph on Garcia's desk—a shot taken at some party not years ago, but embarrassingly recent, where Garcia is holding a beer, a woman underneath either arm, and what looks like a guy in stilettos bent over at the waist, hands on knees in front.

Damn, he needs to find a job with an HR department.

The office door bangs open and Garcia huffs in, face red all the way to his plugs, and he detours to the mini-fridge for a diet cola before plopping into his creaky chair. He pops the tab, and a hiss fills the air between them followed by the smell of fake sugar. He pulls a long sip before settling Blake with a stare hard enough to crack molars.

"What is it with you, Fields?"

"Must be my boyish charm," Blake responds before he can stop himself. "Men can't keep their hands off me."

Garcia drops the soda to the desk harder than necessary and says, "I never had a peep of trouble before you. Give you the bell, and suddenly there's fights in here every weekend."

Blake grimaces at the reference to the choker all the servers wear—a black velvet strap with an obnoxious bell that tingles with every step. He grumbles, "Not every weekend."

"Go home." Garcia takes another sip. "Get your pheromones under control and come back Monday."

Icy horror splashes in his guts. "But I have a shift tomorrow!"

"Not anymore." He draws again from the soda. "Get it together. This is your last chance."

He should say something. Tell Garcia about his mom in the care home, about his empty fridge or about the phone bill he's not sure he can pay this month. The shattered dreams that clang in his head like an out-of-tune piano. But it all dries up inside his throat and his shoulders sag. It wouldn't do any good. Garcia is an alpha, and the last thing any of them care about is other people. He slinks away to the locker room to change, the sound of Garcia burping following him out.

***

Sunlight blinds Blake as he steps out of the café into the city, and he ducks his head and pulls his shoulder bag up higher in a rush to put as much distance as possible between himself and the site of his disgrace. He hooks a corner and leans against a brick wall papered with fliers about the current war. His stomach lurches at the stern face of Mikhail Volkov, king of Servos across the sea from here. He rips one down in a futile display of autonomy, tearing it into as many tiny pieces as he can manage.

Around him, life buzzes in Remun City. Honking stop-and-go traffic, blinking crosswalks, a sea of digital billboards urging the masses to *buy, buy, buy* anything from the latest mech companions to virility supplements. People crowd every sidewalk and alleyway, alphas, proud heads held high and a swagger in their step, betas, the majority of the populace with their subdued aromas and general amiability, and omegas, the lowest of ranks and, in werewolf terms, easy prey. The weather is remarkably clear—Remun City, on the west coast of Atlas (formerly the US of A), spends most of the year lashed with rain, but this early spring day is tainted only by the smell of exhaust and sweat that clings inexorably to the city. It burns Blake's nostrils as strongly as that flat-nosed alpha's acetone scent.

He wipes his face like it might clear the stink away and tries to problem solve his way out of this situation. No work for the rest of the day or tomorrow. That means being down at least one bill. The power bill was late last month, so maybe this month he can squeeze out some pity from the landlord. He sticks the tip of his thumb under a canine as he thinks and chews at it. Maybe he can snag a last-minute gig mopping tables or scrubbing dishes somewhere. It would be better than—

"Hey!" A deep voice cuts into his thoughts, rising over the city's car horns and construction. Blake jerks his head around. Jogging toward him is a familiar muscular profile. The second alpha, the one who'd stepped in and punched Flat Nose, makes his way across a street and waves.

Nope.

Blake heel turns and breaks into a sprint. Not today. Not now. Not ever. He makes it to the next crosswalk before the man catches up.

"Hey, wait!"

Blake fidgets desperately in a pocket for some pepper spray. It has to be here somewhere.

"I'm in a hurry. My friend's expecting me," he lies in a rush. Got to peel this guy off him. He switches to the other pocket before realizing with a waxing horror that his pepper spray is in his jacket back at the café. Idiot.

"Whoa, it's cool. I'm not going to try anything, all right?" The alpha puts both hands up in front of him, palms out. He tilts his head to one side to expose his neck, a classic sign of deference.

Blake ignores him to stare straight ahead, tapping one hand on his bag's strap as the traffic light flicks to red and the cars grind to a halt. The people around them press forward in a mass, always more concerned with where they're going than where they are, and Blake propels himself away from the street, barely short of running, beelining for the subway.

"Look, I'm not trying to cause you trouble." The alpha keeps pace with him. Must be easy with those long legs. "That asshole grabbed something from you. I want to give it back."

Blake sighs and slows to a stop beside a red neon sign advertising ramen. The smell of pork, salt, and seaweed wafts out of the curtains, and Blake's mouth fills with saliva. He swallows and faces tall alpha, crossing his arms and putting on his best war face.

"Here." The alpha holds something at arm's length, and a flash of sliver chain catches the light.

Well, shit. Blake drops his frown like a hot plate and sucks in a breath. His pendant! He grabs the collar of his shirt even though he knows it won't be there. He can't believe he didn't notice it was missing. Guilt flares now, and the alpha might see it in his expression, because he forces a smile and motions for Blake to take the necklace.

"Thank you." Blake barely gets the words out. All he can see is his mom's face, shrouded in disappointment. If she remembers it exists, she'd be so upset. Although lately she hardly remembers *he* exists.

He reaches for the pendant, half expecting the alpha to snatch it away at the last second, but it drops solidly into his fingers, and he exhales a breath he didn't realize he's been holding. He tears his eyes from the insignia to finally get a proper look at the man who's saved him twice now, and all the feeling dissolves from his tongue.

To Blake, men fall into two categories:

1. Sleazeballs who are better off left far, far away, and

2. Handsome, charismatic ones who should be kept even farther away.

This guy isn't just category two, he's a category all to himself: 3. Trouble, capital T.

He wears gray sweats, which barely conceal his broad shoulders and muscular build. The guy must do a hundred reps of everything a day, and the pull of the fabric on his chest and biceps tells the tale of someone who starts each morning with a double shot of protein powder. A tattoo peeks out of the cuff on his right sleeve, a tease of something more, and a ponytail tames a shaggy head of shoulder-length hair. Blake tears his eyes from his build—best not to be caught gawking—and gets a hit of magazine-worthy charm. Stubble shades the alpha's cheeks, like he'd just rolled out of bed that morning and knew he looked good enough not to shave. Flecks of gold gleam in his deep brown eyes—a sure sign he descends from a fullblood line of alphas. Blake wonders if the guy can shift to wolf form. Not everybody can, and he beats away the impulse to ask. He does, however, take a deep breath to get a lungful of the alpha's personal scent. Grass after a fresh rain, earthy and comforting.

Yep. Trouble.

He tears his eyes from the man and focuses on the pendant. The titillation of his new acquaintance leaches from his body as he realizes the clasp is broken. Stupid Flat Nose snapped it clean off. Must have been when he got hold of Blake's shirt. The pendant itself seems undamaged, but the chain is now short several links with no ends to connect.

Blake sucks in a breath, but his lungs cramp, and it lodges in his throat. Don't panic. Take a breath. Easy in. But the air doesn't want to come, and all he can imagine is his mom's face the day she'd given him the necklace, strained and already older than her years, fighting for her life against an unseeable, unknowable enemy.

"Whoa, hey, it's all right." The man doesn't reach for him but holds both hands out like he wants to. "I noticed it, too. Not a big deal. Easy fix, you know?"

Not that some alpha would know anything about it. Blake replies in a flat voice, "Look. I appreciate your help, but I'm done with today. I just want to go home and sleep, so could you leave me alone forever now?"

"I can fix it," the alpha urges. "Or, anyway, I know someone who can."

"You do?" It's out before he can stop himself. Better not to walk this path. Better to stay away, find some means of fixing it himself, than rely on someone else for help. Especially an unfamiliar alpha. But the urge to see it in one piece again tugs at his conscience like a lingering melody.

"My packmate," the alpha says. "He's good with this kind of stuff. His shop's a few blocks from here, if you don't mind walking it."

Blake clicks his tongue. He can't afford a jeweler and wouldn't even know where to start fixing it himself. Another memory flashes: his mom, silhouetted at a piano, silver nestled in her clavicle. The promises he'd pledged. Guilt burns his throat like bile. Some things are worth the risk.

"All right. But my friend is waiting for me. This better be quick."

The alpha grins, and the smile lights up his whole face like the midday sun. Blake glances away as the feeling in his tongue dissipates again. It's got to be the alpha's scent that's making his head so light. It's the only logical reason. Obviously.

Oblivious to Blake's thoughts, the alpha falls into step beside him and proclaims, "Name's Jay." His voice is deep enough to resonate over the bustling city.

"Blake." Jay has to lean closer to hear him, and a whiff of soft earth plays in his nostrils. He's not doing this. Not after years lived alone, instincts aching for a pack. Today is not the day he crumbles. He clenches his fists.

"Nice. Sorry again about that jackass. Smelled like he didn't have a mate, but that's no excuse."

No, it's not. Weird to hear another alpha say so. "Thanks," Blake says, trying to keep things polite, to keep Jay at arm's length. "For stepping in. You got kicked out for me."

"Eh, I don't think that was really my kind of place anyway. I just wanted some coffee, and it was on the way." Jay flashes that easy smile, and Blake's head goes numb. "What's it like working at an omega café? Do you like it?"

He snorts. "Hell no. Boss is an ass, and so are the customers. Well, most of them." He returns Jay's smile, the numbness in his head dulling out the warnings. This is dangerous. Cut out now and go home. But he finds himself talking again.

"So, Jay the Alpha, what kind of guy are we going to see? Who makes the cut as your packmate?" He can't help the playful tone in his voice. Something is clearly very wrong with him. Damn werewolf pheromones.

"Why? You applying for the honor?" Jay tips him a wink.

Oh god, they're flirting. Stop it. Abort. *Abort.* Yet somehow his mouth is still moving.

"Curious about my savior, that's all." He feigns innocence. "It's not every day at work an omega gets fought over."

"Well, not every omega is worth the fight." Jay's smile broadens as they exchange lines.

He gets the sense that Jay is the sort of man who would fight for anyone's honor, and suddenly the cooler spring weather feels a thousand degrees hotter.

"But to answer your question," Jay continues, "the guy we're going to see is good with his hands. I guess you could say fixing the little things is his forte."

A packmate that's good with his hands has exactly one meaning in this day and age.

He fights the urge to ask if they're a Thing. He's pretty sure that's how packbonding works. As if he would know. A lifetime without a pack leaves a lot of details in the dark, and school textbooks and romance novels hardly parse the specifics.

"And what about you?" Blake dares to ask. "Are you..." *Don't say 'good with your hands'. Don't say 'good with your hands'.* "...good with your hands?" *You suck.*

Jay laughs aloud and delivers an equally corny line, waggling his eyebrows to complete the smarm. "Baby, I'm the best."

They laugh together at that one. Somehow it feels like the ten minutes they've known each other is more akin to ten years.

Danger, whispers that little voice again. You have to stay away. Stay alone. He shoves it aside.

"You'd better tell me about yourself if I'm following you downtown. People might talk, and I have a chaste reputation to uphold."

"Oh yeah? Never heard of a saint working at an omega café. Who's talking?"

Blake rolls his eyes playfully. "Oh, you know, all two people in my life. I'm quite the social butterfly."

"Ooh, let me guess. Nights reading under the blankets with a flashlight and..." He taps his chin as he considers it. "Love songs. Those country ones about broken hearts."

Blake laughs. "One for two. Reading under the blankets, definitely. Country music not so much. I'm more of a classical guy. You know, 'Eine Kleine'." He gestures as though conducting a baton.

"Ah, we'll have to differ on that account, but I won't hold it against you. Promise." The twinkle in his eye and small smirk are infectious. Even if he doesn't appreciate the finer points of Mozart.

"My turn to take a guess. You can bench press your body weight, and you watch action movies." He holds up a finger to interrupt Jay's retort. "But you secretly love rom coms."

Jay's turn to bark a laugh. "How about I leave that to mystery? I'll give you this tidbit though: last flick I caught was *When Harry Met Sally*."

They both laugh, and Blake doesn't care if it's a joke or true. But he can't help but love the idea of curling up with a bowl of popcorn and binging some ancient movies together. Reminds him of the nights spent with his best and only friend, Terri, tossing popcorn at the screen when characters kiss and booing the saccharine happily-ever-afters.

Jay interrupts his thoughts. "Almost there. He should be in; doesn't usually take his break until later."

They round a corner and stop in front of an electronic shop that sells the latest in laptop models and mech companions. It's sleek, the kind of shop fullbloods would patronize, all dark colors, chrome, and minimalist logos. In the front windows, a series of companions stand on display, their smooth faces blank and inactivated, waiting for a master. The elite in modern android technology, capable of home tasks, computing, and social function. Blake's seen them around town before, running errands and accompanying families, but he's never been up close. They look like anyone else, except for a strip of LEDs on their hairlines. Atlas might be behind the rest of the world in magic, but technology is the country's specialty, and in this shop, it's on full display.

He glances at the price tag. Yikes. At least half a year's rent. A lump forms in his chest. No way this works out.

"Um..." he starts to speak, but Jay cuts in.

"Don't worry about the place. Elliot's a good guy. He can fix anything, and he owes me a favor, anyway."

Blake shifts his bag to his other shoulder, still uneasy. "All right."

"Hey." Jay catches his eyes, even though he's trying to look away. "It's cool. I'm not dressed for the occasion either." There's that flash of charming smile again, and Blake suddenly doesn't mind his own loose jeans and slouchy cap. He smiles back, and they enter the shop, Jay holding the door open for him.

"Nope!" A voice calls over the large showroom before they can even close the door. Blake recoils, tries to flee the scene, but Jay stands resolute behind him, making it impossible to retreat. He bumps into a (much too sturdy and warm) chest. "Jay, not now," the voice continues, "I'm not fixing your craptop again. It's your fault for downloading all that porn. Learn your damn lesson."

"Hey, hey, Elliot, c'mon, man." Jay holds up a placating hand. "Just here to help out a friend, yeah?"

"Meaning you're here to cash in a favor. You're out of I.O.U.'s." A tall, slender man walks toward them, dark hair slicked back and stylish glasses catching the display lights. Elliot's jawline is smooth, his alpha odor smoother.

Blake swallows. These two in a pack together is a double dose of Trouble. They look like super models. He squirms in place, feeling frumpy and disheveled. He *had* put on deodorant today, right? Of course he had, it's a workday. Oh god, but what if he hadn't? Resisting the urge to sniff himself (like that would do him any favors) he attempts a disarming smile. Feels more like a grimace. His face never listens to him when he needs it.

"Don't be like that," Jay cajoles. "I help you out plenty. And it's super simple. Bet you could fix it in a minute."

"So you *do* want something fixed." Elliot looks to Blake. The man's pointed gaze could skewer a fish. "And who is this? You're taking home random omegas now?"

Blake can't tell if he's picking up hurt in Elliot's voice, and he wonders again what the deal is between the two. A hand landing on his shoulder startles him out of his thoughts.

Jay says, "This is Blake. Some jackass alpha tried to get in his business, and I put a stop to it."

Elliot's eye twitches ever so slightly, and he replies, "And, what, that makes him your ward now?"

Jay chuckles in the face of the man's wilting attitude. "Only want to help him out. Look, he's got this necklace. Clasp's broken. Could you fix it?"

Blake, all too aware that he's stuck in the middle of some years-long issue between these two and very much wanting to duck out, holds up his necklace for Elliot's inspection. The symbol—a two-headed wolf with emeralds for eyes—catches the light.

Elliot doesn't even look at it. "And why would I want to do that?"

No escaping the situation. Better to dive in deeper than back out, so he finds his voice. "This is my mom's. I hope it's not too much trouble." He tries a tiny whiff of pheromones, something soft and conciliatory. It's manipulative, but it's the best tool he's got.

Elliot falls silent, eyes flicking between Jay, Blake, and the necklace. At last, he holds out his hand and motions for Blake to pass it over. A spark of anxiety flares as Blake drops it into his hand. He's never let the pendant out of sight before, and when Elliot takes a glance at the symbol, his chest hitches. *Please don't look too close.* Elliot's attention passes to the chain ends.

"I can fix it," he announces. "Not now, but I'll attach a new clip. I have to run the shop for an hour, but I'll do it on break. Come back around two."

Relief floods him. Elliot seems competent. Trust—never Blake's strong suit—comes a little easier than normal. Then he falters. "I don't have much money..."

Elliot waves a hand. "No charge. Just don't let this goob cop a feel, okay? He doesn't deserve it."

Blake side-eyes Jay, who laughs, though this time he sounds like a pup caught sneaking candy. "Hey," he says with a shrug, "wouldn't dream of it."

"Uh-huh." Elliot's dry reply closes the conversation, and he walks off with the necklace, returning to the counter and pulling out his phone. The latest model.

"Don't mind him," Jay says with a wave. "He gets protective, you know? He means well."

"I fully expect my honor to remain intact today," Blake says, wagging a finger. Part of him begs to differ. He beats that down hastily.

"I am nothing if not a gentleman." Jay bows at the waist.

"Gentlemen listen to classical music."

"I guess you'll have to send me a playlist."

Blake feels the corners of his mouth pull upward. "That can be arranged."

Jay's back to all grins. "So. We've got a couple hours to kill. You like video games?"

They're talking the same language. "Who doesn't?"

"Well, I happen to have a membership to the Friendly Fire Arcade, and I can bring someone, if you're interested."

Oh, hell yes.

"Are you kidding? I would die to go in there! They've got the latest Apoc game."

Jay's grin is more impish than friendly now, though no less charming in its gleam. "I'll kick your ass. I'm on the leaderboard."

"Oh, we'll see about that, Mr. Too-Perfect!" It's out before he can stop it, but he barrels on anyway. "I clocked in three hundred hours on the last one. I think I can take you."

Jay slings an arm over his shoulders. "Challenge accepted. But no crying when I wipe the floor with you."

"I'll wipe the floor with your tears when this is over," he shoots back. He can't stop smiling. Be it Jay's alpha aroma or adrenaline, he feels like a hummingbird vibrating in the air, full of energy.

Jay leads him outside, arm still slung over his shoulders. Blake makes no effort to distance himself. Even that warning voice in his head quiets down. They exchange game talk all the way to the arcade, and by the time they get there, Jay's arm has snuck to his waist and settled in a way he can't help but enjoy.

Trouble, capital T.

Chapter Two

Haydn's "Little Serenade"

J ay had always been a sucker for cute blonds. Most of his hookups involved one (or two; no need to be a prude about it), and a blond omega like Blake set his blood to boiling. It was only natural; their werewolf ancestry had hardwired them for attraction. Alphas might be at the top of the food chain socially and politically, but nothing broke through their armor quite like an omega. Jay didn't consider himself particularly in touch with his wolf, but something about Blake ignited his instincts. To provide, protect, and in the darker corners of his mind, claim and dominate. He shook it off. Nothing worse than an alpha who couldn't control himself. This was the civilized age, where fights between packs were settled in courtrooms and, on a larger scale, with political treaties. Never mind that he'd gotten into a scrap that afternoon. He had ended it, anyway. It wasn't like he'd stand around and watch some poor guy get harassed. Blake didn't deserve it. They weren't animals.

Still, he felt an instinctual magnetism to omegas. They smelled like heat and sex and every good thing he'd ever tasted. But even among the omegas he'd known, Blake stood out. The guy outshone the arcade's neon. Definitely dating material. His family would disagree; Blake was obviously strapped for cash and not accustomed to upper-class environments, but what did it matter now? It was Future Jay's problem.

For now, he wanted to lose himself in Blake. The man was a whirlwind of energy and scent, and—Jay couldn't help but notice—completely unbound. No mark on his neck, not even the smell of a pack. The odds of meeting a loner omega these days were about as good as catching a shooting star. How he survived without pack affection, Jay didn't know. He'd have to ask Elliot about it later.

"How's that for a high score?" Blake crowed as his initials overtook Jay's on the leaderboard.

Jay snapped out of his reverie and smiled. "I bow to your superior skills." He mocked a genuflection, which elicited a laugh from Blake. The sound made Jay's stomach flood with warmth.

Around them, the arcade cabinets blinked and beeped and sang out, calling to passersby for coins. A row of racing games, the kind you could sit on and control as the motorcycles swerved back and forth, took up one wall. A VR setup dominated another corner, some shooting game framed like a horror B-movie. Between them, a digital clock proclaimed the time: two p.m. They should head out to meet Elliot, but a tugging in Jay's gut insisted he extend this a little longer.

"You hungry? We could grab a bite."

"I'm okay." Blake didn't meet his eyes.

"My treat," Jay pressed. "I was thinking hot dogs. The food counter is decent here."

Blake fussed with his bangs as he mulled it over. His hair shone softly, even in the harsh arcade lighting. Finally, he looked up, giving Jay full view of his brilliant green eyes. Green! Jay might have met two people in his life with green eyes; the werewolf blood had basically wiped it out of the gene pool. Everyone these days had brown or gold or occasionally blue eyes. But green... He could lose himself in those eyes and never turn back. He coughed as he realized Blake was speaking and forced his focus onto the words.

"It'll be my treat instead," Blake declared. "I want to thank you for helping me today."

Wow, not many people passed on the opportunity for a free lunch. During his last date, (not that this arcade outing was a date, or anything) Jay had paid for everything from dinner to the chick's cab ride home. He liked Blake's style.

"Thanks," he said. "You're not so bad, you know that?" And he winked to emphasize his good humor.

"And you're probably the coolest alpha I've ever met."

Blake's words from earlier sprout in his mind. *Mr. Too-Perfect.* Jay's heart sped up. It felt suddenly too tight in this arcade, the heat and the noise almost overwhelming. It was perhaps a little too tight in his pants, too, but he could force that down. Thank God he'd worn sweats today.

They approached concessions, and Blake bought them both hotdogs with a wallet overburdened from single bills.

"Sorry," he said, eyes sliding away from Jay's again. "Haven't made it to the bank yet. It always looks weird when I buy something with cash. Somebody asked me once if I was a stripper." He forced a laugh, but Jay got the feeling he didn't find it amusing.

"Probably wishful thinking. I bet they didn't have a mate."

Some people these days went crazy without mates, resorting to dodgy consort services and growing more desperate and obsessed the longer they stayed alone. Jay wondered again how Blake kept himself together without a mate or a pack. As far as he knew, omegas needed to be bound. It was in their nature.

Blake flashed a real smile, enough to melt the concerns from Jay's mind, and said, "Yeah, I bet. You wouldn't believe the kinds of people we get at the café. Some real pieces of work. Nobody like that guy this morning, usually, but a lot of them say some sideways stuff or try to grab a handful. It's hardest on the unbound omegas." He rubbed the back of his markless neck, leaving Jay to wonder if maybe he was looking for an alpha, after all. Someone who could keep him safe, hold him at night, cover him in warm, open-mouthed kisses—

Cool it, man. You hardly know the guy.

Their food arrived, and they gathered it to go, eating on their way to meet Elliot. Jay slathered his in ketchup and mustard, but Blake opted for relish.

"I don't know how you put up with it," Jay commented between mouthfuls. Waiting tables was one thing, but being treated like he was on the menu? No way. "I'd punch a sonuvabitch."

Blake snorted. "You did."

"I guess you're right."

Music floated toward them from down the sidewalk. A busker stood on the corner, playing something Jay didn't recognize on the violin. Blake shifted his hotdog to his left hand and tugged his wallet out of his bag with his right. After some careful maneuvering, he retrieved a small stack of ones and dropped them into the violin case. Jay copied. The musician smiled in appreciation.

They crossed the street, and Jay offered his unprofessional opinion. "Nice violin."

Blake snorted at him. "It's a viola."

"What's the difference?"

Blake laughed for real this time and shook his head. "Maybe you're not quite as perfect as I thought."

"Wait, no, come on. What's the difference?"

"Violas are bigger. Deeper sound."

"And you could tell just from that?"

Blake shrugged. "I like music. Even if some of us choose to have poor taste."

"What can I say, I live at the whims of our pop culture overlords. Maybe you can rescue me."

"I'll take that challenge. What do you say to some opera?"

Jay grinned. "Maybe someday we can arrange that."

They rounded the corner toward Elliot's shop. Jay tossed his hotdog wrapper in a trash bin and took a breath.

Now or never.

He stopped and caught Blake's arm. A dab of relish splashed to the concrete.

"Hey." He put on his best smooth tone, sincere and charming. It got him into as much trouble as it got him out of. "I want to see you again. Don't disappear after you get your necklace back, okay?"

Their eyes met, and electricity shot up Jay's spine. Blake smiled. "Wouldn't dream of it." He licked his lips—absolutely kissable—and added, "Even if you don't know the difference between a violin and a viola."

"Scouts' promise, I'll learn every instrument in an orchestra. Can I call you?"

He pulled out his phone, a limited-edition model that Elliot had hooked him up with. He swiped the contacts page open and prompted Blake to recite his number. It saved the number automatically, no input needed, but a flash of inspiration propelled him to type a message and send it off. Blake jumped when his pocket vibrated.

"Check it later." Jay tried on a smirk, hoping he looked cool. He felt more like a dweeb than he would have liked to admit. "Come on. Elliot's probably waiting for us. He prefers things to be prompt."

Sure enough, when they entered the store, Elliot stood at the counter, arms crossed and eyeing the clock. Two-twenty p.m.

"I know, I know." Jay waved a hand at Elliot as if to swat away his discontent. "We had to grab something to eat. My stomach was digesting itself. So-rry." He drew out the word as he said it, toeing the edge of sarcasm.

"You don't sound it," Elliot replied curtly. He turned to Blake and passed him a small box along with the solemn pronouncement, "You're too good for him."

Blake took the box, opened it, and brightened like a supernova. "It's perfect! Thank you!"

Whoa. Jay thought he might melt under the force of Blake's joy—his scent alone was enough to overpower a city block. Elliot didn't reply at first, seeming just as overwhelmed by the sudden wave of excited aroma. He and Jay met eyes, and Jay nodded to confirm they both sensed it.

"Not a problem," Elliot said when he recovered. "Be careful with it, though. Those are real gems."

"Oh. Yeah." Blake quieted as swiftly as he had exploded. "Yeah, I know. I messed up letting it out of my sight like that. I was just so..." He shook his head. "I'll be more careful. Thank you. This means so much to me." He clipped the pendant around his neck and tucked it under his shirt.

"Glad to be of service." Elliot graced Blake with a genuine smile.

Jay felt the corners of his own mouth turn up. Always nice to see a packmate smile. Filled him with the warm fuzzies.

"I really should be going home." Blake tucked a few strands of hair behind his ear. "I've got things to do, and the trip is kind of long."

"Yeah, and your friend is waiting."

Blake blinked like he'd completely forgotten. He chuckled and rubbed the back of his head. "Right. My friend." He moved to the door, and Jay called after him.

"Be careful going home. You never know what crazy is out there."

Blake looked back, a playful grin on his face. In that moment, the afternoon sun silhouetted him, giving him an aura of golden light. Jay's heart nearly choked him.

"I don't know what crazy is in here," he replied in his melodic tenor. He had a point.

Jay smiled as Blake left. The city absorbed him in its restless embrace, leaving Jay to hope they'd meet again sooner rather than later. His smell lingered after him, sweet and succulent, begging Jay to chase after.

Elliot cleared his throat. "You know—"

Jay heaved a sigh, the moment of fantasy broken. "What? That my folks would hate him? Or I'm being irresponsible?" He could practically hear Kimiko's voice in his head, telling him to stop projecting onto Elliot all the time.

"No," Elliot replied. He sounded unphased, but the way he adjusted his glasses spoke volumes. Jay winced. "I was going to say, he's cute when he smiles. Don't you think?"

Mm, yes, Jay did think. He bowed his head slightly, a habit he'd picked up from Kim. "Sorry. Shouldn't have jumped on you like that. My bad."

"Indeed." Elliot's way of accepting an apology. He switched to a friendlier tone. "Don't go falling in love, now."

Jay chuckled. "Yeah. What would my parents say?"

Elliot waved a lackadaisical hand. "Screw them. They don't own you."

Jay grinned and threw an arm over Elliot's shoulders. Sometimes, Elliot just got him. He had a way of seeing through bullshit, which was invaluable when navigating Jay's family. Twenty-six years of dealing with them, and he still hadn't maneuvered out of their clutches.

"Yeah," he said, and leaned his forehead sideways against Elliot's. "Screw 'em."

***

Don't think about his smile.

Blake's feet hit the pavement in a series of eighth notes. Now away from Jay, his head has a chance to clear. Somehow it stays foggy.

Don't think about his smell.

He hops a ride on the subway heading north, and the lingering grassy scent dissipates in the face of raw public transport aromas. Mostly nicotine and piss. It strengthens the closer he gets to home.

Don't think about his voice.

He hops off at his stop and hits the pavement up top. The sounds of a protest echo in a park square. Not so much a park these days as a gathering place for drug dealers and homeless people, but in a city like Remun there's space for everyone to come chasing a dream only to find disaster around the next corner. The farther north he goes, the more the pristine metal buildings give way to old, collapsing brick, the manicured grass and healthy trees dwindle into weeds, and graffiti, not flashy digital signs, color the concrete. Blake rushes past broken fire escapes and shadowed alleyway gaps.

He can't do this. Not after so many years of stalwart loneliness. Not after what Mom had done to keep him safe.

He ducks around the street to his apartment building, and the smell of sex hits him like the cannon fire in Tchaikovsky's "1812 Overture". An alpha leans against the wall by the door, a woman on her knees in front of him, head bobbing. The alpha grins at him.

"Wanna make a buck?"

An obscene slurping noise punctuates the question.

Blake wrinkles his nose and shoots back, "What, you need an audience to get off or something? I'd think twice about that if I had a dick as small as yours."

The guy flips him the bird, and he returns the favor with the most city-hardened "Piss off" that he can manage. Just another lovely day in the neighborhood.

He gets to his apartment without any more scenes, though it takes three jiggles of the key to get the lock to turn. Once inside, he bolts the door and considers pushing a chair against it. Huffing a sigh, he abandons the thought. It's all cheap particle wood anyway; it wouldn't make a difference.

He drops his stuff to the ground and plops onto the beanbag he uses in lieu of a couch. One of his neighbors down the hall screams something about the lights. Nothing new there. Sometimes at night he hears sobbing from the wall behind his bed, followed by the thump of someone else jarring the floor with a broomstick. Remun is the kind of place where you can get lost in a sea of people, you can feel like one bee in a buzzing hive of millions, a cacophony of misery unlike any other place in the world. Not that he had ever been anywhere but here. Remun suits his needs perfectly. If you want to disappear, this is the place to be, and in Blake's case, he needs to be invisible. A specter. One note in a symphony full of ceaseless noise.

So far so good, anyway.

He pulls out his phone and flips it open. No LCD screen for him; he makes do with a used artifact from yesteryear. Jay's text greets him.

You owe me that playlist.

Uh-oh. Suddenly he's no longer one note among millions—the thought of Jay pulls him from his solitude, makes him wonder what they'd sound like together. What would their unique chord be?

He should delete it, but he doesn't. Instead, he's typing a reply and sending it before he can stop himself. Before good sense can intervene.

Wouldn't dream of welching.

He hovers his fingers over the buttons, considering if he should save Jay to his contacts. But that's one step too far, so he just shuts the phone and tosses it aside.

Somehow a library book finds its way to his hands, but when he stares at the pages, all he sees is Jay's smile.

A loopy warmth fogs his brain.

"I am in so much trouble."

As if agreeing with him, the neighbor down the hall screams for help.

***

Jay's text messages dominate Blake's life for the next week. He feels like a live wire, crackling with electricity at every buzz and beep of his phone. He mixes up orders at work. He fumbles his fingers while practicing piano. He forgets a call to his mom. If this goes on, he might short circuit and blow out entirely.

Now he sits at his best friend's house, unable to think about anything except Jay. He hasn't texted yet today. Disturbing how quickly the lack of some guy's innocuous **Good morning** could wreck his life like this. Pathetic.

He heaves a sigh and sinks into Terri's couch. Her TV plays images and sound, but nothing penetrates his malaise.

"Hey." Terri drops her controller. "You're not even playing. What's going on?"

"I don't know what you're talking about." He reaches for the popcorn bowl. He hasn't mentioned Jay to anyone (never mind that Terri is the only 'anyone' in his life), and that conversation can wait.

His fellow omega clucks her tongue in disapproval. "I'm talking about you, airhead," she says, though not without affection.

He barely hears her as Jay's laugh plays in his mind again. Damn, that guy looks good when he smiles. What would Terri think of him? She's got alpha experience under her belt; maybe she could deflect his charm. Hm, but then again, Jay is on a whole other level. He's the Olympic champ of charm.

"Hell-o!" Terri pokes his temple. "Come in, Blake, all I'm getting is static."

He blinks, handful of popcorn halfway between the bowl and his mouth. "Oh. Sorry. A lot on my mind lately." It's the truth; no need to tackle those nasty details.

"Uh-huh."

He recognizes the tone—the same one Elliot used with Jay back at the electronics store. God, that feels like a year ago.

"Hey!" Terri prods him again. "I'm seriously going to start worrying about you if you don't tell me what's up. Is it..." Her voice drops to a near whisper. "Your mom?"

That pang of guilt flares again. He can't lie to her. "No." She heaves out a relieved sigh. "Nothing like that. It's kind of stupid, actually."

"You're kind of stupid," she replies, smiling. She tucks her feet under herself to assume the Gossip Position, ever popular at their childhood sleepovers and an immediate indicator he has her full attention. "Come on. Tell me what's up."

Blake tosses the popcorn back in the bowl. It's cold, anyway. "I met a guy," he starts, and she makes a squeaking noise he knows prefaces a gush of questions, so he holds up both hands to stymie the flow. "Hang on! It's not serious. We've texted a couple times, but that's it. We don't have plans or anything."

"Bla-ake!" She sing-songs his name and wraps him in a hug. "I'm so happy for you! My little pup is all grown up!" A pretend wipe of her eyes.

He pushes her away. "We're the same age! Anyway, it's no big deal." Except his dreams lately have been less and less about music and more and more about a certain broad-shouldered alpha.

"So. Dish. How'd you meet? What's his name? Do you have a pic?" She waggles her eyebrows at that last one.

"At the café, Jay, and no, you pervert. We barely know each other."

"Wait. At the café? Does that mean...?" She leans in, all seriousness. "Sweetie, is he an alpha?" Blake makes a noncommittal sound. "Blake!" She reels back, squealing, half-excitement, half-concern. "You know what that means, right?" Her voice drops low, and she looks at him through mascara-laced eyelashes. There it is. The 'I'm about to talk sex' look.

No, please, not tonight.

Sex is fine and dandy—Terri certainly thinks so—but his practically lifelong dry spell makes the topic unbearable. Thoughts of Jay (and those muscles) do nothing to help the issue.

"Yes, I know what it means. No, I don't need to hear all about it." He doesn't intend to sound snippy, but it comes out as clipped as a buzz cut. And despite his attitude, there are certain alpha, ahem, *features* he has yet to tackle in real life. Damn that werewolf DNA and its ability to create massive problems. Emphasis on massive.

He pushes the thoughts away and attempts a subject change. "Jay's not like the usual customers. Some asshole tried to get into it with me, and Jay defended me."

Terri tuts. "Honey, be careful. A macho alpha is tough to handle. You could—"

"It's okay." No need to hear the next words. "Nothing's going to happen to me. Like I said, we've barely even talked. He's probably not interested like that."

The last bit is more lie than truth, based on the text messages they've exchanged. Two days ago, Jay sent a simple, **Thinking of you**. Blake isn't a flirtatious person (no, really!), but something about Jay brings it out in him. Then he remembers he hasn't heard anything from the alpha since that text and a pit gnaws at his stomach. Shit. He'll be mortified if he has the wrong idea.

"Hey." Terri's sincere tone demands his attention. "Seriously, don't mess around with alphas. They take that stuff for real. It works out when you both want the same thing, but if you met him at the café..."

"I told you; he isn't like the usuals. He helped me out a lot. I think—" He stops himself short. There's no way they could be on the same wavelength. Only a fool would dream about a life with Jay. The guy is so far out of his league they aren't even on the same field. Blake drops his eyes and hisses a breath through his teeth.

"Look." Terri wraps an arm around his shoulders. "I'm just saying don't jump the gun. Alphas can be great, but you've never even dated one before. Don't go into this unprepared."

"Yeah." His voice sounds like a frog crawled into his throat and died. This conversation breaches territory he isn't ready to confront. Better to brace himself. Fall back on his old self-reliance. "I didn't really want this anyway. Things have been fine. I can keep going like this and it wouldn't matter. Jay's just a distraction. We'll probably lose touch in a week."

And then life would resume, alone and agonizing. Late nights curled up in bed, body aching for a connection with someone, anyone. But he can't afford to dally with anyone seriously, anyway. A lifetime lived in hiding makes it kind of difficult to maintain relationships. And he has his mom to think about, too. Shit, if she knew about this, she would be so worried. He's being maximum irresponsible.

"Yeah." Terri bows her head, voice saddened. "Sure."

An awkward silence floats between them now, and Blake is about to declare he's going home when his phone pings a loud message beep. They both look at it where it sits on the table, closed. The small screen on the front announces the name of the contact without divulging the text—Jay.

"Oh," Blake says. All of a sudden, his head is full of helium. He reaches for the phone and wonders whose arm extends to grab it. It can't be his; he would be able to feel it. The stranger's hand closes around his cell phone and flicks it open. Beside him, Terri makes little squeaking noises and cranes her neck to see. He reads the text. "Oh," he repeats.

"Dammit, what's it say, already?" Terri looks ready to jump out of her skin.

"'Got a reservation at the Wood And Stone Grill tomorrow night. Packmate bailed. Wanna join?'" Blake reads. Wow, along with his arm, someone has apparently possessed his voice, too.

Terri gasps. "That place is crazy bougie! Oh god, Blake, you *have* to go!"

He wants to say he doesn't *have* to do anything, but his fingers are already texting back a reply to confirm his attendance. He'll figure out the details later. He hits send without re-reading it. Silence stretches out in an infinity of seconds while the two stare at his phone. It beeps again.

Great! Pick you up at 7?

It is great, and Blake does want to be picked up at seven, but what is he supposed to do about the fluttering in his chest? Surely, he's having a coronary. This is how people die. In the distant world that is Terri's living room, his best friend lists off all the things they need to get to prepare for his—get this—*date* with Jay.

Something, something, clothes, something—wait, condoms? That one almost snaps him out of his Jay-induced reverie. Almost. But too strong are the memories of Jay's smile, scent, and the warmth of his arm on Blake's waist.

Blake's heart hiccups. Oh yeah, this guy is going to kill him.

Chapter Three

Saint-Saëns's "Aquarium"

Blake spends the next day with Terri, who picks out clothes from her packmate's closet ("It's only for a night, I *swear*! I'll dry clean it for you!"), buys him a haircut ("You really needed one, anyway."), and somewhere along the way slips an alpha-sized condom into his bag (she's mum on that topic, go figure). They end back at her apartment on the east side, where Jay will pick him up. At this point, Blake's stomach has relocated to his throat.

He sits on Terri's couch. Or rather, he watches from a strange, floaty, disembodied position as someone who looks an awful lot like him sits on Terri's couch. Her cat clock ticks away every second with a whoosh of its tail.

Why did you agree to this?

His stomach does a pirouette and flourish. Ten points.

Why the hell *did you agree to this?*

Terri flits about in the background, straightening things that don't need to be straightened. She tries to straighten Blake (ha ha, never had a chance there), but he only slouches deeper into the cushions. Tick-tock goes the kitty clock.

"You'll wrinkle the suit!" She tugs at his jacket.

At a minute to seven, there comes the dreaded knock, knock, knock on the chamber door. Terri pulls him to his feet and frantically adjusts his clothes.

"Go, go, go!" She prods him forward.

Blake moves through the air as though it's molasses. His mouth tastes like he's eaten cotton balls, and his stomach has apparently retired from the gymnast circuit and flown to another body altogether. That's okay. Dinner dates don't require stomachs. Blake reaches for the doorknob.

The door isn't opening. Oh no. This must be a dream, a nightmare. One of the bad ones he gets sometimes. He'll be stuck here for eternity trying to open the damn door while Jay waits for him outside and knocks and knocks and knocks and oh god, make it st—ah, right, the door's locked. Blake turns the bolt.

The door swings inward, and there stands Jay with a hand halfway up to knock again. Damn, he looks good in a suit. All crisp lines and broad shoulders. The bit of stubble he sported when they met is shaved neatly off. Jay drops his hand and smiles.

"Hey," he says.

"Hey," Blake replies. Not the cleverest of lines but there's no way he can think straight when gazing into those gold-flecked eyes.

"Hey!" Terri proclaims, bowling into their moment with all the grace of a beached whale.

"Oh, nice to meet you." Jay's smile tightens. "Are you...Blake's packmate?"

"Something like that." Terri takes in Jay's muscular frame, shaggy hair (no ponytail this time), and tailored suit. She lets out a low whistle. "Blake, you really outdid yourself this time. This guy's got to be an underwear model, right? How many abs have you got under there? Blake, promise you'll count."

Jay's eyebrows fly up, and Blake groans. This is clearly Terri's first attempt at testing the alpha, and if so, he knows he doesn't want to hear what comes next.

"Terri, now's really not—" he tries to bail them out, but Jay suddenly cracks up.

"I'll let it be a surprise," he responds. "Hate to ruin the thrill."

Terri grins back at him and sticks out a hand to shake. First test passed, apparently. Jay gives her hand a solid pump.

"I hope you realize Blake means a lot to me, and, therefore, a lot to my pack." Terri lets the implication hang.

"I wouldn't dream of returning him in more than one piece," he assures her.

Blake feels somehow relegated to an observer position, an audience to the train wreck that is evolving before him. Should have known Terri's insistence that they meet at her place was less a kind gesture and more about vetting his potential boyfriend.

Ack. Boyfriend. The one word makes him feel like he's got a volcano under his skin.

"I hope you two have fun, but understand: Blake's never *been* with an alpha before, got it?"

Oh no. The train is officially off the track and careening straight for his dignity.

"Terri!" he hisses, "Come on, not now!"

Jay, still maintaining his smile, responds with a smooth, "My intentions are nothing of the sort. Not yet, anyway." He smirks at Blake.

"Just make sure he has a good time. I don't think he's had an orgasm since high school."

There it is: the sound of the train colliding with Blake's soul and exploding into a burning heap of destruction.

Blake wheels around on Terri and declares too loudly, "Ok, you met him. We gotta go now. Bye-bye!"

He pushes her into the apartment and dashes out, slamming shut the door in time to hear her cry out, "Make sure to wrap it up first!"

With the hook of his elbow, he snags Jay's arm and drags the man away. Doesn't stop dragging until they're at the sidewalk.

"Nice girl." Jay's grinning, somehow unphased by Terri's blatant attempts to shake him. "She's...protective."

If only he could rewind time and delete this whole conversation. Now Jay will ask him about his history, and then what'll he say? 'Extenuating circumstances limit my dating capabilities'? Like that'll fly.

Jay, to his credit, doesn't pursue the topic. He smooths the wrinkles from his suit jacket and says, "My car's around the corner. You look good, by the way."

"Thanks." Belatedly, he adds, "You, too."

In his pocket, his cell beeps. He flips it open. A text from Terri, of course.

An oversized eggplant emoji looms at him, followed by three water droplets.

Why, Terri, why?

If he blushes any more than this, he might pass out from the blood rush. He slams the phone shut and shoves it deep into his pocket. Jay doesn't comment on it, thank every deity out there.

"So." Blake declares, voice ringing too loud in his own ears. "Wood And Stone Grill. What kind of packmate stands you up on a place like that? Isn't it impossible to get a table there?"

"It's not really her fault. Family emergency. Had to leave town for a bit."

"Oh." *Looks like I'm the asshole.* "Sorry. I didn't mean to—"

"It's cool." Jay waves a hand. "Don't worry about it. How's your necklace holding up?"

"Good as new! Tell Elliot 'thanks' again from me. I would've been messed up without it."

"From your mom, you said? Family heirloom or something?"

They arrive at Jay's car, and he opens the passenger door for Blake. Blake marvels at his reflection in the car's finish. Jay must be loaded. Not just anyone can afford to drive in this city.

"Something like that," he replies. Time to change the subject. "Nice car. What do you do? Don't tell me you're actually an underwear model."

He expects a laugh, but Jay sidesteps the question. "It's not a big deal. Some family business stuff." He shuts the door and rounds the car to the driver's seat.

Ack, red flag. God, it's so obvious. Jay's physique, the car, his downtown connectio ns... It all points to one crushing fact: the mafia. There was no way someone like Jay was anything but muscle for a lead pack.

What the hell have you gotten yourself into?

Random alphas at his job are one thing, but an alpha mafia family won't fly. Hell no is he going to wake up with a decapitated wolf head under his blankets. He sticks the tip of his thumb under his canine and chews at it. He'll have to play it cool before he can wiggle out of this.

"We should have plenty of time to get there." Jay's voice cuts into his ruminating, and warmth fills the pit of his stomach at the sound. Despite the news that Jay is clearly not a viable partner, his body is still betraying him.

Jay clips on the seatbelt and taps a button on the car's console that brings the engine to life. Blake's heart jumps to his throat. He can count on one hand the amount of times he's ridden a car in his life.

Please let Jay be a safe driver. Also, not a murderer.

"So what about after dinner?" He dares to probe.

Jay shrugs. "Up to you. If dinner is enough, then I'm happy with that." They swing out into traffic, and Blake's stomach resumes its acrobatics.

Better to be diplomatic. "I guess this is all pretty new to me. I hope I haven't said anything wrong."

Jay glances at him and back to the road. "Relax." Then he chuckles. "Easier said than done, huh?"

Blake nods. "Yeah." A pause stretches between them, and he scrambles to cover it. "Look, I'm not really good with people. Especially alphas. Sorry if I've already messed everything up."

"Did I do something to make you feel that way?" Jay asks, and for the first time, he sounds less than confident, like Blake has poked a hole in his life preserver and they're both watching the air hiss out.

"No!" Blake waves a hand, now the one off-kilter. "It's not you. I think you're really interesting, and I don't want to mess this up."

Or end up on some mafioso's shitlist.

"Yeah, that I can understand."

"So, tell me about yourself," Blake forces out. "I know you like video games and have a great workout routine. Not to mention you're a connoisseur of rom coms." This earns him a smile. "But what else do you like?"

"Cute blonds, for one." An inscrutable expression crosses Jay's face after the words pop out, and he backtracks "Sorry. That was, uh—"

"No, that was cute." Blake smirks. "The look on your face, I mean."

"Oh, so I'm the cute one now?"

Before his brain can signal him to shut right the hell up, he blurts, "Oh, come on, you know how good you look. You're like one of those ancient Greek statues. All muscle."

"Are you comparing me to Adonis?"

Oops. Time to pack it up. "If that means this conversation ends and I can die of embarrassment, then, yes, okay, I am."

Jay laughs. "Okay, okay. Let's leave it. We're both cute. Call it even. Look, here's the place. Why don't we enjoy some food? We can be cute together."

Together is good. Blake likes together. They pull up to the restaurant, and the valet workers—the latest in mech technology—open their doors with a bow.

"Hello, sirs," one says. "Welcome to the Wood And Stone Grill. We're so pleased to have you." Somehow, they look even more real than the ones in Elliot's shop. The only distinction from flesh and blood is a thin strip of LED lights along their hairline. No uncanny valley here.

Jay exchanges the car for a ticket and offers his arm to Blake. He can feel Jay's bicep flex underneath the sleeve. The man's scent—warm earth with a dab of cologne—Intensifies at this distance. Good-bye, rational thought. They walk inside together, and Blake realizes the extent of the disparity in their heights. He barely comes up to Jay's shoulder. This guy may as well be a mech companion engineered for physical perfection. *Damn, Terri's really going to hound me for deets on this one.* They step inside, and the thoughts drop clean out of his head.

Holy shit. Blake gawks from glass ceiling to floor-length red drapery to, yes, that is indeed a tiered fountain. He cranes his neck to see deeper into the establishment. It does *not* look this big from the outside. The architect had gone all out and built the restaurant in the style of an amphitheater. You could fly a kite in here.

"Good evening, Mr. Reed and Ms.—" The hostess cuts herself off and glances from them to the reservation list. "My apologies," she says, "We have a Ms. Oshiro here on file."

"She had to cancel," Jay says. "I managed to find someone to join me though."

"Oh. I'm Blake," Blake offers, tearing his eyes away from the chandelier, which sparkled with what had to be real diamonds, "Blake Fields."

"Well, Mr. Fields, it's a pleasure to have you with us tonight." The hostess writes the correction on her list. "Please follow Derek to your seats. Enjoy your meal."

They follow him down past the tiered seating set in concentric floors, all the way to the bottom. Blake damn near salivates when they pass a grand piano, which rings out a luscious timbre. The greatest thing he's ever wanted is to play on a piano like that, to feel the smooth keys beneath his fingers and see the joy on another's face at the music he makes. He packs that dream in with a well-practiced hand. Attracting attention is the last thing he needs, and playing piano in front of groups definitely counts as showy.

Candles flicker at their table, and Blake sits in a plush, high-backed chair across from Jay. He has but a moment to admire the tablecloth (damn, the thing probably has a higher thread count than his bed sheets) before he gazes at his date and, *no*, stomach, you stay put! In the soft lighting, Jay could be a movie star. Mafia family or not, those intense eyes drag Blake into their depths.

"This place is amazing!" Blake exclaims. *Don't make it awkward.* "I bet all your dates put out after eating here!" *That's it. No more talking from you.*

A bemused smile lights Jay's eyes, but he thankfully changes the subject.

"Do you like steak? They have the best chateaubriand in the city. At least, that's my opinion."

"Sure." Steak is steak, as far as he's concerned. Blake flips through the menu and notices a distinct lack of listed prices. Oh boy. He glances back to Jay, who peruses the wine list.

The waiter, dapper in a vest and bowtie (no uniforms like that at Blake's job), delivers their bread, a spiel about specials, and takes Jay's wine order.

"Is a bottle okay?" Jay asks. Blake can only nod. He doesn't know a cabernet from a cabaret.

Blake leans in and whispers, "This is incredible. Thank you for inviting me."

Relief loosens Jay's face. "I'm glad you like it. I really enjoyed being with you the other week. I'd like to get to know you better."

"I'd like that, too." Starting with whatever the hell his family does.

"So besides working at an omega café, what do you do with yourself?"

Blake shrugs. "You already know I like reading late nights. Borrowed a copy of *Pride and Prejudice* from the library last week." He puts up a hand. "No judgment, Mr. Rom Com. But I spend most of my time taking care of Mom. And piano. I can't go a day without that." He glances again at the grand piano, whose player is currently coaxing out a flawless rendition of Mozart's "Piano Sonata 16" from its keys. He could die happy to play a piano like that instead of his keyboard. No cheap plastic on that beautiful instrument.

"Your mom? I thought she wasn't around anymore."

Blake shakes his head, "No, she's sick. She gave me her necklace right before she went into full time care. I guess you could say she's gone, though... She doesn't exactly act like herself anymore." Blake's eyes cast to the table. "I wonder if she would've liked this place. Nah. She'd probably hate it." The laugh he wants to let out catches in his throat.

"I'm really sorry," Jay sounds genuine. "Let's talk about something else."

"What about you?" Blake shoves aside thoughts of his mother. "What do you do most days?"

"I guess you can already tell I'm a gym junkie." Blake chuckles and nods. "But as far as other things go, I like gardening."

"You keep surprising me, Jay," Blake says. "Never met an alpha interested in growing something over tearing it down."

"I think you've only met shitty alphas. Sure, most of us suck, but it's worth getting to know one once in a while."

"I think I'm starting to see that."

And now he needs to get Jay to open up about his work. Ticking through the options, Blake figures he's a bodyguard at best. A hitman at worst. The waiter returns with their wine and writes down their orders. Alone again, Jay raises his wine glass to toast. Blake mimics him.

"To wonderful company." Jay clinks their glasses together.

Blake takes a sip and does a double-take at the smooth flavor.

"That's no boxed wine. You know how to pick them." *You sound like an idiot.*

Jay chuckles and swirls the wine around in the glass with an expert twist of his wrist. "It's kind of a requirement in my life."

"Meaning?"

"It's like a birthright. My whole family loves wine." He makes a vague gesture with his free hand.

"Oh yeah? Do they own a vineyard somewhere?" Keep it casual. Breathe.

"Eh, not really important." Jay's gaze slips elsewhere. "I kind of hate my family."

"Sorry," Blake says, but the information churns in his mind. Maybe Jay hates the work and wants out. Maybe he isn't a cold killer, after all.

"All good," Jay says and reaches to cover Blake's hand with his own. He speaks with a sudden intensity. "Maybe one day I can tell you about it. Tonight... let's just enjoy this, okay?"

Oh God, his hand is warm. Alphas run hotter than betas or omegas, and the heat seeps into him, making him dizzier than the wine ever could. Blake can practically feel his pupils dilating.

"Yeah. I really like being with you. You're—" The waiter returns with salad. Hands separate and tend to their forks.

But the heat lingers in his fingertips.

***

Somehow, Blake navigates the rest of dinner. He has a moment while staring at the cutlery where it hits him that he doesn't have an ice cube's chance in hell of picking the right fork, but Jay, a perfect gentleman, pretends not to notice. All too soon they're back outside Terri's apartment. They linger beside the car, neither willing to call it a night just yet.

"This was great. Really." Blake taps his fingers together. "Thank you for inviting me."

"And thank you for joining me. Kim would've been great company, but I have to admit, I enjoyed yours."

Blake beams his appreciation.

"Hey," Jay breathes, voice suddenly husky. He closes the gap between their bodies and settles his left hand on Blake's hip. The right reaches for his face.

Blake swallows a thick lump in his throat. His nerves crackle with electricity as the heat practically suffocates him.

"Yeah?" His brain buzzes like a beehive. He locks eyes with Jay, whose mostly brown color seems to shift all the way to honey gold.

"I'd hate to end tonight here. Promise you'll go out with me again soon?"

His thumb brushes over Blake's cheek, and Blake's knees weaken. Blood rushes south, leaving him even more lightheaded. He leans into the touch and fights the urge to close his eyes. Jay smells as welcoming as a fresh shower.

"I want to see you again, too. I'm free Thursday."

"Thursday, then." And Jay leans forward close enough to feel a puff of breath across his lips. "I'll call you."

Unable and unwilling to control himself, Blake leans up, extending his legs so he stands on tiptoes. He closes his eyes and tilts his head, lips parting ever so slightly. Jay's nose nuzzles his own, and the heat that built in Blake's mind explodes when their lips touch. Jay tastes like wine and fine food and wonderful, burning sex. Blake presses himself closer and winds his fingers through that wavy hair, barely registering the silken texture. The hand at his hip wraps around his waist, and a little growl rumbles in Jay's throat. Blake's head spins as Jay flips their positions, pushing him against the side of the car as he deepens their kiss. The world melts into wet heat as Jay's tongue caresses the inside of his mouth. Their bodies press flush together, and a familiar hardness grinds against his hips. Jay's hand roams from waist to the hem of Blake's shirt, groping for flesh but fended off by the tucked-in fabric. Blake moans and arches his back. He can't remember the last time someone touched him like this. He can't even remember his own name as Jay's mouth moves from lips to neck, trailing a line of heat down to his collar. Blake moans, and the needy sound surprises him enough to shrink away. Jay immediately freezes and pulls back.

"Sorry!" Blake untangles his hands from Jay's hair.

Jay pauses as he collects himself. He takes a step back, and the night air, even though it's the start of a warm summer, blows cold against Blake's heated skin.

"No, I'm sorry." Jay runs a hand through his mussed hair. "I shouldn't have—"

"No, really! It's okay!" Blake straightens his clothes and steps away from the car. "I liked it. It was nice." He barely gets the words out. His dick throbs so hard he can't think clearly. "But maybe let's save some for later? I don't want—" He's going to say, 'to mess this up', but the words don't come fast enough.

"No, no, I understand!" Jay insists, breaking into Blake's sentence. He takes another step away. "I didn't mean—"

"It's okay. It was nice. Really. I just—I should head up. Um, Thursday, right?"

"Yeah, Thursday."

They linger. Blake takes a step in Jay's direction, hesitates, then breaks away and hurries up to the apartment with a hasty, "Good night!"

***

Jay stood for a while beside his car in a darkness lit by streetlamps and passing headlights. That better not have screwed the entire situation.

"Calm down," he hissed at his crotch, which currently stood at full attention, threatening to pop a seam in his pants. "Seriously, don't mess this up for me."

A moment of deep breathing, and things settled. He climbed into his car and drove off. The wine had been good tonight, but he could use another drink after all that. Or maybe a whole bottle.

Chapter Four

Chopin's "Butterfly Étude"

After a round at a nearby bar, Jay decided the only place worth visiting was Elliot's apartment. He plugged in the address to his car's GPS and settled back while it drove him over. His mind, boozy and distantly aroused, spun with thoughts of Blake. He rode the elevator to Elliot's flat and knocked. A moment later, his packmate greeted him with a cocked eyebrow.

"Date go wrong?"

Jay ran a hand through his hair and didn't quite meet Elliot's eyes. "No, not really. Just need a drink."

As if things were ever really just drinks between them.

To send the message home, Elliot replied, "'Just' a drink?"

Jay huffed and stepped past him into the apartment, kicking his shoes off on the way. He ignored Elliot's pointed stare, knowing the man wanted to chide him about scuffing real leather, but none of that bullshit mattered to him. Instead, they headed to the kitchen where Elliot fetched a bottle of bourbon and poured two glasses. Jay held the glass up briefly before tipping it back and swallowing deeply. It burned, not unpleasantly, and the cloud around his head lightened. Elliot sighed, topped him off with one meticulous pour, and returned the bottle to its home.

Steady eyes trained on Jay's, Elliot asked, "What happened?"

He grimaced. Elliot always got straight to the point. He grumbled, "Omega's got my head messed up. Nearly lost myself, like some chump alpha." He took another draw from the glass, irritation with himself burning more than the alcohol. "I hope I didn't push him too far. He's..." He made a waggling motion with his hand. "Skittish."

"So you're thinking with your dick again."

Jeez. No need to say it like that.

But Elliot watched him squarely, the sharpness in his eyes easily reading between the lines.

Still, Jay huffed. "I didn't say that."

"You implied it. Don't try to talk circles with me. You could have spoken to Lance or Kimiko, but you came here."

Jay wrinkled his nose. "Neither of them have met Blake. Anyway, Kim's out of town."

Elliot rolled his eyes and directed Jay to the living room. They passed the hall that led to his workshop (he was always tinkering with some new gadget), music room (couldn't remember the last time he'd heard Elliot play guitar) and bedroom (would the night end there? Did he want it to?). A stack of magazines took up space beside the couch: tech, magic, and modern news. The top one proclaimed to be a complete history of the war between their country, Atlas, and Servos, across the sea. Leave it to Elliot to keep up with all that stuff. They sat side by side on the couch, and Elliot unstacked two coasters for their cups. Mahogany table—he'd be pissed if they left rings behind. Elliot had always appreciated the finer things more than Jay. Maybe because he'd had to work for them.

Jay polished off the liquor in his glass and flopped sideways, crossing his legs over Elliot's lap. The latter didn't move him, merely leaned back and sipped from his tumbler.

At last, he asked, "What do you expect to get out of this relationship with Blake?"

He sounded like a therapist.

Jay grunted. "Don't call it that. It was one date. One kiss. That's it."

Inside, he berated himself. Jay, the eternal bachelor. It was practically a personality disorder at this point.

"And?" Elliot pressed.

Jay groaned. "And plans for next Thursday."

"So you're feeling bad because you want something more than he wants? Because you want something less? Or," and Elliot deposited his glass on the table, "is it because you want something more than you're ready to admit?"

Jay growled annoyance in his throat. Bullseye. He flung a distressed arm over his eyes, knowing he was being dramatic, the booze making him not care, and muttered, "Maybe I just hate myself."

Elliot nodded sagely. "That's likely."

The haze in his mind had grown thicker and thicker as he lay there, spinning uneven circles through the alcohol. Now he sat up suddenly, almost quickly enough to turn his stomach. "What do you think of him?"

"Blake?" Elliot paused as he considered. "I think there's more to him than meets the eye."

He was trying to imply something, but the buzz made it impossible to discern. All he could think was...

"Yeah, like, probably a great ass..." He made a circular motion in the air.

Elliot poked his forehead. "Thinking with the wrong head again. What do you really know about this guy? What did he tell you tonight?"

He couldn't tell what Elliot was getting at. Jay frowned, forcing his dancing mind to focus.

"His mom's sick with something. I guess all the money he makes goes to her bills. He plays piano, don't know how well. Likes video games, reading..." His brain faded back to their moment outside the car, how warm Blake had been in his arms, supple, yielding. "And he tastes like strawberries."

Elliot clicked his tongue. "You want my advice?"

Jay nodded.

"Be careful. I don't know if getting involved with some mysterious omega is the best idea." He must have seen a look on Jay's face, because he sighed and added, "You'd better stay here tonight. You look one drink short of trashed."

He felt it, too. But the booze told him it was a good idea to lean in close and murmur. "Be honest. Are you jealous?"

Sober Jay never would have asked that. Too delicate a topic, too close to home. They were packmates, and with that came an instinctual sort of longing. A desire to be close, to be physical. That he was seeking out sexual partners beyond the pack could be a sore spot. Elliot had always been touchy about it. But Sober Jay wasn't here, and that meant a free-for-all on way too personal questions.

Elliot, to his credit, didn't flinch. He put his palm on Jay's face and pushed him away.

"I only want what's best for you, you dumbass. You're absolutely hopeless without us."

"You *are* jealous," Jay accused. Sense had apparently flown out the window. "You want me aaaaall for yourself."

Elliot snorted. "Hardly."

That was fine, though. Way too sleepy to bother chasing the topic. Jay stretched back against the couch arm and closed his eyes. "It's cool. I like you, too. Glad we're packmates."

It was a mumble more than anything, and before consciousness reasserted itself, he'd passed out into a drunken sleep.

***

Jay met Blake again on Thursday. They'd opted for a walk in the city's sprawling park, and Jay came equipped with a cooler full of sushi and riceballs. Kim had taught him how to roll them some years ago, and he'd spent the morning carefully arranging fish and vegetables and hoping Blake wasn't averse to chopsticks. Remun City resided on the west coast of Atlas, with only a ten hour flight between them and the capital of Oceana (once upon a time known as Asia, though these days werewolf pack rule reigned supreme, and a coalition of countries had shifted all the borders), and so it seemed nearly half the restaurants here were Oceanese. Probably Blake knew how to use chopsticks.

Blake jogged towards him from across the street. It seemed he took the subway everywhere. Jay had never ridden a public subway. They looked horribly sticky on TV. Painful to imagine Blake riding in a crammed car, body pressed up against a bunch of strangers, maybe even some rogue alpha. Hopefully his sweet scent wouldn't be spoiled by trash and cigarettes.

"What's that look about?" Blake slowed to a stop in front of him and cocked his head to one side.

Jay shook his head quickly, banishing the thoughts. Blake smelled as amazing as he had the last time they'd met, when Jay had him pressed up against his car, and that soft, breathy moan had escaped his mouth.

"Okay, now what's *that* look about?" Blake crossed his arms, bemusement in his eyes.

"Nothing. Sorry. My mind ran away from me." Jay cleared his throat and hoisted up the cooler as a distraction. "Do you like sushi?"

The gambit succeeded. Blake brightened and clapped his hands together. "I love sushi! Terri took me to that place on Masters, do you know the one?"

"Bento." He'd been there a few weeks ago with Kim. "Sorry to say, this won't be as good as theirs, but it is fresh." Then with a hint of pride, "Made it myself."

"What? You cook, too?" Blake looked flabbergasted.

Jay shook his head. "No, not like that. Just a couple things. Sushi, mac and cheese, waffles. Although, those come in a mix..."

Blake laughed. "That's fine. I was worried I had stepped into a TV drama. You know, where all the omegas faint and the alphas look like..." He trailed off and made a general motion in Jay's direction.

"Nope. I'm the real deal." Jay flashed his smile.

The smile worked on everyone, and Blake was no exception. The man blushed and tucked some hair behind his ear. He dressed plainly, jeans and a green t-shirt, with a slouchy knit beanie on his head. Too hot. The V cut on his shirt exposed enough collarbone to make Jay's mouth water.

Calm down. Don't scare him off.

Blake's eyes traveled elsewhere across Jay's body, the cooler now forgotten. Jay couldn't help but notice they lingered on his abs. He'd picked a tight black t-shirt for the occasion, hoping it would have exactly that effect. Then Blake paused on his right arm.

"How long did it take to do that?"

Half the tattoo sleeve he'd gotten years ago with Kim was exposed to the light. It featured the four cardinal legendary animals, as Kim had described them. A dragon twisted around his forearm along with a prowling tiger, a phoenix covered the upper half, mostly obscured by the shirt, and a turtle resided around his shoulder blade. She'd told him the names once, but he'd forgotten them now. What mattered was what the tattoo represented: his bond with Kimiko.

"A few sessions," he replied and offered Blake his arm. Blake traced the intricate lines with his fingertips almost reverently, and, a little cheeky, gave Jay's bicep a squeeze. Jay's grin broadened. "The worst part was the inside of the elbow." He directed Blake's fingers to the spot. "Hurt like hell."

Blake smoothed his thumb over the area, sending little tingles straight to Jay's dick. The distance between them was so slight; he could grab Blake and kiss him and he'd barely have to move. Then Blake withdrew.

"It's really nice."

"Happy you approve."

They struck up a slow pace around the perimeter of the massive lake that dominated the center of the park. Some paddleboats drifted lazily across it, couples on dates and kids with their parents. A flock of geese honked overhead before banking and landing on the opposite shore to pick at the grass. It was barely summer now, still cool with spring breezes, and the air smelled like fresh flowers. The dahlias were blooming, and clumps of them dotted the landscape, pink and white and burgundy, their faces lifted to the sun.

"Had a good week? No more alphas getting in your business?"

"As long as you don't count the guy who asked me for a 'sweet slice of my cake', then we're a-ok."

Jay snorted. "You're kidding me. That's got to be the lamest thing I've ever heard. You need a new job."

"Tell me about it. What kid dreams of running coffee all day and pretending to flirt for tips?"

"What did you want to be when you were a kid?"

Blake hesitated at this, like it was a secret he didn't want to spill. Then, in a soft voice he said, "Concert pianist. I wanted to play at the symphony. I wanted to go to Juilliard or the Royal Academy of Music. But some dreams aren't meant to be real. Reality is a lot stronger than a childhood obsession."

Jay felt a sympathetic pang in his chest. "Never too late," he said. He half-believed it.

Blake cringed and shook his head. "It won't happen. I don't play for people. No one but Mom and Terri."

They were treading a sensitive topic. Jay decided to lighten the mood. He needed to see a smile on Blake's face again. "Want to know what I dreamed of being as a kid? Leon Kennedy. From the Resident Evil games. I thought he was the baddest badass ever."

To Jay's relief, Blake cracked a smile. "Not Lara Croft? You sure you didn't want to strut around in booty shorts?"

"You know I'd rock those."

Blake burst into a laugh at the image. "Ok, so one of us lives in reality, and the other one's a hopeless romantic. I should've known you'd want to do something as ridiculous as blow up zombies."

"It's only ridiculous until the zombies are trying to eat you."

"Noted. I'll rely on you if we ever hit the apocalypse."

Blake took a pause to open his shoulder bag and produced a to-go baggie of birdseed. He must have bought it specially for the occasion. He tossed a handful to a group of ducks, who quacked excitedly and picked at it in short, jerky movements.

"Duck butts are cute."

Jay wanted to tell him he was cuter, but bit back the words and merely watched the gentle curve of a smile on Blake's lips.

More ducks poured in for a bite, squawking and flapping, and causing something of a ruckus. Some pigeons took notice and joined in. Blake hesitated, unsure what to do with this sudden flock, and the ducks turned hungry eyes on him.

"Uh-oh."

The largest bird flapped its wings mightily and darted forward at Blake, who tossed him a handful, but the bird would not be satiated. The geese now took note, and a dozen of them joined the kerfuffle.

"Let's go before this gets any worse." Jay caught Blake's wrist and tugged him away from the shoreline.

The birds would not be deterred. A squad of them gave chase, and Blake yelped, "We're getting mugged!"

"Drop the food! Give them what they want."

Blake tossed the contents of the baggie behind them and stuffed the empty plastic into his satchel. The birds, triumphant, flapped and hissed and snapped at each other over the mountain of food. Blake and Jay put distance between them, stopping under the shade of a tree to look back.

"Okay, maybe that was a bad idea." Blake looked at Jay, and they both burst into laughter.

"Mugged by some birds. What the hell?" Jay wiped his face as his chuckling dissolved. "So much for Leon Kennedy."

"Duck butts are much less cute when they're coming at you like a death squad."

"Let's go a little farther before we have lunch. Don't need those jerks stealing our sushi."

They settled on a gently sloping grassy knoll, away from the majority of people. Once in a while a cyclist or stroller passed them on the path below. The grass smelled fresh here, the stalks cropped short from a recent mowing, and Jay dropped the cooler in some shade. Blake sat beside him on the grass, close enough that he could have leaned his head on Jay's shoulder, but he kept a polite gap between them.

Jay unpacked lunch, tucked away in two bento boxes someone had bought him years ago. He didn't miss the eager look on Blake's face.

"You okay with chopsticks?" He offered a pair of smooth wooden sticks carved with cherry blossoms.

Blake plucked them out of his hand. "No problem. I grew up on the east end, in the Oceanese district. We lived above a noodle shop." His eyes went distant for a moment as he reminisced. "It always smelled like dashi."

"Cool. I thought only immigrants lived over there."

Blake stiffened and replied quickly, "Rent was cheap. Mom waited tables until she got sick. Then I took over."

"How old were you?" Maybe he shouldn't be prying, but Blake's life was so different from his own that he could barely fathom what it must have been like.

Blake tapped his fingers together as he counted back the years. "Fifteen or sixteen, but I started work earlier than that. When I was twelve, Mom got me a part time job washing dishes in the back of her restaurant. I did that for a few years every day after lessons, and then eventually waited tables, too. Guess I haven't changed much, huh?"

"There are worse things to be. You could be a politician."

The corners of Blake's mouth twisted, somewhere between amusement and thoughtfulness. "I guess you're right. Thanks for listening to my sob story. Not every day someone cares."

"Happy to. You're an interesting guy, Blake Fields. Thanks for putting up with me."

Blake laughed and said, "What about you? What's your deal?"

"Me? Nothing much. Got a degree in marketing. It's as boring as it sounds."

"So where do you work?" Blake took a bite of sushi and chewed nonchalantly.

Jay balked. Blake must know about his family.

Don't tell me he's a gold digger.

"It's not really important. Family business."

"Ah."

Tension settled in. Blake shoveled fish into his mouth like it would cure everything. Jay tapped his chopsticks on the side of his bento box and offered a few words of consolation.

"I don't do that much, anyway. Just some side projects here and there. It's really more of a token job than anything."

That seemed to ease Blake's mind somewhat, and he smiled again.

"This tastes amazing. You did a great job. Thank you for making it."

"Happy to provide." And he was. The alpha pride in him glowed at Blake's compliment.

They returned their empty dishes to the cooler, and Blake laid back on the grass, arms behind his head, to gaze up at the clouds.

"I'm glad we're doing this." He tore his eyes away from the sky to look at Jay. "This is nice."

Jay leaned back on his palms and replied, "We'll have to hit the arcade again, too. I need to win back my honor."

"Good luck, Cowboy. That high score ain't goin' nowhere." Blake affected a drawl as he proclaimed it.

Jay couldn't disguise a grin. Seeing Blake like this blew away his doubts. His lips were a perfect, kissable pink, and the sweet smell of him intoxicated Jay. His family didn't matter. They didn't need to know about Blake, and Blake didn't need to know about them. He could handle this. Besides, the sunlight illuminating Blake's eyes damn near blinded him. No way he'd worry about something so trite as family politics when Blake looked like that.

He wondered if he could coax Blake out of his shell. Get him to play some piano, to admit it was safe once in a while to harbor a dream. No one should have to sacrifice their happiness for a crap job and a crap life. Jay had connections. There might be something he could do.

Blake stretched, and the hem of his shirt lifted high enough to expose a band of skin above his belt. Pale and creamy, and absolutely delicious. Jay laid next to him, tried to look at the sky and put the thoughts out of his mind.

"Terri thinks you're hot, by the way." Blake blew a strand of hair from one eye.

"Oh?" This should be good.

"Yup. Called you 'total sploosh material'."

"Heh. And what are your thoughts?"

Blake rolled to his side to look at Jay. "What, fishing for compliments?"

Jay mimicked him, and they lay facing one another amid the grass. "No, just curious."

The hair fell back in Blake's eye, and Jay brushed it aside for him without thinking. Blake looked as surprised as Jay felt.

Well, no taking it back now.

Jay curled his hand around Blake's cheek and drew his face closer. He offered no resistance, instead tilting his chin up and holding his breath. The heat radiating from his skin matched the desire in his eyes. Their lips met, tentative at first, but when Blake gasped a small noise of pleasure, Jay pulled his body flush and growled in delight. Blake's hand, which had been resting above his head, abandoned its position and grabbed Jay's waist. His hips moved, slow and tantalizing, against Jay's.

Jay could barely stand it. The taste of Blake nearly dropped his canines. He separated their mouths and pushed Blake onto his back, crouching over him like a lover in bed. He leaned down to kiss, to claim, to mark Blake as his own, when a voice called out from the path below.

"Yo! Jay!"

He knew the voice, and it couldn't have come at a worse time. He couldn't smell Lance at this distance (not with his senses full of strawberries), but he glanced over his shoulder to see the familiar black hair and lithe frame. Dammit. He knew Lance liked to jog here every day, but he'd thought his routine took him by in the mornings.

"Lance," he greeted, rolling off of Blake and trying to calm the blood pounding in his nethers.

Blake propped himself up to see who'd interrupted them. His cheeks were flushed, and his beanie, already knocked askew from their groping, fell wholly to the ground.

"Who's this?" Lance grinned impishly from Blake back to Jay. "You didn't tell me you were dating again."

"Not everything is your business." He tried not to sound petulant and didn't quite succeed.

"When it involves pack, it sure is."

"Well, it doesn't, and I'd appreciate you keeping your nose out of it."

Lance was a good guy, but he liked to talk, and if it meant so much as getting a conversation in with Jay's sister, then Lance would probably sell him out in an instant. At this point, his crush on Cat verged on unbearable.

"Hey, whoa, no offense meant." Lance raised his arms in a defensive position. "Just give us a warning if you start bringing in other people, you know? Maybe vote on it, or whatever?"

Jay ground his teeth. "I'm not 'bringing' anyone in. Sometimes it's nice to have some company, okay?"

"Okay, okay." Lance didn't sound convinced, and he didn't leave them alone either. Instead, he jogged up the hill and introduced himself to Blake. "Nice to meet you, anyway. I'm Lance."

"Blake." He leaned forward and gave the air between them a little sniff. "You're the pack's beta?"

"Yup, that's me. I rein in these crazy bastards." He shook his head. "Do you know how hard it is to be a beta in a pack of alphas? They think I talk too much, but if I didn't they'd've killed each other already." Then he leaned in with an appraising look. "You're an omega, right?"

"Yeah."

"Well, watch out. They'll all fight over you. Alphas, man. They have the worst egos." And he made a show of shrugging.

"Not all of them, though. There's got to be some good ones out there." Blake sounded uncomfortable. Jay could've punted Lance across the damn park.

Lance laughed. "Sure. Of course there are. Anyway, I'll see ya later, Jay. And don't worry—" he held up his hands again as Jay started to speak, "your secret's safe with me. Won't say a word. Not even to Catalina." He waved at them one last time and jogged back to the path before falling from view.

"Well, that was…"

"Annoying." Jay filled in the final word for Blake. Lance and his inexplicable ability to land timing. Maybe it made him a good storyteller, but he'd better keep his lips shut about this one.

"He seemed nice, though. Your pack really cares about you, I bet." Blake failed to keep a note of jealousy from his voice.

"Yeah, I guess they do."

A pause.

"I agree with Terri, so you know."

"Huh?"

"About you. Total sploosh material." Blake grinned.

Ah, dammit, now he couldn't even be mad about Lance anymore.

He stood and proffered a hand. "Let's go. We can grab some ice cream, if you want. There's a place around the block."

"Sounds great. I could go for some strawberry."

Jay looked at Blake's lips. *Yeah, me, too.*

Chapter Five

Handel's "Passacaglia"

He must be losing it. He's never felt so alive, so thrilled at every beep from his phone, every memory of his time with Jay. Blake plays back their kisses in his mind, tasting his new partner, knowing deep inside it can't keep going like this, he can't throw away a life carefully lived for the sake of some alpha. But then he dreams again of Jay, body hot to the touch, mouth full of liquid fire, and all caution melts.

He's survived alone long enough. Most omegas would've lost it by now—he's heard an endless supply of stories about loner omegas falling into depression and taking drastic measures. He's stronger than that, though. He's a fullblood, even if he'd never admit to anyone. His heritage, while troublesome, does offer some benefits—stronger pheromones, sharper senses—though it's as much a curse as a blessing. It means alphas stick to him like chewing gum, and the last thing he needs is extra attention. It's kind of hard to hide when people come sniffing around all the time.

He's out now, shopping with Terri. It mostly involves holding her bags and zoning out while she tries on clothes, so it leaves him with plenty of time to daydream. She's hounded him relentlessly about the relationship. They've known each other since they were pups, and even though he turned down an offer to join her pack, she feels a certain responsibility for him. And, of course, a burning curiosity about his new beau. She directs colorless jokes at him about alphas and sex and alpha sex, and no amount of sarcasm or eyerolling or pleading stops her. Sure, she's slept with alphas before, knows the ropes, but he's not ready to hear his best friend dole out tales of the birds and the bees. He's seen enough porn to know what's packing in an alpha's pants, thank you very much.

"Blaaaaake, sweetie, you don't understand," she says as she flips through a rack of clothes at the department store.

They're in the fashion section of 911, the largest skyscraper mall in Remun. It's famous for its overseas styles, rooftop dining, and outrageous prices. Blake stands at a window overlooking traffic some eleven stories below and tries to block out the conversation. Terri won't have it, though. She abandons the rack and closes in on him, a pile of dresses draped over her right arm.

"You need to be ready to deal with what's going on down there. Alphas think with their dicks, and sooner or later he's going to show you what he wants."

"Ugh, drop it, already. Can't I have one nice thing? One?"

"I want you to enjoy yourself, really! But not if the reality is going to crush you. Has he really not made any moves yet?"

Oh, there have been moves. Mostly contained in their respective pants, but *something* was moving, all right.

"Look, we've kissed. It was nice." More than nice, but she doesn't need to know that. "Leave it. Jay's a good guy. He won't push me."

Terri shakes her head and lays a palm on his arm. "Please tell me you know he's got a kn—"

"Yes! Fucking hell, Terri, I know what a knot is!" He hisses it too loudly, and a nearby woman shoots him a disgusted look. He shrivels.

This is officially The World's Most Uncomfortable Conversation.

"Okay, okay." She placates him with a pat on his arm. "I just want to be sure. You were with that beta once, right? What was his name? Sammy? Sonny?"

"Sebastian." Yep. Worst conversation of his life.

"Oh yeah! Sebby! God, he was a jerk. Glad you dumped him."

If only he could disappear between the clothes racks. Curl up in a little ball forever. Memories of his pseudo-relationship with Sebastian plague him. He wishes he could throw them up like food poisoning.

"Anyway, my point is, you've never had much luck with these guys, and I want to be sure you're not getting in over your head with some macho alpha. I mean, come *on*, have you seen those muscles?"

He has, in real life and in dreams. He opts not to respond.

"Guy's got to have an ego with a build like that. And alphas are different from betas." Terri wags a finger like a schoolmarm. "Way less chill. You thought Sebby was a bad time? What if Jay—"

"Stop it. Seriously." And something in his tone freezes her in her tracks. He thinks again of Jay's possible mafia family, of what blood might be on his hands. Takes a breath. "I know what I'm doing." A big part of him doubts it. "Sort of. At least, I know I like this guy and I want to see where it goes. Let me have that much, okay?"

Terri backs off, smiling a little, and nods. Without needing to, Blake barrels on.

"Anyway, his pack seems cool. I don't think a jerk would have a pack like that."

Uh-oh, now he's done it. Terri's face lights up, and she exclaims, "You've met his pack?"

Blake, face hot, turns away and begins walking toward the exit, bags in his arms swinging. Terri hounds him on his heels.

"O-M-G, Blake, I can't believe you didn't tell me about them! Did they like you? Were they alphas?" Then, voice sultry, "Are they hot?"

"You're killing me!" Blake waves his arms, and the bags flail to and fro. "This is cruel and unusual torture!"

"Deets!" She squeals. "Deets!"

"We bumped into one of them, that's all!"

"You said you met his pack!"

"Not all of them! Just Lance and Elliot!"

"That's two! How many are there?"

"It's not important! Leave it alone already!"

The woman from earlier coughs pointedly, and Blake glances around. Eyes on him, too many eyes on him. He drops his arms to his sides.

"Look," he says in a low voice, "I've met two guys. One's a beta, the other's an alpha. And," he swallows, "yeah, they're hot."

Terri erupts a squeal of rapture, but he'll have no more of it. He grabs her shoulders and spins her around, pushes her to the dressing rooms.

"Go already! I need to pick my dignity up off the floor."

"Oh, honey, better leave it down there. A pack of hot guys will have you on your knees anyway." She giggles before disappearing into the changing room with her armful of clothes.

Blake gawks at the space she'd been standing in. She was incorrigible. Absolutely, mortifyingly incorrigible. When did decency disappear in this town? He snorts. As if. The Howling City is known for its promiscuity. He's the odd one out, not her.

Not like it's his fault, though. Mom forbade him from dating anyone for so long. He grew up alone, lives alone. He doesn't know the first thing about pack bonding.

He glances around himself to make sure no one else is staring. The lady is back to her browsing, thank God. But then someone across the room catches his eye.

He squints and then gasps as he recognizes the wide, flat face and deep-set eyes. The alpha from the café! The one Jay had roughed up. It had to be a coincidence...right? The guy looks away quickly and pulls his collar up, as though it might erase what Blake saw.

His stomach drops like he took a tumble down some stairs. This guy is some kind of stalker! Palms sweating now, Blake glances from side to side, searching for an escape. But the safest place is in public with a friend. He swallows. The guy sidles up and out of the store as though nothing strange has happened at all, but one last glance back in Blake's direction tells him everything.

Some rough alpha has learned his scent, stalked him like an old werewolf tracking prey, and means to do... to do... Blake's mind buzzes as he inserts images into the blank space, each one more horrifying than the last. He shudders.

He can't tell Terri or Jay, and definitely not the police. No background searches, no entanglements. No, it's better to keep quiet entirely. The guy probably wanted a stroll around the mall. Thousands of people come here every day. He's no different from them.

He manages to calm his heart with the thought. It's a coincidence, nothing more. He has pepper spray and a lock on the door. He'll be fine. He doesn't need anyone's help.

Terri exits the dressing room with her first outfit—a white summer dress that compliments her dark skin beautifully—and gives a twirl.

"What do you think?"

***

A third date later, Blake decides to tell his mom about Jay. Not an easy decision considering her condition, considering how even in her prime she disapproved of anyone coming near them, threatening to break up their carefully lived life. He can't blame her—after what she sacrificed to get him here, keep him safe... To throw it away for a fling is unconscionable.

But this is Jay, someone so wholly different from anyone he's ever met in his life that it seems possible, somehow, that he might be able to settle down, outstrip his past and plant a future. Again, the thought that he might dare to dream of having more than this one shot at life plagues him. The dangers from his past—no, he won't think about that. Jay is the present, maybe even the future, and his mom deserves to know about him.

He visits her every week, always slipping his eyes from the meager care home's dull light and peeling wallpaper. It's all he can afford, and it's better than nothing. He would have no chance of taking care of her on his own. It's always a crapshoot if she's lucid enough to recognize him, and it pains him to look at her, thin and weak in her nightgown, blond hair, originally so soft and flowing, now wiry and dull. She's the shriveled shell of the beautiful woman he remembers from childhood, the one who baked pies and taught him how to play piano and always made sure they had a roof over their head, even if it meant working three jobs.

The nurses do their best to take care of her, but there's too many patients and too few staff, and sometimes she smells like they haven't bathed her since the week before. Often, she lies in bed staring wide-eyed at the ceiling, watching the ghosts of her past with twitchy, moaning focus. Sometimes she treats Blake like an old family member, a brother or a cousin, but not her son. Sometimes she grabs him as hard as her bony hands allow and hisses, "He's after us! Mikhail can't know!"

Those moments are the scariest, because he thinks, *What if she tells someone? What if she doesn't realize what she's saying and tells someone?* But he always holds her hands and soothes her with promises that they were safe, no one knows. No one will ever know.

He tells her stories about his week, what piano pieces he's practicing on his old keyboard, what book he has checked out of the library. He tries to reminisce with her, tell her stories from the days they lived together, and sometimes she smiles and remembers with him. Sometimes she pulls away and turns her back.

He hates the world that put her here. Whether it's God or fate or his own ineptitude that struck her with this illness, he hates it. She's young still, and sometimes when she turns her eyes on him, he can see the shade of what she'd been, the beauty that led them here, all the way across the sea. She ran away from her old life to keep him safe, and look where it landed her. Unfair. The world is so fucking unfair.

Blake passes the yellow hallways of the nursing home, checks in at the desk, and approaches her room. He imagines her as she'd been last week: twisted up in the bedsheets and moaning with a pain that seemed to have no source. Wonders what version of her would greet him today.

He knocks on the door and pushes it open gingerly. "Mom?"

"Oh, honey, it's good to see you!" She's sitting up in bed, a faded green shawl around her shoulders, with a pile of magazines in her lap. Her fingers—usually trembling and weak—pluck at photos and tear them out with precise, tiny movements. A little collection of them lie scattered on the sheets: flowers and cars and various words in different fonts, as eclectic as her own failing mind.

The sound of her voice shakes him to his core. It's as though nothing is wrong at all—he's just come home from school instead of working a shit shift at a shit job. He can practically smell the pie baking. She'd taught herself how to make them, apple and cherry and strawberry, and he aches to taste a slice again.

"You look good today." Legs too weak to carry him farther, he sinks into a chair beside her bed.

"What, I don't look good every day?" She winks at him to show she isn't offended. She's tearing out a picture of a chrysanthemum, hands moving like they used to when she played piano, confident and steady. "They won't let me have scissors," she explains to Blake's unasked question. "Say I could hurt myself. Silliness! I'm not a pup!"

His throat catches for a fraction of a second, and he has to swallow back an urge to hug her, to climb onto the little bed beside her like he did when he was four and had a nightmare about the bad man coming after them. Instead, he clears it and says, "It'll look better this way when you paste them in your book. The edges will have some flair."

Her face brims with pride. "That's my boy. Always seeing the bright side."

He has to grip the chair arms to keep himself stable. His throat is a pinprick, and air barely wheezes through it. She hasn't been this functional in months. He dares not believe she could be recovering. He picks up a magazine and thumbs through it for something to add to her collection.

As they sit together, plucking little images of balloons and cake and pretty girls from their pages, she prods him for conversation.

"Tell me what you've been up to. Practicing anything new?"

He flips a page and stares at an underwear model. Tries to push Jay from his mind. "Rachmaninoff. *Prelude in C Sharp Minor*. I love the opening chords."

She nods. "A powerful piece. I remember Mikha—" A shade flickers over her eyes, and Blake's stomach drops. Now it would come. The pain, the other side of her. With every old memory of her life before Atlas, she slides a little closer to the edge, where he fears she'll forget him entirely.

Her breath hitches, eyes miles away, in another time, another life.

"Mom?" His voice couldn't overpower a mouse's squeak.

Her eyes well, shining blue in their sunken holes. She blinks, and a tear slips down her cheek. Without breaking her staring contest with the abyss, she whispers, "They're after us. You have to hide, Blake."

He reaches across the gap between them and takes her hand. "We're safe. We've been safe for years. It's okay, Mom, come back."

She pulls in a haggard breath, and another tear splatters the sheets. She tears her eyes away from whatever she sees in her past and stares at him. He can see the whites all the way around her irises.

"Tell me you've been careful. Tell me no one knows."

He squeezes her hand. "No one. Not even Terri. I promise."

She shudders under his gaze.

"Your eyes... just like..." She groans and falls back against the pillows.

"Mom!" He leans over her, and his necklace slips out from beneath his shirt and dangles above her face. Silver and green flashes in the yellow lamplight.

"Where did you get that?" Her face twists into a dark snarl as she stares at the pendant. A storm brews in her battered mind.

Blake steadies himself and reaches for her hand. "You gave it to me. A year ago, remember? Before you came here."

She jerks her hand out from under his and snatches at the necklace. "Give it back! You stole it!"

"I didn't—"

"*It's mine!*"

She gets a hold of the pendant and jerks, yanking Blake down by the neck until the chain snaps. By now, footsteps hurry down the hall, and in burst two nurses to check what the commotion is about. Nurse McConnall rushes over and presses her back into the pillows while Nurse Stevens administers a sedative.

Blake recoils from the scene, staring in horror as his mom struggles against them, all good will gone from her features. His fault. All his fault.

"Mom?" He tentatively reaches for her, but she jerks away from him, chest rising and falling in short, shallow breaths. "I love you. I'll visit again tomorrow, okay? I'm sorry." He swallows an acid flavor. "I don't blame you, okay? It's not your fault."

Her fighting ceases, and she watches him through half-lidded eyes. "Thief," she hisses and falls into a sweaty, limp sleep.

All around lie the crumpled pictures they'd torn out, like a battleground pockmarked with craters. Dazed, Blake picks up the chrysanthemum and smooths it out.

Nurse McConnall pries the necklace from his mom's grip. "This what set her off?"

He takes it from her, the flower dropping from his fingers to the scuffed floor. "She gave it to me before she was admitted. It's like a family heirloom. I guess she forgot about it."

"She's forgetting a lot of things." Nurse McConnall says it with tenderness, but it fails to comfort him.

He wraps the pendant chain around his hand and presses it to his chest. The links are broken again. "She was having such a good day. Like old times. I was going to tell her..." He trails off, the hurt too deep to continue.

"That'll happen, too." The nurse pats his shoulder in a distanced sort of way, like he's a twice removed family member or maybe the pet dog. "She'll have good days and bad. Stuff sets patients like her off. It's not your fault."

She's not some patient. She's my goddamn mom.

He forces a smile and nods. His muscles feel like music wire tuned too tightly. He tries to linger in the room, to adjust his mom's hair and make her comfortable, but the sickness in his guts nearly overtakes him. He leaves, head down, heart throbbing, and barely looks up until he's home again. He sits on his bed and presses his face into his hands. The smell of the nursing home's antiseptic lingers on his skin, bitter and sharp. The necklace dangles from his fingers, once again broken and unwearable. He doesn't cry. His tears dried up a long time ago, somewhere between the years he spent in kitchens and the sight of his mom screaming from a pain no one could identify. He manages a few shaky breaths and lies down. Maybe tomorrow will be different, but somehow he doubts it.

Chapter Six

Rachmaninoff's "Little Red Riding Hood"

The following morning Blake lies in bed—futon, really—staring out the window in his studio. It opens onto a fire escape with a practically unfettered view of the opposite building's gray brick wall. Usually, local taggers keep a revolving selection of art pieces to admire from this vantage point, and today is no exception. Blake traces the lines with his eyes, pinks and greens and purples, all coalescing into a massive, erect dong.

For all their art, the local taggers aren't very creative.

Beside him on the nightstand, his phone buzzes. His malaise keeps him from immediately reaching for it. Heaped next to the phone is his necklace, chain snapped and twisted. The phone doesn't buzz a second time, and Blake almost ignores it, but something about looking at that splotchy pink and purple dick on the wall makes him pick it up.

Doing anything this weekend?

Jay.

Blake plops back against the lumpy mattress and holds the phone over his head. He stares hard at the words, searching in his gut for some reaction that isn't apathy. He finds it a second later when another message follows.

A selfie of Jay at the gym, towel over his shoulders, grinning with a thumbs up. Damn this tiny screen. He can barely make out the shape of Jay's pecs. His junk jumps anyway just thinking about the sweat glistening on that neck.

He glances back at the message. **Doing anything this weekend?**

You, hopefully.

He shakes his head. Better not send that particular thought. He has some self-control at least.

He types back, **Hanging out with you?** And adds a smirking emoji.

The response is immediate. **Oh, I'm hung all right.**

Blake rolls his eyes. As if there was ever any doubt.

Keep it in your pants, Mr. Macho Alpha. How about pizza? I know a place.

Can I get pineapple?

Ew. No. You're a monster.

I see how it is. I send you a nice photo and now I'm a monster. Tongue-out emoji.

Before Blake can think of a witty reply, a second message follows up.

Quid pro quo?

He swallows. Jay's asking for a photo. He's sent one dirty picture in his entire life, and that was a disaster. He'd snapped a picture of his dick and accidentally sent it to Terri, who had responded with a bunch of wide-eyed emojis and a small eggplant. He grinds his teeth at the memory.

Trying to worm his way out of it, he texts, **I'm in bed. Not much to see here.**

Jay responds, **Thinking about me in bed are you?** Followed by a winky face.

Fine then, if that's the way he wants it. Blake positions himself with his boxers pulled down ever so slightly and his hand beneath them, appearing to tease himself. He starts with one photo: a smirk and the caption, **Thinking a lot about you.** Then he sends a second photo, his hand removed from his pants and flipping Jay the bird. **While I was thinking, I found this.**

A moment, then the reply arrives. **Touché.**

Blake chuckles. Jay has scrubbed his bad mood away with only a few messages. He had planned to spend his day holed up in his room, but now he feels more like getting out. Maybe a walk downtown. Maybe he can get his necklace fixed again. He scoops it off the nightstand and pulls on some clothes. Not his style to go begging for a hand, but hopefully Elliot will help him out one more time. He locks up the apartment and hurries down the metal stairwell with a bounce in his step.

***

Elliot's shop hasn't changed since Blake's last visit. Still richer than his palate can handle. The door dings as he enters, and a new face greets him from the counter.

"Good day, sir. May I help you with anything?" The woman smiles and tilts her head slightly to the right, exposing her neck politely. Not that it matters, with her being a mech and all, but it's a custom they programmed into her, and Blake smiles in return.

"I'm looking for Elliot. Is he here?"

"Mr. Smolders is in his office. One moment, please."

She dips inside the back, and a minute later Elliot appears dressed in a tailored jacket and slacks.

"Oh, you're back." He sounds surprised.

"'Smolders'? That is *not* your last name." It's out before Blake can stop himself.

Even more surprised, Elliot responds, "Is that a problem?"

Shut up, you need his help.

"Are you secretly a model or something? That sounds like a stage name."

"It's Servan. Been around for generations. I'm not making it up." His lips twist up in amusement.

"No, I'm pretty sure you're a model. Or a superhero. Did you come from another planet? Maybe your whole pack did, and that's why you're so—" The word 'perfect' dies in Blake's throat.

"So what?" Elliot arches an eyebrow, and Blake gets the vibe he's practiced this expression, probably on Jay. He's more elegant than Jay, anyway, with a smell like caramelized sugar and cream. He isn't as tall, but he's lean and self-assured, with that easy confidence that comes with being an alpha. Really, he's more feline than lupine, as though his family might have mixed blood. Vampire Union, maybe? Blake's never met a vampire—they're awfully rare unless you live overseas.

"So..." and Blake makes a general motion in the air as if Elliot, himself, is the answer.

Elliot crosses his arms and taps a long finger on his cheek. "Why are you here, Blake Fields?" He doesn't seem mad, only amused.

"I don't remember telling you my last name." Blake leans forward and squints at him. "Are you stalking me?"

You never shut up, do you?

"No, I just have packmates who love to gossip. A few drinks, and it all comes spilling out."

"Hopefully that's *all* that comes out."

"I don't kiss and tell."

Blake frowns. So that's how it is. "What's it like?"

"Sex with Jay? Not the conversation I imagined having today."

Blake waves a hand to shut him up. "Having a pack, I mean. Someone always being there. Like...like a family, right?"

"So you really don't have one." Elliot steps forward, bringing their bodies only inches apart. He sniffs lightly at the air to confirm it. "No, I don't smell anyone else. How old are you?" No judgment in his voice, just open curiosity.

"Twenty-four in June."

"And you've gone your whole adult life without a pack. That takes fortitude. What drives a man to live alone like that? Especially an omega."

Elliot still hasn't pulled away. Their bodies are practically touching, and an electricity seems to jump through the air between their skin. Blake barely dares to breathe, lest he drown in that caramel aroma. But he holds his own. Stares Elliot down and says, "Maybe I don't like people."

"Maybe."

A pause, one filled with an unspoken accusation. Elliot knows something, and their eyes lock together; a silent battle of wills and pheromones unfold between them. At last Elliot says, "You didn't answer my first question. Why are you here?"

He's going to have to push things. He can't give ground now. Better to act like nothing is strange about him. He pulls out the pendant and holds it so Elliot can see the break in the chain.

"I had another accident. I was hoping you'd fix it."

Elliot's eyes don't even bother to look away from his. "I thought I told you to be careful with it."

"Yeah, well, shit happens."

The tension is grinding his nerves, making him snippy. What does Elliot want from him? A confession? To back off Jay? He'd be damned if he—

"I'll fix it." Elliot plucks the necklace from his fingers and walks away to the back room, leaving a breadth of cold air in his place.

Blake runs a shaky hand through his hair. Elliot knows something. Dammit. If he's figured him out, knows his real identity... Blake swallows. He could be blackmailed, sold out, traded over to the government, anything.

"Shit."

Elliot returns with a pair of pliers in hand, the type with the pointy tip. He lays the necklace on the counter and turns a lamp on. White light blasts the area, and he rotates the broken chain to get a better angle. Blake glares at him from the middle of the room, hugging his arm to his body.

"Let me ask you something else." Elliot doesn't look up from his task.

"What's that?" He forces his voice steady.

"Do you know where this necklace comes from? What the symbol means?"

Ice splashes Blake's guts. Elliot asked it casually, as though there's not an ocean of implication in the words.

No doubt about it, Elliot knows exactly what the necklace means.

He tries to cover. "I don't know what you're—"

"Because I do. And if you plan to continue this relationship with Jay, I need to know you're not going to cause him problems." Elliot draws the broken ends of the chain together and aligns them.

"I'm not trying to cause anyone trouble."

He can't figure out what Elliot wants from him, but he refuses to squirm. He steps forward instead, approaching the counter like he might a wild animal.

"You originally came from Servos, didn't you? That crest matches the royal family's." The words—and their truth—are like a punch in his gut. Then Elliot continues. "You're a refugee, aren't you?"

Blake has to stop himself from sighing in relief. It's technically the truth, even if it's not the whole truth.

"Yeah. My mom ran away when I was a baby. I grew up in Atlas. We're not spies, or anything." Anyway, the truth is almost too unbelievable even for him.

But Elliot shakes his head. "Yet you just so happen to run into Jay and start dating. Seems convenient." He crimps the chain links into place with a few dexterous pinches of the pliers.

Blake frowns. "What does that mean? Jay came to my shop. I didn't—I'm not *seducing* him, if that's what you think."

Elliot glances up from his task and studies Blake. The electricity is back between them, implications and accusations sizzling the air between their eyes.

"No," he says at last. "I don't. But Jay's had his share of gold diggers, understand? I don't want to see him invest himself in someone who's interested in the wrong thing."

Damn, how rich is Jay? The thought of some mafioso giving commands to off the snooping omega dance in his mind. Then he realizes Elliot might be part of it, too, if they're in a pack together.

Ah, shit. He's probably sending a message, and Blake went and got his wires crossed. He waves both hands. "I'm not looking for trouble, either. I don't want to be on anyone's bad side."

Elliot passes the necklace back to him, good as new. "You're not on my bad side. I'm simply concerned with Jay's well-being. He's my pack leader, after all."

"You're in on it, too, aren't you? God, I'm such an idiot. What have I gotten myself into?" He clutches the chain to his chest. "Just tell me, okay? Please. What kind of family is he part of?"

"Don't you know?" Elliot stares at him hard, like a man trying to solve a riddle. "I thought for sure you knew."

Blake squeezes his eyes shut like it might cushion the blow. "Just tell me. I can take it."

Please don't be a hitman.

"He's the youngest child of the Reed family." The amusement creeps back into his voice. "Really, how could you not have known?"

Blake blinks. It sounds familiar. The hostess at the restaurant called him that, but he can't figure out why it's so important. He squinches his face as he considers.

"Reed." Elliot repeats it like he's astounded they're even having this conversation. "As in, Colin and Sara Reed. The Reed Foundation. Reed Dynamics. He's Julian Reed."

He's WHO now?

A merciless giggle escapes Blake's lips. Suddenly lightheaded, Blake breaks into a laughing fit.

No fucking way.

Elliot stares, mouth slightly ajar, and the sight only makes Blake laugh harder.

"You're kidding me!" He wheezes out. "There's no way! He's not—" He hiccups a breath of air. "He's not *that* rich! I've seen him wear sweatshirts! We—" and the memory sets off another roll of laughter. "We were attacked by ducks at the park. Rich people don't get attacked by ducks."

"You really didn't know." Elliot shakes his head. "You're something else."

This can't be right. The worst case was supposed to be that Jay killed people for a living. Not that he's in politics.

"Okay, but for real, though? He's not a mafia hitman? He'd better not be. I was hoping we'd hook up soon." The laughing fit has apparently made him loopy and now all kinds of nonsense is spilling from his mouth. He has such a way with words.

His laughter seems to be catching, though, because Elliot chuckles at that. "That's what you thought? No, I can assure you he is not some mafia hitman. I've seen him prune tomato plants. He couldn't kill anybody if he wanted to. His sister, though..." and he laughs again at the private joke.

Right. He has a sister. And an older brother, if Blake isn't mistaken. And, like, more money than anyone in their right mind would know what to do with. The Reed family is one of the three lead packs in Atlas. They basically run the west coast. It's their job to maintain and oversee relations with the nearest border, Oceana, and make sure no wars or scandals break out. They have their hands in other world politics as well, and they're basically the go-to name on the west half of Atlas.

So much worse than the mafia.

"This is insane." Blake shakes his head, and the laughter peters out, replaced with a growing sense of horror. "I didn't sign up for this."

His mom would lose it. He had been raised to keep his head down, stay low, never make a scene. No alphas and no attention. Somehow, he's broken those rules utterly and flippantly. The Reed family could end him with a snap of their fingers.

"You may want to discuss the matter with him yourself. You seem perturbed." It's a polite way of saying he looks terrified.

"I may be having a minor panic attack or three. Am I breathing? I'm not totally sure I'm breathing."

"This isn't the way I'd imagine anyone reacting to the news that their partner is fabulously wealthy."

"Guess I'm full of surprises. Am I..." Blake's head spun dangerously. "I might faint. Oh no, he promised me this wasn't some TV drama. I'm dating a liar."

"I don't know what you're talking about but come over here. Sit." Elliot guides him to a chair on the other side of the counter. "Breathe already."

"So I'm not breathing. I knew it. This is how I die." Another giggle erupts from his chest.

"You don't need to worry about his family. They won't deport you."

"Oh god, I hadn't even thought of that. Give me a bucket. I might throw up."

Elliot hesitates, unsure if Blake is kidding or not.

"Will you see Jay soon? Perhaps a serious conversation is in order. I may have overstepped my boundaries telling you all of this. Sorry."

"You mean *Julian*?" A hysterical bark of laughter escapes him. "Does he even look like a Julian to you? I don't think Julians spend all their time at the gym. Julians go to afternoon tea and opera houses and charity dinners."

"He does prefer his nickname." Then, helplessly, Elliot repeats, "Sorry."

"When was he going to tell me?" Blake shoots an accusatory glare at the alpha.

Elliot shifts under his gaze and gives a little shrug. "Most likely he assumed you already knew. Would you like me to call him? He's not working on a project this week. He could come over."

"Ha! Yes, not like us plebeians. Jobs, who needs those when you have more money than God?" The shock transforms into a bitter anger that surprises him. It isn't Jay's fault he was born into the Reed family, but it would have been nice to know a little sooner.

Yeah, and then I could've gotten out before I started feeling all these pesky emotions.

Alphas, man. They really screw with your head.

Elliot taps his fingers on the counter nervously. "This is not how I expected this conversation to go," he admits.

"Because you're an alpha," Blake accuses with a jab of his finger. "You always expect everything to go your way."

"That isn't—" Elliot cuts himself off with a little hum.

Gotcha. One point to Fields.

"Look, I need some time to think this over." Blake gets his feet under him and exhales a long breath. "I have a date with Jay this week. I'll talk to him about it then. Thanks for fixing my pendant again." He starts to leave, but Elliot calls after him.

"Why are you so scared of who Jay is?"

Because someone could spot me. Because I've been hiding for two and half decades, and this could trash all of it.

"Because I'm Little Red Riding Hood, and he's the Big Bad Wolf. I don't want to get eaten alive."

He leaves without waiting for a response.

* * *

They meet two days later at a pizza parlor downtown. Blake's spent the intermittent time questioning if he should ghost Jay—just throw his phone down the sewer and never show up again. But if Jay really is a Reed, he'd have connections, ways of tracking him down that he couldn't avoid. No, better to talk this out and break things off gracefully.

The pizza parlor is a step up from a hole in the wall, but they make great food, evidenced by the fact that there's nowhere available to sit. People cram in, grabbing slices and whole pies, garlic knots and calzones. It smells like parmesan and red pepper and grease—heaven under any normal circumstance. This is not a normal circumstance.

"You seem tense. Want to grab a pie and find somewhere less crowded?" Jay is all smiles and good humor and, as always, fantastically handsome. He wears a hooded jacket over a red V-neck and a pair of jeans with purposeful rips at the knees. The sight makes Blake's resolve waver.

"Somewhere private would be nice," he manages.

"How about my place? I'm around the corner."

His place probably smells better than the pizza shop, though for different reasons. They could sit on the couch and eat lunch and maybe Blake could get his hands under that shirt to feel every contour, maybe even get the shirt off.

Stop that. That's not why you're here. You're supposed to break up with him, not bang him.

Harder than it sounds, really.

"Okay. But no pineapple."

Jay shakes his head. "My pizza genius is unappreciated. What would you like, then?"

"Pepperoni. And peppers."

"Might I interest you in mushrooms?" Jay runs his hand down Blake's arm, sending sparks of heat through his body.

"I could be convinced."

Jay winks and leaves him to wait in line. Blake calls after him.

"See if they'll throw on some extra basil!"

Might as well have a killer pizza before everything falls apart. Then they could console themselves with the leftovers.

Blake idles in a corner as Jay puts in their order. His heart accelerates as he watches the man—the friendly smile, casual grace, affable charm. It seems impossible that he's actually the youngest member of the most influential family in Remun City. Damn his luck that he wasn't a normal guy. Then things might work out. But there's no way. Not when the secret he's been harboring his whole life could tear them both to shreds. Jay deserves better. Blake chews at the tip of his thumb, lost in thought. He almost doesn't notice the man sidling up beside him, but then the smell hits him.

Cigarettes and acetone.

Blake wrinkles his nose. He knows that smell. A hand falls on his elbow, gripping firmly. Not a friendly grip.

"I've got some questions for you," a deep throaty voice hisses in his ear, thickened with an accent.

Blake turns and locks eyes with the broad, flat-faced alpha who'd been at the department store, who'd grabbed him in the café, whose nose is still splotchy and bruised from Jay's punch.

His heart leaps into his throat, and he instinctively jerks away. The man tightens his grip painfully and growls, "Come here if you want to keep your boyfriend out of this."

Blake responds with a snippy, "He's not my boyfriend."

Good job. Because that's the most pressing issue here.

"Whatever he is, he doesn't have a part in this. We're leaving. I've got questions for you."

"You said that. Do you always repeat yourself?"

He feels loopy again, but one thing seems clear: keep talking. Distract the guy. Hold out for Jay to come back.

The alpha growls low, a sound meant to threaten and play on his omega instincts. Obey. Concede. Surrender. But, being a fullblood, all it does is irritate him.

"Is this just a thing you do? Grab some poor guy and haul him off? It's never going to get you laid."

Yeah, dingus, unless he forces you. Don't piss him off.

Too late. Flat Nose jerks painfully at his arm, and Blake opens his mouth to shout. Then he feels the sharp, cold point of something nestle into his side.

"You want to stay quiet and follow me," hisses the man. "One foot in front of the other. Come on."

Blake takes a few halting steps toward the door, eyes darting to Jay, whose back currently faces them. The point in his side presses in harder, pricking him through his shirt. The spit evaporates from his throat. He allows the man to lead him outside.

They round the corner and walk down an alleyway, out of sight of people. Blake's heart triples its speed, outpacing them like it's trying for a world record sprint. Then the guy shoves him up against a wall, and he swears it stops entirely.

"What's your name?" Flat Nose growls in his ear.

"If you wanted to date me, there's better ways to get my info." The hysteria is back, along with a heaping pile of panic.

The man grabs his shoulder and shoves his face harder against the brick. All Blake can see is red and black. An ant scuttles over the bricks by his nose, ignorant of his struggle.

"Your name. Where you're from. Why you have that pendant. Now!"

There it is. The icy reality catching up to him. The thing he had known deep inside would happen all his life. The worst possible scenario.

This guy doesn't want sex. He wants Blake's head on a platter.

"Hey!" A shout from the other end of the alley, deep and familiar, full of anger and command. Jay. "Get off him!"

Flat Nose stiffens, then releases his grip. The knife disappears from Blake's side, followed by the sound of fleeing footsteps echoing away down the alley.

Blake heaves a breath, then his legs go to jelly. He melts to the ground, hugging himself and shivering. Someone knows who he is. Someone dangerous. All these years of dodging others, maintaining distance, all meaningless now. Someone knows who he is, and that means he's as good as dead.

Warm hands grab his shoulders and pull him close. He falls against Jay, not crying, but not steady either. Jay hugs him tightly, surrounding him with the scent of earth and flowers and soothing rain. The heat eases his muscles, blanks out the stress in his brain. This is only him and Jay, and that's all that matters.

My alpha.

"Did he hurt you?" Jay sounds pissed. Blake shakes his head, still too shocked to speak. "I'm sorry I wasn't there. I won't let it happen again." He squeezes, and Blake's heart melts.

Impossible. The whole situation is impossible. Everything he's ever worked for is going down in flames. He can't let Jay be a casualty, too. Time to find the right chance to break the news.

Even though his every instinct screams to hold Jay close, he knows it's time to pull the plug.

Chapter Seven

Ravel's "La Valse"

Jay leads Blake away from the scene and toward his place. At Blake's insistence he stops to pick up the pizza. Blake holds it as they stroll down the busy street blocks, consoling himself with the smell of cheese and pepperoni. Jay keeps a firm arm around his waist and mean mugs anyone who gets too close to them.

"It's okay. I don't think they want our pizza." Blake feels numb despite his casual tone.

"You were attacked! How can you be so blasé?"

"I don't think it's hit me yet. I can't process this on an empty stomach."

"Who even was that guy? Who attacks someone at a pizza place?"

Guilt washes over Blake. He shouldn't feel at fault for being attacked, but he feels it anyway.

If I was just some normal guy this wouldn't have happened.

All the more reason to break it off with Jay. If someone is after him, Jay's going to get dragged into it. But he has nowhere to go. A cold fear grips his stomach, washing out the hunger for a distant panic that makes his breath catch. Flat Nose proved he could track Blake down, which means he could find Mom next. There's nowhere to go. He can't take her out of care. They can't flee to another country. This is it. The finale. His swan song.

"Blake?" Jay stops walking.

The thoughts have frozen Blake in place, welded him to the ground. He whimpers.

"Hey, it's okay. You're safe now. Let's get to my place and we can talk about it. Come on." He gives Blake's waist a little tug.

With a heaving effort, Blake steps forward. One foot in front of the other. Clear out the thoughts and move. It's all he can manage now. He's nothing if not a survivor. He can do this.

They arrive at a condominium a few minutes later. A porter greets them with a bow, swipes a key card, and the door swings open for them, letting out a gasp of air conditioning scented with lemon. Blake glances up from the pizza box.

The place is plush, gleaming tiles on the floor, two elevators side by side polished to a shine that reflects Blake's haggard face back at him. Wood walls, potted plants in the corners, and delicate hanging lamps that light up the hall with a soft white glow.

Despite everything, his interest is piqued to wonder what Jay's place will look like. He supposes he'll find out in a minute as the elevator dings and slides open for them.

Jay punches the button for the third floor, and they stand in silence as the elevator rises smoothly to its destination. A soft song plays as they travel: Chopin's "Nocturne in C Sharp Minor". Blake's fingers twitch at the melodic piano, a nearly Pavlovian reaction from years of playing.

The elevator slides to stop and announces their destination with a high *ding!*. The doors open, and more tile and plants greet them.

Jay steps out and offers a hand. "Might I welcome you to my humble abode?"

Blake takes his hand and follows, pizza box balanced on one palm.

"Which one is yours?" Blake nods at the three doors.

"All of them. I own the floor. That's an office," he points, "and that leads to my home gym. You don't want to go in there unless you like stinky gym socks."

Blake pulls a tense smile. "And that?" He points to the right.

"Everything else." Jay starts toward the door, and Blake tags along next to him.

So he owns the whole floor of a luxury condo. Seems excessive for only one guy, but that's the Reeds for you. Honestly, Blake is just relieved he doesn't live in a palace.

"Welcome home, Jay," a voice calls to them when Jay opens the door. So maybe he doesn't live alone.

"Roommate?" Blake cocks his head to one side, searching for the source of the noise.

Jay chuckles. "Not really."

A man rounds the corner and bows politely. Blake would be confused if it isn't for the lights glowing beneath the man's skin and the serial code stitched into his uniform.

"You have a mech! That's nuts!" He shouldn't be surprised, but there it is.

"A gift from my sister. She thought I needed company or something ridiculous like that. Charlie, this is Blake. Blake, Charlie."

"Hello, Blake, it's a pleasure to meet you." Charlie tilts his head to the right.

"Hi." Unsure if there's a particular etiquette when dealing with a mech, Blake resigns himself to saying almost nothing. It's a new strategy for him.

"Would you like tea? Ms. Oshiro left some leaves I could brew. Longjing from the mainland."

"That sounds good," Blake pipes up. Strategy unsuccessful.

"You heard the man. One pot of tea, please."

Charlie bows and leaves for the kitchen. Blake looks around for the first time unfettered. The condo is modern with large square windows bordered with chrome and wooden floors. From here, he can see the living room clearly, decorated in blues and silvers, with an entertainment system spanning one wall and a glass door leading out to a porch. An open staircase connects to a landing above the room that seems mostly unused, just a few boxes stacked neatly along the back edge. Across from there, a dining room furnished with what appears to be a solid wood table and chairs sits clean and untouched, probably because the bar at a cut through to the kitchen is cluttered with newspapers and a tablet. Through the cut out, Charlie is heating water in an electric kettle. Everything is well lit, clean, and nearly entirely covered in plants.

They're in every corner and crevice: ferns and flowers and succulents. A large pot in the dining room grows what appears to be a lemon tree. It all smells like Jay. Warm earth with a sweet fragrance like lilies or maybe daffodils. Blake could curl up here and never move again.

He must be gawking, because Jay says, "It's a little cluttered, I know, but—"

"It's great! I can't believe you live here! I mean, I can, it smells just like you, but it's so nice! Not that I think you wouldn't live in a nice place. I'm just not used to nice places. I mean, shut up, Blake." He zips his lips before more nonsense can spill out.

Jay laughs and leads him to the large, overstuffed couch in the middle of the living room. Crossing the hall, Blake can see down both ends, each leading to closed doors. They sit together on the couch, close enough to touch, the pizza occupying the table in front of them. Jay wraps an arm around Blake's shoulders.

"How are you feeling? Really."

With no other answers, Blake opts for the truth. "Stressed."

"Did he hurt you?" Jay sounds deadly serious. Like he might track the guy down and crack his skull against a wall in return.

Blake shakes his head.

Silence now. They need to talk. *He* needs to talk. Apologize. Tell him they have to end things. But nothing comes out.

Jay wraps both arms around Blake and pulls him close. He tosses off Blake's beanie and buries his nose in his hair. Blake almost stops breathing, except that this close to Jay's chest he can smell the alpha musk, and he never wants to stop smelling it. He takes in a long breath and presses himself to Jay's body. It seems impossible that he's lived without this for so many years.

A sudden spark of need flares in him. Tingles shoot down his skin, coalesce in his groin, and he lets himself melt. He presses a kiss to the side of Jay's neck, then another. He can't help himself. His mouth always has a habit of running away without him, and there it goes again. He knows he's not doing either of them any favors by giving in like this, but right now all he wants is Jay.

Jay's hands slide lower, one finding Blake's shirt hem and slipping underneath, the other groping over his clothes to find his ass. A giddy throb leaps inside Blake's chest. He pushes back, and they topple sideways, Jay falling against the couch arm, Blake perched atop him. He leaves Jay's neck to find his lips, warm and wet and full. Another round of tingles passes through him. He's fully erect now, straining against his pants, and there's no way Jay doesn't notice. The hand beneath his shirt roves to the front and finds his right nipple. A light pinch elicits a moan that he barely recognizes as his own voice. His hips, moving entirely of their own accord, grind against Jay's. The alpha is just as turned on it seems, and when their cocks slip against each other, even through the barrier of clothing, Jay lets out a grunt and bucks back.

Blake's heart pounds. Gone are the thoughts of breaking it off, gone is the memory of Flat Nose and his demands, all that exists—all that ever had or ever would exist—is Jay.

He tugs at Jay's shirt, stretches it, tries to peel it off, but the fabric doesn't yield. A little whine escapes his throat that absolutely couldn't be him. He's never sounded so needy in his entire life. Jay growls in response and nips his bottom lip. His canines have lengthened—definitely fullblood alpha—and the sensation nearly drives Blake to madness. He sits up and grabs his belt buckle, what little mind he has left made up that he will fuck this man, fuck him so thoroughly that they'll both lose all feeling in their legs and probably never walk again.

Then voice calls out, "Your tea." A little clatter as Charlie sets the tray of teapot and cups down on the table beside them. "Will you be needing anything else? Lube, perhaps?"

They both freeze. Blake blinks a few times, then a giggle bursts out of him. Jay groans and releases his grip to facepalm.

"No, Charlie, that'll be all."

"Very good. I'll be nearby if you need anything else." He strides down the hall and disappears into one of the rooms.

They study each other for a moment, the sudden onset of passion utterly ruined, and Blake retreats to the opposite end of the couch.

"Sorry about that," Jay mumbles, and Blake can't tell if he's referring to their make out session or Charlie's interruption.

"No, it's fine, I'm sorry, too." Blake fusses at a lock of his hair and wills his dick to shrink.

Jay grunts and sits up. After another moment of silence, he opens the pizza box and offers Blake a slice. Blake's stomach immediately leaps into action. He takes the offering and bites into it like a starving man. The cheese has congealed, but the taste is still astounding thanks to the extra basil. They eat, piece by piece, until most of the pie is gone. Jay tosses a crust back into the box and groans.

"No more. That's way too much pizza. Why did we get a large?"

Blake plucks his crust out of the box and nibbles at it. "I regret nothing."

"Do you know how many sit ups I have to do now?"

"Mmm, ten?" Blake licks some grease off his fingers. He doesn't work out usually, but he walks everywhere and sometimes only eats one meal a day. This much pizza won't affect him.

"Like a hundred. But you're right. No regrets."

"Do you do those upside-down crunches? Those look pretty effective. That's got to be the equivalent of twenty crunches."

Jay chuckles, and Blake relishes the deep tone. "I don't think it works that way."

"You should try it. I bet they work just like that." Blake mimes a crunch as though it proves his point.

"So, what do you want to do now? I have some AR games we could play."

It sounds wonderful, but Blake hesitates. Too much at stake now, and he needs an out. He can't put Jay through whatever comes next.

"That guy still on your mind?" Jay presses a hand to Blake's shoulder.

"I spoke to Elliot the other day," he blurts.

Jay cocks his head to one side. "You saw Elliot? He didn't mention it."

"Sorry. It's just." Blake huffs and finally squeezes out the words. "Julian, huh?"

Jay winces. "He told you, did he? Honestly, I thought you already knew."

"Yeah, you'd think I'd pick up on the hints. But, nope, I'm just that thick."

Jay brushes bangs away from Blake's cheek with a soft touch. "It doesn't change anything. Who I am doesn't affect how I feel."

Blake's heart jumps at the thought that Jay would feel any such way towards him, but then he reminds himself that isn't the point of today. Today is all about the exit strategy.

"Look," he starts, shying away from Jay's hand. "I don't know what to think about it all. It's...a little much."

As if his own history isn't worse.

Jay drops his hand and says, voice guarded, "I know. I get it. My parents are terrible, and I thought maybe I could keep you separated. You don't have to deal with them, and they don't have to know about you. I don't really spend time with them, anyway. I'm kind of the family disappointment."

"You? Yeah, right. You're fun and charming and—" Blake cuts himself off before he convinces himself not to do what he has to do.

Jay smiles faintly. "Thanks, but it's not exactly the standard my family judges on. More like I'm unwilling to be in the spotlight and make friendly with some foreign dignitary for political gains. They have different priorities than most people."

Blake bites his lip. Just what Mom hates. Just what he needs to avoid.

"Jay," he starts with a deep breath. He has to get this out. Let it be the end of them. Return to a life in obscurity, dodge the alpha that had caught his scent, and keep his mom safe. Keep Jay from getting tangled up in it and hurt. Nothing else matters.

Especially not his own happiness.

"Wait." Jay catches his wrist and leans in. "Don't say it. Not yet. Give me a little more time." His thumb rubs a warm circle on the inside of Blake's wrist, coaxing him closer. Blake wavers, then leans in towards Jay, wanting that heat, that body all around him, wanting for once in his life to be close to someone.

But he can't.

"I'm sorry, Jay," he wheezes. "You don't understand. I can't—"

Then the front door bursts off its hinges with an ear-shattering crash.

Jay jumps to his feet and whirls around while Blake yipes and tumbles backwards over the couch arm. A towering wolf charges into the room with a howl, its shaggy black fur up on its hackles. It bares teeth at them and snarls, gray eyes gleaming with bloodlust. It's easily three hundred pounds of muscle, claws, and teeth, and all of it charges directly at

Jay. Jay jumps back in time for the monster to land on the edge of the couch, shredding open its stuffing and over-ending it. Blake stumbles back, lands on his ass, and scuttles backwards until he bumps up against the glass door leading to the balcony. It feels like his eyes might bulge out of his face.

The wolf rounds on him, stalking over with a low, menacing growl rumbling deep in its chest. Blake pants panicked breaths as it closes in, all at once too much and not enough air pouring in and out of his lungs. Drool slobbers over the wolf's muzzle as it bears down on him, and Blake recognizes the gray eyes. The man's face is no longer so flat now that he's transformed into a wolf, but he still stinks of cigarettes and acetone.

This is it. Goodbye, world. Wish I could have at least done it with Jay.

It isn't the most dignified of dying wishes.

The wolf's jaws open, and hot, stinking breath pours over Blake's face. Its teeth seem sharp enough to cut even the air. Then the wolf howls a sound of pain and jerks away from Blake as a loud crunch echoes in the room. Wood splinters and flies out. Something falls in Blake's lap. He stares at it. A chair leg. He blinks and stares at the wolf, who looks as dazed as he feels. It's collapsed sideways against the couch, the remnants of one of Jay's dining chairs exploded on its side. It whines and twitches. Jay stands over it, heavy, angry breaths rising and falling, fists clenches around a piece of wood.

"Son of a bitch!" Jay raises the wood—the back of the chair, Blake realizes—and throws it at the wolf.

The wolf howls and flinches as the remaining piece of chair bounces off its flank. Then it opens its eyes and snarls. It raises itself up, though favoring its left side, and stalks toward Jay, teeth bared. The chair assault is ultimately unsuccessful.

It crouches, coiling its back legs and readying a pounce, when someone else leaps on it from behind. Blake goggles at the sight. Charlie came up on it quietly and jumped on its back, now grabbing it under the jaws and pulling its head back. It thrashes, but Charlie holds firm, apparently programmed for bodyguard application as well as household chores. He punches the wolf twice—two sharp raps in the throat—and the wolf staggers before dropping to its belly. When it seems subdued, Charlie relents.

"Holy shit," someone mutters, and Blake realizes he's the one who's said it, so he says it again. "Holy shit."

"Jay, I am contacting the police," Charlie informs. "As well as your family." He stands and closes his eyes, processing an email.

Suddenly the wolf springs up, but this time it dashes for the door instead of an attack. It runs off limping, but no one gives chase. Blake and Jay stare at each other, and at last Jay says, "I swear this isn't a normal thing for me."

Blake exhales a shaky breath and replies, "I don't even know what normal is anymore."

Chapter Eight

Tchaikovsky's "Valse Sentimentale"

A flurry of questions consumes the rest of their afternoon. Police come and go, taking a description of the attacker and assuring Jay they'll be on high alert. Of course they'd bend over backwards for a Reed. If this had happened in Blake's neighborhood, the police might not have even shown up. Blake spends the time dodging as many questions as he can and diverting attention back to Jay, which, honestly, the police seem more than happy to do.

Finally, they're gone, leaving the two in a condo with a destroyed door and torn up couch. Blake collapses into a chair in the dining room and plops his head in his hands.

"How'd that guy even get up here?" He grumbles.

"Tricked the porter. Told him he had a delivery for me to sign. He must have come in human then shifted outside the door. Guess he tracked us after attacking you in the alley."

"Shit." Blake drops his forehead to the dining table and huffs at the indignity of it all. "What the hell even is life right now?"

A hand falls on his shoulder, warm and tender. "Stay with me. I won't let anything happen to you."

"But who saves your ass?"

"Hm. Charlie, I guess."

Blake twitches up the corners of his mouth. "He was pretty cool, huh? Guess you owe your sister a thank you."

"Ugh. Never. I'll die first."

A voice calls over to them from the edge of the dining room, rich and sharp, like a French horn. "What was that, Julian?"

Blake drags up his head from the table and blinks. Someone has strolled in through the broken door like they own the place.

Please don't let it be another shifter.

"Cat!" Jay's voice turns syrupy and sarcastic. "To what do I owe the horror?"

A tall woman made taller by red spike heels stands before them in a red jacket and knee-length skirt with a blazing color of lipstick to match. Her brown hair curls around her shoulders in waves that would make a shampoo ad jealous, and she eyes them with a cold detachment befitting a queen or a runway model.

Blake can practically see the lower third announcing her identity: Catalina Reed—Sister, Alpha, Takes No Prisoners.

"Charlie contacted me regarding your little altercation." She crosses her arms over her ample chest. Really, whoever designed (and Blake has no doubts her clothes are designed specifically for her) that jacket is a master magician, because regular buttons surely would have long ago been beaten into submission and dropped off. He forces himself not to stare. Somehow the people in Jay's life bring out the gawker in him.

Catalina catches him, though, with a careless flick of her eyes. She doesn't bother to address him. "Really, Julian? You're taking in stray omegas now?"

Jay grinds his teeth so hard Blake swears he can hear them creaking. "None of your business. I didn't ask you to come here."

"Yet here I am, interrupting a meeting with the princess of Euphracia. You know she's only visiting for a week."

"You were on a lunch date!" Jay throws up a disgusted hand. "Probably gossiping about your love lives. You two have talked every weekend since grade school!"

She sniffs truculently. "All the more an affront to her. You're lucky she's a forgiving sort." She shrugs, which gives Blake genuine concern for her top button. "Betas, you know."

Blake glances back and forth between Jay and Catalina as they shoot remarks like a tennis match. They fight as much with their scents as their words, and now alpha musk clings to the air like aerosol. It stinks like overinflated egos.

He crosses his arms. "Jay, is everyone in your family super hot, or is this a sibling thing?"

The remark—tinted with as much sarcasm as he dares use—catches both alphas off guard, and Catalina stares at him like he's grown a third eye. Obviously not accustomed to big mouth omegas. To her credit, she recovers herself smoothly and sticks out a hand for a shake. "Catalina Reed, Julian's older sister. I take it you're Blake?"

Blake stands and circles around the table to accept her hand in his own, staring up at her determinedly, even if he has to crane his neck to do it. He lets out his own pheromones in counterattack as he grips her hand firmly. She rewards him with the kind of handshake reserved not for business meetings, but for crushing the dreams of your enemies.

He doesn't break away, but holds on, feeling the bones in his palm shift. Forces a smile. "I haven't checked today, but lately everyone's been calling me that."

Her eyes narrow. She releases his aching hand and dismisses him to address Jay. "You never said he was funny."

"I never said he was anything! Who told you his name?"

"Charlie, of course." She flips her hair over her shoulder, and a rich smell of cinnamon and chocolate permeates the air. "He's been a wonderful insight into your personal life. Sends me all kinds of updates."

Jay's jaw drops. Then he works himself up to his full height (normally impressive, but compared to Catalina's stilettos, only eye to eye) and growls at her, "You've been spying on me."

"Dearest little brother, why else would I buy you a mech?" She shakes her head. "I would've thought you knew that from the start."

The fight leaks out of Jay, and he slumps into the seat where Blake had previously sat. "You're the worst. All of you. Did you gossip about this with Mom as well?"

"No, I haven't, and you should be grateful. They'd lose their minds if they knew you were slumming it."

"I'm right here, you know!" Blake snaps at her.

"I have eyes," she snips back. Returns to Jay. "You know they always hoped you'd mate Kimiko. It would be a perfect match, politically speaking."

"Not going to happen." Jay grinds the words out through his teeth. "How many times do we have to have this conversation?"

"She's too good for you anyway. How you convinced her to packbond, I'll never know, but she really deserves to be the alpha leader, if you ask me. She's much more savvy." Jay groans loudly and petulantly, but she presses on. "And that's really neither here nor there. What exactly happened today?"

"None of your business." He refuses to look at her.

"It most certainly is!" Suddenly Catalina abandons her haughty stance to sit beside Jay and place a hand on his shoulder. When she speaks, her tone is serious and hushed. "If this was an assassination attempt, we need to know. You could be attacked again." She enfolds both of her hands over Jay's. "Are you really going to make your big sister worry about you?"

Blake doesn't understand the history between them, but the words—or maybe it's her sudden softness where she had previously been all sharp edges—do the trick. Jay leans back in the chair and says, "I don't know what else it could have been. The guy followed us back from lunch and burst in here. I think—" He glances at Blake, who feels his guts seize up. "I think he tried attacking Blake to get to me."

Ack, not quite.

The guilt ratchets up. The guy, no question, has to be a Volkov agent. Fullblood shifters all either come from prestigious families or work for one. Blake has no doubt Flat Nose came here for him and him alone. Jay is just collateral damage.

But there's no way he can explain that. He shifts uneasily. As much as the guilt tears him up, it's better to let them think it's all about themselves. Probably rich people are accustomed to thinking that, anyway. And maybe, maybe he can use this to his advantage. No way Flat Nose has the guts to stick to him while he's with the Reeds. The war between their countries has been at a stalemate for years, and attacking a lead pack would probably cause more problems than it would fix.

He'll have to hope.

Catalina clicks her tongue. "That's a problem."

"You're telling me."

She settles a gaze on Blake, who finds himself stuffing away thoughts of the Volkovs and Servos as though she could read his mind. "How do you feel about this?"

Time to turn on the charm. He spreads both hands out and gives a helpless smile. "Somewhere in my life I walked on set of a telenovela, and everyone just kept filming. When do I get my union card?"

"Sorry," Jay mutters, putting a hand over his eyes. "I really should have warned you about all this. I swear I've never been attacked before."

Catalina considers Blake for a long moment and then declares the five most dreaded words in werewolf history.

"You should meet our parents."

Oh yes, wonderful. What's he supposed to say to *Colin and Sara Reed*? 'Ah, yes, hello, Mr. and Mrs. Reed, who could crush everything I am with a wave of your hand. I would very much like to boink your son.'

Luckily, Jay seems to be on the same page. "I don't think that's a good idea."

Catalina's sharp edges return with a vengeance. She feigns a high-pitched innocence that would honestly sound more natural coming from the mouth of a demon. "Odd, because I thought you'd be concerned about his safety. Big, scary man after him now. Who else can keep him safe? I guess we'll throw him to the wolves."

Dirty trick, but it works. Jay's shoulders drop. "Fine. But give us a day, all right? I think we're both pretty shaken up."

"*Bueno.*" Catalina says it as though it is not, in fact, *bueno.*

Jay rolls his eyes. "Don't pull that with me. You're not grandma."

She lifts a finger. "I'll get out of your hair today, but you have to promise me you'll stay somewhere safe tonight. This place needs a new door and five more security systems. What happens if that wolf comes back?"

Jay avoids her eyes. "We did all right."

She leans in, voice pleading, eyes missing their cold detachment. "You can't shift, Jay. You versus wolf doesn't have good odds."

Jay retreats from her concern with a deep frown. He walks to the kitchen cut out and leans on it, showing them both his back. Catalina opens her mouth to say something else, but he speaks first, voice low.

"I might not be a shifter, but I'm alpha enough to protect the ones I care about. We'll be fine."

He cares about me. It makes Blake's insides feel warm and gooey.

Catalina pauses, fusses a moment with her jacket cuff, then replies, "All right. You've heard me out. Thank you. I'll be in touch later about tomorrow. Take care of yourself."

She starts toward the not-door, then glances back at Blake.

"Watch his back for me, would you? Big sis can't be everywhere at once."

"Yeah." He nods firmly. "Promise."

They share a silent moment, a silent assessment that both sides pass. Then she strides out the door, and he and Jay are alone again.

Blake glances back at Jay, and the tension in his back and shoulders looks ready to snap. The grimace on his face matches.

He needs comfort. He's freaked. Stop lipping off and be a proper omega for once.

He crosses the distance between them and wraps his arms around Jay from behind, leaning his cheek on Jay's shoulder blade. He focuses inside, finds the little tug of instinct that controls his pheromones, and pushes out a sense of comfort around himself.

Calm.

Relax.

We're safe.

The tension dissolves from Jay's muscles, and he turns to embrace Blake fully. They stand hugging for a minute, then Blake says, "I'm sorry things are so messed up right now." It's the closest to a truthful apology he can manage. Dragging Jay into this had never been his intention, and now the thought that he'd have to use the man and his family for his own benefit makes him feel like the biggest jerk in the world. The least he can do is smooth things over and bring Jay some comfort.

"The only one getting messed up is that asshole if he shows his face again," Jay growls. "No one threatens my omega."

Blake could float to the ceiling and bounce around like an untethered balloon. *His* omega. A moment of fantasy overtakes him: the feeling of Jay's teeth on his neck, biting, marking, bonding them together. Goosebumps tingle his skin at the thought.

"Sorry," Jay says, breaking into Blake's imaginings. "Not everyone likes that possessive alpha crap. You probably never want to look at another alpha again."

"Is it okay if you're the exception?"

"I can live with that."

Blake leans up on tip toes and kisses Jay softly. He pulls away before it picks up speed.

"I have to see my mom."

Mood effectively killed.

"Isn't she in a nursing home?"

"Yeah, but what if that creep finds out about her? What if he goes after her?" He shakes his head. "I have to keep her safe."

"And who keeps you safe?" Jay runs his thumb over Blake's jawline.

"Are you applying for the job? Open interviews today."

"As long as it comes with benefits."

"Oh, yes, plenty of those. I've been known to bake once in a while. Do you like muffins?"

"I'll eat every muffin you make. Even zucchini."

Blake pulls back from him. "Gross. What is it with you and the weird food?"

"I don't like weird food."

He holds up a hand. "Exhibit A: pineapple pizza."

"Lots of people like pineapple on pizza!"

"Insane people. Really, I should be concerned for my safety around you. You're clearly a madman. Anyway, shouldn't an alpha like red meat? Burgers and steak and venison? Not sushi and pineapple."

Jay shakes his head. "I'm not actually a wolf. You ever met anyone who only eats steak?"

Blake clicks his tongue, outdone by the logic. He hesitates briefly before daring to ask, "So you really can't shift? Even though you're a fullblood?"

Being directly descended from werewolves usually means being a shifter, unlike most hybrids these days. If he can't shift, that leaves him susceptible to attack from fellow fullbloods—a vulnerability most can't stand.

Jay winces. Obviously, it's a sore subject. He doesn't pull away, though. Instead, he leans close and nuzzles the top of Blake's head.

"I never got the hang of it. My whole family are shifters, and here I am, odd man out. Some alpha, huh?" He shakes his head in disgust.

Overcome by a need to console him, Blake keens a soft noise in the back of his throat. "Best alpha I've ever met."

"Like you've met any good ones."

"Meeting you is enough."

Silence absorbs the words; at last Jay breaks it with a gruff, "Thanks."

Blake nods. For now, anyway, it will have to be enough. He takes a chance. "So, you'll come with me to see Mom?"

"Of course. Let me tell Charlie to stay here. He can watch out in case anyone comes back."

Just the thought of them meeting turns Blake's knees mushy. Even in her best mood, his mom hates alphas, and Blake can't blame her. She's told him stories of her life in Servos before fleeing here, and the idea of it—bred from a young age to marry an alpha, trapped, bound, claimed, like she had no agency of her own... It makes him shudder. How could she ever feel anything but disgust for them?

And here he is, falling for one, and not just any alpha, the son of a lead pack. It's like he's throwing away everything she's ever done for him. Choosing her old life over the freedom she fought to give him.

"Dammit," he mutters as the guilt threatens to engulf him.

"Something wrong?"

"It's just." He takes a breath and finds the words. "Fair warning. Mom doesn't like alphas. At all. And she's not always all there. Try to keep your scent down, okay?"

"Sure."

"Please don't be mad at her. She really can't help it."

"Why would I—"

"Please."

"Not a problem. It'll be okay." Jay kisses his forehead. "I'll make sure she's safer than safe."

"I hope so."

***

Jay drives them to the nursing home after insisting they avoid public transportation. As far as Blake is concerned, they would have gotten there quicker on the train. Cars might be fancy and expensive, but the traffic holds them up at every turn. Navigating it agonizes him, every stopped light and flared brake a needle in his frayed patience. Hell, walking would have been faster. So he tightens his fists and jiggles his leg and wills every car in front of them to *move the hell out of the way.*

They don't.

One eternity later, they park in an empty lot and approach the building. The plaque by the door welcomes them to the Bertram Full Time Home, though it's mucked over and almost impossible to read. To his credit, Jay makes no comment about the peeling paint on the stucco or the dim lighting. They walk down the hall, check in at the desk, and face Theresa Fields's door.

Blake chews his lip. "I don't know how she'll be. It's roulette every time."

Jay grasps his hand and squeezes. "I'll be good."

"It's not you I'm worried about," he mutters. He opens the door and pokes his head in. "Hi, Mom."

She's sitting up in bed, turned away from him to look out the window. One of the nurses must have opened the curtains for her. At his voice, she glances back. She squints at him as though trying to figure out who he is or why he's bothering her, but then the realization dawns, and her face lights up in a smile.

"Hello, honey."

Blake steps inside and waves a hand behind him to stop Jay from immediately following.

"I brought someone with me."

"I've been looking at the sky." She speaks as though he hasn't said anything. "Sometimes birds fly past. Do you think I'll leave someday? I feel like I've been here forever."

Blake flinches. "Maybe we can go outside today. Take a walk around the building."

She's usually too gone to do such things, but the idea that he's been neglecting her physical activity pains him.

She smiles a sad smile and says, "Maybe."

Blake takes a step toward her. "I brought someone with me," he tries again. "I'd really like you to meet him."

"All right." She seems resigned, capitulating to forces beyond her control. Maybe her whole life has been that way. Maybe Blake is just another person who locked her up in a room she can't escape. His stomach curdles at the thought.

"His name is Jay. He's a," he pauses, searching for the right words, "good friend of mine." He steps into the room the rest of the way and waves Jay inside. "Jay, this is my mom, Theresa."

Jay enters, and the tiny room suddenly seems all that much smaller. He's a tall guy, layered with muscle, and it seems the room can barely hold the three of them.

"Hello, Theresa. It's nice to meet you."

"Hello, Jay, how did you meet—" And the awful realization crosses her face. The thing Blake has dreaded from the moment he started dating Jay. "Alpha," she hisses, a mixture of fear and hatred twisting her features. "Get out of here!"

Blake rushes over to her and grabs her hands. "It's okay! He's not a bad guy. He's not like those other ones."

She jerks away from him and snaps, "You know I hate them! All of them! How could you bring one here?"

"Mom, please, he wants to help me. There's been trouble." He lowers his voice to barely a whisper and kneels next to her, trying to look into her eyes, impart the gravitas of the information. "Someone's after us."

A flicker of confusion dances across her face, followed by grim understanding.

"That's it, then," she says. "They'll kill us. Or worse, drag us back there."

He stands and tries to cover for their quiet conversation. "But Jay can help us! His family has connections. He wants to protect me! Please just let him meet you."

The sour look doesn't leave her face, but she says, "All right." She stares hard at Jay, sizing him up from feet to forehead. "Do you want to claim my son?"

Blake's face warms. He shakes his head fiercely. "Mom, not the right question."

"I don't see why not. How can you not understand what he wants? What they all want." She glares at Jay and repeats, "Do you want my son?"

"I do. I won't pretend otherwise."

Ack. Not helpful.

Jay crosses his arms and meets Theresa's petulant gaze with his own steady eyes. "But only if he wants me. What matters now is keeping you both safe. I can arrange a new caretaker for you. Get you out of here to somewhere more secure. Would that be okay?"

She jerks her head away to look back out the window, effectively ignoring him. Blake sighs and stands.

"This wasn't my most stellar idea."

"Let me make some calls. I can set you up somewhere better, at least for tonight."

Blake has to shove down the immediate reaction to turn him down. He's not used to handouts. "Are you sure? I can't afford—"

"Don't worry about it. I got you into this, and I'm going to help you out of it. If you're worried about your mom, then I am, too."

He tries not to wince. Jay only wants to do the right thing. He, on the other hand, is lying and putting Jay in danger.

Shit. I've got to fix this.

"I'll get her medical information. Thanks for this. I swear if you get to know each other..." He shakes his head. "Who am I kidding?"

***

The next few hours are a blur of shuffled paperwork and long phone calls. Finally, they sit in a room on the opposite end of town, in a private hospital Blake has never even heard the name of, though the large, clean rooms, well-equipped with televisions and coffee machines, speak for themselves.

"This place is like a hotel suite!" Blake holds his arms out and spins in a circle. Neither hand brushes the walls. "Do not tell me how much it costs. If I know, I might end up in one of the beds with a heart attack."

His mom blinks owlishly at them. "I'm sorry, where are we?"

Blake sits beside her and holds one hand in both of his. "Jay's helping us out. It's better here. Don't you feel more comfortable?"

"Who is...?" Her eyes flicker like she's been struck with an electric jolt. She moans and lays back against the pillows, lips twitching.

A nurse appears immediately, checks her airways, then calls in a report to the doctor.

"How frequent are these seizures?" He asks as they wait for the doctor.

"They usually happen when I'm around," Blake mutters. "A few times a month. She takes medicine for it, but—" He shrugs helplessly.

Ultimately, the doctor pronounces her safe and under control. They'll try a new medication and run some tests. Ashen-faced, Blake avoids asking how much those will cost. Jay seems unconcerned.

"Whatever it takes," he replies.

That leaves them alone in his mom's new room while she sleeps. Blake fidgets in his seat, feeling all at once relieved, tired, and uncertain.

"You're sure she'll be safe here?" He's asked it about twenty times since they moved her. Once more won't make a difference.

Jay smiles indulgently. "Positive. This place is top notch. No tricking some porter to get in. My family's known Dr. Dunn since before I was born, and there's no way he'd let something happen to your mom."

"Right. Thanks." Blake turns his tired eyes to Jay's. "You're some kind of boyfriend, you know that?"

"You inspire a lot of dedication in me."

"Or you really want to get in my pants." Blake laughs and slaps himself. "God, stop talking for once."

Jay stands and holds out a hand. "I called Elliot and Lance already. How does a sleepover sound?"

"Do we get to eat popcorn and play spin the bottle?"

"I can arrange for one of those."

"Oh good. Because I really like popcorn."

He kisses his mom's cheek and takes Jay's hand. Things are complicated, but not impossible, he tells himself. Jay makes him feel safe... comfortable in a way he's never felt with anyone else. Sure, there are certain issues they need to work out, but as long as Blake keeps the truth tamped down, his identity a secret, then there really isn't any reason they can't be together.

Sometimes lies are so much prettier than truths.

Chapter Nine

Brahms's "Hungarian Dance No. 5"

"I have to go back to my place first," Blake announces as they step into Jay's car. "I need clothes. All my stuff is there." He needs his official papers in case this all leads to some problems with the police. Plus, his keyboard is in there, one of the first gifts his mom ever gave him. Sometimes playing it is the only thing keeping him sane. At a skeptical look from Jay, he adds, "I have work tomorrow. I need my uniform."

"I thought we were meeting my folks tomorrow."

"I can do both. What? I have bills to pay. I can't miss a day."

"You don't think it might be a good time to call in sick? You know, having been attacked, and all that?"

He has a point. The Volkov agent knows where he works. He'll be a sitting duck until they catch the guy. Blake taps his fingers together while Jay puts the car into reverse and backs out of the parking lot.

"All right. I'll call in this time, but I can't lose this job. The work is garbage, but the customers tip well."

Jay drops the subject, though from the tightness around his mouth it seems he has more to say. Blake doesn't press him. One win is enough.

"How do I get to your place?"

Blake gives him the address, and off they go, the buildings growing shabbier and shabbier and the roads emptier and rockier as they drive.

"You live here?" Jay doesn't mask the shock in his voice.

Defensive, Blake replies, "We can't all afford to live in the heart of downtown, you know. I've lived in worse places." He winces because he sounds less reassuring and more pathetic loser.

"Sorry, I didn't mean to offend you. I've never been to this side of town."

"Well, welcome to the other ninety-nine percent. That's my building. You better stay here while I go up."

"You shouldn't—"

"I mean, those guys over there will probably tag your car or leave you on cinder blocks if you're not around." Blake points at a trio of men slouching in the next alley over. One of them makes a provocative gesture with his fingers and tongue.

"Yikes."

"You're an alpha. They won't mess with you. Stay in the car, and I'll be right back."

"I could just get you new clothes. We don't have to stick around here."

"My keyboard's up there. And I've got a gallon of milk in the fridge. You want me to waste good milk?"

It's actually a half gallon, and the fridge is a mini he thrifted from a secondhand store, but neither detail matters. He's getting that keyboard come hell or high water.

"It's just milk!"

"Jay, I've lived here for years. A few minutes to grab some things won't kill me." Then he realizes something. "You're not worried about me; you're scared of being alone out here!" He chuckles. "Big bad alpha is scared of the thugs."

Jay's turn to get defensive. "They could have guns or something. Do you have no self-preservation instinct at all?"

Blake leans across the car and pecks Jay on the cheek. "I'll be right back. Don't let the scary, malnourished jerks get you." He hops from the car before Jay can retort.

He jogs past the alley to a series of X-rated catcalls to which he shouts back, "Up yours!" and rushes to his apartment. His heart speeds up as he approaches the door. He has no idea where the Servan agent is right now; he could have already trashed the place looking for him. Or worse, be waiting inside with his wolf jaws slathering for blood.

He pauses with his keys in hand and strains his ears for any noises inside. Silent as a musical rest. Still, he digs around in his shoulder bag and brings out his pepper spray. He does have *some* self-preservation instinct, after all.

A little click of the lock, and he pushes the door creaking open. Sweat prickles his palms. He pokes his nose in and holds his breath.

Everything is exactly as he left it this morning. No looting or foreign smells. Nothing broken or out of place. Relieved, he pushes the door in all the way. Before gathering his things, he does a quick sweep, emphasis on quick. There are maybe two places someone could hide in here. The closet, which is really only big enough to hold a few shirts, and the bathroom. Both are empty. He sighs and plops on the bed, dropping his bag to the floor. The studio apartment is at least convenient for easy searching.

He digs out a bigger bag and folds clothes into it, followed by a book and his official papers, unhooks his keyboard and tucks it away into its case, then he walks to what amounts to his kitchen (a mini fridge and a shelf from a thrift shop) and browses for a snack. Who knows when he'll get back here with everything that's happening? Best to be thorough. He finds a sleeve of butter crackers and pops one into his mouth. A reward for all his stress. He gets the half gallon of milk out of his fridge and shakes it. Two-thirds left.

He strolls over to his bedside and uncaps the milk, sniffs it to be sure, then takes a sip. His last moments here, most likely. How is it he's getting wistful over a shithole apartment? He reaches across his bed and pulls the curtain open to see what graffiti adorns the opposite wall today.

And comes face to face with Flat Nose.

Blake gapes. The alpha's jaw drops. He stands on Blake's fire escape, one leg up on the windowsill. For a moment, Blake imagines a surreal picture of a dog taking a piss. Then the man's lips curl into a snarl and he raises what looks like a metal club and smashes Blake's window open.

He might've shouted, he doesn't know, but as Flat Nose clambers through his window and over his bed, Blake does the one thing he can think of. He throws the open milk jug at the guy's face. It bounces off and splashes white liquid everywhere, getting in the man's eyes and stalling him long enough for Blake to dash to the bathroom and lock himself in.

He climbs on top of the toilet like the attacker is actually a cockroach scuttling on the floor. His heart pounds so hard it feels like his eyes might pop out of his head. He flails looking for something—anything—to fend the man off. His pepper spray lays abandoned outside by his bed, probably covered in milk.

The doorknob twists and jangles, then comes a grunt as Flat Nose attempts to kick the door in. It buckles but holds. Blake yipes and grabs at the shower curtain, yanking it down. The rod it hung from holds fast, and when he jerks at it, it resists fully and stubbornly, welded to the wall so tenants can't take it on the way out.

Blake's heart kicks into prestissimo. He might pass out, his blood pressure is so high. He scrabbles again at the shower curtain and then hears a sickening crunch from outside the door, followed by an inhuman snarl. The man has shifted forms. The door screams its last protests as a three-hundred-pound wolf bashes it in. This guy really has something against doors.

Blake shouts and holds up the shower curtain, feeling absurdly like a matador taunting a bull. He throws it over the wolf, who snaps and jerks and gets tangled up in the small space. This is not a bathroom meant for anyone larger than Blake. As the wolf jerks sharply side to side, curtain flapping around it, Blake gets his fingers under the toilet tank's lid and pries it up. It comes loose, nearly overbalancing him as he crouches on the seat, and he raises it up, up, up over his head. The wolf claws out of the curtain with snapping jaws, pauses long enough to see Blake bringing the heavy toilet lid down with maximum force, and Blake can swear in that second he registers the wolf's gray eyes saying, "Oh, shit."

A loud *CLUNK!* as the tank lid—ten solid pounds of porcelain—crashes over the wolf's head and breaks in half. The wolf collapses in a spray of blood. The curtain, which flew up when the wolf slashed through it, flutters gently down over its form like a flag of surrender. Blake stands still on the toilet seat, chest heaving short, panicked breaths. The wolf doesn't stir.

At last, he crouches and jabs the wolf with his foot to be sure he isn't faking. Nothing. He hops off the toilet and skitters out of the tiny bathroom.

"That's it," he mutters as he scoops up his belongings (some of which are coated in milk), "I want a new life. This one's broken." He dashes out of his apartment, not even locking the door behind him. Outside, Jay's car gleams in the setting sun. Blake throws his stuff in the backseat and flings himself into the front.

He must have some kind of wild-eyed look, because Jay asks him, "Are you okay? Did something happen?"

"I think I killed a man." Blake stares at his hands. They shake as though he's been stricken with palsy. "In my bathroom. Oh god, I hope they don't charge me for the toilet lid."

"What?" Jay's tanned skin loses its color.

"He broke the window. Do you think I'll get my deposit back?" Blake isn't sure what nonsense is pouring from his mouth, but it isn't exactly helpful.

"Are you hurt?" Jay catches his shoulders and twists him side to side, searching for wounds.

"No. But the door's broken. And maybe his skull, too. I hit him." Blake mimes the motion with both hands. "With the toilet lid. He stopped moving."

"The guy from before?" Jay sounds as shocked as Blake feels.

"Well, he was a wolf at the time. Do you think I killed him? I really hope I'm not a murderer. That doesn't jive with my worldview."

"If he was a wolf, probably not. When he shifts back, he'll heal. We should get out of here; he could still come after us." Jay swings out into the street and blows past the apartment building. "When we get to Elliot's I'll call in a report."

***

Elliot's apartment is a high rise downtown near his shop. Twelfth floor with a view overlooking the western half of the city, out into the bay. It's cleaner than Jay's, almost sterile, with a black and red accent theme. Inside, Elliot and Lance wait for them, Lance holding a tumbler of golden liquid, Elliot a steaming mug.

"This should be a good story," Lance says congenially as Blake puts his stuff down. Elliot waves a roll of paper towels at him, and he sets to wiping off the remnants of milk from his bags.

"I have to call the police again. Give me some time first." Jay walks past a staring Lance and into another room, leaving Blake alone with the other two.

"Elliot tells me you found out Jay's identity," Lance says, all smiles. "What do you think about the limelight? I mean, he's never had anyone come after him before, but I guess it was bound to happen eventually."

"Funny thing, that," Blake replies as he scrubs at his keyboard case. "I guess an adrenaline junkie would get off on it. Some guy bursting in with enough teeth bared to give the Cheshire Cat a run for his money. And then waiting for me at my place, like I'm some deer he's stalking. It's enough to give a guy a hernia."

Lance and Elliot exchange looks. "He came after you at your place?"

"Oh boy, did he ever." Blake gives up on the stain and focuses his efforts on a splash across the front of his shoulder bag. "You want a story? How about 'Little Red Busts The Big Bad Wolf In His Big Bad Skull'?"

"Maybe you'd like a drink first." Elliot walks to the kitchen and opens a cabinet. "Wine or something stronger?"

"Something stronger, please. And maybe a new life. One where I'm not accidentally killing guys in my bathroom."

"I can't tell if he's joking or not," Lance says to Elliot. "Do you think he's cracked?"

"No, but my toilet lid is. Along with that guy's skull." And Blake lets out a hysterical chuckle before clapping a hand over his mouth.

Elliot returns the bottle he picked up (a brandy from the looks of it) and selects instead a clear bottle with the number 180 on it. What a night this is going to be. He pours Blake a shot.

"It won't taste good," he says as he passes Blake the glass, "but it should do wonders for your anxiety."

"Self-medication." Blake takes the glass and holds it up in a toast. "I can appreciate that." He tips it into his mouth and immediately coughs as the alcohol displaces all the liquid in the back of his throat, turning it into a burning desert. He struggles the shot down and wipes his eyes. His head is already light, but that could be for any number of reasons today. "I think I should watch out," he says as he passes the shot glass back. "You might be after my life, too, with shit like this."

"Special occasions only." Elliot accepts the glass but doesn't pour him another. "Let me know if you need another pick-me-up."

"Hoo, not right now. Right now, I need to sit down and review my life choices. Do you remember in school when the teacher would circle all your wrong answers in red pen? I need to do that with my entire life."

"I can see why Jay likes you. He has a thing for sassy chicks." Lance chuckles.

"One." Blake holds up a finger. "Not a chick. Two." He adds a second finger. "I keep the sass to an acceptable minimum. I'm really quite pleasant."

Lance leads the way to the couch and replies, "Duly noted. One acceptably sassy omega. I should watch out. You might steal my job."

"You're not sassy," Elliot responds crisply. "You just have a big mouth. There's always a place in this pack for a beta who talks too much."

"Is that supposed to comfort me?"

"Not really."

The three settle onto Elliot's couch, Blake sitting in the short part of the L-shape a suitable distance away. Lance sits beside Elliot, hooking one arm over his shoulders casually. Jay's pack keeps things close, it seems. Physical touch and affection are not strangers. He wonders if all packs are like that. A tiny yearning calls in his gut, the remnants of instinct for a deeper connection with others that he thought long since stamped out. He tugs a pillow into his lap and fiddles with the tassels. Alone is fine, he reminds himself.

"Tell us, Blake," Elliot says over the rim of his mug. "What happened today?"

He takes a deep breath, calms the fuzziness in his head, and launches into the story, carefully omitting the details about him and the Volkovs and certain complicated histories. Jay returns to the room when Blake is at the part about the wolf barging into his bathroom. He's gotten into the story at this point, helped along by the buzz in his head, and he makes a big gesture as he describes hitting the creature with his toilet lid. Lance and Elliot are enraptured. He catches up to the present and ends the story by saying, "And then you gave me a shot of 90% alcohol, and now I feel like I could do karate on your coffee table."

Not even Lance has something clever to say. He and Elliot look to Jay for confirmation about the whole thing and are rewarded with a nod and a shrug.

"I can't believe he tracked your apartment." Lance shakes his head. "This would make a great movie."

Elliot pokes him. "Turn off the screenwriter brain. I doubt Blake wants to sell his life rights."

"I'm partial to my privacy," Blake agrees. If only they knew.

Jay sits beside Blake and ruffles his hair, knocking his beanie askew. "I'm sorry for all the trouble."

"You're worth it. But you better put out after all this." Blake blinks, realizes the half-joke that popped out of his mouth, and retreats. "Not that I'm pressuring you, or anything. I get it if you don't want to. I mean you're..." he waves at Jay with both hands, "and I'm..." he gestures at himself like that explains everything.

Jay snags his hand and kisses the back of it. "You're drunk is what you are. I can't believe I leave you alone for a few minutes, and my pack liquors you up. You're all irresponsible."

"Says you," Lance retorts, but Elliot elbows him.

Jay shakes his head. "It's getting late. I'll sleep out here with Blake. I doubt we'll see that guy again, but I'd rather be sure."

"I'll get you some blankets."

The group splits, Elliot dropping off some spare blankets to the couch before retiring to the back with Lance. Jay lays back on the couch and motions for Blake to join him. Blake's heart leaps. He expected to curl up on the short end of the couch. Cuddling hadn't occurred to him. He shuffles over to Jay, clutching a blanket to his chest. Jay holds his arms out.

"Come here, Buttercup."

Blake's face warms at the pet name. Or maybe he's already warm from the alcohol. Either way, he lays down on top of Jay, snuggling up under his chin. Jay wraps strong arms around him and breathes out a satisfied sigh. They lay in silence, relishing the contact and steady heartbeats. Through the alcohol's influence, Blake feels a little jump inside his chest. The wolf instincts beg him to breathe in the smell of his alpha, nuzzle his own smell against him, mark Jay as his own. He presses his lips to Jay's neck then nips lightly.

"Hey, now, careful with that mouth. It's a registered weapon. Don't point it unless you mean to use it."

"Mmm...fine. But soon, okay? I want this soon." He grinds his hips against Jay, rewarded with sensation of Jay's dick hard against his leg.

"Soon. But not when you're drunk." Jay strokes Blake's hair. "It's been a long day. Sleep. You've earned it."

Already edging on sleep, Blake nods and closes his eyes. He's out in less than a minute.

***

Jay laid awake a while longer, listening to Blake breathe deeply. He ran the day's events through his mind, tracing them like a wolf tracking a scent. He'd never been attacked before; in fact, despite the ongoing war, he'd lived a pretty peaceful life. He couldn't piece together why now all of a sudden someone would come after him. Maybe his parents would have some answers. They'd meet tomorrow and take whatever steps came next.

Ugh. They were going to hate Blake.

He grimaced and shoved the thought away. If only Kim was here. She always had a level head. Cat was right; she really should have been their pack leader, not him. Kim could move a mountain with merely a word. If that didn't say alpha, nothing did. But she'd wanted him to take charge, be the one the pack relied on. Him, without a wolf form or the strength to command other alphas. It baffled him to this day. He shirked most pack responsibilities when he could, leaving Lance to glue them together, relying on sex to keep their bond strong. He didn't have enough presence to do it with scent alone. He sighed, feeling, not for the first time, like a sham.

Blake stirred against him, murmured a soft sound, and nuzzled his chest. Jay's breath caught. This wasn't a responsibility he could abandon or shrug off onto someone else. Blake needed protection, someone to rely on. And as he lay in the dark, Jay realized he wanted to be that person. It wasn't only about sex or pack dynamics. He wanted Blake to trust him, and he wanted to be worthy of that trust. He let out a breath through his teeth. He'd never felt so strongly about someone before. Blake made him want to be a better person, and what did that mean?

He pressed his nose into Blake's hair, inhaling strawberries, and murmured the answer. "I love you."

Chapter Ten

Beethoven's "Moonlight Sonata"

J ay roused the next morning to piano music drifting softly nearby. He twitched and blinked, realizing his person-blanket had abandoned him, and glanced around for an indication of where Blake might have gone. Sitting at the other end of the room beside a window, Blake had set up his keyboard and currently coaxed soft music from it.

Jay sat up all the way and studied his omega. He knew Blake played piano but hadn't imagined it could sound so gentle. His fingers slid up to the higher notes and back down again in a repeated motion, and he swayed with the music. Jay's heart surged as he watched the exultant expression on Blake's face. There was no doubt about it, Blake loved playing music.

Jay stood and crossed the room, and the sound of his weight on the floor startled Blake out of his reverie. His hands shrunk away from the keys.

"Sorry. You can keep playing."

"It's all right. I don't really play for people. I just wanted to make sure it wasn't damaged after yesterday."

"You sounded amazing. What was the song?"

"The *piece* was 'Liebestraum Number Three'. Franz Liszt."

"Oh." Like that meant much of anything to him. "Well, it sounded great. Why not play for people?" He stood behind Blake, who had folded his hands in his lap and avoided eye contact.

"I don't like to, that's all."

If that wasn't the end of a conversation, Jay didn't know what was. He let it go.

"Well, you obviously know your classical music. When am I getting that playlist, hm?"

Blake perked. "I promise I'll make you one. When our lives aren't at risk of wolf attack."

"We should grab some breakfast and get you something to wear for today."

"What, my clothes aren't good enough?"

Jay rubbed the back of his head. "Ah, frankly no. Sorry. We need to give you the best chance possible of making a good impression on my parents, and that means a suit and tie."

Blake turned wide eyes on Jay. "They're going to hate me, aren't they?"

"No! No, it's going to be fine. They'll see how great you are."

But the truth was, he wasn't exactly confident.

***

Blake makes up his mind. Affluent people are ridiculous.

He and Jay stand in the shadow of a mansion on the outskirts of Remun City, staring up at its four stories of windows and flanking towers. Blake wears the suit Jay bought him that morning, and it suffocates him around the collar and cuffs. He wants nothing more than to fidget with it, but he caught Jay staring at him on the car ride over as he tugged at the fabric.

Lesson One: Rich people do not fuss with their clothing, even if it makes them feel like a trussed turkey.

"I'm scared," Blake whispers as two figures approach their car.

"It's fine. My parents are people like everyone else." Jay doesn't sound very sure about that, though.

"How do you even talk to someone that rich? Is there protocol?"

"You talk to me just fine."

"Not the same thing."

"Okay." Jay takes him by the shoulders and smiles. "If you get too nervous, just remember we haven't always been the Reed family."

"Meaning?"

"My great grandparents came from the south. Surname Rodriguez. They changed it to blend in with the higher-class packs."

"What?" Blake barks a gale of laughter. "That's ridiculous."

"That's politics. So remember: we're actually super low class. We just fake it."

Blake wants to kiss him for the reassurance, but the figures arrive. The pair of slender, well-dressed mechs bow low enough to show them the backs of their necks after opening the iron gate.

"Master Julian, it is a pleasure to see you again," intones the one on the right.

"This is Blake." Jay jerks a thumb at him. "We're here to see my parents."

"Master Blake, we are honored by your visit," chirps the mech on the left.

Jay passes them the car keys and starts up the path to the mansion. One mech stays behind to park the car while the other hurries in front of Jay. Blake glances between the topiaries and rose bushes, then stumbles after them both. It's practically a hike to get to the front doors.

"Jay." Blake catches his hand before they step onto the stoop. "You'll have to forgive me when I mess up."

"Impossible. You're perfect. They just need to see it."

"What if they don't?"

"Be yourself. They'll fall in love with you, too."

Before Blake can ask about the 'too' in that sentence, the mech opens the doors and announces, "Now arrived: Masters Julian and Blake from central Remun."

Blake marvels at the foyer. Marble pillars flank a grand staircase made of polished white stone. Large paintings adorn the walls, softly lit with their own lamps, and a magnificent stuffed tiger prowls beside some tall potted plants, as though it leaped straight from the jungle and into this bizarre alternate reality where everything he could touch is worth more than his annual salary. He lets out a breath he didn't realize he's been holding.

The family waits for them. Four people accost them as they enter, each redolent in suits or dresses. He recognizes Catalina, wearing a red halter neck dress and heels so sharp they look like they could puncture someone. The other young man must be Gabriel, Jay's older brother, looking trimmer than Jay in a suit that to his estimation is probably worth the GDP of a small country. The last two stand side by side between them, pressed suit and shimmering gown like they're fit to grace a gala with their presence. Jay's parents reek of alpha, power, and blood, meaning they smell like proper werewolves—not at all like Jay's calming earth scent.

"Julian, it's wonderful to see you," gushes Sara Reed. She sweeps over, gown flowing like snake scales, and kisses Jay's cheek. "When we heard about the attack, we were so worried! I'm glad you're well."

"It's been weird," Jay admits. "But we're okay. Both of us." He puts a hand on Blake's shoulder. "Mom, this is Blake. He was there when the wolf attacked. We've been dating for a couple months now."

"Oh?" Sara turns a cold eye on Blake, and he feels his guts shrivel. She sweeps her gaze over him like a mech scanning for data. Whatever she finds must be lacking because she says, "Dear, you really could do better."

Blake splutters. He expected a lukewarm welcome, but that level of bluntness rocks him.

Jay winces. "I'd appreciate it if you gave him a chance. He's a great guy."

"Mm-hm." She turns her back to whisper something in Colin's ear, who nods. She glances back at them. "What, exactly is so special about *this* one?" Her words are not so much venomous as exasperated, as though they've been through this dog and pony show a million times.

Blake shifts uncomfortably. There's nothing he could possibly say that won't dig him in deeper.

Jay rubs his temple with one hand and says, "Could you cool it? You don't have to attack every person I bring home."

"Maybe if you brought someone with some character there wouldn't be a problem. We're only looking out for you, Julian." She practically sticks her nose up.

"Always so great to see you guys," Jay grumbles through grit teeth.

"You're a bad liar," Catalina interjects. "You should practice more."

Sara waves a hand. "Dearheart, don't provoke your brother. I swear you two bicker like pups."

Jay stiffens and mutters, "Maybe all of you should leave it alone. What's wrong with being happy?"

"Happy?" Sara sighs. "What a pedestrian thing. I thought we raised you better than that. *Duty*, Julian. Duty above all else."

"I think Jay can decide what he wants to do with his own life." Blake crosses his arms. Out of the corner of one eye, he sees Jay grimace. Too late to stop now. He barrels on. "He's a great person. Although now it seems like a miracle, seeing how you treat him."

The silence that follows his declaration of war aches like a rotted tooth. Sara turns her cobra gaze on him, then, off all things, smiles.

"And what would you know about family, dear? A little stray omega, a runaway from a foreign country. Don't think we haven't looked you up. What have you to offer but debts and a sick mother?"

Blake's eyes narrow. *She's a bully. You have to stand up to her.* But they know too much already, and he's walking a dangerous plank. The last thing he needs is to make an enemy of some of the most powerful people in the country. Not that it's stopped him before.

Before he can snap back a retort, Colin steps in.

"We're getting off on the wrong foot. Clearly, Julian sees something in this boy, and it's not our place to judge so harshly. Let's retire to the conservatory. We can get to know each other there. It doesn't do well to stand in the hall all afternoon."

Instinct screams at Blake to back out and flee, but he's in too deep, and sometimes to get out you have to go straight through. Sara sidles up next to him and takes him firmly by the elbow, one hand over his like they're old friends. As she guides him out of the foyer, she murmurs under her breath, "My son is worth more than his money. He may not see you for what you are, but I do. You're not the first who's come sniffing around him. I'll exorcise you like all the others."

Blake twitches away from her, but her grip, like a viper's jaws, is firm and unrelenting. She's a force of nature. No wonder Jay hates coming home.

"This is the grand hall," she announces as they step into the next room. "Used for pack gatherings and holiday parties. I do so love a party. One day we'll hold Julian's mating ceremony here, won't we?" She continues before Jay can fight back. "Of course, only the highest society will be in attendance. Only the best."

The implication that he's not invited in any capacity isn't lost on Blake. He sets his jaw and ignores the jab. They cross into the next room.

"An art room." She waves a free hand. "Original works that date back before the Pack Years. Are you a fan of classic art, Blake?"

"I like Monet. Do you have any of his?" He means it to be snarky, but she takes it in stride.

"Upstairs we have his *Woman with a Parasol*. My grandmother acquired it from a collector who specialized in preserving art threatened or damaged by the Lupine Wars. Quite a few treasures were lost when the werewolves fought over territory rights. Shame our ancestors were such brutes. We would have so much more culture if they hadn't burned everything they could touch."

She's right, of course, but he can't stand to agree with her. He keeps his mouth wired shut. They move on.

"The conservatory. We keep plants from around the world here. We have a beautiful collection of orchids that Julian oversees. They're quite delicate."

The room is built of pristine glass, walls and ceilings both, and decorated with plants, overhead and on the ground. The sunlight plays brightly against their leaves and petals, spilling into the room and casting away any shadows. It's bright and beautiful, and the air smells like fresh spring. But that isn't what catches Blake's full attention.

There, in a curved alcove under a hanging lamp, stands the most beautiful, flawless grand piano he's ever laid eyes on. He sucks in a breath at the name carved into the side of the wood.

Bösendorfer.

"No way." He shakes his head and breaks off from Sara's grasp. He walks to the piano and stares at the letters as though they might be lying.

"That's genuine, you know." She hums and slides up next to him. "I have connections with the world market. A friend of mine has a particular interest in antiques."

"But weren't they all burned?"

"Most of them, anyway. A few were saved, including this one here. It's a gem. Have you an interest in music?"

Blake licks his lips, fingers itching. "It's everything," he murmurs reverently. "I play on a keyboard, but nothing as beautiful as this. Mom taught me when I was little. She had a friend with a piano, and we would go over and play for hours. Nothing is as wonderful as music." He reaches a hand to touch the piano's finish, then pulls back. "I'd love to hear it, if that's all right." He's all but forgotten his hatred of Jay's family.

Sara sets him with an inscrutable look, a silent judgment. Then she smiles, sly as a fox, and replies, "That would be wonderful, except none of us play. Do us the honor?"

Blake freezes. "I don't really play for people," he admits in a halting voice. Too late, though. She has him backed into a corner.

"Well, since none of us play the only way you'd be able to hear it is by playing yourself. Pity, I would have loved to hear something beautiful."

"Stop pressuring him," Jay grumbles. "If he doesn't want to, he doesn't want to."

Blake eyes the sleek ebony instrument and flexes his fingers. This could be his only chance. From what he can tell, Jay's parents are just this side of insane, and he might need to find another new identity to escape them.

Not to mention the old dream washing over him. The fantasy of playing to a grand hall, amid an orchestra, the keys beneath his fingers dancing flawlessly. Music beautiful and sincere enough to bring tears to the eyes of patrons. The impossible dream of coaxing the notes of the masters from an instrument finer than any other. And here it is, right in front of him. The only chance he'll ever get.

"I'll play it," he announces. "But," he glances around the room, "it won't sound perfect. The acoustics in here aren't—"

"Don't worry about such things." Sara waves a hand. "This isn't a concert."

No, but it is the next best thing. He hasn't played for anyone except Mom and Terri since that incident at the restaurant when he was six. He'd drawn too much attention, and the tongue lashing his mom gave him had never truly worn away. He doesn't perform for people. But if Mom were here, she'd be able to play the Bösendorfer flawlessly. When it comes to the keys, she's unmatched. Still, once in a lifetime can't be passed up. He lays both hands on the cover reverently. The finish is cool to the touch. There can't be many of these left in the world. Handmade perfection. Blake opens the cover. There they are: the extra black keys. It really, truly, is a Bösendorfer. He glides his fingers over them, not yet pressing down, just savoring the smooth texture. He hasn't played on a real piano since childhood. The sound will be richer, fuller, the plinking of the keys more satisfying, the control sublime. Every note a benediction.

Colin clears his throat.

Right. He said he'll play, and now he's just standing in front of the thing dumbly. None of them understand. They look impatient or just bored. Jay, though, has a soft expression in his eyes, a light curl to the corners of his mouth. Blake's heart jumps. He knows exactly what to play.

He adjusts the seat and settles in. It's a simple start, soft and slow, a warmup for his fingers. He knows the piece back to front; Mom drilled him for hours as a pup. One of her favorites. He hits the first notes, and the breath whooshes out of him. The sound resonates through his fingertips, as though the piano tickles him in return. Softly, softly, he plays.

Beethoven's "Moonlight Sonata".

The triplets pour from his fingers with a mournful grace. It's as if the piano itself lights up at every press. Gentle, coaxing movements caress the music from its keys, first pianissimo, as quiet as spring raindrops. He sways with it, feels it penetrate the core of his heart. The sonata's first movement is a lamentation, a call from the ghost that is his past. He plays, and the ghost weeps.

He pours everything into this, every time he's beaten down this dream, every moment he's lived alone. Everything has led to this.

As he hits the final chords, he doesn't draw his hands away. Two movements remain, and they tell a tale he won't truncate. The allegretto comes next, the cheerful piece between two storms. The chords bounce from his fingers; he plays a touch too swiftly to be accurate, but the joy of it has spirited him away. Jumping from spot to spot on the piano, the notes play leapfrog. Before he knows it, he reaches the end of the movement. The final piece, the presto agitato, bears down on him with thunderous force.

His fingers fly, breaking into rising arpeggios, crashing fortissimo on the chords. The third movement of the sonata is a whirlwind of emotion and depth, the most challenging of the pieces, and utterly unstoppable. A droplet of sweat prickles down his cheek, flicking off into the unknown as he nods his head in time to the chords. His mom seems to float beside him, guiding his fingers up and down the keys, reminding him to keep time, don't lose himself.

But he's far gone anyway.

As the notes cascade downward, he slows momentarily before launching into a final round of arpeggios. The ending chords ring out, foreboding in their intensity, before resolving into scales up and down the keys and the last twinkling of music. He comes to rest on two chords, leaning over the instrument as though the whole performance has pained him, when in reality he feels intensely, absurdly alive. Reluctantly, he removes his hands from the piano and sits back. He lets out a shaky breath. His communion has ended.

"Shit, Blake, you're incredible." Jay stares at him with a look bordering on awe.

"Mom taught it to me years ago. She loves that sonata." Blake wipes his face with his sleeve, remembering too late how expensive the fabric is.

"Interesting." Sara's expression holds something new in it now, something predatory. "Your mother taught you well. Where did she learn such a skill?"

Blake bites the inside of his cheek. The truth is, she was raised to play music for the Servan royal family. Everyone in that pack plays music. Mikhail himself supposedly plays incredible violin, a thought that makes Blake sick. Mikhail is a dark shadow over his past, a Bad Guy, in all sense of the words. Bad Guys don't play incredible violin. But there's no way he can say any of that.

"She learned when she was little, like me." Leave off the details, play it safe.

"I see." Sara narrows her eyes, apparently aware when someone holds out on her. "And why is it you toil away in obscurity when you could just as easily make a living as a pianist?"

Blake barks out a laugh. "Me? I couldn't. I told you I don't play for people."

She leans into him now, bringing her face uncomfortably close to his. "You're telling me you would rather work a dead-end job than play music like that?"

Blake's throat dries. Well, when she says it like that...

No. Too easy to get noticed when you play in concerts or make a scene. Too easy to become the center of attention.

He shakes his head. "I'd rather not. I've got...stage fright." It sounds lame, even to him.

"Stage fright." She repeats the words like they're little lumps of bullshit, which they honestly are.

"Leave him alone about it." Jay rescues him. "I swear, you can't let anything go."

Sara straightens up and smiles again. "Regardless, it was an excellent performance. Credit where credit is due."

Wow, so he's managed to do one thing right at least.

"Come, let's enjoy a snack and discuss matters together."

Blake reluctantly stands from the piano, feeling like he's leaving a piece of himself behind in those keys. This will have to be enough. He swallows, like it might help tamp down the regrets life has left him. He aches inside but knows it will have to be enough.

They settle into wicker chairs with fat cushions and high backs, a table between them that soon holds a magnificent crudité, courtesy of a mech. Blake tries to eat a carrot stick and finds himself unable to swallow. He folds it into a napkin as discreetly as possible.

"So, Blake," Sara launches into a new line of questioning. "Where did your mother flee from again? I know you're an immigrant but remind me from where."

Damn her. She knows exactly where he's from, and they both know it. He glares at her across the table. No choice but to play her game.

"Servos. I don't remember anything about it. I was a baby."

"I see." She snaps a celery stick between her teeth and chews thoughtfully. After swallowing, she asks, "And what is it your poor mother has now? She seems to suffer so."

His jaw tightens. "Dementia. Early onset."

"Early indeed. She's hardly middle aged. It must run in the family, poor dear."

"I wouldn't know."

"You wouldn't, would you? Little stray omega."

She's jabbing him, looking for a weakness. She won't let on how much she knows, and he can't let her trick him. He needs to calm things, redirect.

He licks his lips and says, "My whole life it's been me and her. That's all that matters. She looked after me when I was little, so I take care of her now. I'd do anything for her." He lets out a little puff of pheromones along with the words, just enough to soothe over the situation. He does it all the time at work, and it comes naturally now.

Sara cocks her head to one side, and for a moment Blake thinks she's caught his manipulation. Then she goes on.

"My, what a dedicated son. You could learn a thing or two from him, Julian." She sends an emphatic look at Jay before returning her attention to Blake. "And what was it she was running from? To leave behind an entire life for a new country, it must have been something drastic."

Shit. There's no way she doesn't know. She's as sharp as a dagger, and she's ready to plunge one right between his shoulder blades. He tries to cover. Takes a sip of water, but nearly chokes on it. Eyes watering, he says as coolly as he can manage, "The war broke out. We had to get away. She didn't want me to grow up in a place like that."

"I see." Sara sits back and taps her chin with one manicured finger. "It would have just happened, hm? The war. Only right as you were born. You couldn't have been older than a few months."

"Which is why I don't remember any of it," he shoots back. "Mom did what she had to do. And I'm glad to be here. It's the only home I've known."

"Well then." She settles Blake with a look that's much too knowledgeable. He tightens his grip on his napkin. "A final question. What do you hope to get out of this relationship with my son?"

He hesitates, not really knowing the answer. At last, he replies truthfully, "I don't know. I didn't exactly plan any of this. He showed up in my life one day, and things have been different ever since."

"Not to mention now you have a shifter to deal with," Jay grumbles. "You must be sick of this."

Blake takes his hand and squeezes it. "Worth it." No need to say the shifter is really his fault, though the pang of guilt in his chest begs to differ. He adds, "But what do we do about him?"

"It would probably be for the best if you both stayed here for a time. It's much safer than downtown." Sara says it like it's the most reasonable thing in the world, not the words of a crazy person.

No way he can stay here. They'll eat him alive.

Luckily, Jay seems to be on the same page. "It's fine. We can stay at my place."

"There's hardly enough security—"

"They're putting in a new door today with electric locks. Plus, we have Charlie. It's plenty safe."

And, most importantly, away from the crazies.

"That's good," Blake pipes up hastily. "I'm okay with that." Take what win you can get.

Sara and Colin exchange skeptical looks but concede. "All right. Be sure your mech is in guardian mode."

"Fine."

Tenuous treaty struck, they move on to other topics.

"If you insist on continuing this relationship, we'll need to present you appropriately to the rest of the world," Sara says thoughtfully. "A fitted suit is in order."

"Who, me?" Blake glances at Jay and back.

"Of course you. What, didn't you think the media would find out about you eventually? Julian does his best to stay out of the tabloids, but they're bound to catch wind of you. Better to cut them off at the pass. A party is in order, I believe." Her eyes sparkle at that, like Christmas came early. "And anyway, I wouldn't want our friends overseas to think we haven't considered them. Princess Daphne will be heartbroken, poor dear. She always had a soft spot for you, Julian."

Jay rolls his eyes. "She's way too old for me. You think I'd let you ship me off to a cougar?"

Sara chortles. "No, but we had always hoped you'd mate Kimiko."

"You're dreaming. She'd never have it."

"Well, regardless, we're here now and we need to make plans. Blake, what do you say to a presentation ceremony in your honor? Nothing huge, a hundred people or so. I have some particular names in mind for the guest list. Last year, Catalina and I attended a formal gathering at the VU. Say what you will about their history, but vampires *do* know how to throw a ball! I would very much like to invite the Headmistress. Show her our brand of hospitality."

Blake gapes at her. How'd she go from hating him to throwing a party for him? There's no winning here. Better to let go and let the crazy wash over him. He'll wiggle out somehow.

Jay, however, has his own opinions on the matter. "No vampires. I'm not dealing with that."

"Julian, dear," Sara sighs. "I thought you got over that little prejudice."

"You know how he holds a grudge." Gabriel plucks a cucumber stick from the crudité. "One little prank, and he's scarred for life."

"I was *five*!" Jay bursts at his brother.

"She wasn't going to do anything," Gabriel shoots back.

"She practically ate me!"

"I assure you, Madame LaRoche has matured into a lovely young countess. She even inquired after your health last year." Sara spears an olive with a toothpick and pops it into her mouth.

"Yeah," Catalina adds, "she was worried you might become anemic." She sips her tea.

Jay sinks back into his chair and puts his head in one hand. "I need a painkiller," he mutters. "I need a drink."

Blake sympathizes.

They spend another hour in company before Jay finally extricates them with a forceful, "We're going now." Blake half expects Sara to proclaim the mechs have lost his car keys and would they like to spend the night here?

Luckily, she plasters a smile on her face and says, "Of course, love. Let us know when you make it home. Wouldn't want me worried sick all night over you."

Blake has the feeling she'll know exactly when they get back, because by now she's probably had Jay's apartment bugged.

I'm in the snake pit. Nothing will get her jaws off me.

They stroll out to the lawn, where the sunlight has lowered to the western horizon. It feels like he's been here for a year instead of the afternoon. A mech brings the car around and opens the door for him. He slides in without looking back.

***

Jay lingered after Blake got in his car. The visit had been nothing short of a disaster, and he'd be lucky if his omega didn't run to another country after this. Still, there was a final thing he needed to do.

"Cat." He caught his sister's wrist as she was walking to her own car.

"Mom was in rare form, wasn't she?" Cat shook her head. "I swear you can see the wolf in her eyes."

"It's not that." Even though they were alone under the setting sun, Jay kept his voice low. "Well, yeah, she's a monster, but there's something else. I need you to teach me how to shift."

Cat's red lips parted ever so slightly in shock. "I thought you didn't want to. Weren't you set on being the family pariah?"

Jay shook his head. "I'm not doing it for them. If another wolf comes after Blake, I need to be there. I need to be able to fight." He put every ounce of sincerity he had into his voice. Cat would tease him, but she had to understand how critical this was.

Instead, her face drew serious. "It won't be easy. Shifting is for pups to learn. It's going to hurt."

"Don't care. I need to know. Please teach me."

"You're really falling for this guy, huh? My little brother, all protective of some omega."

"He's not just 'some omega'."

"Right. He's some kind of virtuoso."

Jay shook his head. "No. He's Blake. And that's all that matters."

Cat's tawny eyes studied him, and then she smiled. "You've got it bad. Okay. Call me tomorrow. I'll see what great knowledge I can impart. Better get going. Your omega is watching us."

Jay glanced over his shoulder to see Blake staring at them from the passenger seat. "Right. Thanks, Cat. Means a lot."

"Good night, Jay." Still smiling, Cat opened the backseat of her car and climbed in. Her driver steered the car away, and they disappeared down the road.

Jay nodded to himself and took to the front of his car. Blake stared at him.

"Everything okay?"

"My family is crazy."

"I might have noticed."

"But Cat's pretty cool."

"Good to have at least one person in your corner."

Yeah, true. And of all people, he'd rather it be her.

"Let's get home. Did you want to call your mom? Make sure she's okay?"

Blake smiled, despite the tired lines at the corners of his eyes. "You know me so well. And then can we eat, like, an entire carton of ice cream? Or donuts. Ooh, let's do donuts. There's got to be someplace open."

"One dozen donuts, coming up." Jay swung out onto the main street and turned east, toward downtown. Anything to make Blake happy. Anything to keep him safe. The wolf in the back of his mind howled a possessive cry. He reached across the seat with his right hand and sought out Blake's left. It closed over his, warm and delicate and entirely satisfying. It was all he could do not to imagine a life forever at Blake's side, so he drove them home and hummed the "Moonlight Sonata".

Chapter Eleven

Debussy's "Clair de Lune"

Jay's condo is blessedly free of more damage, mess, or werewolves when they arrive, box of donuts in tow. Blake eyes the couch, where claw marks still slash open one cushion.

"I'll get that replaced this weekend." Jay tosses his keys onto a hook by the door. "Would you like a bath?"

Together? Please let it be together.

"Sounds great. Let me make a call first."

He dials up the hospital to check on his mom, and after reassurances from the nurses that she's sleeping and better not to wake her, he hangs up. He opens his mouth to report in, but then his stomach speaks for him, rumbling a loud demand.

"That sounded feral. You better eat something before your stomach comes to life and swallows us all." Jay flips open the donut box and offers it.

"I skipped dinner, okay? No judging. Who can eat celery sticks and salami when your mom is foaming at the mouth?" Blake selects a jelly-filled and takes a bite. He stares at it grumpily. No jelly. It's all congealed on the opposite end of the pastry. A donut sin, if ever there was one.

Jay winces. "Sorry about her. My parents are constantly playing chess with my life. It's all I can do to disappoint them."

"I think I get it. How did you avoid turning into them? Aren't we all destined to become our parents?"

Jay groans. "Don't say that. You'll give me nightmares." He walks to the kitchen and rummages in a cabinet, speaking to Blake through the cut out. "I didn't actually grow up in Remun. I went to a boarding school on the east coast. I had a longer leash than Gabe or Cat. Got away with a lot of bad behavior I probably should've been called on." He retrieves a small bowl and a jar, then selects a tub of something from the fridge. "It's actually where I met Lance. We stayed in the same tower."

"Wow, what was that like?" Blake takes a bigger bite of his donut, and a spurt of jelly erupts out the back end. He catches it with his hand before it splashes on the polished floors. "Damn."

"Not bad. Lance is a good guy when you get to know him." Jay comes around the kitchen to Blake, bowl and spoon in hand with some kind of white slop sprinkled with brown powder. Blake wrinkles his nose as he licks the jelly off his fingers.

"What's that?"

"Yogurt and protein powder. Makes a good night snack. Did you expect me to eat donuts at this hour?"

"Why else did we buy a dozen? You think I can eat this many?" Blake nibbles at the jelly donut, now excised of its filling.

"No, but you were having fun picking them out. I wasn't going to stop you."

"Good boyfriend quality: indulgent. Check."

They sit at the dining table (now minus one chair) and eat. Blake finishes his disappointing jelly, then moves on to a chocolate and finally a cinnamon sugar.

"So, about that bath," he says as he licks his sugary fingers. "Are we talking bubble?"

Jay drops the spoon into the bowl and leans back in the chair. "Whatever you'd like. Kim left me some salts; says they're good for the skin. You can have rose, lavender, or grapefruit."

"I'll bite. Lavender, please."

They leave the kitchen for the back of the condo where Jay's bedroom waits. A flighty bird in Blake's chest begins to beat its wings.

"Sorry if it's a little messy, but the tub's through here." Jay hesitates at the door and glances back at him. He opens his mouth, then closes it and shakes his head before turning the doorknob and letting them in.

His bedroom stretches out before them, with a bookcase, dresser, and some kind of fern on one side. A shelf over a door on the opposite side holds a series of small robot models that Blake recognizes from an arcade game. But the dominating feature of the room is—

"Holy shit your bed is ginormous! What is that, three beds bolted together?" Blake gawps at it. It covers most of the span of wall across from them, made up nicely with a blue comforter.

Jay chuckles. "It's an alpha bed. The pack sleeps here sometimes, and we all need space."

"Everyone?" It's easy to imagine four people in that bed with plenty of space, but that level of intimacy makes Blake anxious.

"Yeah, you know. Pack bonding. Especially on full moons. We get together and sleep."

"Just sleep?"

"These days, yeah." Then he backtracks with a tight voice. "Sometimes we have sex. If there's been stress or drama or something. Kim's not into it, and Lance is straight, but it's the easiest way to stay bonded." He adds in a rush, "It hasn't happened in a while. Kim's been out of town for weeks now, dealing with some family problems, and Lance has been a good arbitrator."

"But you and Elliot...?" He doesn't know why he's pushing, but it feels important to know. Pack sex isn't technically cheating, socially speaking; as far as he knows every pack in Atlas gets up to it, but he wants to know what he's getting himself into. If things get more serious between them, if Jay marks him, then he'll join their pack, too, and that means full moon cuddle nights or anything else they might get up to. Better to know off the bat.

Jay runs a hand through his hair. "We've had our trouble. Haven't always seen eye to eye." Then he huffs a sigh and says, "Look, I'm not going to bullshit you. Elliot and I hook up. It's not easy having a pack with three alphas in it. I can't blame Elliot for not wanting to take my shit all the time. Kim is happy going along, and I'll never know why." He adds bitterly, "She'd be a much better pack leader if she wanted to."

Somehow, they've tread on a sensitive topic. Blake swallows and says gently, "But they follow you. They must love you."

Jay's shoulders drop. "Maybe you're right. Sometimes it's hard to see why."

On an impulse, Blake reaches out and wraps his arms around Jay's waist from behind. He leans his cheek against Jay and lets out a soft keen from the back of his throat. It seems to do the trick. He realizes as he nuzzles Jay's back that he's released a calming pheromone on instinct. Maybe he could do the omega thing, after all. It's an omega's job to soothe a pack, keep them strong without the need for sex or scent marking. Three alphas in one small pack must be difficult to manage. A brief fantasy overtakes him: joining them, belonging, for the first time in his life, with other people.

Then he recoils. He can't. Not with the Volkovs out there, searching for him. It's bad enough already that Jay's involved. He can't drag a whole pack into this mess, too. He needs to handle this the way he's handled everything else in his life: alone.

Jay turns to wrap arms around him. They stand in an embrace for a moment, two men thinking wildly different thoughts, then Jay pulls back with a smile.

"You've got some kind of magic, don't you?"

"Just instinct, like the rest of us."

Jay shakes his head. "I've met other omegas. None of them were like you." He leans over and brushes his lips across the sensitive skin on Blake's neck, where it meets his shoulder, where a mating mark would go. Blake shivers at the intimacy. "No one's ever smelled so good to me. You're sweet and succulent, and everything spring." Teeth graze Blake's neck, sharper than normal, and oh so tantalizing. "I want you, Blake. I want to keep you."

Blake opens his mouth to say something witty, to diffuse the tension with some sarcasm or a pointed joke, but all that escapes his lips is a shaky sigh. Against his better judgment, he reaches up to thread his fingers through Jay's hair, to pull him closer as he cranes his neck in offering. Something hard presses against his leg: Jay's cock, straining for contact. His own jumps in response.

"You would let me?" Jay whispers. "You would let me claim you?"

All of Blake's logical objections to mating float away under the force of his hormones. What does a lifelong commitment matter when Jay smells like sex and desire, and his teeth keep scraping teasingly over one of his most sensitive areas? He's about ready to demand that Jay take whatever he wants, that they fall into that massive bed and explore each other until the next full moon.

But good sense reasserts itself as he remembers the predatory gleam in Sara Reed's eyes and his own mother sick in bed after a life spent protecting him from alphas. He blinks rapidly and pulls back. Jay immediately takes a step away.

"Sorry." Jay runs a hand through his hair, now mussed and fluttering around his face. "Too soon, I know. I shouldn't have." Little flashes of his canines, long and pointed, peek through his lips. His eyes are a deep amber from lust. Blake has to force himself not to tackle him right into that bed.

"No, it's fine. I lost it, too." He squirms a little, uncomfortable with the tent in his pants.

"One step at a time, right?" Jay forces a smile. His alpha teeth gleam.

Blake licks his lips, dying to press them against Jay's, but instead uses them to say, "About that bath?"

"Right!" Jay seems relieved to have something to do. He jumps into action, crossing the room to the door on the left. "I'll start it for you."

***

Steam clouds the large bathroom when Blake enters. Jay had run him a hot bath, and the air smells lightly of lavender. The tiles beneath his bare feet are warm to the touch, and a gentle bubbling sound greets him.

"So your tub's just as big, huh?" Blake eyes the huge thing, made of cream porcelain and taking up half the room.

"Everything about me is big," Jay replies with a wink. Blake doesn't doubt it.

He sits on the edge and dips his fingers into the water, hot but not too hot, and rolling with bubbles.

"It's a jacuzzi, too?"

"I can turn that off if you'd like."

"Nah, it's perfect. Exactly what I need after a day like this."

Or at least the next best thing to getting sexed up.

"There's a towel on the rack." Jay points. "And I'll leave some clothes on my bed. Take however long you'd like."

"If I drown in here, promise you'll come find me. This thing is so big it could use a lifeguard."

"I'll have Charlie download a swimming protocol." He kneels and kisses Blake's cheek before leaving him alone in a room full of steam and the sound of merry bubbles.

Blake peels off the suit and does his best to hang it on the rack beside the towel. Maybe all the steam in here will press out the wrinkles. He can hope. He climbs into the tub and settles in the deepest part with a long sigh. He doesn't think he's ever taken the time to soak in a tub, certainly not one like this. He closes his eyes and lays his head back against the tub's lip. The heat penetrates his skin and eases the tension in his muscles across his back, shoulders, and limbs. The bubbles do their best masseuse work. Truly divine. This part of dating Jay he can get used to. Maybe not his parents or the politics, but the giants bathtubs and beds can stay.

As he luxuriates, he considers the night ahead of him. Jay won't push him, but Blake knows what he wants. Better to be prepared. He shifts his hips and drops his hand between his legs. It's been at least a year since he last got laid, but he flies solo enough to know what to do. An alpha might be a little different, but it's not like he can't handle that. Nothing lube can't fix.

His fingers work one at a time inside himself, slowly, carefully, and sending little sparks of pleasure to his dick. He resists wrapping a hand around it. This is purely prep work. He'll save the real pleasure for the bedroom. Hopefully, Jay will have the same intentions on his mind.

***

Jay did, indeed, have the same intentions on his mind. He returned to the living room and paced a little before flopping down across the couch and tapping his hand on the coffee table. His cock ached terribly just thinking about Blake naked in his bathroom. He wanted to jump that slim body, press him up against the tub, and fuck him silly. A part of him had wanted to snatch Blake from the beginning, from the moment he'd set eyes on him in the café, wearing that ridiculous uniform—frilly crop top and way too tight black pants, a collar with a bell like he was some sort of pet—and now he was wondering where Blake kept the outfit, and if it was something he might consider wearing privately, for reasons other than work.

Jay shook his head roughly.

Keep it together, man.

Blake might want to just sleep tonight, might not even want to share a bed. It wasn't Jay's place to pressure him.

But, damn, the man looked positively edible. Those wide green eyes made him shiver, and the thought of Blake's full lips around his cock drove him mad. He'd been agonizing for weeks over the fantasies. His hands, those were the best part. Slender, tapered, elegant and fine. Watching Blake chew his thumb when he was nervous or thinking too hard was a tease in and of itself. Jay had felt those fingers in his hair, gripping, stronger than they looked, and seen them play music with startling precision—he could only image what else those hands were capable of.

He stood and paced over to the kitchen to pour a cold glass of water. He nearly threw the contents over his head to keep himself in check.

He was about to start ruminating on how Blake would taste (would his cum be as sweet as he smelled?) when his phone chirped a familiar text tone.

Kim.

He snatched up the phone and swiped to see the message. It was abrupt and to the point, Kimiko-style.

I'm back in town. I need to speak with you. Tomorrow?

He typed off a reply (**Of course. Come over for lunch?**) and hit send.

A moment later, the phone chirped again.

I'll be there at noon.

Jay sent her a little emoji heart and tossed the phone back to the counter.

Now he had to distract himself for the rest of Blake's bath.

***

Blake finishes a while later, refreshed and loosened up, ready for whatever Jay throws at him. He drains the water and towels off before peeking into the bedroom. A pile of nightclothes sits on the bed, but no Jay. He must be in the living room. Blake picks up the clothes and puts them to his nose. They smell like his alpha, warm and inviting. He pulls the shirt on, and it falls to his knees, much too large but impossibly comfy. The pants are a lost cause. He could tie the waist off, but they're so long he'll be tripping over them all night. Just boxers, then. He leaves to locate Jay.

The alpha sits on the couch, not quite lounging, flicking through his phone. Blake pads over to him and offers the pants.

"They don't fit."

"I could try to find other ones. Lance might've left some clothes around."

Blake doesn't miss the way Jay's eyes travel up his legs. Time to just go for it. "It's okay. I was hoping I wouldn't wear this much longer, anyway."

He relishes the way Jay's eyebrows jump up. He likes that he can have that effect on him, surprise him even when the sexual tension between them has been thick enough to choke someone. Still, he enjoys the way Jay looks like he's won the lottery.

"What?" Blake murmurs mischievously. He straddles Jay's hips and pushes him against the couch arm. "Don't tell me you're having second thoughts." The nightshirt rides up his thighs, and Jay's hands find the skin there, pulling him closer. He leans over Jay, vision hazy with desire, and says, "I'd rather we not think at all."

Jay's fingers dig into the flesh of his thighs, and he all but growls, "You say the word, Buttercup, and I'll fuck you so hard you won't remember how to think."

Without waiting for a reply, Jay's mouth finds Blake's collarbone and sends a line of heat across the skin as he trails kisses to Blake's shoulder.

Blake sucks in a breath and closes his eyes. It's like every nerve ending in his body is alive, shooting sparks through his body. He can't imagine doing this with anyone but Jay, can't imagine wanting anyone the way he wants this man.

"Fuck yes," he groans. The nightshirt slips from his shoulder, and Jay's hands creep from his thighs to his ass and grope possessively. Blake pants and arches his back. Can't remember the last time someone touched him like this. It shocks him, in the remaining space in his mind, how badly he wants to be wanted.

He slips his hands under Jay's shirt and rubs his pecs, savoring the firm muscle, then tweaks his nipples. Jay twitches and growls, apparently sensitive. Their lips meet, opening for each other, desperate for more. Blake feels Jay's cock straining and rolls his hips in response. Jay's fingers grope farther, left hand slipping between the cleft in Blake's cheeks and teasing the skin there.

Blake shudders and breaks from the kiss to bury his face in Jay's neck, where he can smell the alpha pheromones strongly enough to send his head spinning. He moans unabashedly. The desire burns a hole in his gut, makes his limbs weak, his pulse too rapid. He's about to lose control, and he can't care less.

"Bed," he grunts, barely able to get the words out. "Please. Fuck me already."

Jay nips his shoulder and says, "Anything for you." He brings his right hand up to run through Blake's damp hair, then trails his thumb over his bottom lip. "I'm going to fuck all the sass out of you."

Blake bites Jay's thumb roughly and responds with his best sassy voice. "That better be a promise. I'd hate to be disappointed."

Without warning, Jay scoops Blake up in both arms and stands, tossing him over one shoulder like he weighs nothing. Blake barks out a surprised laugh. Jay beelines them to the bedroom, nearly knocking over a potted plant on the way. Anticipation curls in Blake's stomach, and, feeling high on the thrill of seduction, he giggles and flails his legs.

Jay practically kicks the bedroom door in and tosses Blake onto the bed. Blake bounces with a giddy laugh and then feigns weakness, throwing in the back of one hand to his forehead. He affects a southern belle accent and declares, "Oh my, what *am* I to do? Big, strong alpha. I sure hope he doesn't take advantage of little ole me."

Jay grins at him, teeth sharp, eyes amber, and replies in a bad cowboy drawl, "End of the road, mister. You've seduced your last alpha."

Blake cracks up at this, half from Jay's terrible accent, half from the idea that he might have seduced anyone. He pushes his luck and runs a hand under his nightshirt, hiking it up his chest and exposing his boxers. Somehow, he doesn't even feel ridiculous, just madly in lust with this other man.

"Go ahead," he purrs, eyes locked on Jay's. "Take what you want."

Jay closes the gap between them, snags Blake's wrists and pins them to the bed sheets. Teeth scrape over Blake's stomach, and a tongue dips into his bellybutton. Before he knows it, his breath is coming in short pants, and Jay's mouth is pressing against the fabric of his boxers, teasing his barely concealed dick.

"Jay," he moans as the alpha nuzzles him through the fabric, breathing him in and growling delightedly. His mind buzzes with pleasure, and when Jay releases his wrists to tug off the underwear, he gasps and arches.

His cock, free now and already dripping, springs up between them. Jay grasps him with one hand, and Blake hisses pleasure. The first stroke nearly sends him over the edge. He reaches out and catches Jay's wrist.

"Hang on," he pants. "You. Strip." He almost regrets the command as Jay releases him to yank off his clothes nearly fast enough to tear them.

Blake hitches a breath as he takes a mental picture of Jay's naked body, from the carefully sculpted muscle to the trail of hair leading from his bellybutton to his swollen, dripping cock.

Out loud, he murmurs, "Holy shit." Internally, he thinks, *It'll never fit*, with a near glee.

He grips Jay with both hands, amazed at the heat radiating off him. Jay's head falls back, and a delicious groan escapes his lips. Blake crouches at the edge of the bed and moves his hands to Jay's hips, thumbs settling into the divot along his hip bones. He nuzzles Jay's dick.

"Fuck," he breathes, almost drunk on Jay's pheromones. He's never felt this *need* before, to have someone inside him. He wraps his lips around Jay's tip, tasting salt and earthy musk, and dips his head as low as he can. Fingers thread through his hair and pull, firmly but not painfully, and he bobs in response, wanting more than anything to give Jay everything he wants.

He listens to Jay's heavy breathing as he works his tongue against him, relishes every catch of pleasure in his throat. He dips deeper and sucks, and Jay's hips jerk as he gasps, and Blake has to break away to cough. A thick strand of saliva drips to the bedspread. He barely has a chance to wipe his mouth and catch his breath before Jay puts hands on his shoulders and shoves.

Startled, Blake falls back against the pillows, sinking into the softness. Jay rummages through the drawer of the bedside table and produces a bottle of lube. Blake licks his lips and shifts his weight, prepares to flip around.

Jay catches him and pushes him back against the pillows. "Don't turn around," he says gruffly. His hand moves to Blake's thighs and pushes his legs up, hooking them over his shoulders. "I want to see the look on your face when you cum."

Blake groans and grips the bed sheet as Jay coats his fingers in lube and presses, one at a time, into his body. A shock of electric pleasure courses to the tips of his fingers and toes. He throws the crook of his elbow over his eyes and moans as Jay stretches him until he's loose enough to handle an alpha-sized cock. Heat pools in his lower half, threatens to explode, but he chomps his bottom lips and forces it back.

Then the fingers are gone, leaving him horribly empty and longing for more.

"Jay," he whimpers, reaching for the alpha's shoulders. "Please. I need you." He's releasing omega pheromones, ones meant to attract a mate, but he's long lost control over it.

Jay, practically drugged by Blake's scent, smears lube over himself and aligns their bodies. Their eyes meet, desperate and needy, and slowly, so slowly, Jay presses into him. Sparks shoot through every nerve ending in Blake's body. He hisses air between his teeth, unable to take a proper breath. No toy or partner has ever felt like Jay, heavy and thick inside him. They kiss between gasps as Jay carefully pulls back and pushes in again. The friction is enough to set Blake on fire. He moans helplessly into Jay's mouth and claws at his back, fingers grappling the skin for purchase. Jay hisses as Blake's nails dig in too deeply. Blake retracts immediately, mentally swearing at himself. He'd lost control, and his nails had sharpened to wolf claws. Damn fullblood DNA.

"Sorry," he pants. "You okay?"

"Fine." Jay seems less concerned with the scratches on his back and more interested in what he can do in return. Blake has no objections.

Jay moves again a little quicker, a little surer, then again, until they strike up a pace together, bare skin thudding in a room filled with sounds of their gasps and groans.

Jay shifts his weight, brings Blake's hips higher, hoisting him off the bed for a better angle. He thrusts again, and Blake's world explodes in light.

"Ah!" Blake feels the words rip his throat as his claws tear at the sheets. "Right there!"

Jay's pace is relentless now, and every stroke lights up Blake's world like fireworks. They fuck like nothing else in the world matters, like they'll never get enough of each other. It only takes a few more thrusts, and Blake loses it, dick erupting a string of cum across their stomachs, filling the air with a tangy sweet scent. He goes rigid as pleasure ripples through him, every pump of Jay's hips another crack of lightning to his senses.

The scent of him is more than Jay can handle. He thrusts fully once more, then shudders and jerks a few shallow times as heat and musk fills Blake. Finally, he stills, leaving nothing but the sound of their panting.

A few seconds pass, bodies still joined, breath still in sync, then Jay pulls out, and Blake feels the thick trickle of seed down his thighs. "Fuck," he moans, which sums up the sensation quite thoroughly.

Jay collapses onto the bed beside Blake and wastes no time pulling him close for a cuddle. He buries his nose in Blake's hair. They lay for a while like that, catching their breath, pulses slowing, until Blake finds the strength to murmur, "I'm gonna need another bath."

"Tomorrow," Jay grunts. "I'm not done with you yet."

If Blake's dick were capable of jumping at that moment it would have. Instead, he yawns and says, "So the rumors about alpha stamina are true?"

"As true as omegas."

Damn, Jay has him there. In the proper mood, Blake can go for hours. And this is definitely the proper mood.

"Hey," he says suddenly as the thought occurs to him. "I thought alphas had knots. Where's yours?" He reaches between them and feels for Jay's dick, giving it a gentle squeeze.

"Mmm." Jay's eyes slide shut and he nuzzles Blake's neck. "Not mated. That's for mating." Then he says in a wicked voice, "Wanna try it, though?"

"Whoa there, Cowboy." Blake removes his hand from between them and runs it through Jay's hair. "I don't think my body could take it."

And anyway, neither of them is ready for what mating entails. At least, he doesn't *think* Jay is ready.

Oh god, Jay might actually be ready to mate.

He dislodges the thought with a shake of his head. They're sex drunk, that's all. All these pheromones in the air (most of them his fault). No one could think straight in this fog.

"But could you go another round?" Jay's fingers trail down Blake's back to ass and massages there, smearing cum over his skin. "Now I want to fuck you from behind."

This time, Blake's cock really does jump.

He kisses his alpha and murmurs, "I still feel a little sass in me. Better take care of it."

Chapter Twelve

Bach's "Prelude and Fugue No. 2 in C Minor"

B lake wakes the next morning to sticky sheets and tacky skin and the glorious sensation of Jay holding him, breath puffing against his collar. He relishes it for as long as it takes him to remember there are leftover donuts in the kitchen, then he extracts himself by carefully relocating Jay's limbs to his side of the bed. He scoots to the edge and climbs out, grateful that Jay is still asleep to miss him stumbling like a newborn giraffe as he gets his legs under him. He feels sore and used up and utterly satisfied. He finds his nightshirt discarded on the floor and pulls it on before padding off, images of coconut creams dancing in his head.

He sidles into the kitchen and gropes for the donut box. He squints. It's much too bright in here. They must have left a light on overnight.

"Good afternoon. Are you the reason Jay is late for lunch?"

Blake jerks, yelps, and loses grip of the donuts. They tumble like descending notes of a chromatic scale, rolling and bouncing across the kitchen tile. He stiffens upright and snaps his head around. A woman sits at the dining table, steaming cup in her hands, appraising him with eyes so dark they seem black. She's Oceanese, with velvety tan skin and soft features. Her hair, shiny black silk, hangs loose around her shoulders and out of sight past her waist. She doesn't smile but doesn't seem particularly threatening either. She simply watches Blake with an inscrutable expression, as though she already knows more about him than he does.

"Oh, um, hi, er..."

What's the etiquette for an unfamiliar woman finding you half naked the morning after sex? Does he have cum in his hair? Jay blasted him in the face at one point last night, and he hasn't gotten around to showering yet...

Focus!

"Sorry, who are you?" he blurts it without much decorum.

She takes a sip from her cup but seems to be hiding a tiny smile. "Kimiko Oshiro, Jay's packmate. And you must be his latest toy. Did you meet at a club? Or are you a stray? Jay does so love disappointing his parents." She speaks with a British accent, of all things.

Immediately irritated, Blake bites back, coating his voice in venom. "I'm the king of freaking France."

"Fine then." Kimiko makes a dismissive gesture with her fingers. "I'm not particularly interested, anyway. Wake him up for me, will you? We have business to attend to."

"What is it with you alphas? Always ordering people around. Some of us try not to step on toes. Some of us think about other people once in a while." Although at this rate, maybe he ought to be taking a note from their books. It certainly seems to yield results.

"You let me know how that goes for you, *Monsieur Monarque*. In the meantime, wake up Jay for me. I'd rather not smell his room right now."

Blake's jaw tightens. The nerve! He ought to throw one of the fallen donuts right at her smug face. See how elegant she looks covered in icing. Instead, he turns on his heel and stomps to Jay's bedroom. He opens the door with a whoosh and declares loudly, "Her Majesty is here to see you."

Jay grunts, twitches, and gropes the edge of the bed, hands seeking Blake. Blake tromps over and pokes him in the temple. When bleary eyes open, most of his irritation melts away. Jay looks delectable with his messy hair and half-lidded eyes. It takes everything in him not to climb back into bed and snuggle close.

"C'm'ere," Jay slurs, reaching for him.

Blake takes Jay's large hand in both of his and presses it to his cheek. Warm and soothing, it eases away the rest of Blake's anger.

"There's a woman here says you're late to a meeting. Should I tell her to go away?" He can't keep the hope out of his voice. The day after first-time sex is meant for cuddling and pizza and more sex. No third wheel factors in.

Jay's eyes pop open though. He props himself halfway up and fumbles for his phone. "Shit," he mutters when he sees the time. He swings his legs over the edge of the bed and stands, gloriously naked if not a little sleep drunk. His tattoo shines in full, delicate lines and swaths of inking across his right arm and shoulder. Again, Blake wants to tackle him, push him back into bed and fuck him until neither of them can move. He restrains himself.

"Sorry," Jay mutters and pushes past him to locate a pair of pants. He settles on some loose sweats and starts for the door. The scratches on his back from the night before shine red and a little irritated. They'll have to clean them later.

"She's in a mood," Blake says as he trots after Jay. "Watch out for her barbed tongue."

Kimiko hasn't moved from her spot at the dining table. She assesses Jay with a silent gaze when he arrives and takes a long sip from her teacup.

"Hey, Kim. Sorry. We got a little carried away last night."

"I can smell that much."

"This is Blake. He's staying with me right now—long story."

"I would appreciate some privacy considering the matter I need to discuss."

Blake can read between the lines. That was Kimiko for 'Get lost'. He humphs and leans against Jay, staking his claim.

Between the two of them jockeying for position with their scents, the room smells positively acidic. Jay groans and takes Blake by the shoulders. "Would you mind? Hang out in my room for a bit? Maybe take a shower? I need some time here."

Of course. They might have had sex (and a lot of it) last night, but Kimiko is pack, and pack always comes first. Blake tries not to show his hurt.

"No problem. Just more strange people in my increasingly strange life. I'll buck up, Buttercup." Maybe he isn't the best at disguising hurt feelings.

Jay winces. "Want Charlie to bring you breakfast? He makes a mean omelet."

Blake sighs, thinking for a flash about the scattered donuts, and nods. "Cheese and peppers, if you've got it."

"Any meat? Sausage?"

"Oh, baby, I'll always take your sausage."

Ack, how did *that* train wreck slip out?

But Jay laughs anyway. "Later. I'll be along as soon as I can." He kisses Blake's cheek, and somehow Blake isn't even mad anymore. He turns away, not bothering to shoot another look at Kimiko, and trots down the hallway.

***

Jay craned his neck to watch Blake go, then shifted his attention to Kim.

"You could've been nicer."

Without missing a beat, she shot back, "You could've been on time."

Jay sighed, chastised, and took the seat across from her. "Charlie," he called out, and a moment later the mech slid into view with a short bow. "Make Blake an omelet, would you? Cheese, peppers, and sausage."

"Would you like one as well?"

"Add spinach to mine. You're a peach."

"I noticed your couch," Kim said as way of icebreaker when Charlie disappeared into the kitchen. "Something I should know about? Or the exact opposite?"

"It's not a weird sex thing, if that's what you're thinking."

"I never can tell with you."

"Shifter attack. Wolf smashed in the door and tore up the couch."

Whatever Kim had been expecting to hear, that must not have been it. Her dark eyes widened, and lips parted ever so slightly. She recovered quickly, tilting her chin up like nothing had phased her in the first place. "This wouldn't happen to have anything to do with your new bedmate?"

"I told you it was a long story. Want the crib notes?"

"As scintillating as your sex life is, I'd rather be spared the details. There's something else I came to discuss. *Obaasama*—my grandmother—has passed."

"Shit." Jay's muscles tightened. Kim had been incommunicado since leaving town weeks ago. That explained it.

The Oshiro clan was the highest ranked Oceanese pack. By rights, that meant Kim owned half the eastern world. Yet somehow news of the leader's death hadn't reached Atlas intelligence. Surely his parents would have alerted him if they knew. Surely people weren't leaving him out of the loop... again...

"We weren't close." She waved a hand. "It's the circumstances of her death that concern me. And before news leaks, I needed to confront you about it." She placed her teacup on its saucer and impaled Jay with a steely gaze. "My grandmother was assassinated, and our intelligence points the blame at Atlas."

A silent moment passed between them. Jay let out a tiny breath.

"Shit," he repeated.

"Indeed." She folded her hands in her lap and turned her eyes out the window. "I know you try to stay out of politics, but if you know anything about this, I would appreciate the clue. I've hushed the clan for now; I'm not ready to plunge us into war without some more research. So I came to you first. Jay, please." Her eyes returned to him. "If you know anything, then I need to know it, too."

"I wish I did. I haven't heard a thing about this. It's been peaceful between us for decades. Why would Atlas strike now?"

Kim hummed to herself as she considered the question. "Perhaps they felt the line of succession was weak. Perhaps they considered that we were packmates, and my loyalties were split."

"BS. You're the strongest person I know. You wouldn't let anything get in your way."

Kim smiled her quiet smile, the one that lifted just the corners of her mouth, like she had a secret. "I never understood why you felt so highly of me, but it is appreciated. For the time being, however, I'll need to do some digging. I have connections at the embassy and among some elite packs. If you hear anything from your family—"

"I'll let you know. I have to see Cat soon. I'll ask her."

"Thank you." She stood and walked to the door before turning back. "And watch out with your new pet. He's left you some nasty marks on your back. Fullblood, is he? With claws like that."

Jay furrowed his brows. "No, he's a..." He stopped himself. *Was* Blake a fullblood? And why hadn't he mentioned it? It would make things a lot easier if he was actually from a prominent family. Perhaps there was a little more to him than he let on, but there was no time to think about that now.

"Say hi to Elliot and Lance for me." Kimiko seemed unconcerned with his abrupt confusion.

He shook it off. "I'll send them your love."

She wrinkled her nose but didn't correct him. And like that, she was gone. Jay sighed and leaned back in his chair. Charlie came around the table, plate in hand.

"Your omelet."

"Charlie, what's it like being a mech?"

"I'm afraid I'm not programmed to answer that question."

"Close enough. Did Blake get his breakfast?"

"He's showering. I left it covered for him."

"All right, then."

He dug into his omelet as he tapped a text message to Cat.

Got any shifter wisdom for me, O Wondrous Teacher?

A moment later, it buzzed a reply.

Yeah, wake up on time. I thought you'd call me hours ago.

This again.

He replied, **Had a late night. Saw Kim. Got some things I want to ask you.**

How is she doing? She's been gone a while.

Never going to happen, Cat. She's not interested.

I don't know what you're talking about. How about this? Come over for coffee, and I'll go over some basics with you.

Let me check on Blake. I'll get back to you.

He polished off his omelet and wandered back to his bedroom, where he found Blake naked in bed, scraping the last few scraps of egg from his plate.

"Charlie should find employment on a cook line. This was great."

"Told you."

"Has Her Majesty left? Wouldn't want to sully her breathing air with my presence."

Jay winced. "Sorry you guys got off on the wrong foot. She's stressed. Her grandmother died."

A flicker of shock crossed Blake's features, then he sighed. "Sorry. I'm being petty. That sucks."

"Maybe when things calm down you two can meet properly. I swear she's actually really cool. She plays *shamisen*. You two probably would get along."

"I guess I'll give it another shot." He stuck his nose up. "But she better not boss me around."

"She can be a bit bossy, huh?" Jay chuckled. "I guess it comes with the territory." He thought again about the claw marks on his back, too deep to be from blunt nails, and almost opened his mouth to inquire, but then some of Blake's aroma drifted to him, and he thought better of it. He climbed into bed beside Blake and nuzzled his neck. He smelled clean—warm water and soap and wonderfully sweet strawberries. Jay murmured, "I know you just showered, but I've got an idea to get you messy again."

"I'm listening."

***

Blake dozes face-first in his pillow. He's aware, in a distant way, of Jay moving around the room, but he's too tingly and sleepy to care. A warm sensation in his gut coaxes him toward sleep. He's safe. Where he's meant to be. Consciousness flickers in and out, one moment a calloused hand pets his hair and lips press to his temple, the next, his phone rings insistently at him.

He slaps the table where he left it, but only succeeds in knocking it to the floor. He groans, rolls, and fumbles on the ground. The phone shuts up just as he brings it to his face. He squints at the front. Missed call from Terri. Oh boy, will she be thrilled to hear about this update in his sex life. He can practically see her brown eyes sparkling.

He opens the phone, but she doesn't leave a message. He tosses it back on the table. That conversation can wait. He needs to clean up again, and these sheets need some serious washing. He clambers out of bed and realizes suddenly that Jay has left. In the living room, maybe. He rinses off and dresses. Brushes his teeth a second time for good measure, then leaves the musky bedroom to search for his partner.

No Jay in the kitchen. No Jay in the dining room. No Jay on the couch. Blake frowns.

"Charlie?"

The mech sweeps over to him and bows.

"Where'd Jay go?"

"He said to leave his apologies, but he went to meet his sister. Important family business, no doubt."

Blake frown deepens. Abandoned already. Twice in one day. And Jay didn't even have the decency to wake him up!

"I guess I'm dead weight, huh?"

"Sincerest apologies."

Blake's phone rings again. He glances at the screen—Terri. Well, she'll at least listen to him complain. He isn't sure if a mech is any good at that. He flips it open.

"Hey, Terri, you won't believe—"

"Mr. Fields," a gruff voice with a thick accent greets him. Blake freezes. "This business of chasing you around has grown tiring. I've enlisted your friend's help in the matter."

Fear clenches a fist around Blake's throat. He wheezes out, a little too high pitched, "What did you do to her? She better not be hurt, you son of a—"

"She is fine, merely resting. This will not continue to be the case if you do not follow my instructions to the letter."

Blake's heart kicks a staccato beat. He purses his lips. "Okay. What is it?"

"You will meet me, alone, and listen to what I have to say."

"I'm listening now."

"I make the rules, Mr. Fields. In person we shall talk." His accent makes it difficult to follow every word. Lantish is clearly not his first language.

"Fine. Where are you? Some warehouse by the docks?"

A low chuckle greets that. "You watch too many movies. I am at the Downtown Howlton Hotel, room 513. You come to me, and we have a little chat. No outsiders necessary."

"And you'll let Terri go?"

"Of course. Your friend is my friend. Now hurry up. Be here in the next twenty minutes."

A beep indicates the man has hung up. Blake lets out a shaky breath and drops his hand. He stares blankly at the floor as the information turns over in his mind. Jay would want him to call, to bring backup, to do absolutely anything to ensure he'd survive the encounter. But he has to play it carefully or his secret will come spilling out. And he can't risk Jay again. Not after last time. This is his problem, and he'll deal with it like he deals with everything. Alone.

Decision made, he turns to Charlie. "I have to go. If I don't get back in an hour, call Jay and tell him to check the Downtown Howlton Hotel, room 513. Tell him the shifter's there, bring backup. And..." He blinks, aware of how ridiculous confessing feelings through a mech is. "And that's it. I'll see him soon. I hope."

He scoops up his shoulder bag from beside the couch, relocates the pepper spray to an easy-to-snag front pocket, and pulls on his shoes. He dashes out the door and down the elevator, trying to calculate how quickly he can walk to the hotel. Twenty minutes should be just enough.

Hang in there, Terri. Calvary's coming.

Chapter Thirteen

Vivaldi's "Summer"

Blake rushes through the hotel lobby and up to the fifth floor. As he draws nearer to room 513, the sickness in the pit of his stomach burbles stronger and stronger, until it feels like he might puke all over his sneakers. No one around to see him approach the room. Will this be the last anyone ever hears from him? Some half-assed message through Charlie could be his dying words.

This is stupid. You're being stupid.

But Terri is in there. The only friend he's ever had, who's stood beside him for years. Maybe she's hurt or drugged or tied up, and it's all his fault.

He musters what courage he can and comes face to face with 513. Will a wolf be waiting on the other side?

No, stupid, he said he wanted to talk. Can't talk if you're a wolf.

Blake huffs a breath, shakes out his hands, and adjusts the strap on his bag. He knocks weakly, then a second time with some more umph behind it. The latch on the other end clicks, the bolt slides, and the door creaks open.

A gray eye peers out at him, bloodshot and deeply lined. The voice to match rumbles from behind the cracked door. "You come in. No one else."

"No one's here," Blake grumbles. He really hopes Jay doesn't hate him for this.

"That better be true."

The door slides open enough for Blake to step through. The man gives him a few feet, and then Blake's inside, door clicking shut firmly behind him.

The man stares at him with a frown, assessing him.

"Put the bag down," he finally says.

"Where's Terri?" Blake counters. The room, as far as he can tell, is a normal hotel room with a single bed, TV, and sitting desk. No place to hide Terri, unless she's in the bathroom.

"Bag first," the man snaps.

Blake keeps his face blank as he unshoulders the bag and places it at his feet.

"Go stand by the lamp," Flat Nose instructs. It's the furthest point in the room, by the back corner. Blake hesitates. "Go. Or your friend suffers."

He steps over his bag and across the room. Once standing by the lamp, wondering if he could smash the window open, he repeats, "Where's Terri?"

"Idiot boy," Flat Nose sneers. "She's not here. I stole her phone."

Blake gapes at him as the wheels click into place. Terri isn't in danger, never had been. He had just assumed...

"You fucker!"

"You are a fool. So willing to believe a stranger. But you will stay here, and we will talk." He stands, arms akimbo, and looks Blake up and down. "Pretty shoddy prince," he proclaims.

"Pretty lousy agent," Blake shoots back. "Who gets beat up twice with furniture?"

Flat Nose's bloodshot eye twitches. "You have none of the grace or presence belonging to the Volkov name. You're a runt. I do not see why the Great Wolf wants you back."

"Must be my winning personality. Did you drag me here to berate me, or can I go?"

He shakes his head, walks to the desk, and picks up a folded booklet with a picture of a plane on the front.

"Tickets," he says like that explains the matter.

"Very good!" Blake pours on the sarcasm. "You must be acing those remedial Lantish courses." Stress really brings out the bitchiness in him.

"You will go," Flat Nose says as though Blake hasn't spoken. "Back to Servos. These will take you to the Great Wolf. He has business with you."

"So you *don't* want me dead?"

"You are my ticket home. Dead does not help me. The Great Wolf has made it clear that you are to meet him in person." He sneers a grin. "Call it a family reunion."

"Not interested. My only family's here."

Flat Nose pulls back his lips, transforming his smile to a snarl. "Yes. Rotting away in hospital. Brain too weak to remember her own name."

"Shut up!" Blake snaps, his overworked nerves unleashing a load of fury. "You don't know anything about it."

Flat Nose chortles and waves the tickets. "I know plenty. You want her fixed? You go home first."

Fixed. Despite himself, Blake perks up. Damn, this guy knows how to yank his chain. From his bag, his phone rings. Flat Nose eyes it like it might explode. Blake sidles a few steps away from the lamp.

"Stop that!" he barks, waving the tickets. "You will take this plane. Your documents are prepared."

"What did you mean 'fixed'?"

Flat Nose sighs exasperatedly like Blake is a misbehaving pup and says, "Wild magic. A spell. I will tell you no more. Go to Servos. Find your answers there."

Wild magic. It's easy to forget that other parts of the world have such things, when Atlas is so technologically inclined. Maybe some spell could cure her. He's never even considered it. His phone stops ringing and then immediately starts again.

"Shut that thing off!" Flat Nose snaps. "Who goes to a hostage situation with their ringtone on?"

"Oh, sorry," Blake replies, rolling his eyes, "because I've been in *so* many of these."

Flat Nose shuffles back a few steps and kicks Blake's bag. It tumbles over, and the flap falls open. His phone flops out, buzzing madly, and Flat Nose stomps it so hard the plastic frame explodes across the room. The ringing sputters and dies.

But something else skitters out of the bag. A little cylinder rolls to the middle of the room, stopping a few feet short of Blake. His eyes widen. The mace! Flat Nose notices it, too, and they both dive forward, arms reaching.

Blake kicks off the ground to give himself a few more inches of reach and snatches the spray out from under Flat Nose's hand. He hits the carpet, scraping his knees through his jeans, and dodges sideways as Flat Nose tackles the space he'd just occupied.

He scrambles, gets his feet under him, and uncaps the pepper spray. They've switched sides now, putting Blake's back at the door. Flat Nose growls at him, teeth lengthening. Blake holds the pepper spray as far away from himself as he can, points directly into those gray eyes, and presses.

A thick, orangey liquid spurts out, covering the man's eyes and nose. He screams and paws at his face, dropping immediately to the ground.

Blake groans and blinks rapidly, eyes watering. The mace has left a poisonous cloud of particles in the air, and he nearly chokes on them. He ducks, covering his mouth and nose with his arm, and grabs his bag.

Then he notices the booklet of tickets on the ground. Sinuses screaming, he makes his decision. He's on his own, and no one else will bail him out. If this could be the end of it, then better to go at it swinging. He snatches the booklet and stomps out of the room, coughing like a lifelong smoker.

***

Blake's feet hit the pavement outside the hotel in a run. He puts a few blocks of distance between him and Flat Nose and stops to wipe his face. His skin burns around his eyes and cheeks, and he blinks away a few tears. That mace is some serious shit. At least it should keep the guy down for a bit. He opens the booklet to get a look inside.

A passport greets him, along with two tickets. One plane departing the local airport, a stop on the other side of the country, then arriving in the Servan capital. Behind the tickets is another document, written in eastern Servan so that he has no earthly clue what it says. His picture features in the top right corner. He studies the plane tickets again. The first one departs in an hour. He chews his thumb tip. The subway has a stop at the airport, so he could hop it in twenty minutes, but he may not have enough time to get through security. "Priority", the ticket reads. Maybe that will give him a chance.

Damn, without his phone there'll be no time to contact Jay. He shakes his head. It doesn't matter. It's time to clean this mess of his life up, to stop dragging other people into it. He doesn't need the help. He can do it alone.

Even if it's a death warrant.

But Flat Nose said the Volkovs could fix his mom...

Anything, he told Sara Reed. He'd do anything for Mom.

He breaks into a sprint, booklet clutched in a fist, directly for the subway. He doesn't even notice the squad of police cars roaring down the street except for their sirens blaring in beat with his heart.

Five minutes later, he's catching his breath aboard the subway, rocketing toward his destination.

***

Jay paced in his sister's house, phone to his ear.

"Come on, pick up already!"

Cat sat quietly at the bar, tapping out messages on her phone.

"Shit! It's not even ringing anymore!" Jay ran a hand through his already mussed hair. His stomach jumped to his throat since Charlie first contacted him a few minutes ago, and now it threatened to choke him with acid. "What the hell was he thinking?"

"Police should be there soon," Cat reported. "I'm in touch with Commissioner Harrison."

"I can't believe him! I leave him alone for an hour, and he goes off right into the guy's lap!" He resisted the urge to throw his phone across the room. "Why the hell would he do that?"

"He must have his reasons." Cat tapped the counter with one nail. "As stupid as they probably are."

"Shit." Jay ceased wearing a hole in Cat's carpet and collapsed onto the couch, head in hands. "He could be dead!"

Cat crossed the room and laid a hand on his shoulder. Jay snapped his head up, jaw set.

"We have to go over there."

"We'll get in the way."

"I can't stay here."

"You can't go, either."

"Watch me." He shrugged her hand off and stood, striding to the door.

"Jay," Her voice held command in it. Alpha voice. "You have to stay here. I'm getting updates every few minutes. You'll know sooner if you stay here."

He whirled on her. "And what? Abandon him? He probably did this because he doesn't trust me to help." He threw his hands up. "I'm fucking useless."

"Look, stay here until we get news. Then you can go on your rampage. Hell, keep up this anger and you might even shift. You're not a lost cause."

"I can't believe this."

"You've got a troublemaker on your hands."

"If that guy does anything to him—"

Cat's phone pinged. She reported in, "They're on the scene. Found the guy throwing up in the hotel room. Seems like Blake maced him."

"That's my boy."

"No sign of Blake, though. They're doing a sweep of the area."

Jay resumed his pacing. Blake was probably all right. Signs said he got out of there. But Jay can't imagine a good enough reason to make him go in the first place. He groaned and coughed. The acid reflux ramped up with a sickening burn.

They'll find him. And when he gets back, I'm never letting him go.

Chapter Fourteen

Handel's "Sarabande"

B lake was gone. The police had searched the entire hotel, along with nearby streets and alleys. Asked around the area for anyone matching his description. Checked security cameras. They only knew he fled the scene after macing the Servan agent and now remained at large.

The agent—Victor Litvin—waited at the police station and said nothing other than a request for representation from the embassy. An embassy that was no longer active due to the war. So it was stalemate.

Jay stood now at the window looking into the interrogation room where Litvin resided. It had been eight hours since Blake disappeared. His nerves were flayed, his throat raw from stomach acid. Blake was going to give him ulcers.

"No touching, no moving to his side of the table. Keep things civil. Being here is a privilege, got it?" Officer Maclean stood by the door and ran through the protocol for the umpteenth time.

"Yes. Got it. Best behavior." Jay opened and closed his fists, as if to remind them it was not, in fact, time to throttle this guy.

Maclean unlocked the door and let him in, following close behind. Jay crossed the room and stood at the table to glare down at Litvin. The man sat, wrists chained to the metal furniture, and returned the glare with matching force. The skin around his eyes and nose was horribly red and inflamed, puffy as though he'd had an allergic reaction. From the depths of his swollen skin, his gray eyes glittered like steel.

Jay sat across from him, jaw tight. He loosened it enough to ask, "Where's Blake?"

Litvin said nothing.

"What did you do to him?" His voice raised a little, but he wrested it under control.

Nothing again.

"I swear to God, if anything happened to him..."

"You'll what?" The man sneered, accent thick through his thicker lips. "Cry to mommy and daddy? You are a powerless pup playing at world politics."

Jay's fist twitched. Litvin was taunting him; better not to rise to it. He took a breath.

"Tell me where he's gone. I don't care about politics. I don't care about you or who you work for. Where did Blake go? That's it."

"I will talk to embassy."

"There is no embassy!" Jay slammed the table with his fist. It rattled. Officer Maclean cleared her throat, but he couldn't care less. "Do you know how Atlas handles spies? You're a war criminal. There's no out for you here."

"Then I have no reason to talk." Litvin barely seemed to move as he spoke, didn't even change the direction of his gaze. He was like an alligator, watchful and nearly silent.

"I'll give you a reason." Not a threat. A bargain. "You know who I am. You call me powerless, but I still have influence. I can pull more strings than you imagine, and those can either go in your favor or against it."

The alligator stillness of him didn't break. He replied, "You have no motive to help me once you have him back. And I will not take a promise like it's candy. I am not so trusting as your little pup."

He was as immovable as a mountain. Jay sighed and leaned against the chair back. One last card to play.

"You haven't been speaking, but that doesn't mean we don't know anything about you. It's easy enough to do a little digging. You aren't some highly trained military agent. You're barely even an officer." Jay tapped the table with one finger. "Victor Litvin, forty-three. Exiled from Servos for dereliction of duty. You've spent every day of the last decade looking for a way back, any way to appease Mikhail Volkov and receive a pardon. Mess with the lead Lantish packs, return home, be treated like a hero. That's what you want, right?"

Litvin sucked his teeth, but otherwise gave no response. Jay pushed on.

"You help me out. You tell me where Blake is, and I'll pull the right strings for you. Your family could come here, live peacefully with you again. No war crimes, no record at all. Just you, your wife, and your daughters. All you have to do is help me get Blake back."

Silence now, as Litvin processed everything. Slowly, he reached across the table with one cuffed hand. He laid it over Jay's wrist and leaned in, eyes bright.

"It is too late. He took the tickets. The little pup is across the country now, if he's on that plane. On his way to the Great Wolf. He is out of your reach. Good luck with him, *nevolk*."

A surge of stomach acid erupted up Jay's throat. He jerked his hand away and stood.

"I'm done," he snapped.

Maclean let him out, and he paced to the front desk to pick up his phone. He ran a hand through his hair, dislodging it from its ponytail. As he turned the phone back on, a beep informed him someone had left him a message. He swiped.

'Maybe: Blake', the alert read.

He never hit play so fast in his life.

"Hey, Jay, it's me. Blake, I mean." A dry chuckle. "You know, the guy you just banged silly?" A sigh like he was regretting that one. "Look, I don't have a lot of time. I'm doing something stupid. Like, a-one-star-review-of-Casablanca stupid. But, um, sorry-not-sorry? That came out wrong. What I mean is please keep an eye on Mom and I'll be back as soon as I can. Oh, right. I'm going to Servos. Long story. Not something somebody explains over a payphone. God, we really *are* in some telenovela, and it's all my fault. Shit. I gotta go. Hold tight for me, okay? I have to kick Mikhail Volkov's ass."

It cut off with a prolonged beep.

Jay stared at the phone, replayed Blake's voice in his mind, tried to fill in the blanks.

What the everloving fuck was going on?

He caught the officer at the front desk's attention. "I need a call traced. Where's Commissioner Harrison?"

Maybe if they acted fast enough, they could track Blake down. Jay tried to count back the hours to figure where on his trip Blake could be. If he was taking a direct flight, then he'd be halfway there by now. If there had been a layover, then maybe there was a chance. A chance to snatch him out from under Mikhail's grasp.

But as the minutes ticked by, it felt more and more like the hand was closing.

***

Blake shifts in his seat. He's never been on a private charter plane. The first plane was commercial, a seat from west Atlas to east, but then he'd taken a train to a private airfield where a sketchy-looking Servan man wearing a pilot's hat accepted his ticket and ushered him onto a tiny jet. It isn't uncomfortable, but the only other person on his side of the cabin is a woman dressed in a severe black skirt and suit jacket who'd grabbed his chin when he first said hi and stared so close at him their noses almost touched. She'd nodded and released him, then proceeded to pointedly ignore him the entire trip. He thinks she understands Lantish, but she avoids conversation like a cat avoiding water. So he sits in silence at a window and watches the clouds pass. It's dark out, and sleep drags the edges of his eyes, but his nerves jangle, and he can't bring himself to close them.

Jay must be so worried.

He'd called on a public phone before catching the second plane. Left a message in a failed attempt to explain himself and reassure Jay everything would be fine. Honestly, if he does make it back, it'll be a miracle if Jay forgives him.

Can't think about that now. One thing at a time.

He wonders how much farther they'll fly. A few hours, maybe. No messages come in from the pilot. All he has on him is his bag, and it contains the sum total of his life: a library book, a wallet with some change, and a packet of gum. He'd had to trash the remaining pepper spray back at the airport.

He shifts and sighs, leaning his forehead against the cold window. Tries to rehearse what he'll say to Mikhail when they meet.

Hello, Father, good of you not to kill me.

Doesn't quite have the ring he wants.

The clouds pass, and his eyes slip shut. Dawn on the horizon. A new country to set foot in. A despot to confront.

Somehow after all these years of fending for himself, he finally wants someone to back him up.

***

"He's out of the country now. Some private flight. It won't respond to any hails." Gabriel reported. "It crossed into Servan airspace an hour ago. Nothing we can do."

Jay let out a hiss of breath. He sat in his parents' lounge, Cat on one side, Mom and Dad on the other. Gabe sat across, a tablet in his hands.

He continued, "I've been in contact with the Travers pack, and they're sending a message overseas. But now we wait."

"Wait?" Jay spat. "Wait? No, we go over there and we get him back."

"Dear." His mom faced him and placed a hand over his. "You aren't thinking clearly. There's no way any of us can enter Servan territory without invitation. We're formally at war."

Jay twitched his hand away. "You expect me to wait around? Wait for news that he's dead?"

"I hardly expect Mikhail to simply kill the boy," his dad said. "Too much effort to bring him overseas. Perhaps we can strike a bargain."

"We wait," his mom said crisply, "and we take advantage of any opportunity that presents itself. Obviously, Blake is special; I've had my suspicions since we met, but there's nothing we can do until we get word from the Volkovs. Don't worry yourself into a rut. We'll sort this out."

How his mom could be this confident, he'd never know, but there wasn't any sense in fighting her. He huffed again and stood.

"I need to clear my head. I'm taking a walk."

"I'll go with you." Cat followed.

No sense fighting her, either.

It was dark out, but the lamps around the garden shed enough light to walk by. Clouds obscured the waxing moon, and the distant light of the city blocked most of the stars. Cat fell into step beside him.

"Don't waste this time," she cautioned.

"What are you talking about?" Jay stopped at a row of hyacinth and inspected the petals for signs of drought or malnourishment.

"Shifting. You can still learn. You're pissed off enough, anyway. And the moon's full in two days. I can take you running."

"How am I supposed to concentrate on that now?" His fingers lingered on the leaves of a yew bush sculpted into a perfect cube.

"How can you not? He's your mate, right? So shift for him!"

Jay flinched at the word. No, they weren't technically mates, but he felt it in his gut.

Mine, hissed his wolf instincts, *mate, omega.*

Couldn't deny it.

"I'll try. I have to talk to my pack. We're usually together on full moons."

"Can't Kimiko shift? Maybe she should come along." Cat hurried after him as he headed to the center of the garden.

"She has other problems right now." He paused. It was the first time he'd thought of Kim's words all day. "Do you know anything about a target on the Oshiro clan?"

"I haven't heard anything." She narrowed her eyes. "Did something happen?"

Jay sighed. "Kim's grandmother was assassinated. She claims Atlas is at fault. I told her I'd ask around."

They stopped at the heart of the garden, dominated by a massive bay laurel topiary shaped like a howling wolf. The fragrance filled the circle like a soothing balm. Jay lingered.

Cat, impatient, crossed her arms. "How do we not know about that already?"

"She hushed it. Doesn't want to spark a war before she gets all the facts." Jay checked the undersides of some leaves and circled around to head to the grove in the back.

"That means she has to take over, doesn't it? She'll have to move back. Sorry to hear that."

She did sound sorry, but it didn't quell the tightness in Jay's chest. Two people leaving him now, and he was entirely powerless to stop them. He tried forcing a brave face.

"We'll figure it out. But see if you can't get some information for me. Find out who might have wanted the attack. If it really was Atlas..."

"Then they were working outside our control." Cat shook her head. "Our family is the primary liaison with Oceana; no way will we allow someone to get away with this. You can assure her I'm personally handling the matter. I do wish she would have come to us directly, though."

Oak trees lined the back of the yard here in twos, creating a path to stroll down. At the very end, a massive wisteria vine shaped into a tree draped purple flowers over the grounds. It had started as a cutting when Jay was a pup. A gift from the Oshiros. He remembered watching them plant it together, a show of solidarity. It thrived now, and they walked beneath the petals.

Suddenly nostalgic, Jay said, "Kim's always been aloof. Do you remember when we first met her?"

Cat chuckled. "She made you cry."

He rolled his eyes. "I meant how she didn't talk to anyone. I thought she must have been a statue or something."

"How did you get her to open up? I never figured it out."

"Persistence, mostly. I was a stupid kid. I thought if I kept bugging her, she'd talk to me eventually."

"It worked."

"No, she just hit me with a *bokken*." Jay laid his hand on the trunk of the vine as though he might feel its pulse.

Cat laughed outright then. "That's why you were crying? We never figured it out."

"I hated her for a while after that, but we kept seeing each other. Eventually I mistook those feelings for love. Funny how the two can be so similar to a kid."

"I wonder how she feels about that."

"When I confessed, she told me," he put on an accent to mimic her, "'You're not in love with me. You're in love with a me that doesn't exist.'"

"Ouch."

"She was right."

"She usually is."

"Then we became friends. She always hated being caught up in a lead clan. We bonded over that. It took years to get her to trust me."

"Your point being that she doesn't trust us. The Reeds or Atlas."

"Bingo. She won't approach you directly if she doesn't have to."

Cat clicked her tongue. "International relations will be hard if she can't come to us with troubles."

Jay nodded. He sat on the ground, leaning up against the vine and looked up through the petals. The sky turned amethyst with their blooms.

Cat went on without sitting. "She may want to abdicate, if she feels uncomfortable leading the clan."

Jay shrugged. "That's her business."

They stayed silent for a while after that. Jay thought over the last couple days. The werewolf attack, meeting his parents, his night with Blake (his hands, firm and delicate, all over Jay's body), seeing Kim again, and now Blake's disappearance. He realized with a sigh how tired he felt. Too much, too quickly.

"I need a drink," he muttered.

"How do a few shots sound? My treat."

"You're speaking my language."

"Come on, little brother." She held out a hand for him. "Let's get you trashed. You have to promise me you won't start bawling over your omega, though."

He took her hand and stood. "Please. I'm an adult now. I can hide in my room and cry alone like the rest of you."

Cat snorted and led the way back to the house. They took her car to her place, and she rolled out a selection of tequilas and rums for the two of them to sample. Jay found a tequila he liked and sampled half the bottle. He woke up the next day achy, exhausted, and nauseous. And thinking of Blake.

He'd better be okay, wherever he was on the other side of the world.

Chapter Fifteen

Schubert's "Der Erlkönig"

Blake hesitates outside a door twice his height. Music pours through from the other side, a violin perfectly picking out the notes of a piece he knows he should recognize, but whose name escapes him. Blame the stress. His stomach, luckily empty, feels like it might revolt and unburden itself all over the palace's pristine stone floors.

He arrived in Moskva, the Servan capital, two hours ago. Midday sun shone on him as he disembarked, and guards hustled him through a private security building. The woman who'd been on his flight accompanied, barking orders to this guard and that, then dragging Blake along until they stepped out into the city. Blake had all of a minute to absorb the sight—more towers and domes than Remun had skyscrapers—until a black limousine pulled up, and the woman shoved him unceremoniously into the back. Gazing through the nearly black tinted windows, he could see different colored buildings rolled out over the landscape like art pieces, each with thin pointed tips or bulbous curved domes and archways everywhere. Moskva was ancient compared to Remun, and the history showed. The buildings weren't blinding metal and glass, but stone and brick and wood, different textures and shapes. How he wished he could roll the window down and stick his head out. But the woman kept a heavily mascaraed eye on him, so he settled on pressing his face to the window.

When they arrived at their destination, Blake marveled. And he thought the Reed estate had been big. This was a palace, a genuine palace. He couldn't even count all the windows, there were so many. White walls, pale green roof, and golden tips on the towers. They passed some checkpoints and cruised into a courtyard before the driver pulled over and opened the door for them. Guards flanked him, the woman strode ahead, and he hurried along behind, trying to peer into every crevice possible.

The walls inside were mostly white with so much gold detailing he thought he might go blind. Here and there, a red accent popped up. Every inch was sculpted and detailed, from the ceiling to the doorknobs. If the war with Atlas was fought with opulence, then Servos had won. They twisted through the hallways until he was completely, hopelessly lost in some spot deep in the building. Finally, they stopped outside a door, and the woman faced him.

"You go in," she said, voice an elegant waterfall of vowels and consonants. He thought for the first time that she was really quite beautiful.

"What do I do then?"

"Talk. You are good at that."

"So I've been told."

"I will wait here. Go nowhere else."

Now Blake hesitates, studying the massive arched door. The Volkov crest, a two-headed wolf with emerald eyes that matches the pendant around his neck, taunts him from the wood. Music spills out from inside as though it leaks from another reality. One where his mom never left Servos with him, never stole him away in the night to save their lives.

His nerves tighten. He'd spent an entire life without a father because the monster on the other side of these doors wanted him dead to push his political plans. A surge of mixed feelings turns his mouth sour. Hatred, determination, fear, and the tiniest, most despicable touch of regret. Regret that he'd never known the man playing the most soulful violin music he's ever heard.

He knows the piece now as he hears familiar plucking notes. Ernst's violin solo for Schubert's "Der Erlkönig". He's never heard it so intense and haunting before. Precision and emotion, all wrapped into one. He closes his eyes to listen.

The violin screams several high notes, and his heart shoots to his throat. No more waiting. No more fear for this shadow over his life. He yanks the door open.

Mikhail Volkov stands facing a window on the opposite side of the room, coaxing sweet notes from the violin in his hand. He moves with a practiced grace, bow drawing short and long over the strings, fingers flying. He sways with the music, body almost jerking as the Erlking's melody takes over. His pale brown hair is pulled into a neat tail at the base of his neck, and he wears a pressed blue suit.

Blake stares at his silhouette as the violin shrieks. This is the man who tore his mom's life apart. Who threw their countries into war. Who dragged him, over two decades later, across the sea to finally set things straight.

He's shorter than Blake expected.

He can't see Mikhail's face at this angle, only the violin and the side of one cheek, the bow waving across both like a mad hacksaw.

The music slows. The door falls shut behind Blake. Mikhail runs a finger over the strings, plucking them, before articulating the final chords. The bow stills, and he relaxes his stance.

Damn him, but he's a magnificent violinist.

Mikhail takes a moment to lower the violin without turning. It's as though he's in no rush to meet his estranged firstborn. He reverently places the violin and bow on a polished wooden table and adjusts his suit cuffs.

Anyone else would be dwarfed in this room, Blake is sure of it. But there is something about Mikhail that takes up more space than his slim build. A presence that fills the cavernous music room.

At last, Mikhail turns. Blake tenses, the grip on his bag stiff to the point of pain. Even from across the room, he can make out the man's features. He'd know those eyes anywhere. Large and bright green, his own eyes gaze at him from this despot's face.

He doesn't know what he expected—fear to be facing this man, the urge to cower and expose his neck—but it doesn't come now. Instead, a hot rage rushes him, makes him lightheaded.

"You!" He starts, almost breathless with fury, with twenty-four years of pent-up daddy issues. He wants to scream, to swear, to claw this fucker's eyes out. The rage is so palpable it chokes him.

Mikhail steps forward and holds out both hands. "Welcome home, son." Barely a hint of an accent and even less animosity.

"How. Fucking. Dare you," Blake starts, hands curled, nails sharpening. His senses flare, werewolf instincts heightened for a fight, then a scent crosses his nostrils, something somehow nostalgic, somehow soothing, and the anger, as acute as it is, burns itself out in its intensity. Blake's shoulders slump. "Why?" It's all he can get out, the only way he can demand answers. He wants to spew more: Why did you try to kill us? Why do you want me back now?

Why didn't you love me?

But the single word would have to be enough.

Mikhail considers him a long time before choosing his words. "I've missed you, *syn*. Thank you for coming. You can't imagine..." His brow furrows, and he tries a different sentence. "I've thought you dead for twenty-three years."

Words fail them both. They're left in a silent bubble, encapsulated by two decades of distance, bound by blood and a lifetime of unspoken words.

"You tried to kill me." Blake almost chokes on the accusation. He registers the surprise on Mikhail's face, but barrels on anyway. "I was a fucking baby, and you tried to kill me."

A shadow passes over Mikhail's face, dangerous and intense. "Never," he says plainly. "Your mother stole you from me. Filled your head with lies. At first, we thought Atlas was to blame. A kidnapping, or worse. I didn't know you lived until months ago." His lips tighten, almost imperceptibly. "To lose my firstborn son. You can't imagine the pain."

The anger flares again, leaving him lightheaded. "How about the pain of growing up alone? Of living in hiding my whole life? Scared of you. Of what you'd do if you found us." He jabs a finger at Mikhail. "Because of you, I never had a dad. I had a bogeyman."

They stare across the room at each other, accusations made, never to be unmade. At last Mikhail takes another step forward, closes the distance between them. Blake refuses to back down, even as he steps near enough to touch.

His scent is floral, of all things. Sweet, like lilies. Underneath it lies something sharper, though, an alcohol tinge. His face isn't hard lines or a strong jaw, like the alpha stereotype, but softness to the point of beauty. They're nearly the same height, Blake a mere inch or two shorter. He sticks his chin up defiantly and glares at Mikhail, daring him to make the next move.

Mikhail studies him, light and shadow flickering in his eyes. Then he reaches out and brushes his fingers over Blake's hair. Before Blake can smack his hand away, he speaks.

"You look so much like her. I don't understand the circumstances that took you both away from me, but know I never intended to hurt you. Whatever Nadine told you, this is the truth. I loved you, *syn*. If you know anything, know that."

He's almost dizzy from the impact of the words. He can't believe them. His whole life, he's known one truth: Mikhail Volkov is an evil bastard who would rather kill them than see them happy. An angry lump forms in his throat, only making him angrier. How dare this son of a bitch affect him this much. That scent wafts again, easing his rage, confusing him on an instinctual level. Still, the resentment is hard to let go.

The years of aching loneliness. Watching his mom waste away to nothing. Working to exhaustion and then working more. All because of this bastard. And he has the nerve, after all of that, to greet Blake with welcoming arms.

"Screw you." He wants to scream it, but it comes out barely a whisper. "You don't get to walk back into my life and be dad of the year."

Mikhail closes his eyes, takes a slow breath, then opens them and says, "Then why come here? If not to reclaim your birthright, then why?"

"My mom. She's sick. Fix her."

He nods slowly. "Nadine still lives."

"That's not her name anymore!"

They stare at each other again, and Mikhail takes another breath as though he's a saint of patience. "She will always be Nadine to me. I loved her, you know. Even though she hated me. I loved you both."

"I don't care!" Blake snaps the lie like it means nothing to him. His chest aches horribly.

"You are upset. It's understandable. Perhaps we should discuss this later."

Now it's Blake's turn to close his eyes and take a breath. *Cool it. You'll never get what you want this way.* He opens his eyes and says in a steadier voice, "No. I flew across the world to have this conversation. I left my home, the people I love, the life I know, to have this conversation. I need to know what's wrong with her. I need you to fix it."

Mikhail steps away from him, turns to a sitting area to the left of them. "Come. Sit. We'll talk. It's overdue."

Blake takes a breath and follows him. They sit across from each other on facing couches. Mikhail spreads both hands and says, "Tell me about yourself."

Blake is flabbergasted. Of every scenario he'd imagined going into this, curious and regretful dad did not make the list.

He struggles to find the words, to not inject them with venom. "I'm a nobody. I have no pack. I have one friend. I live in obscurity because if I made any connections, if I made a scene, you might find me."

"My son," Mikhail murmurs, a twist of sadness on his face. "It's true I can't imagine your struggles. Can you accept that I'm sorry? Sorry that the world did this to you."

He wants to say the world didn't do this, *you* did, but the accusation dies in his throat. He sighs and hangs his head. "I just want Mom to be okay. Please. If there's anything you can do. Please."

Mikhail taps a finger on the couch arm. "There might be something. I will need to research. Speak to the court mage. In the meantime, would you stay here? I would like—if you would have it—to get to know you. For you to get to know me. Do you understand?"

Blake looks up at him. Considers the remorse and frustrating hope on his face. Feels that spark of anger again, then that familiar scent hits him, and he sighs.

"Okay. I'll try."

Mikhail smiles. It's tight and doesn't look often used, but it's real.

"There's so much to discuss," he says. "Tell me, have you learned anything about music?"

***

The full moon shone over the empty soccer field where Jay stood beside his sister. He stared up at it, so large and bright it blocked out most of the stars. It almost looked red in the night sky. He felt the old pull on his blood, the power of it ushering him toward his ancestors, calling on his instincts. Somewhere inside himself, a wolf howled.

Off to the side, Elliot and Lance sat on the bleachers. They'd come in a show of solidarity. Having his pack close soothed him, but he longed for Kim's presence as well. They'd not spoken in two days, though he'd sent her a few messages. Unlike her. Cat stretched and unbuttoned the top of her blouse.

"You might want to take that shirt off. Shifting tends to wreck everything you're wearing. Did you bring a change?"

"Yeah." The clothes sat folded atop a towel on the bench.

"Good. Now focus in. You feel the moon?" She pointed.

"Yeah." He didn't have much more to say. Truth was, he was nervous. The few times he'd tried shifting as a kid had always ended in painful failure. He'd broken his arm once trying to do it, and since he hadn't figured out the full shift, it didn't heal back automatically. He'd had to go to the emergency room and get pins in it. Hadn't tried since.

"It's like the tides, isn't it? The way the power pulls on you. Shifting is the next step in that, the natural progression of the moon's power. Get good enough and you can even shift in daylight. You need to feel that gravity in your soul. Right here." She tapped her chest, above her heart. "Let it pull you. Go along with it. It's always there, you just have to let go."

Jay tried to focus internally, then sighed. "That's too abstract."

"Hm." She considered him. "You can shift your eyes and teeth, can't you? I've seen them drop when you get pissed off."

"So what?"

"So it's that feeling, but all over. You try too hard to be in control all the time. Always fighting it. The wolf is in you, let go and let him out."

Jay screwed up his face in concentration. The moon pulled, the wolf howled, but still nothing happened. Maybe his skin itched a little.

"You need more motivation." Cat tapped her chin with her forefinger.

"What do you think about when you shift?"

"Power. Blood. Dominance. I don't think that'll work for you. Hmmm. Think about Blake instead. Think about his smell. The way he feels when you hold him. The way he tastes. Think about him in trouble. What it would take to protect him."

Jay closed his eyes. Focused on Blake's scent and the sound of his voice. His smile. The fear in his eyes when the wolf burst through the door.

He felt his teeth drop into fangs. Felt his nails lengthen. Felt a prickling all across his skin and through his bones. Tried to pull on it, to coax it through.

Then it receded and he felt nothing again.

"Shit." He raked both hands through his hair.

"You're trying too hard again. You just let it out. Let it go. Watch."

Cat unbuttoned the rest of her blouse and discarded it. Immediately, fur rippled across her body. Her face lengthened; her hips realigned. She dropped to all fours, her pants and underwear split off as the change completed. A fluffy tail burst out behind her. She shook and then fixed him with a steady stare. Her eye color hadn't changed, but everything else was wolf. Ruddy red-brown fur and long, elegant legs. It had happened in under a minute.

"Damn, you make that look easy."

She barked at him and raised a paw. His turn.

He inhaled a long breath and closed his eyes. Blake. Mate. Protect. The wolf in him pushed, reaching for freedom. A surge of power shocked him like static, and he shuddered and backed off. Cat barked. Again. He pressed for the energy, tried not to shy away. Felt patches of fur on the backs of his hands.

Come on.

He pushed. A sharp pain in his gut doubled him over. He gasped and dropped to a knee. A quiver passed through him, leaving him alternately hot and cold. He moaned. His bones didn't crack or move, but the power twisted up inside him, threatened to tear him open. A cold nose nudged his cheek. Cat. He met her eyes, and she shook her head. He let go of the power, let it wash back and settle in its usual hiding spot. The pain subsided.

"Do you need to stop?"

Elliot had come up behind him, reached as though to touch his shoulder, then withdrew.

Jay grunted, couldn't quite get words out. His teeth ached at the roots.

Lance jogged over. "Call it, Jay. You're hurting yourself."

"I can get there," Jay panted. The stubborn streak hurt almost as much as failed shifting.

Lance shook his head. "Shifting isn't a big deal, man. Most of us can't do it. It's not worth hurting yourself."

Wolf Cat tapped her paw on the turf. The three looked at her. She raised her head and howled, haunting and long. Almost mournful, the sound echoed through the soccer pitch.

Jay felt the surge one last time. Felt the call from the moon and the returning howl of the wolf inside himself. Felt it resonate, grow stronger, erupt fur across his arms and back, felt his jawbone click, then he fell against the ground and writhed as his bones shifted. Pain coursed through him, too much, too much. He scrabbled at the dirt and ground his teeth together.

No! His mind screamed.

Everything receded. Darkness washed over him, and the pain jolted to a stop with unconsciousness.

***

Jay awoke with dirt in his mouth. He coughed and spat, and a tuft of grass fluttered down. He realized he was lying on his side, covered in sweat. Something moved next to him.

"He's coming to. Jay? Would you like some water?" Elliot's voice.

Jay groaned. Tried to speak, but his tongue felt swollen. An arm propped him up, and a water bottle pressed to his lips. He sipped.

"Shit, I thought he had it for a second there." Lance this time. "Do you think he needs a doctor?"

Now Cat's voice joined them. "If he's still in pain, then yes. It's always possible something inside didn't shift back all the way."

Oh great.

Jay pawed at his stomach. Pressed around like his organs might have squished loose. It didn't hurt, thank God. His head still felt like a lead balloon, though. He dropped it against the turf.

Cat crouched over him. The robe she now wore swished against his arm. "Maybe we give it a rest. Try again next month."

Unable to argue, Jay nodded. A beetle crawled across the ground in front of his nose. Lance and Elliot scooped him up into a sitting position, and he accepted more water. Everything itched and ached, like his skin wanted to peel off. He shook his arms out.

"Maybe I'm adopted," he muttered. "Maybe I'm not actually fullblood."

Cat rolled her eyes. "Excuses. You'll figure it out; you just need more practice."

"Back to my place?" Elliot asked, interrupting what could have been the start of an argument.

"Yeah," Jay grunted. "My sorry ass could use a nap."

"Still no word from Kimiko?" Lance held out a hand to help pull Jay to his feet.

Jay took it and winced as his joints popped. "Nothing."

"Something's up. That's not like her."

Jay dusted dirt off his clothes. "We can try calling when we get back. But if she wants privacy, you know how she is." He faced Cat. "Thanks for the lesson. Heading back to your pack?"

"As much as I'd love to entertain you, yes, I have other things to do."

"Let me know if you hear anything."

"Of course."

They didn't hug, but Cat patted Jay's shoulder and dropped Lance a wink before walking away from them.

Lance let out a whistle. "I think she's into me."

"Not a chance in hell." Jay shook his head. "She's messing with you. Has been for years."

"You don't know that."

"She's my sister. I know her well enough to know when she's playing a game."

Lance shook his poor, delusional head. "Man, you don't know. I have charm. Catalina's flirting."

"Keep telling yourself that."

***

At Elliot's apartment, Jay stripped and headed to the shower. He scrubbed quickly, with water hot enough to singe his skin bright red. It eased some of the aches. Toweling off, he wandered into the living room. Lance had the TV on, and he stood, remote in hand, in front of it. Elliot appeared to have been fixing tea but froze with the kettle in his hands.

"What's going on?" Jay rubbed at his hair with the damp towel.

"Um." Lance, for once, lost for words. He stepped aside.

A press conference displayed on the television, morning sun shining on a podium bearing the two-headed wolf of the Volkovs. A banner ran along the bottom of the screen announcing footage from Moskva, broadcast a few minutes ago. Mikhail Volkov stood behind the podium, face set and chin up, as he spoke in eastern Servan. A group of people clustered around him, and a translation subtitled the screen.

"Twenty-four years ago, I lost my son to Atlas in what became the spark that lit the flames of war. I spent these last years thinking him dead at the hands of killers from another country. Atlas has long proclaimed me responsible for his death, as though a father could do something so abhorrent. Despite our bickering, neither side had an answer to the question: what happened to my wife and son? Now, all these years later, I can finally say I have the answer."

Jay crossed the room and stared hard at the people forming a half circle around Mikhail. A familiar head of blond hair shone among the dark colors.

Mikhail put an arm out toward the blond. "My son, Blake, has at last returned home."

Applause broke out from the reporters. He waved it down with a subtle twitch of his left hand.

"Allow him to tell you his story."

Jay watched with equal parts shock and horror as Blake replaced Mikhail at the podium. He wore a tailored suit in a color to match his father's. Even from across the world, Jay could tell Blake was nervous. He kept touching the hair on the right side of his face as though to smooth it, and he avoided looking at the cameras. Still, he was undoubtedly Blake, alive and unharmed—and somehow in the middle of a press conference with Mikhail Volkov.

"Hi." Blake took a breath and released it with a whoosh. "My name is Blake. I've been living in Atlas my whole life. In hiding with my mom. She always told me if someone finds out who I am, I'd be dead." He tugged at a tuft of hair then dropped his hand. "But Dad never wanted me dead in the first place."

Jay's throat closed. There was no way this was happening.

Blake went on. "I'm home now. And I'd really like my mom to come back, too."

Jay felt his jaw slacken with the wrongness of it all.

Blake stepped away from the podium, and Mikhail took his place. "According to my son, his mother is currently under the hands of the Reed pack in Atlas. I am formally requesting a meeting between our clans to discuss her well-being and the future of our countries. Don't delay. Let us take steps in the right direction."

The broadcast switched to the newscasters, who began discussing the announcement. Lance muted it.

"You never said he was a prince." Lance halfheartedly chuckled.

"He never—I didn't know. Shit, what is he thinking?" Jay's mind swam with the implications. "He never trusted me," he muttered. "And I'm idiot for not figuring it out."

"I'm the fool," Elliot said. "I saw his pendant. It had the Volkov crest. I thought it meant he was a refugee, not royalty." He shook his head. "His eyes alone should have given it away."

Jay's thoughts flickered briefly to the scratches down his back. So Blake really was a fullblood. That explained the force of his pheromones, why no other omega seemed half as attractive. A prince... no wonder his mom had changed her tone so quickly. She must have figured it out. Figured it out and kept it to herself anyway.

"Dammit," he hissed.

"But this is good, isn't it?" Lance piped up. "It means there's no reason for war in the first place. And what Mikhail said, 'the right direction'. Wouldn't that mean peace?"

Elliot shook his head. "He never said that directly. And the fact that they made this a public announcement rather than making private contact puts pressure on Atlas. People will see this and think if we don't reach an accord that Atlas is to blame."

Jay ground his teeth. "They're using Blake. Bastards."

"You should talk to your parents. Maybe you can join them in the discussion with the Volkovs."

"They're acting like we have his mom as a hostage!" Jay began pacing. "We're helping her, dammit!"

"Get it out of your system now, because you can't be pissed off if you go with them." Elliot returned to brewing tea. "At least you know Blake is safe."

Jay grimaced. 'I'm home now,' Blake had said. Home. As though he was never coming back. Jay growled low in his throat. His skin tingled again, like it had earlier in the soccer field. He wouldn't believe it until Blake said it to his face. Home.

Wasn't he home enough for Blake?

Chapter Sixteen

Saint-Saëns's "Danse Macabre"

Blake stares out the window in the music room where he first met Mikhail. It affords a view of the courtyard, hedges trimmed and sculpted in a series of concentric circles. His body aches with exhaustion, like someone has set a weight on his shoulders and progressively added more and more until he can barely take it. He's slept a little since arriving—no complaints about the softness of the beds—but his mind reels. He has an escort everywhere he goes, not just to guide him through the cavernous rooms and hallways, but certainly to also make sure he doesn't try anything disastrous. Mikhail assured him it's in everyone's best interest that a bodyguard stay close.

Mikhail. His father. The man who's overshadowed his entire life from a continent away. The man his mom reviles. He grits his teeth at the conflict of emotion the thoughts conjure.

Somehow, he's nothing at all what Blake expected. A little distant, maybe, but curious about Blake's life to the point of being intrusive. Blake peppers him with stories about growing up in Atlas, about his mom and music and the hours he spent working in kitchens. They share meals together in a small room with a fireplace, and Mikhail explains his life in return. His new wife, Alina—the stoic woman from the plane—and their son, Kirill, who's off studying something or other in West Servos. He speaks most passionately when the subject of music comes up, and last night the two even laughed as Blake rang out the opening notes of Paganini's "Caprice 24" on some wine glasses like a drunken party trick.

Things have changed so much.

His whole path went in one direction, and now he's off messing around in Servos while the most important people in his life wait for him across the sea. He wants to tell himself this is all part of the plan—get on Mikhail's good side, get the cure for his mom, get home. But some part of him can't help, no matter how hard he scolds himself, but enjoy the attention. It's exhausting to think after all these years of fear and doubt, the great king of Servos never wanted them dead at all. He can't wrap his head around it. It's worse to think there's a part of himself that still wants his love and approval.

He watches some birds flutter across the grounds, then turns away from the window. Despite all this, he misses Atlas. Misses Jay. A quiet fear has been mounting in the back of his head over these days that Mikhail might be pretending, only stringing him along to use him for political gains. That he never intends to give up the cure for whatever is ailing his mom, and that Blake will be trapped here for the rest of his life, a prisoner in a gilded cage.

After all, Mikhail had insisted he make an appearance on television, promised to use it as a way to reach his mom, but it's been two days since then, and he's not heard a peep on the matter. Could be he's just a pawn, a piece for Mikhail to play.

His stomach roils at the thought. He needs to clear his head.

He glances around. Musical instruments decorate the room. Here a harp, there a series of flute cases. A grand piano dominates one corner. Blake eyes it. Not a Bösendorfer, but still elegant and polished to a shine. The kind of thing he'd always dreamed of touching. He crosses the room to it, runs a hand over the keylid. He shoots a look over his shoulder to the guard at the opposite corner. He doesn't seem to care what Blake does, as long as he doesn't break anything.

So he scoots the bench out and takes a seat. He needs a break, needs to be somewhere else for a while. He opens the cover. The white and black keys gleam at him, whispering promises of sweet melodies. He tests them for pitch, although he doesn't expect them to be any less than in top condition. Mikhail loves music as much as his mom does. Blake learned from her as a pup because when he played, she smiled like she'd never been prouder of someone in her life. All he's ever wanted is to make her happy, and now here he is, trapped across the sea, back to where she had tried to free him, while she wasted away every day a little closer to the edge.

He swallows. If he doesn't make it back in time he might never—

He cuts himself off, replacing the noise in his mind with the sound of music.

His fingers decide on a piece, starting first slow and mournful, haunting low notes in a set of three. Rachmaninoff's "Prelude in C Sharp Minor". The chords resonate through his fingertips as he plays his way back and forth across the keys. It picks up after the first minute into a series of rolling notes up and down the piano growing louder as they go, like a mounting rage. Then back to the three chords, fortissimo. As things slow again, softening into regret, he feels the strain of the last few days crash over him. He blinks back a burn in his eyes.

The final chords ring out, and he drops his hands. Soft footsteps tap the stone floor behind him. Then, a voice.

"You inherited your mother's skill."

Blake rubs his right eye before facing Mikhail. "She's better than me. She could play 'Winter Wind' like it was 'Twinkle Twinkle Little Star'."

"You light up like her when you play. She always shone the brightest when she was at the keys." A moment of nostalgic silence. "Would you play a duet with me?"

Blake balks. "I've never played accompaniment before."

A wry curve of smile twists Mikhail's lips. "Yes, you're more of a soloist, aren't you? Fitting for my son, I suppose. Do you know Saint-Saëns?"

Blake tries guessing which piece he's referring to. "'Introduction and Rondo Capriccioso'?"

"I was thinking more 'Danse Macabre'."

Now Blake is interested. He had a recording of the orchestra piece as a child. Listened to it over and over again, even when his mom tried encouraging other composers. Eventually he also took to Liszt and Chopin, but the old melody echoes in his mind like the repeated lines of a poem.

"All right. Do you have sheet music? I haven't played the accompaniment before."

Mikhail crosses the room to a filing cabinet and rifles through it before returning with a folder. Blake flips through the pages in silent study, hearing the notes as they dot the staff. His father regards him in equal silence.

After reading through the pages, fingers tapping on his thighs, Blake says, "Yeah, I can play this."

"Excellent. Allow me to get my violin."

While he fetches the instrument and checks the tuning, Blake arranges the score on the music desk. He was nervous—ages ago it seems now—when he played for Jay and his family. He no longer feels that way. Mikhail's efficient competency and unquestioning confidence buoys him. Blake holds no question that the man would not bother to play music with someone he considered inferior.

In a moment, he stands beside the piano, violin on his shoulder. "When you're ready."

Blake plays a chord and nods as Mikhail mimics his sound. They find a matching tone together, then recede from the notes so the piece can start.

Mikhail plays softly at first, a few D pizzicato notes, and Blake comes in with a gentle spring of chords. At twelve plucks of the violin, midnight strikes, and out comes the devil to start the dance of the dead.

Mikhail's violin screams a dissonant tone, bow streaking across the strings with an unearthly rhythm. Blake picks up the accompaniment, matching his speed. As the violin sings out eighth notes, Blake echoes, swapping the melody between them. The sound consumes him, a deathly waltz full of shocking highs and lows. Dread builds in the music, a combination of the violin's erratic notes and the piano's bass chords.

Blake flies through a descending arpeggio, and Mikhail draws the bow forte across the strings, their eyes meeting in the moment. They don't combat each other with their playing, but rather in a series of crescendoing notes, dance around each other, each instrument supporting the other until they wrap back around to the melody, higher pitched and more frantic than ever.

Now the violin trills a series of triplets as they reach the finale. Dawn on the horizon. They speed up together, both swaying with the notes. Intense chords rock the music room, sharply back and forth from violin to piano. Blake rumbles low notes, the beginning of the end. Mikhail's violin sings out soft vibrato as Blake rests. At last, they come back together, unleashing the final notes. Sun has risen, and the dead lay back to rest. They drop their positions.

"Excellent." Mikhail graces Blake with a rare full smile. "A thrilling duet."

"When can I contact my mom?" The words burst from his mouth so suddenly that even Blake is shocked. He catches a breath and adds, "I want to know she's okay."

Mikhail sighs and lays his instrument down on a table. "I'm afraid I'm still waiting on word from Atlas."

"Why wouldn't they contact you right away?"

He has to believe Jay still wants him back, but a tiny voice of doubt chirps in his mind.

"It's a delicate matter. There are many steps between every message we send and receive." Mikhail takes the sheet music from the piano and returns it to its home.

"I could talk to them. Let me reach out to Jay; he'll listen."

No response at first but the gentle click of the filing cabinet. Then Mikhail straightens and says, "It's not so easy. Our clans have been feuding for longer than I've been alive. Since before the Pack Years. If one conversation could fix generations of blood, don't you think we'd have done that by now?"

"Maybe it's easier than you think. Maybe both sides are sick of fighting."

"You may think me a despot in Atlas, but I am not the sole leader of this country. They call me king, but I have a parliament to report to. Some of those members want nothing but blood."

"So what happens to my mom?" Blake's hands tighten to fists. "What if she gets worse while I'm gone? What's even wrong with her?"

Mikhail strides to the window and stares out, considering his question. At last, he says, "You are aware of the use of magic in high courts? Casters who utilize shifting magic for spells?"

"I've heard a little about it..."

"Atlas is a young country compared to the rest of the world. Your magic is technology. Perhaps some mages exist there, but it's not like in the old places. Our lead packs each have a mage employed, for use politically and personally."

"What's this got to do with Mom?"

Mikhail levels a gaze on Blake. "Your mother is cursed."

Blake takes a steadying breath and says, "What kind of curse?"

"A bonding curse, used by my family for generations to ensure loyalty between mates. Being separated over time, it deteriorates the mind, wastes the body. A nasty thing."

Blake's mouth is a desert. Years she's suffered, and this is why. Stupid political magic. She must have known when she left Servos that she would rot away. She knew, but went anyway...

He clears his throat. "Is there a cure?"

Mikhail turns from him, replies softly, "I'm not aware of any way to break it. I'm very sorry."

Cold washes over Blake. He sucks in a breath and holds it. Nothing to do. No way to break it. She would wither and die in misery.

"Come," Mikhail says, motioning for him. "Would you like lunch? The chefs will make anything you want."

"Sure."

Not hungry. The exhaustion seeps back into him, but he forces his legs to stand and cross the room. He needs to go home. To see Mom. This trip is a failure, and he can't waste any more time here.

If only he knew what it would take to make Mikhail let him go.

***

Jay stared at the wall across from his bed. He wasn't laying in it, moping, but he was sitting up, knees to his chest and glowering. Not the same thing. Two days since Blake's appearance on the news, and the Lantish packs hadn't made a move. His own family had remained silent on the matter. After an irritating call with his mom that ended in him shouting at her, he'd retreated to his room to sulk.

No, not sulk. He wasn't a child. He just needed to clear his head. Figure out what to do from here. He'd travel across the world himself to pick up Blake if he had to. Damn the consequences.

His phone rang. Not this again. He could ignore it, drop it in the toilet and never talk to anyone again. But he picked it up instead to see Kim's name and photo displayed. He quickly answered.

"Hey, Kim! It's good to hear from you."

"Jay." She spoke curtly, but that tended to be her way. "Could you meet me at my estate? There's some things I want to discuss."

"Already on my way. We've been worried about you." Jay hopped off the bed and grabbed his keys. Out the door in less than a minute.

"I'm fine. We can catch up over lunch."

Jay climbed into his car and backed out. "What are you talking about? It's breakfast."

"Maybe for you."

Jay chuckled. "Fair point." Kim woke up blazingly early most days. He never could figure out when she got any sleep at all.

He said goodbye and hung up, racing to get across town to the southwest end. Kim lived on a decent chunk of land, not far from her main business, an Oceanese health resort that catered to the social and political elite. She had confided once that it was initially an intelligence gathering endeavor, but she'd come to enjoy the peaceful atmosphere. It was a slice of home to her, and now Jay wondered if she'd give it up to return to her family. That sparked his nerves. The thought of his pack without her was downright painful.

He arrived, and a mech led him to the courtyard at the center of the building, a square garden with a pond and cherry tree she'd imported. She sat on a cushion watching the clouds, lit cigarette in hand.

"Good to see you," he greeted. It was true. Her loose hair cascading down her back, the smell of her, even over the cigarette; she was childhood and comfort and fond memories.

"Thank you for coming." She took a drag and exhaled a plume of smoke. Jay sat beside her. "I saw your boytoy on the news. I guess he wasn't being sarcastic about being royalty."

"Hard to tell with him."

She eyed him from the corner of her eye. "How did you manage to find him?"

"Some guy was roughing him up at his job, and I stepped in. Turned out that same guy was Servan. Started stalking Blake. Turned into a wolf. It was a whole thing."

"And now he's over there, in their hands." She flicked ash off the end of her cigarette. "What are you doing about it?"

Jay huffed indignantly. "Trying to find someone who gives a shit, I guess. My parents keep insisting it isn't up to them. It seems like whenever there's a real issue, no one's in charge."

"Pack troubles. Sometimes I think the world before the wolves had a better sense of leadership. A system, even flawed, still allowed policies that helped people. There's less government now, but those of us at the lead don't always want to be there."

"Are we talking about your family now?"

Kim puffed on the cigarette. "I have a proposition for you. You want Servos and Atlas to talk? They won't do it without neutral ground. Establish a meeting in Oceana; I'll oversee negotiations. Who knows, maybe you'll get your boy back."

"You don't always have to be so derogatory toward my partners. Blake isn't just some bed warmer."

"The way you sleep around, could've fooled me."

Jay winced. "Okay, maybe I deserve that. But since Blake I haven't been with anyone else. Haven't wanted anyone else."

Kim regarded him over the smoke of her cigarette. "Are you planning to bring him into the pack?"

He scratched the back of his head. "I'd like to talk about it, at least. See what he thinks. Elliot and Lance already like him."

"Which makes me the odd woman out."

Jay gave her a small smile. "Yeah, but you never like anyone at first. It's part of your charm."

She huffed a little, but he spotted the upturn at the corners of her mouth. "If I'm being honest, he didn't smell bad. Naive maybe, but not like a bad person."

"Sounds like him."

Kim stubbed out the remainder of the cigarette and dared to ask, "Will you mate him?"

Jay avoided her eyes as he sidestepped the question. "Have to get him back before I can think about that."

"All right, don't answer me."

"Fine. Question to you first. What are you going to do about your family? Are you leaving us?" *Leaving me?*

Kim stood and shook out her long hair. It fluttered, shining in the morning light. She offered him a hand. "I've thought about practically nothing else since *Obaasama* passed. And yet I still have no answer."

"Sayori could—"

"Trust me, I've considered it. My sister would love nothing more than to take over for me. But is it the right choice? Do I do this for myself or for my people?"

Jay took her by the shoulders and pressed their foreheads together. He had to lean down to do it. "You're so serious all the time, Kim. Not everything needs to be life and death."

"When those are the things on the line, then, yes I must be. Someone killed my grandmother, she swore it on her deathbed, and I still don't know who. I have suspicions, but..."

"But no one's talking."

"Nothing from your family?" She pulled back from him, though not far enough to break from his hands.

"Cat had no idea. Said she'd poke around. She seemed pretty pissed about it."

"That's fine. It's my hope that if Atlas and Servos meet in my territory, I might glean some more information from either side. I'll put out a formal offer to the packs. Maybe we can both get what we want."

Jay's stomach took the opportunity to growl. Kim smiled. "Perhaps we break for a meal. Are Elliot and Lance free? It would be good to see them."

He dialed them up. Good to have the whole pack back together, but he couldn't help but feel like a certain omega was missing from their fold. Blake deserved a spot among them, and he would see to it that the next breakfast they shared would include him.

Chapter Seventeen

Mozart's "Turkish March"

"Wake up."

The harsh voice rouses Blake from a fitful dream. Something about his mom in bed with tubes running throughout her body. He shakes it off. Alina stands over him, a severe frown on her face.

"We must go today. I've instructed the maids to leave out proper clothing for you. Get dressed and follow your guard to the car. We'll be waiting."

She doesn't wait for him to reply; probably knows he'll question her. She leaves him, groggy and confused, with the clicking of her heels echoing behind her.

So much for hospitality.

He fumbles with the heavy sheets and steps barefoot onto the cool stone floor. Sure enough, a pale suit waits for him on a hanger. He wrinkles his nose. If he ever wears another suit, it will be too soon. Stuffy and starched and wholly uncomfortable they all were. He much prefers his loose jeans and short sleeves. He scratches his head. Hasn't worn a hat since leaving Atlas. He misses his slouchy beanies almost as much as he misses Jay.

Maybe that's an exaggeration, but as the days tick on from his appearance on the news, he grows more frustrated with Jay. Not a peep from him or anyone else. A concern grows in his gut that he isn't worth much after all. Not to Atlas and not to Jay.

The little voice in his head he assumes must be his conscience reminds him he's done nothing but lie to Jay since they met, and now he's run off without warning across the world. Of course Jay would hate him now. It's all he deserves.

He rubs his face with both hands. Need a shower. Alina can wait that long at least. She'll glower at him, but he'll be quick. Five minutes, tops.

Ten minutes later, he towels off and dresses. Ties: those are another thing he can live without. Reminds him too much of his uniform at the café, with its stupid chiming bell. Maybe from now on he'll exclusively wear V-neck shirts just to let his collar breathe. Maybe when he gets home, he can go shopping with Terri and let her dress him up like she always wanted. Casual clothes only.

He hopes Terri is okay. Wonders what she must have thought seeing him on TV. Shakes his head. He'll have some explaining to do when he gets back.

The guard waits outside his door and silently leads him to the courtyard he first arrived in. A limo idles there, black tinted windows up. The driver opens a door for him, and he climbs inside to find Mikhail and Alina sitting across from him.

Alina, face sour, shoots him a dirty look. Par for the course. After all, he's nothing but a reminder to her that she was never Mikhail's first choice. Her own son isn't even technically next in line. He tries to give her a disarming smile.

Mikhail ignores the discomfort and says, "Apologies if you were unable to eat breakfast. The news came last night, and we need to be off early today."

Blake settles in, and the car starts. "Off to where?"

"Oceana." Blake makes a garbled sound, but Mikhail presses on. "We're meeting the Atlas leaders on neutral territory. The Oshiro clan is hosting."

Kimiko. The thought of her judgmental eyes and haughty voice chafes him.

"It's no game to play at world politics," Alina cuts in. "You're only there to make an appearance. Nothing more."

Mikhail's lips thin as she speaks. He adds, "It's appropriate for you to be there, but I ask that you stay quiet during negotiations. These are delicate matters."

"No problem." Hopefully Jay will be there, too. Hopefully this is his ticket out. "How long is the trip?"

"Ten hours, give or take. Once we arrive, we'll have to pass the Oshiro private security."

"And your security?"

"Tailing us, of course. These trips are always cumbersome."

Somehow in a week, Blake will have visited two entirely different countries on private flights.

Oh, the places life takes you...

If only it would take him somewhere without itchy clothes.

***

They touch down in Oceanese territory many hours later. Blake ate on the flight, but his stomach churns queasily and his skin, despite his earlier shower, feels like it needs that degreaser fry cooks use to clean flat tops. How is it long distance travel makes you so gross?

They pass security checkpoint after security checkpoint in the small private airport, until finally the three of them and their entourage of bodyguards emerge in the cold night air.

All Blake can see are the lights of the distant city. They appear like a colorful sun on the horizon. Above him, some stars twinkle, and the moon, now waning, waits for sunrise. A series of Oceanese guards and diplomats greet them, bowing and ushering them toward another limo. More travel, it seems. Blake stifles a yawn. He needs sleep before this meeting business. He needs to be clear-headed so he can find his escape.

It isn't that Mikhail is a bad man—he doesn't think he thinks so at this point, any-way—it's that he doesn't belong in Servos. And, whispers a morose voice in his head, his mom can't have that much longer left. He needs to be with her.

He rubs one eye and stares out the limo's window. Full dark, no streetlights. The city gleams in the distance. But it becomes increasingly clearer that they are heading to the outskirts and not the heart of it. Probably to the Oshiro estate. Trees pass too quickly to identify. Then some grand houses built with sloping roofs and flanked with statues. And finally, they slow outside a massive wrought iron gate with a dragon carved into the front.

Blake has been half-dozing throughout this, barely catching the details, but now he blinks away sleep. The gates rattle open, and the car slides smoothly inside. It's too dark to see much at this point—it has to be around midnight here, surely—but it's impossible to miss the massive building that looms over them.

Perhaps not quite as sprawling as the Volkov home, but it has the building beat in style. Multiple stories of curved roofs and shingling cover pillars and circular windows and massive, arched doors. Two large wolves carved from some precious stone flank the entrance. They're stylized with beautiful, arcing shawls in the air around their heads. Blake's seen this kind of art before in movies, but the sight in person, even in the dark, takes his breath away.

The shifter culture in Oceana is a little different than the rest of the world, from what he understands. Werewolves started in the mafia families and took over from there. And there are more than wolves here. Foxes, predominantly. And he's heard some kind of raccoon shifters live among people as well. The families are older, more tied to tradition than Atlas. He wonders now, looking at the intricate carvings on the pillars and doors, what the etiquette is when meeting political dignitaries. No wonder Mikhail wants him to keep his mouth shut. He can barely go a breath without sassing someone. He might get challenged to a wolf honor duel or some ancient thing like that if he talks too much here.

A young woman greets them inside the entrance.

"Good evening. I hope your travels went smoothly."

"No problems," Mikhail replies. "It's wonderful to be in your beautiful country again."

They both bow. Alina elbows Blake, and he hastily bows along. So keeping quiet won't be enough. After everyone lifts their heads and starts into the palace, he follows along.

Mikhail and the young Oceanese woman chat politely as she tours them to their rooms. Outside their doors, she bows again.

"I hope you will find your accommodations comfortable. The Atlas dignitaries have already arrived. We will meet in the morning for meal and discussion, if it is to your liking."

"That would be wonderful." Mikhail bows in return. "Goodnight, Sayori-san."

She departs, and Mikhail and Alina turn to their room. Blake steps into his, adjacent to them. Sleep will be good. Thank God for sleep.

Inside, he finds a soft robe waiting for him as well as a spacious four poster bed. He still can't get his mind around all the luxury these people live in. Excessive, is what it is. A closed glass door leads to a balcony, and he pokes his head out to get a look around. Damn, but the view over the gardens and lake puts his old apartment's fire escape and brick wall to shame. A wave of homesickness washes over him, and he abandons the balcony. A bath and then bed. He deserves it.

He steps into the bathroom, already stripping out of his suit jacket, when a voice interrupts him.

"About damn time."

Blake's fingers slip on the button, and he gawks at the person sitting on the edge of the tub.

"Jay!"

"The one and only." Jay stands and crosses the room, enveloping Blake in a firm embrace. Blake has a half second to regret his greasy skin and hair then melts into the hug like ice cream on a summer day. "Do you know how long I've been hiding in here? I thought they'd stuck you in a different room."

"And do you know how long I've waited to hear from you? I thought you'd given up on me."

"Never. Been trying to reach you since you left." He presses a kiss to Blake's forehead. "I can't believe you, running off like that. I nearly had a hernia."

Blake winces. "Not my smoothest move. I thought I could take care of this myself. I didn't want to drag you in any deeper. I screwed up. I'm really sorry."

"If it makes you feel any better, the guy you maced looks like he stuck his head in a hornet's nest. Nasty stuff you got there."

"Supposed to be able to take down shifted alphas." Blake leans back to study Jay's face. "You don't look like you messed with some hornets, but you don't look great, either. When's the last time you slept?"

"The night we hooked up."

"Please. As if we did any sleeping."

Jay cracks a grin. "There's my Buttercup. Although you owe me an explanation or two, Mr. Prince. Couldn't bother to tell me sooner, huh?"

Blake winces. "I'm sorry. Look, I spent my entire life in hiding. It's not something you just tell someone, you know?"

"I could've helped. We're a team, aren't we? You don't have to do everything alone."

Blake leans his forehead against Jay's chest. "I've been alone my whole life. I'm not used to relying on people. I'll try to be better."

"Good. But you'd better apologize to my couch. It died for you."

Blake laughs. "My bad. I didn't think a shifter would come after me. I was as surprised as you."

"We probably could have avoided all of this if you had told me the truth." A touch of admonishment in his voice, but not quite scolding. Still, guilt curls in Blake's chest.

"I've been an idiot about this whole thing. But..." He considers his words before saying, "I don't think I regret coming here. Mikhail is..." Shakes his head. "Anyway, now I'm ready to be back."

Jay kisses Blake's forehead. "We'll figure it out. Now about that night we hooked up. What are the chances of an encore?"

"Right now?" Blake shakes his head. "You're kidding me. My dad's one wall over. We're surrounded by bodyguards and the world's most powerful packs. And I feel like someone covered my face in greasepaint."

"I can be quiet."

"Down, boy." Blake gives him a friendly shove. "We need to talk about other things. How's my mom? How can I get home? What, exactly, does someone say when they meet the leaders of the world?"

"She's stable, we'll negotiate that, and I would've thought you'd figured that out by now."

Blake props his hands on his hips. "I can't flirt with them. They're not all you."

Jay chuckles. "I don't see Will Travers reacting well to that." He seesaws his hand back and forth. "Guy's kind of a stick in the mud."

"I'm so doomed. I wasn't cut out for this. I'm a waiter, for crying out loud."

"There you go. Smile and give them what they want. And if that doesn't work, call over management."

"And who's management in this scenario?"

"Me. I'll cover your ass."

Blake can't resist a cheeky smile. "Wouldn't want anyone else back there."

"I missed you."

Blake leans up on tip toes and plants a warm kiss on Jay's mouth. Jay wraps an arm around his waist and pulls their bodies flush. The kiss deepens, and for a moment, Blake forgets all about his greasy skin and tired body. Then something hard presses against his leg, and he pulls away.

"Not tonight, I said."

"I can't help it. I've got a Blake addiction. I'm not the one in charge here."

"I'll settle with you. We can cuddle. No funny business."

"Deal."

"I need a bath first. I think I have enough oil on my skin to fry a chicken."

"May I join you?"

"I'll close my eyes, and if someone happens to be in the tub when I open them, I can't exactly kick them out, can I? That would be rude."

Before Blake even turns his back, Jay is already loosening his collar. He sets to running the water and scrounges around for towels and soap. When he looks back, Jay is settled chest-deep in the steaming water. He grins, dumps his clothes, and climbs in after him. Jay pulls him close, back to chest, and Blake lets out a long breath.

At last, things are looking up.

***

The next morning, lying in bed, chest to chest on top of Jay, a hand caresses Blake's back, and another runs up his thigh. He sighs and presses himself into the body beneath him. Being held again, by his alpha no less, is the greatest feeling in the world. He inhales deeply, taking in that warm earth scent and feels his dick harden. He kept Jay off him through the bath and nighttime, but now, with dawn rays peeking through the curtains, a hot desire builds in his gut.

Jay's left hand—the one on his thigh—trails a little higher, cups his backside and squeezes gently. Blake's dick twitches.

"What do you think?" Jay murmurs low in his ear, the edge of sleep not yet worn away entirely.

Blake wiggles his hips and replies, "I don't think there's any lube."

"Don't need it if I'm sucking you off."

"You drive a hard bargain." Rock hard, he can barely think of anything else. "Consider me convinced."

"Good." The little growl is back in Jay's voice, the one that belies his arousal. He flips their positions and crawls down until he crouches over Blake's dick, already dripping precum. He leans forward and licks the tip, eliciting a sharp gasp from Blake.

"Shit, I don't know how quiet I can be..."

"Better work on that."

With no more warnings, Jay envelops Blake with his mouth. Blake claps a hand over his face, back arching. God, it's so hot and wet and perfect. Jay pulls his head back, sucking up his length, and Blake nearly loses it. His free hand digs into the bed sheets, twisting them up in a fist. Sleep is long gone now, replaced with a burning desire that reaches his fingertips. He's back in Jay's arms, where he's meant to be. It's almost too much, the smell of his mate all around him.

Shit—mate?

Then Jay sucks again, and all thoughts spiral out of his mind.

Blake moans and jerks his hips. He clamps a hand on his mouth, trying to stifle every little grunt and groan of pleasure. Jay laps at the underside of his dick with his tongue, and the tip brushes the back of his throat. Electric pleasure courses through him, his body tightens, and then he can't hold it back anymore. The wave crashes over him, and he shoots a load into Jay's mouth. He gasps and shudders, holding in the cry that tries to burst from his throat. Warmth washes over him, from bottom to top, and he sags into the bed.

Jay releases him and swallows, wiping his mouth. "Feel good?"

"Fuuuuuuck yeah."

Jay plops beside him on one elbow. He brushes bangs out of Blake's eyes with a gentle touch.

"I really did miss you."

Half-lidded, Blake gazes at him. Those golden-brown eyes, the tan skin, long hair... Another wave of desire races through him.

Jay blinks as Blake's scent shifts from plain arousal to something more. He doesn't mean to do it, but he's releasing a mating pheromone.

"Blake..." Jay's fingers trail to his neck, rubbing a circle on the soft skin. His canines drop in response to the pheromone, begging to sink into Blake's skin and bond them together.

Blake tries to diffuse the situation with a joke. "Good call, Blake, there's only an entire house of werewolves waiting to kill each other because of you. Yeah, great time to get all sappy." It's a terrible joke.

Jay's brow furrows. "You're kind of giving me mixed signals here, Buttercup." His eyes flick down to Blake's neck, tip of his tongue running over his teeth like he can't wait to dig in. "If you want this..." he leans in closer, "then tell me." His scent shifts as well, an intoxicating rush of mating signals.

Blake can't help it. He panics. Shuts down his pheromones and twitches away from Jay so violently that he rolls off the edge of the bed and splats on the floor. A moment of silence stretches long enough that Blake realizes it's up to him to rescue this disaster.

"I'm just gonna lay here for a while, okay? I'm thinking my brain cells might have rolled under the bed somewhere, and it looks like I can fit under there, so if anyone comes looking for me let them know I went to Narnia or something."

A grumble from above him. "Narnia's in a closet."

"Whatever."

"You really trying to get away from me that badly?"

Blake grimaces. Does the only thing his brain's been programmed to do for twenty-three years. He deflects. "Maybe I like cat and mouse. Or maybe I'm pyromaniac who just wants to burn his life to the ground. Blake Fields: the King of Bad Decisions."

"Or maybe you need to be straight for once and tell me what it is you actually want."

Blake forces a choked laugh. "I tried to be straight once. It ended with me sucking dick."

An exasperated sigh from the bed. Blake thumps his forehead on the wood floor. He's never learned how to let someone into his clamshell of a life.

Try harder, damn you.

He clears his throat. "Um, maybe it's something we can tackle later, you know? When we're home?"

Before Jay can reply, a thump at the door interrupts him.

Blake squeaks and rockets up, reality clicking into place so fast that it gives him vertigo. His dad was one room over while he was getting his dick sucked.

How self-destructive can one guy get?

"Hide," he hisses at Jay. Another knock sounds. Jay ducks under the covers and lays flat. Blake slaps his forehead with the heel of his palm. "Not there!"

"Well, where, then?"

"I don't know, the balcony! Go!"

Jay vaults off the bed and slides naked onto the balcony, slipping the door shut behind him. Blake tugs on boxers and a robe and ties it off before peeking out the bedroom door. Alina glares down at him from the other side.

Blake affects a lean against the door, trying to simultaneously look casual and block the triple-X aromas coating the bedroom. His malfunctioning brain interprets this as a wink and finger guns. "Morning, Mrs. Volkov."

You need to be committed.

Alina's top lip curls back, completely uncharmed by his affect. "Sleeping in again?" Then the inevitable smell of sex wafts out and she wrinkles her nose.

Blake forces a too-loud laugh and says, "Call me 'Sleeping Beauty'. Later today I'll go outside and sing to the animals."

She stares at him like he's grown an extra head, then says, "Breakfast is down this hall and to the right." She points. "I trust you can find us there?" She's already backing away.

"Oh yeah, no problem. I'm great at finding people. Found somebody last night in my bathroom."

Thank God she's already left by the time that pops out of his mouth. He fights back the urge to slap himself, then shuts the door and groans loudly.

Jay doesn't reappear. Instead, his voice drifts from outside.

Oh god no.

Blake crosses the room and slowly floats farther and farther from his body as he makes out the sound of Jay talking.

"Nice morning, isn't it? It's always nice to visit Oceana."

Blake reaches for the door, and the world doubles back in on him as he watches it slide open without feeling it.

First, he sees Jay, hands clamped firmly around a small stone planter with a tall cactus poking out of it. He's standing rigid, the morning sun glowing off his bare skin, the planter held tightly to his body as if blocking his junk from the world. Then Blake's neck creaks as he looks over to the adjacent balcony and sees none other than his own father, fully dressed, staring blankly at Jay.

Mikhail's eyes travel from Jay to Blake, and Blake lets out a hysterical laugh and says way louder than necessary, "Oh yeah, this place is great! They're so, um," his eyes flick to Jay's cactus and back to his dad, "accommodating."

He doesn't know his dad well enough to read the expression on his face, but he assumes it's somewhere in between surprised and overtly offended. Surfended. He steps in front of Jay in a vague attempt to block the man's nakedness and starts backing him up toward the door.

"Alina told me breakfast is soon," he carries on like nothing is weird. He doesn't have a naked man on his balcony in the middle of a decades-long political conflict. "I hope they have something good to eat. Do you know what they serve here? I wonder if we can get waffles." He butt-bumps Jay back into the bedroom and slinks backwards until just his head pokes out. Calls out, "I like mine with extra syrup!" Then pulls head inside and shuts the door.

He stares at his hands where they clutch the door shut as though Mikhail might swoop over and tear it open to confront them. He blinks the blur out of his eyes and lets out a shaky breath.

"Extra syrup?" Jay says from behind him.

"Strawberry syrup," he clarifies numbly.

"That could have gone better."

"I think I might throw up. What are the odds we invent time travel in the next five minutes and wipe this whole morning from existence?"

"I'd say greater than the odds of your dad ever forgiving me."

"Oh shit," Blake groans and slaps his forehead.

"What?"

"I never told him I'm gay. This is *not* how someone wants to find out their son rides dick."

Jay snorts. "You know it's not the 1500s anymore, right? Nobody gives a shit about that. I think you should be more worried that he knows *whose* dick you're riding."

Blake whirls around at him. He's still gripping the stupid cactus like it's a lifeline. "Did we just ruin this whole thing? Like, are we about to enter Super War?"

"Is that war but with more explosives?"

"I don't know; you tell me. And put that stupid plant down! It's staring at me."

Jay drops it on the floor, and they stare at each other.

"I should get dressed," Jay says at the same time that Blake says, "You should get dressed." Then they both choke out a laugh.

"We're so screwed," Jay mutters, running a hand through his hair.

Another knock at the door causes them both to jump.

"Oh god, it's my dad, it's gotta be." Blake starts pacing. "I'll-I'll tell him you were just stopping by to check on me."

"With my dick out?"

"Maybe I can convince him it's Lantish culture? Like, totally polite and normal and not at all meaning we have crazy, banging sex."

"You tell me how that goes. I'm hiding in the bathroom this time."

Jay disappears into the bathroom like he should have in the first place, and Blake takes a breath and approaches the door.

As he opens it, he starts talking. "Good morning, just wanted to let you know Jay was only here because I was having plumbing problems. He was checking my pipes." Then he stops abruptly because the person on the other side of the door is not, in fact, his dad.

A boy stands there in servant garb, head slightly bowed. He's maybe a year or two younger than Blake by the look of him, blond and a little too skinny, like he's the runt of the litter. He lifts his head, and Blake startles to realize he isn't Oceanese. As if the blond hair didn't give it away. It's definitely the same outfit all the servants wear, though. His apron hangs heavy from his waist, pockets bulging.

"You're not my dad," Blake says dumbly.

The boy glances side to side, avoiding his eyes like they're magnets repelling each other.

Still reeling from how badly this morning is going, Blake says, "What do you want?" The boy flinches, and Blake immediately regrets his harried tone. "Sorry. Let's start over. I'm having a bizarro morning. Can I help you?"

"I'm here to help you." The boy's eyes turn to Blake's feet, and Blake finds himself wondering if he has something stuck between his toes. The boy's Lantish has a light accent, like he was raised speaking Oceanese. "Your clothing..." he trails off like he expects Blake to understand what he means.

Blake stares down at himself, still garbed in the white robe. "Uh, sorry, I'm not dressed yet. I'll throw something on."

Before he can back away, he hears Jay say something from the bathroom.

"Hang on. One second. Be right back." He shuts the door and shuffles over to the bathroom. "What?"

"You can't wear western clothes," Jay says through the door.

"What? Why not?"

"You're in the Oshiro house. We all wear formal Oceanese clothes to meetings."

"Why didn't you tell me sooner?" Panic rises in Blake's throat. All he has is the suit from Moskva.

"Don't worry." Jay cracks the door open and peeks out an eye. "There's going to be something in the dresser for you."

"So what's the servant about?"

"I can pretty much guarantee you they left you a kimono. You'll need help getting that on."

"What?" Blake pulls the door open the rest of the way. Jay's half-dressed in last night's clothes, shirt hanging open, pants unbelted. "You're shitting me."

"I've got to get out of here, too, you know. I've got a *montsuki* waiting for me."

"Oh, so *you* get to dress like a guy, but I don't?"

"I'm an alpha. You're an omega. Them's the rules."

Blake gapes at him. "I'm a *guy*!"

"Traditionally, omegas in Oceana are all treated like women and alphas like men. Meetings like this are all about tradition. Don't sweat it. You'll look good. Anyway, it's not like you have to wear makeup or something."

Blake narrowed his eyes. "What, you saying I wouldn't look good in lipstick? Terri's always telling me I'd be great in drag. She keeps pitching me drag names. The last one was 'Ivana Bussy'." Why he chooses to die on this hill, he doesn't know, but the morning has gotten way out of hand.

"Let's put a pin in this one." Jay rapidly buttons his shirt and steps out of the bathroom. "Trust me, I *need* to know where this conversation goes, but I also need to get moving. If we're late for breakfast, then *everyone* will be pissed at us, not just your dad."

"Oh good, my Disappointing People Quota hadn't quite maxed out yet. If I don't let the entire world down by lunch I might as well be slacking."

Jay leans down and kisses his cheek. "Chin up, Buttercup. We'll get through this." He opens the bedroom door and mutters, "*Ohayou*," to the servant, who panics and bows so deeply Blake fears his neck might snap. Then Jay's gone down the hallway, leaving him alone with the other blond.

"Well, better get in here then." Blake steps aside and motions at the boy. After a moment, he creeps past. Blake gets a whiff of mellow chrysanthemum and parchment paper. Definitely an omega. It's a relief, honestly. His life has been so stuffed full of alphas lately he can barely keep track of them all. This is the first time he's had a chance to speak with a fellow omega since leaving Atlas. He aches for a moment for Terri, vowing to catch up with her the moment he can.

"So," he says, slapping on his brightest smile, "How do you handle all these alphas? Pain in the ass, aren't they?" The servant doesn't reply, and Blake pushes for a laugh. "I've been thinking this whole place needs a massive unbunching of their underwear. Maybe we should all just get drunk and have a dance party. Terri says karaoke fixes everything. Can you imagine them all screaming the lyrics to 'Don't Stop Believing'?"

This earns him jack all. Probably not the right approach. This kid looks scared of his own shadow. Blake puffs out a sigh and runs a hand through his hair.

"Sorry. Just trying to be funny. Not so good at it lately." He releases a calming pheromone, something to break the ice. "I'm Blake. What's your name?"

The boy's breath catches, like he didn't expect the personal question. Then he says, voice quieter than ever, "Mashuu. Or Matthew, if that's easier."

Blake beams at him, trying to get him to loosen up. "Nice to meet you, Mashuu. I hear I've got to wear a kimono? I'll be honest with you; I don't know the first thing about foreign clothes. I'm glad you're here. It's good to meet another omega, you know?"

Mashuu nods furtively, like he's too scared to agree out loud. Then he asks, "Would it be all right if you changed now? Please?"

"Oh, right." Mostly naked in front of strangers is not his favorite thing in the world, so he quells his nerves by talking while he unties his robe.

"Where are you from? I didn't think the Oshiros took in foreigners."

Mashuu shuffles to the dresser and unfolds a kimono of beautiful deep blue. He lays it out on the rumpled bedspread and checks for a variety of belts and fabrics as he replies. "I was born here. My mother has served this pack for many years. Even though we look different, we've been treated...well enough."

Blake registers the pause and its implications and tries to ease away the hurt. "It's hard to be different. I've never fit in anywhere. I—" He shakes his head, "It's not enough, but I'm sorry. That sucks. People suck." He shifts uncomfortably in his boxers and waits for a cue of what to do next. Asks, "What's your mom do?"

Mashuu pauses, thinking over his reply. At last, he says, "She's away a lot. Helping the embassy. I..." He looks up and meets Blake's eyes for the first time. "I don't know her very well."

A surge of empathy rolls through Blake. He offers a comforting scent. "I'm sorry. I don't know what I'd do without my mom. She's the most important person in my life." He shakes his head. "Things are weird right now. I didn't know my dad for twenty-three years. Now he wants to be in my life like nothing ever happened." He shrugs and admits, "I don't know how to handle it."

Now Mashuu lets out a soft aroma, floral and charming. "It's hard not to know where you come from. Sometimes I think I don't know where I'm going."

Blake has a sudden urge to hug him, like he's just picked out some piece of his life and slotted it into place. Instead, he holds out his arms so Mashuu can drape the blue fabric over them. Mashuu moves around him, straightening and smoothing the garment. Their scents mingle pleasantly.

"You're cool, Mashuu," Blake says. "Sorry you're stuck obeying a bunch of hoity-toity alphas all day. I mean, come *on*, do you see how much money these people waste? It's ridiculous." He puts on a snooty accent. "Oh, *dahling*, could you pass the solid gold candelabra? I just purchased a fleet of private yachts and want to celebrate by burning a pile of thousand-dollar bills."

Mashuu is crouched out of sight behind Blake's knee, but Blake hears him stifle a laugh. Jackpot. He continues with renewed energy.

"I used to think it was a good day when I got by without ruffling anybody's feathers. Now I think it's a miracle I don't strangle any of these self-important alphas with their own pearls. The last purchase I splurged on was a ten-pound bag of potatoes. I felt like a king eating homemade potato pancakes and mashed potatoes and breakfast hash for weeks. It was like, wow, I can get an extra hundred calories today, I'm really coming up!

"You know what I ate my first morning in Servos? They made a *mountain* of food. Enough to feed me for a month. And there were only three of us! I almost broke down at the table because I can't remember ever seeing that much food in one place. And there's no way I can explain *that* experience to the King of Servos because I'm pretty sure he's never gone a day in his life without a personal servant fetching him every little thing he could ever want. How the hell do you explain poverty to people who only skip meals because they're 'detoxing'?" His throat catches, ceasing his sudden tirade.

Mashuu doesn't reply, but a cooling aroma of flowers eases out the stress that's built in Blake's throat. He's groping beneath the kimono, feeling for something in the fabric, and the back of his hand brushes Blake's thigh.

"There's a loose thread caught on your, ah, *pantsu*. Please be still while I clip it."

Blake holds still, waiting to be told when he can move around again. He's about to ask about Mashuu's dad and their relationship when a sharp pain causes him to gasp instead.

"*Sumimasen!*" A flurry of motion erupts behind him, then a pressure presses against the back of his leg, above his knee. "*Moushiwake arimasen!*"

"What happened?" The sting aches a little, but it was the suddenness that surprised him more than anything.

"I'm afraid I cut you with my scissors. I'm so sorry. I'm a clumsy—"

"Whoa, calm down. It's okay." The dismay in Mashuu's voice and sudden sour smell startles Blake more than the nick. "It's not bad, right? Doesn't feel that bad. Everything's okay. Do you know how many coffees I've spilled? I'm way clumsier than you." He tries to ease the air between them with a dose of a more powerful personal pheromone.

Mashuu stills, and his voice comes out softly, but more calmly. "I'm sorry. I'll bandage it."

Some more rustling comes from behind him, then the pressure relents and something sticky presses to his skin.

"All better!" Blake declares, wanting nothing more than to ease poor Mashuu's mind. "No worries."

Mashuu appears from behind him and bows. "Please accept my apologies."

"It's fine!" His insistence is making Blake uncomfortable. "These alphas really have you on edge. They don't..." he roots around for the right word, "mistreat you, do they?" He's about ready to storm into breakfast with some choice words for Kimiko if that's the case.

Mashuu shakes his head. "No. I have my place and I am expected to stay there. Everyone has a job to fill, even a low omega like me."

Blake knows he's making a face at that, but he can't help it. Damn traditional werewolves. He tries to shake off the displeasure and put on a friendly expression.

"You could leave if you wanted. Do your own thing. You don't have to deal with their bullshit if you don't want to." He pushes out his best soothing scent. It's the equivalent of hugging Mashuu or pressing their foreheads together like they're pack.

Mashuu's fingers twitch, and a tentative aroma replies. Something familiar aches Blake, but he can't place it. Mashuu whispers, "I'm happy here."

"Right." They stand in silence for a minute, a cultural divide separating them from a closer bond. Blake gives in and says, "Anyway, you don't have to worry about me. You're good in my book."

"I should finish," he mutters. "If that's all right, Blake-sama."

Blake's jaw tightens at the honorific. It's all wrong, and he hates it. "Just Blake," he insists.

Mashuu's face slackens, like the idea of calling Blake by just his first name is more horrifying than anything the alphas have done to him.

Blake grimaces. "I guess 'sama' is fine, if it makes you feel better."

"*Hai. Sumimasen.*"

He doesn't recognize the second word, but it sounds an awful lot like an apology. He's going to have to spend some time with Mashuu while he's here. Maybe he can give him a morale boost.

"Okay then." Blake extends his arms again. "How do we tie this thing?"

Chapter Eighteen

Grieg's "Piano Concerto in A minor, op. 16, 3rd mov."

Jay rushed to brush his teeth and dress. Kim helped him out getting into Blake's room last night, but she wouldn't be pleased if he arrived late for breakfast. This was the first event in a long day of discourse, and the last thing he needed to do was blow it by showing up late.

Or, you know, stumbling upon the highest ranked Servan alpha while his dick's out. If they weren't all already at each other's throats by the time he got there it would be a miracle.

He slowed to tie the pants correctly, fingers remembering the crisscrossing patterns he'd learned as a child. It was a custom outfit, emblazoned with the Reed crest (a castle tower with a full moon above) on the front and back. The rest of his family would be dressed similarly.

He straightened the sleeves a final time, checked that his hair was pulled back neatly, and left for the dining room.

Most everyone arrived before him, but the meal service hadn't started yet so he was in the clear. He paused at the door to take it all in. A large, rectangular room housed everyone, with a row of open sliding doors across one side. The doors led out into the garden, and a lovely, sweet breeze wafted in through them. Bodyguards flanked the edges of the room, and servants—not mechs—walked back and forth offering refreshments and welcoming everyone politely. A large table took up the center of the room, the far end populated by Mikhail Volkov and his wife, along with a few members of their parliament. On his side sat his family, three members of the Travers pack, and the head of pack Hunt. In the middle were Kim, Sayori, and their brother, Akira, dressed in plainclothes denoting his beta status. Jay bowed to them before taking a seat beside Cat.

Somehow the room wasn't in chaos, but he didn't miss the way Mikhail glared at him when he entered. He didn't even try to give the man a smile or greeting. Better that they all pretended nothing ever happened this morning.

"Was starting to think you'd be late," Cat mused. "I wonder what kept you?" Her eyes flicked to the other end of the table, a wry curve of her lips implying she knew Blake was also missing.

"Couldn't get my *hakama* tied. You know how it is."

Cat snorted but didn't press the matter.

A few minutes of quiet chatter passed, then the door across from them slid open. A servant bowed and stepped away, leaving space for Blake to enter. He walked carefully, as though he thought he might damage the clothing. The kimono was a deep blue, accented with white and pink peonies down the bottom and sleeves. Jay felt his breath catch. His omega was stunning—beautiful enough to draw the attention of the room. He was, after all, the reason everyone was here.

Blake fidgeted before catching Jay's eye. Jay nodded toward Kim, trying to pass the information on to him. Blake seemed to pick up on it, walked gingerly into the room, and attempted to bow to Kim. He failed, of course, because the sash across the kimono was too rigid to allow a bow at the center. No one had taught him how to do it properly. Kim gave a little wave of her hand to spare him any further embarrassment. Relieved, Blake took a seat on the other end of the table. Eyes didn't leave him, though. He glanced around himself, twitched the corners of his mouth down, and Jay could practically hear his brain forming some inappropriate joke to diffuse tension.

Luckily, before Blake could ask everyone what their favorite sexual position was or something equally absurd, the servants began bringing in food. Roasted fish, miso soup, rice—steaming bowls filled the table. To Jay's knowledge, after the meal they'd discuss pleasantries and introductions, then take a break before the real discourse started. He'd attended meetings like this before, dragged along as a pup, but this was the first time he'd ever felt committed to the process. With the right words, he could have Blake back, put an end to the fighting, start a new year of peace between their countries. Not that he'd do much talking. Like Blake, he was more of a token appearance than functional. Except for the whole 'showing up naked on the balcony across from Mikhail Volkov' thing, which he dreaded would follow him forever, like that story about Will Travers and the scullery maid at a Hunt pack mating ceremony.

Shit, I'm going to be the guy who flashed Mikhail Volkov for the rest of my life.

Kim said a few words, they ate, and the dishes cleared. As water glasses refilled, Jay settled himself for the next phase and tried very hard not to look too long across the room. Kim stood, and everyone turned politely toward her.

"Thank you all for coming," she started. "It's an honor to host the greatest packs in Atlas and Servos here on my estate. As you have heard, my grandmother has passed, and so I have taken on the mantle of the Oshiro clan. I'd like nothing more than for our families to cooperate in the best interests of the world. Rest assured I will do all in my power to facilitate conversation as she would have. You have all the resources of Oshiro at your service. Now if you please," she raised a hand, "let's make introductions." She nodded to Mikhail.

Mikhail introduced himself and his party, then the Lantish pack heads did the same. It was stiff and formal, but it would warm them all up to speaking terms. It would go on like this for a while, forced compliments and icy smiles. The last time these people had been in a room together was when Jay was a baby. Legend had it Will Travers threatened to shift and bite the head off one of the Servan parliament members. Suffice it to say, today's attitudes were less than welcoming.

His own mother beamed a smile all around. She'd told him once, 'Smile, and no one will know what you're thinking.' Seemed she lived by the advice. Her warm gaze and tone thawed even Will's frown. They discussed everything but politics—the beautiful spring weather, the history of the area, anything to keep it light and friendly. It took some time, but they finally circled into a relevant topic, courtesy of his mom.

"Of course," she said, wrapping up a conversation about music, "I'm no expert. I would have to defer to you, Mikhail. Or to your son. He's an excellent pianist."

Blake tensed up, but Mikhail merely smiled politely and replied, "Good taste runs in the family. Blake, would you have a recommendation for Sara? A favorite symphony, perhaps?"

A little mischievous flash crossed Blake's eyes, and Jay felt a jolt of fear for what would pop out of his mouth. Then, with a surprising elegance, he smiled and replied, "Mahler five is excellent. There's a good recording online, but nothing beats hearing music played live."

"Isn't that the truth. Perhaps by the end of the day, you could grace us with some music of your own. I would love to hear you play again."

Blake's smile didn't slip. "I'd be honored." It comes out almost too saccharine.

"Isn't it interesting," his mother persisted, "that he would be so skilled without your tutelage, Mikhail."

"His mother was a gifted pianist herself," he replied.

"And yet she barely knows herself now, suffering the way she is. It's no surprise the boy wants her back."

A quiet descended on the room. Mikhail's eyes narrowed as he calculated her motive.

"That would have to depend on negotiations today. You're the ones who have her."

She tapped a finger to her chin. "She's safe and as healthy as can be expected, considering the circumstances. Though we'd be relying on you for a cure."

Jay frowned. What did his mom know that she wasn't saying?

The corners of Mikhail's mouth turned down. "That remains to be seen."

A silence settled around them for a beat, then Kim spoke up.

"That's enough for now. I think a recess is in order. Everyone, if you please, stretch your legs and get some water. You're welcome to browse the garden." She gestured behind her to the open doors.

Stiffly, people stood and maneuvered around each other. Servants brought in another round of drinks, and Jay met Blake's eyes, nodding toward the garden.

They met outside on the far end, beneath a plum tree. Jay glanced sideways to check if anyone watched them. No eyes, particularly green ones. He let out a breath.

"That could've gone better." Blake flashed a wicked little grin. "But be proud of me. I almost told your mom to listen to '*Leck mich im Arsch*'."

"Based on context clues, I'm going to say you did a good job. Honestly, I'm just happy no one's said anything about this morning."

"Maybe everyone's too uptight to even acknowledge it. Maybe we're secretly safe to do anything we want as long as everybody pretends it didn't happen. All right, place your bets on what happens if I streak across the garden. Come on, let's hear it."

"Hold up. No more streaking. I can't handle it. I'm pretty sure there's already rumors about me."

"What? How?"

"You have no idea how badly rich people gossip. It's practically their national pastime. Haven't you ever watched those Real Housewolves shows? They *live* for drama."

"Well, whatever. What's done is done." A sparkle brightened Blake's eyes. "Let's meet out here tonight. Under the tree. I bet it's real romantic." He waggled his eyebrows.

"You're going to be the death of me, you know that?"

"I don't hear a 'no'."

"Of course let's meet out here. Keep the kimono on. I want to kiss you in it."

Blake snorted. "Pervert." As though he hadn't brought the whole thing up. "After everyone's asleep. Midnight?"

Jay shook his head. "Two. Wolves are nocturnal, you know."

"You're gonna make me wear this thing all night?"

Jay shook his head with a grin. "Ideally, no."

Blake facepalmed. "Ack. Walked right into that one."

"Better head back. They're sitting down again."

"Yeah, and I think Alina is going to burn a hole in the back of your head with those lasers she's trying to shoot out of her eyes."

Jay jerked his head around to see her glaring at the two of them. Blake twiddled his fingers at her. Mikhail was very specifically *not* looking at them. Jay sighed, and they separated to opposite ends of the table, settling in for the next hours of negotiation.

***

Day one: completed. Jay left dinner feeling a little numb and a lot exhausted. The discussions had lasted long into the afternoon and eventually devolved into bickering between two of the parliament members and the Travers pack. Kim had called an abrupt end to the day and invited them all to rest.

But there'd be no rest for him. He had a date by the plum tree. He flopped onto his bed and stared at the ceiling, rifling through events of the day and images of Blake dressed in the formal kimono.

Damn, wonder if he'd buy some clothes like that for home...

Home. No idea how long it'd be until they both got back. It had seemed for a minute like the discussions were going somewhere, when his dad asked Mikhail what steps Atlas needed to take to start fresh, but then one of the parliament members got snappy about some old blight to the pack honor, and things had fallen apart.

Blake was right about alphas and their damn pride. Caused more trouble than it solved. Maybe the world should have been ruled by omegas.

The thought of Blake in charge sent a little thrill to his lower half. Blake on top, eyes closed, head back. Shit, the image tantalized him.

He groaned and stood up. "Thinking with your dick again," he grumbled to the room. He needed fresh air.

He wandered the halls, looking for a spot to sit and clear his head. The garden was to the south, so he padded that way, his socked feet making almost no sound on the polished wood floors. He'd get there early to wait for Blake, maybe pick him a flower. He shook his head. Way too sappy. As he drew closer to the garden, he heard a voice outside. He paused as he translated the words from Oceanese, feeling a little slow and clunky. It had been a while since he'd used the language.

"...Find. Handle it."

Another voice, also unfamiliar, replied, "Yes. As you wish."

Footsteps, walking away. Jay was about to assume he'd walked in on someone scolding a servant, when the voice said in a hiss, "Before dawn."

"Yes," the second voice repeated, and that was that. The footsteps disappeared.

That was abnormal. Whatever and whoever needed done before dawn, it didn't sound good.

Jay peeked out into the garden but saw no one. He checked his watch. One-forty AM. Another few hours until dawn and whatever that was about. He clicked his tongue as he decided whether or not to tell someone about the encounter. For all he knew, it was just someone told to do the laundry. But if it had been about something else...

He abandoned the garden to find Kim.

***

Blake tiptoes out of his room and down the corridor, the unfamiliar hallways somewhat impeding his progress. He winds through the estate until arriving outside the garden doors from this morning. He doesn't run into anybody, not even a patrolling guard. He slides the door open as quietly as possible and steps into the courtyard.

The moon and stars, brilliant silver, cast mood lighting over the garden, turning the water in the pond to rippling mercury and casting deep shadows beneath the leaves and in the corners. He holds his breath for a moment as he calls on his wolf side, and his vision sharpens.

No Jay.

He'd figured his alpha would beat him here. It's hard enough to move in this outfit, and he hadn't exactly rushed through the halls in case he missed the right turns.

He shifts the fabric around himself, feeling a little tight at the waist where it all holds together, and decides to wait by the plum tree. He steps carefully on the path, avoids the rock garden in case any flowing fabric might catch, and finally settles on the grass beneath the tree branches. It's deeply shaded here, and the smell comforts him—fresh cut grass and sweet flowers. Legs folded beneath him, he closes his eyes and waits.

And dozes.

A vague sensation of wind rustling the leaves above. A memory of Jay's hands on his skin. A smell of earth and warmth and the good feelings that follow it. His name on Jay's lips, whispered in the heat of pleasure.

And a sharp rap to his skull, knocking him out of his doze.

He jerks and nearly falls sideways with a groan. His legs are more deeply asleep than he'd ever been, and they prickle and twinge from knee to toe. He rubs his head and blinks up at the attacker.

"What do you think you're doing?" Alina stares him down, frown so deep on her face that it seems someone carved it from stone. One hand grips a wooden fan, presumably used to hit him.

"Ow, why did you do that?" Blake groans again and shifts so his legs aren't quite so bound up beneath him. Shoots of pain make him grimace.

"You're a disgrace," Alina hisses. "Cavorting with that Reed boy while we discuss the future of the world. Do you know what your father has been through on your behalf? The pain he suffered when you ran away?"

"Oh yes," Blake snaps back, sarcasm dripping from his words, "because I had so much say in that. Mom thought he was going to kill us, what do you expect her to do?"

A fire burns in Alina's eyes, and she spits, "Know that Mikhail is a good man who would no sooner harm his own family than himself! Stand by him as any dutiful wife should! She may have been beautiful, but she never deserved him! She's the coldest woman I've ever known!"

That's a step too far. Blake snarls at her, "Maybe she didn't choose to be his wife in the first place! And now because of people like *you*," he jabs a finger at her, "she's suffering.

Dying for a man she doesn't love. How can you ever think I'd be okay with that? That I'd want any part of this screwed up family?"

A light flickers on inside, near the garden entrance. Alina hunches a little, as though it might make them invisible.

"Keep your voice down, pup. Do you want everyone to hear you? I come out here to rescue your dignity, and you treat me this way. Disgraceful."

At last, some feeling returns to Blake's legs. He manages to push himself to a wobbly stand and glares at Alina. "No one asked you to interfere. Atlas is my home, and Jay's my alpha, and I'm not staying away from them. I won't lay down and roll over for you, so forget it. I'm not—"

Alina's eyes widen suddenly, and she shoves him to the side with both hands. Still unbalanced from his numb legs and restrictive clothing, he topples sideways. He doesn't quite have the breath to shout as a black blur blasts past him and tackles Alina. She makes a rasping groan at the impact, then everything falls entirely still.

An oversized black wolf pins Alina to the ground, muzzle twisted in a snarl, drool slipping down its maw. It squats inches from her neck, seconds from snapping its jaws around her and twisting her head off like a champagne cork, and Blake does the only thing he can think of doing.

He jumps on its back and grabs it under the throat.

Coarse, thick fur gives him enough of a grip to latch on and cling for dear life. The wolf jerks and snarls, nipping at its sides, trying to reach any of Blake's body parts. He can smell its breath at this distance, meat and blood. It tries to shake him off, but he clings like a sandspur, determined beyond all rational thought to keep himself and Alina alive.

A shout fills the garden, another light switches on, and he cranes his neck enough to see a figure in the doorway. Then his world topples sideways as the wolf rolls over, mashing him into the ground.

He swears as fur tears off in his fingers, and the wolf springs free. It backs off him and shakes itself, and, dizzy, Blake sits up, silken clothes completely askew.

The wolf's haunches coil, preparing for a leap that will send it directly into Blake's face, where he will feel the stinking breath swallow him up, chomping down, tearing him apart.

Damn. Not even time for a last word.

***

Jay jogged through the mansion, frustrated and alone. He'd been unable to find Kim in her quarters, and there had been no guard stationed there to question. It seemed the manor had slipped into a deep slumber around him, nearly frozen in time. No one in the halls, doors closed tight. Something was off. He realized, stomach sinking to his feet, that Blake was probably waiting for him in the garden. He U-turned sharply and picked up the pace. As he approached, the sounds of a scuffle carried to him. He kicked it into high gear, switching on a light and slamming open a door that led to the garden. The moon, barely waning, still hung large and beautiful overhead, giving him enough light to see what was unmistakably a large black wolf trying to buck off none other than Blake himself.

Frozen, Jay watched as the wolf rolled over, knocked Blake loose, and stumbled back to its paws. Jay sucked in a deep breath, heart pumping in his ears. The wolf crouched to prepare a counterattack, teeth gleaming. His muscles thawed, and Jay ran. Ran full tilt at the wolf as it began to leap.

The pulse echoed in his chest, not his heartbeat, but something more; a need to be more. His feet thudded like jackhammers on the grass, carrying him faster than he'd ever run in his life. Carrying him forward onto all fours. Fur erupted out along his back. The garden was not so dark anymore—the shadows clearer to his eyes. The smells hit him in waves, fear and adrenaline, bloodlust, the heavy musk of wolf pelt. And Blake. The smell of strawberries so close by. He caught the other wolf in midair, tackled it straight to the ground. He was bigger, he could tell by the way their weight hit the dirt that he'd have an advantage. His lips pulled back in a snarl, a fierce cry rumbling from his chest that he barely recognized as himself. He snapped at the other wolf's neck, but it was faster, and he wasn't accustomed to his lupine shape yet. It dodged back, put some distance between them. Jay hunched, looking for an opening. Every follicle of hair on his body felt electrified. He stood between the other wolf and Blake, his instincts burning like a brand on his mind.

Mine. Mate. Protect.

He howled, fervent and alive with shifter energy. The howl of an alpha.

The other wolf snarled at him, but the tone was higher pitched, panicked. Jay could smell it at this distance, fire and nicotine, a little too familiar, though something else ran beneath it. A papery smell. His wolf brain gave it no consideration, and he leapt forward, snapping at the air. The wolf yipped and fled, tail tucked between its legs. It dashed into the shadows, and Jay coiled his legs, ready to take off after it. Then a voice called out, unsteady.

"Jay?"

Every sense in his body went to attention. He padded over to Blake and nosed his cheek. A long, thin cut across Blake's jaw oozed a little blood. Jay whined in concern, but Blake reached up and wiped it.

"I'm fine," Blake said, dazed. His hand fell on Jay's head, sinking into the thick fur. "You're a wolf now?"

Jay chuffed and sat down on his back haunches, tail slapping the grass. The wolf in his mind grinned broadly.

"Oh boy. I know you liked the heavy petting, but I didn't think it'd go this far."

Alina stood, wiping down her clothes, now stained with dirt and grass. She nodded to them. "You saved my life. You have my gratitude. You're the Reed boy, aren't you?" Jay barked once in assent. "And they called you *nevolk*." She shook her head and graced them with a rare smile. "Your wolf is beautiful. Thank you."

Inside the manor, the strange, quiet spell that had seemed to descend broke. Movement rumbled the floors. Jay could smell the people scurrying now, followed by voices.

Alina laid a hand on Blake's shoulder. "I must go to Mikhail. Whoever is behind this might target him next."

"We should stay with Jay," Blake countered. "What if another wolf—"

"*Nyet*. It would be better if he shifted back. Any *volk* is a suspect now. He could be seen as a threat."

"He saved our lives!" Blake protested.

"Please, child, listen to me for once. Mikhail won't be happy we've been threatened. If he sees a wolf near us, then he'll react instinctively. I do not wish for more fighting."

Blake made a face before relenting. "Jay, you can shift back, right?"

Jay closed his eyes, then whined softly. He couldn't seem to find his human form underneath all this fur. Human Jay seemed like another time, another life.

"Uh-oh."

Alina considered him. More footsteps echoed in the halls, and a nearby door slid open.

"Alina?" A voice called.

She pushed at Jay and Blake. "Go now. A private room. Get him to shift again. I'll handle Mikhail." She looked out across the garden and called back something in Servan.

Blake stumbled up to his feet, catching his balance and hurried away beside Jay. They stole away into a side room, mostly filled with neatly organized cleaning supplies. Jay sat down on his haunches while Blake shut the door behind them.

"Okay," Blake said with a heavy sigh. "Now what?"

Chapter Nineteen

Shostakovich's "Waltz No. 2"

Blake stares at Wolf Jay. His fur is a deep russet color, thick and coarse to the touch. His eyes gleam honey gold. Wolf Jay turns around in place as though checking himself out. He's much too big for the cleaning closet, though, and knocks into some supplies, upending a shelf and sending boxes of soap flying. He tries to nose them back into place, but only bumps over a mop before giving up and squatting on his haunches.

This is a new feature, anyway. When did he figure out how to shift?

Blake straightens his kimono, but the garment seems damaged beyond repair. It hangs limply off one shoulder, the bottom hem dirtied and torn. Hopefully Kimiko won't be too mad about it. He blows out a heavy breath and reaches for Jay, petting him behind the head.

"You saved my ass," he says. His fingers thread through the thick coat. "How did you figure out shifting?"

Jay cocks his head to one side.

"Right. No talking. That's fine. I talk enough for both of us." Jay licks his hand, the sensation sticky and a little unpleasant. Blake wipes it on his torn kimono. "We gotta get you back. I don't want a wolf for a boyfriend. It's going to destroy my new sex life."

Jay barks as though admonishing him for the joke.

"Yeah, not appropriate. Sorry. I'm a little stressed out here, okay? I thought I was out of my depth when you took me on our first date. What the hell am I supposed to do with world politics and assassination attempts? I keep waiting for the bottom to drop out. Things are getting weirder, and now my boyfriend's trapped as a wolf, and I really just want to go home and be in my shitty apartment again. At least life made sense there."

Jay leans against him, warm and fuzzy, and somehow still smelling like himself even as a wolf. It's a small comfort.

"What's it going to take to get everything back to normal? I don't even know what normal is anymore. So much changed so quickly. And now it's like I have a dad, and I've never had a dad before, so how do I deal with that? And he's also kind of cool, which is the worst part, I think."

He takes a long breath. Jay watches him patiently.

"Sorry, that was too much."

Outside, voices shout over each other. A commotion's broken out, but Blake can't pick up on any words. He frowns. Kimiko should be here to arbitrate, but he doesn't hear her.

A knock at the door behind them gives him a dash of hope, but instead of her light voice, he hears Catalina's rich tone.

"Alina tells me there's a little lost wolf in there. Mind if I help?"

Blake opens the door for her. "Please do; I'm talking myself in circles over here. It's embarrassing."

She steps in, wavy hair loose and nightclothes somehow not wrinkled, arms full of folded fabric. She cracks a grin at Jay. "Look at you, little brother. All grown up."

Jay barks at her.

"Did you try giving him a kiss? I hear it works in all the fairy tales." She tips Blake a wink.

"Oh yeah, except I'm the prince." He rolls his eyes. "Don't think it works in the opposite direction."

"Just a suggestion." She examines Jay with a critical eye. "Don't you want to be human again? I know it's taken your whole life to be a wolf, but if you really wanted to be human, you'd change back."

Jay closes his eyes for a moment, then opens them, amber and piercing. Still wolf.

"Well, I guess he's an *Atascado*."

Atascado. The Southern word for someone trapped in their shifted form. Supposedly whole gangs of them ruled the Southern countries, where things have been essentially quarantined from the rest of the world. The South is not exactly welcome in polite society.

Jay shakes himself from head to toe and closes his eyes again. Still nothing.

"What do we do?" Blake glances uncertainly at Catalina.

She shrugs. "It'll pass eventually. I hope."

Not good enough. Blake squats beside Jay and wraps his arms around him. The coarse fur tickles his nose.

"Come on. I want you back." Then, on a whim he adds with a puff of pheromones, "Don't you want to kiss me again?"

Jay moves beneath him, at first as though to stand, then Blake feels the ripple of energy below his skin. Jay's wolf body cracks and twists, and in moments, stubbly skin replaces the shaggy fur. Blake leans back to give him a once over. Jay, naked and fully human, sits on the ground beside him.

Without a word, Jay grabs Blake and presses their lips together. Blake grins through the kiss, but wiggles away when Catalina gives a pointed cough.

"Not that I'm not pleased for you both, but that's my cue to leave. Congratulations, little brother, you're officially a Reed."

Jay wrinkles his nose. "Take that back."

"Never." She leaves without another word, tossing the pile of clothes that she'd brought at them.

Blake runs a hand down Jay's chest. "I'm glad you're back. I really didn't need a pet for a boyfriend."

Jay pulls on the loose pants and ties them off. "Is that over the line? No wolves in the bedroom?"

Blake's turn to wrinkle his nose. "No thanks. I like you this way just fine."

More voices had gathered outside, and Blake swears he can hear the sound of a wolf snarling. Goosebumps break out across his arms.

"What's going on out there?"

Jay frowns. "Whatever it is, it's not good. At first it was all in Servan, but then I heard some Oceanese, too. I think—" He cuts himself off, looking disconcerted. Shakes his head. "Here, you change, too." He tosses a robe from the pile over to Blake. "We need to see what's going on."

Blake hurries to tear off the kimono. It comes off much easier than it went on. He shrugs on the robe and ties it. Jay fidgets from foot to foot as he changes, eyes glued to the door as though he might see straight through it into whatever is happening outside.

"Come on." Jay snags his wrist as soon as they're both dressed and tugs him along.

Blake blinks as they step back into the garden. The packs are gathered from the looks of it, each side split and surrounded by personal bodyguards, glaring down none other than Kimiko, who stands resolutely, arms loose at her sides, hands in tight fists. She seems to struggle to keep her face blank. A mottled gray and white wolf, hackles up, faces her, lips drawn back in a snarl.

"I promise," she's saying, "I will find whoever is responsible for this and deal with them. I will not stand for my guests to be treated in such a manner."

Mikhail steps forward from within a throng of guards and barks a command to the wolf in Servan, who snaps to attention and circles back to him to stand at his side. Mikhail addresses Kimiko tersely, "Have you no leads already? There's someone in this house attempting to murder my family. Where are your guards? Your security tapes? *What happened here tonight?*"

Kimiko tenses and motions for someone to come over. A man dressed in black approaches her, taking a knee to whisper something in her ear. Her expression turns severe, and she snaps something in Oceanese, her cool demeanor slipping for a moment.

"Shit," Jay mutters.

"What?" Blake grips his arm, trying to steady himself amid the sour stench of adrenaline and simmering anger.

"Sounds like the security system was down. No records of the last hour."

"What? How is that possible?"

"Somebody hacked it. Or..." he pauses as though not wanting to say the next bit. "Or it was someone inside the Oshiro family."

Blake chews his lower lip. "Who would do that? Who was that wolf?" He glances up at Jay, sees an uneasy storm in his eyes. "Jay?"

Jay blinks, pulled out of his thoughts. He meets Blake's gaze and fails to smile. "Whoever it was...smelled a lot like Kim."

Blake's eyes widen. The implication sinks in as he stares back out at the garden, trying to gage Kimiko's expression. Jay can't actually think...

As if reading his mind, Jay mutters, "Not her. Can't be. It's too messed up."

"Then who?"

"I don't know. Someone's got it out for her."

He steps forward, intending to approach her, but Mikhail catches sight of them and waves them over. They pass the Lantish packs as they cross the grounds, and Blake notices the severe look on Sara Reed's normally smiling face. She says nothing, however, and they stop in front of Mikhail, who immediately takes hold of Blake's shoulders and tilts him to one side, studying the cut that streaked blood down his cheek and neck.

"It's not as bad as it looks," Blake says in a futile attempt to disarm the bomb that's about to explode.

"This is unacceptable." Mikhail glares back over to Kimiko. "How dare you allow someone to spill blood during our negotiations?" Kimiko actually flinches at that, and Blake feels a wave of anxiety on her behalf. Mikhail presses on, "There is a wolf here who smells of my son's blood. Find him." He addresses Jay next, taking a moment to glare at him as if admonishing him for this morning, before clearing his throat and saying, "Alina tells me you saved them both. You must have gotten a scent when you fought off the attacker. Can you track it?"

Jay hesitates, gaze sliding to Kimiko and back again. "I'll try."

A new group of people approach them, spearheaded by Kimiko's sister, Sayori, expression dark. Behind her, their brother, Akira, follows along with a handful of guardsmen. They stop a few feet short of Kimiko, and a silent communication seems to pass between the sisters.

"Have you news?" Kimiko asks.

The corner of Sayori's mouth twitches downward. She takes a step forward and announces to the whole gathering, "We have a suspect. Based on a guard's account, a lean black wolf fled from the garden fifteen minutes ago. While we were unable to catch it, he did get a scent." She turns her hard eyes on Kimiko. "Where have you been tonight?"

A ripple of shock passes through Kimiko's features. Slowly, she replies, "Seeing to a security issue in the western hall. Satou informed me of a broken camera, and I spent the time investigating the area."

Sayori addresses a tall, bulky man with a scruff of facial hair standing behind her. "Satou, is this true?"

"Yes, but..." He glances at Kimiko the stands ramrod straight and declares in a formal voice, "Apologies, alpha, but I only spent a few minutes there. Master Oshiro dismissed me to check the surveillance room. I wasn't beside her for the remainder of the night, and the camera system was down. By the time I brought it back up, the attack had already happened. My greatest apologies for this failure."

Sayori's lips press into a line so thin they nearly disappear. She locks eyes with Kimiko. "Sister?"

Haltingly, Kimiko admits, "This is true, but I never approached the garden. I found out about the attack only as everyone gathered."

Mikhail jumps on the accusation. "You arrived later than all of us. You expect me to believe that you were ignorant of this attack until now?"

"Whoa, hang on," Jay says, hands up. "Kim would never—"

Mikhail rounds on him instead. "What did that wolf smell like, boy? You know better than anyone."

All eyes on Jay now. Blake grips his arm so hard it must hurt them both. Jay and Kimiko share a look, then he glances away to stare hard at the ground.

"It wasn't her. I know it wasn't."

Mikhail isn't convinced. He says something to the wolf beside him, and it walks to Kimiko, nose forward, snuffling. She tenses, but lets it sniff around her legs and hands. It suddenly pulls back and growls, low and persistent.

"Your pockets," Mikhails snaps.

"There's nothing—"

"Your pockets," Sayori repeats.

Kimiko reaches into her pockets, first the front—nothing—then the back. She frowns, a deep line creasing her brow. She brings out a handkerchief. The wolf snatches it from her and delivers it to Mikhail, who unfolds it and takes a slow breath.

Then, with a fire in his eyes that Blake has never seen, he snarls at Kimiko, "You dare attack my family and then lie to my face about it! This," he throws the handkerchief at Sayori, "is my son's blood."

Sayori sniffs it, then releases a resigned sigh. "Kimiko." She tilts her head up, face set. "As next in line to the Oshiro name, I claim you unfit to lead this clan and hereby assume the title of alpha. You'll be placed under house arrest as we investigate this matter. I promise," she addresses the crowd now, "that I'll make amends for this. She'll be handled as any traitor would. You can be assured that no more harm will come to your packs."

"Not good enough," Mikhail counters, voice a growl of contempt. "Who was she working with? She couldn't have done this alone."

"She didn't do it at all!" Jay snaps at him.

"Julian!" Sara Reed steps forward, face set in a frown so deep it's hard to believe she ever smiled at all. "That's enough. It's clear your packmate is not trustworthy."

Jay won't stand for it, though. "She would never do something like this! She's the most honorable person I know! She—"

"Jay," Kimiko says in a soft voice, almost tender. "It's okay. Don't do this."

"How can you say that? You know you didn't..." he trails off studying her. "Don't give up, Kim." Blake has never heard Jay plead before, and the sound breaks his heart.

The guards step between them, surrounding Kimiko. She gets one last look at Jay before they march her off, somewhere into the heart of the manor. Jay's shoulders sag.

Sayori clears her throat and announces, "I'll deal with this matter personally. Please set your guards at your doors and stay inside until this is settled."

Mikhail crosses his arms. "I expect this to be a swift meting of justice. We should convene tomorrow to discuss it."

"Agreed," Sara says. "It's only proper that we're involved in the process."

"Tomorrow," Sayori concedes. "We'll meet after dinner to give my pack time to investigate."

"Fine." Mikhail reaches for Blake. "Come, I do not wish anyone to disturb you." He shoots a solid glare at Jay and emphasizes, "*Anyone.*"

Blake glances up to Jay, head a storm of uncertainty. At last, he releases his iron grip on his alpha's arm and steps away to stand beside his dad. He can't do anything else. Everything's spiraled out of control.

As they walk away to their rooms, he hears Jay mutter, "This is bullshit."

He can't agree more.

***

Jay stormed into his room and sat heavily on the bed before standing up again and crossing to other side to glare out the balcony. Unable to be still, he crossed back to the bed and kicked one corner.

He had to clear Kim's name. There was absolutely no way she would do something like this.

He dug out his cell phone and pressed Lance's name. It rang once, twice, and as he was swearing out loud, it clicked, and a huffing voice came on the other end.

"Jay? What's going on?"

"Lance! I knew you'd pick up."

"Yeah, man, I'm in the middle of a run. What is it, like, 3 AM where you are? What's up?"

"I need you to get Elliot and meet me at the Oshiro estate."

"What? In Oceana?"

"Kim's in trouble." He took the phone away from his ear and put it on speaker so he could tap through it while talking. "I'm setting you up with a private flight. You know where our hangar is. Get there as soon as you can. I need you here yesterday."

"Say no more. Anything we should bring other than passports?"

"How about a big fucking club to beat someone with. I'm not sitting around while they do this to her."

"Whoa, man," a note of unease in Lance's voice, "you need to tell us what's going on. Is she hurt?"

Jay finished messaging the private airport his family kept and switched the phone back to his ear. "No. Not yet. But there's not much time. Get Elliot and get over here."

"Roger. Send me an email with the info. I'm already on my way."

No waiting for goodbyes. The phone beeped as Lance hung up. Jay typed off a quick email with the important details—flight information along with Kim's predicament—and sent it to both of them. He considered calling Elliot, too, but figured it would just slow them down. Lance could take care of it. He needed to think. They'd be here by noon tomorrow, if the trip went smoothly, and he needed the time to figure out what to do next.

He needed to see Kim.

***

The guard outside Kim's door wouldn't let him in, the bastard.

"Hey, do you know who I am?" Jay snapped. "Let me talk to her."

"No visitors," the guard intoned firmly. "You may speak to the alpha if you'd wish to request a formal meeting."

"Kim *is* the alpha!"

"Not anymore."

Jay fumed, glaring down this man with all the force possible, the childish part of him wishing he could melt this dumb goon's face off with the power of his mind.

"You're full of shit," he spat.

"Jay." A muffled voice called his name from behind the door. He leaned around the guard to better listen. "You always make such big scenes. Have some dignity."

Jay bristled but broke into an anxious laugh. Go figure Kim would admonish him for coming after her.

The guard tried to stonewall him, pressing his bulk between him and the door. Jay ignored him and said, "What's going on? Who set this up?"

"I have no idea. The only person I saw was Satou. Speak with him. I will meditate on what I can do."

"No visitors," the guard huffed, actually laying a hand on Jay's shoulder and pushing him.

Jay snarled a guttural sound at the guy, and he recoiled enough to give him the chance to say, "I'm going to figure this out, Kim. Elliot and Lance are on their way."

"Jay." Kim sounded so far away, like speaking through bulletproof glass instead of paper and wood. She sounded small in a way he'd never heard before. "Please don't get hurt."

The guard shoved him with both hands this time, and Jay stumbled backward. He pointed at the guy and said, "I'm not forgetting that." He left to seek out his next target.

***

Blake spends most of the night sitting up in bed, worrying. Jay is going to do something drastic, no doubt. He needs to be there, needs to squeeze his way out from under his dad's grip and find Jay. But Mikhail placed a guard at his door, instructing that he isn't to leave without the full entourage. It seems after twenty plus years of absenteeism, Mikhail is going into parental overdrive.

Jeez, Dad, overcompensating much?

The hours creep by, and around six AM a knock comes from the other side of the door.

"Yeah?" He's still in his robe from last night and can't much care.

The door cracks open, and Mashuu pokes his head in. "I hope I'm not disturbing you."

Blake rockets out of bed to greet him. "No! You're not! Come in."

Mashuu slips inside, silently shutting the door behind him. He holds a tray of food in both hands.

Blake nearly pounces him. "Is there any news? Is Kimiko okay? Where's Jay?"

Mashuu goes paler than usual and stammers unintelligibly.

Blake takes a long breath before saying, "Sorry. Too much. But is there any news? What do you know?"

"I'm afraid I don't know anything."

"Right. Sorry. I didn't mean to jump on you. I'm sick of being in this room. Trapped in here like a princess in a tower. It's so irritating."

"I've brought you a meal, if you like." He lifts the tray of food.

A smell wafts over: roasted fish and fresh rice along with the undeniable aroma of dashi. Blake licks his lips.

"Okay, fine. No use going on a hunger strike. But come here, have some with me." He waves Mashuu over to the sitting table in one corner and pulls out the chairs.

"Ah. Ehhh..." Mashuu's eyes flick sideways and then land on the floor. "I'm very sorry..."

"No, none of that. Come on. Just a bite. Smells great, right? We can talk. I'm going nuts in here by myself."

He knows he's put Mashuu in an uncomfortable position, but he needs company or he'll lose it. He sits, and Mashuu reluctantly follows, laying the tray between them. Blake leans across and uncovers the bowl of rice. A puff of steam flourishes in the air.

"Ah, that's amazing. I love the food here." Blake plucks the chopsticks and digs in before pausing and offering them to Mashuu. "A taste?"

Mashuu goes beet red, hands folded tightly in his lap. "*Anoooo...*" He glances up at Blake's earnest face once, twice, then reaches for the chopsticks with a shaking hand. "*Itadakimasu,*" he whispers before taking a bite of the rice.

"It's good, right? Perfect texture." Blake sips some miso soup with a smile. "I could eat this every day." He lets out a little calming aroma that blends with the food, and Mashuu's shoulders drop their tension.

"This is crazy. The attack, the lockdown. My dad's livid. Won't let me out. Ridiculous. I've survived three wolf attacks in two months. You'd think I could handle myself at this point."

"Three?" Mashuu's pale eyes widen. "Who did you anger?"

Blake laughs and shakes his head. "I don't know. God, maybe. Or fate." He bites into the fish and sighs happily. "It's not all bad, though. I've had more food in the last week than I ever ate in my shithole apartment."

Mashuu dares to take another mouthful of rice, chews thoroughly before asking, "Are you afraid? Of the alphas?"

Blake snorts. "As if. Bunch of prissy—" He cuts off his tirade to sigh. "It's my mom. She's sick. I don't know how much longer she has. I've been gone a while now, and she's just getting worse. I need to get home to her."

"I'm so sorry," Mashuu murmurs. He downcasts his eyes.

Blake rakes a hand through his hair. "All I've ever wanted is to make her happy. She risked so much to give me a safe life, to get me out of Servos and give me a fighting chance. She's sick because of it." He takes an unsteady breath and mutters, "It feels like my fault."

The sound of the chopsticks clattering to the table startles Blake out of his remorse. He looks up to see Mashuu covering his face with both hands.

"You okay?" Blake reaches out and touches his shoulder, pulling back when he flinches away. There's that aching familiarity again, an almost déjà vu sensation.

"I'm very sorry," Mashuu wheezes.

"It's not your fault. I just need to get out of here and see her again." He has to choke out the next words. "I don't know if I'll ever get another chance."

"You love your mother very much," Mashuu says with a force of emotion in his voice. Something like wonder and guilt and regret. He smells like chrysanthemum and parchment, and Blake finds himself reaching out to grasp his hand across the table.

"I'd do anything for her. I thought I came here to find her cure, but I guess it's too late for that."

"I wish..."

"What?"

"I wish I had a family like yours."

Blake locks eyes with him, studies his cheekbones and lips, and a spark of inspiration hits him.

"You can help me."

"I can?"

He leans over the table and takes Mashuu's hand in both of his. "Please. Give me your clothes. Let's swap. You stay in here, and I can leave and figure out what's going on. The guard won't know any better if I keep my head down. He'll think," he puts on a deep voice, "'Another blond omega.'"

Mashuu jerks back from Blake, freeing his hands to wave them in front of himself. "I'm sorry!"

Blake's figured out by now that this is his way of saying 'no'. But it's not acceptable. Not this time.

"Please, Mashuu. Just for a few hours. I'll stick up for you if anyone gives you trouble. Us omegas gotta stick together, right? Like a family." He spreads his hands in front of himself. "If this isn't solved, there's no way Mikhail is sending me home. I'll never see my mom again."

Mashuu clasps his hands in front of himself and closes his eyes, thinking it over. Finally, a little whisper floats out of him. "If it would help you, Blake-sama, then I'll do it."

Blake practically launches himself across the table to hug him. "You're amazing, thank you! This means so much, you don't know."

Mashuu squeaks, and Blake quickly releases him and wolfs down a few more bites of breakfast before stripping out of his robe. Mashuu takes longer to change, hands slipping on the garment's ties. Soon, Blake wears the servants' garb: a red pants and top combo made of light cotton with an easy tie at the waist, and probably the most comfortable thing he's ever put on. He sighs in satisfaction. He can actually move in this thing.

"When I get home, I'm stocking my closet with these," he announces.

Mashuu unties the matching handkerchief from his head and helps secure it for Blake.

"Ah," Blake says, catching himself in the mirror. "A commoner once more. What a relief." He laughs.

"You must keep your head down," Mashuu instructs quietly. "And say to the guard, *'Sumimasen'*."

"*Sumimasen*," Blake echoes.

They practice the word a couple times, and Mashuu shows him the proper way to bow as an omega, hands folded demurely in front.

"Don't make eye contact. Show the back of your neck. Don't speak unless spoken to."

"Got it. I'll stay out of sight. All I need to do is find Jay." He smiles at Mashuu. "Thanks again. You're a good friend."

Mashuu glances away. "You're a nice person, Blake-sama. I'm sorry."

"You're sorry for a lot of things, huh?" Blake shakes his head. "You didn't do anything."

"Oh!" Mashuu faces him again. "If you smile, please cover your mouth."

"Lot of rules, huh? I'll do my best."

"*Ganbatte kudasai.*"

Blake gives him a bemused smile, then remembers to cover his mouth. "*Hai.*"

He gathers the food tray and starts to the door but hears Mashuu murmur something and turns back around.

"What's that?"

"I..." Mashuu shakes his head. "*Nandemonai.* It's impossible to say."

Blake squints at him, something bothering him in the back of his mind, a little itching of some truth that he can't quite put a finger on. But there's no time to dig for it now. He has too much to do. He turns his back and slides the door open.

He steps out of the room with his head down and whispers to the guard, *"Sumimasen."*

The guard doesn't even grunt. He passes by, heart thumping, and forces himself not to hurry as he walks down the hall, beyond his dad's room and into another wing of the manor.

Most everyone is squirreled away in their rooms, and, given the early hour, he doesn't run into anyone more than another servant, who never even tries to make eye contact. He finds a place to stash the food tray and steps back into the main hall to decide what direction to go next.

He supposes the logical thing to do is to find Jay, but that's probably the first place people will look for him if he's found missing. No, he'll need to strike out on his own for this task. Maybe he can get back to the garden and trace that wolf's steps. It had to leave some sort of clue behind.

As he's considering it, two voices drift down the hall toward him. He stiffens and almost lays flat against the wall, then straightens up and peeks to see who's coming.

He nearly squawks when he recognizes Sayori and Akira striding resolutely side by side and speaking in rushed Oceanese. He bows deeply, making sure his face is completely out of sight. They approach, ignoring him, and begin to pass by, almost behind him, and the jackhammer that is his heart starts to slow right as Sayori pauses and calls something in his direction.

Shit.

His muscles lock up, and she calls again, impatiently. He unthaws enough to turn around and croak, *"Sumimasen?"*

He can almost hear Sayori rolling her eyes at him. "You're that *gaijin* servant, aren't you?" Thank God, she's switched to Lantish. "Follow us. I have a task for you."

Well, shit. He murmurs, *"Hai,"* and follows behind, brain churning out options to get away from them both.

Somehow, he thinks 'shove Akira through a door and run' isn't in his best interests.

The two resume their speedy pace, and Blake tags along behind them, hunched as deeply into himself as he can. They continue whatever their discussion is about, and Blake distinctly picks up the name 'Kimiko'. They take a flight of stairs to the next floor and stride across to the other side of the mansion. Sayori's tone grows hotter as they travel, almost to a snapping point, but Akira stays neutral.

Damn, I'm learning Oceanese when I get out of here.

They stop suddenly outside a door, causing Blake to slip to a halt. Sweat's broken out over his forehead, but he forces his breathing to steady. Sayori addresses him.

"My sister has been moved here for now. You will see to her needs. Bring her only food and drink and do not speak to her. You are bound by duty to follow the words of your alpha. Do you understand?"

He bows lower, feeling his back creak. "*Hai.*"

She pauses as if studying him. He doesn't dare move a muscle.

"Keep her whereabouts a secret," she says at last. "No more of her packmate attempting to get to her. Go on."

He swears he can feel himself developing scoliosis as he hunches for the door. The siblings' eyes bore holes into him as he passes. He's pretty sure he's stopped breathing entirely.

Please don't smell me. I'm just a random foreign omega. I'm no one.

He lays a hand on the sliding door, slowly pushing it open. Still, the Oshiros hover.

"Have you forgotten something?" Sayori's tone is sharper than a chef's knife.

He freezes. "*Sumimasen,* Oshiro-sama." It's all the Oceanese he can speak.

He hears her tapping her foot. "Work on your manners, omega. My grandmother may have allowed you to stay here, but your mother's past work only earns you so much grace."

He wonders what the Oceanese words are for 'fuck off', but the sounds of their footsteps retreating from him echo in the empty hall. He waits a beat longer to cool his head. How dare they talk about Mashuu like that. Damn alphas. He gives himself a minute to grind his teeth before unkinking his back and staring at the door.

Kimiko's temporary cell. Time to get to the bottom of all this.

He slides the door open and steps into a dimly lit room. As he shuts it behind him, her voice drifts from the other end, a mixture of exhausted and exasperated.

"Who have they sent to me now?"

He steps forward to look down at where she sits, and grins as her eyes light up in surprised recognition.

"Blake Fields at your service, Your Majesty."

Chapter Twenty

Tchaikovsky's "Piano Concerto No. 1"

Close to noon, Jay welcomed Elliot and Lance with a bear hug that cracked joints. Lance wheezed. "Give a guy some space!"

They broke up, and Elliot appraised Jay's looks. "Did you sleep in a gutter?"

"Who could sleep at a time like this?" He put on a serious face. "I don't know where Kim is anymore. They moved her somewhere. We have to figure out what's going on before dinner. If they decide she's a traitor, they might—" He choked a little on the words, but Elliot and Lance knew the penalty for treason in high-ranking wolf packs. Since the old days, werewolves would fight it out in shifted form. Death by combat.

"We'll do whatever we can," Lance said, laying a hand on Jay's shoulder. "Tell us whose kneecaps we need to break."

"Let's start with that guard, Satou. He has to know something. He's the last one who saw Kim before the attack."

"Let's go, *le capitaine*," Lance walked into the mansion, a man on a mission. Then he turned back and said, "Where is anything here?"

Jay, despite everything, nearly smiled.

***

"I know nothing more," Satou intoned in his flat voice, dark eyes staring straight through them. "I have already told the alpha everything."

Jay growled at the guy, more frustration than an attempt to intimidate. "You have to know something. You were the last person who saw her!"

"With respect," Satou rumbled in his deep bass, "You are not my alpha. I owe you no allegiance."

Jay stared, unable to think of more to say. This guy stank. There had to be more to it all. He threw his hands up and stalked away, and Elliot stepped into his space.

"Satou, please tell me what you told Miss Sayori."

Satou sneered at him. "I have to tell you nothing. You come from no lineage. You command no power. You are all pups. Leave this place and return home to your Lantish mechs and greasy food. Let Oshiro handle Oshiro business."

"We're not getting anything out of this guy," Lance grumbled. "We should regroup. Figure out where Kimiko is."

"Dammit." Jay glared at Satou, who didn't move an inch. Frustrated, he stormed up to the man and stuck his face uncomfortably close. "You're not getting away with this," he spat.

Satou narrowed his eyes. "There is nothing to tell you. Leave now. I have work to do." Hot breath puffed from his mouth, the scent of anchovies and seaweed. And something else. Jay frowned and pulled back.

"Right," he muttered. "Guess we're wasting our time."

He motioned for the others to follow him, and they abandoned Satou's quarters.

"We're doing this the wrong way," Elliot said softly. "We need to make friends, not enemies. No one trusts us. No one will help us."

Lance sighed. "They all hide when we come around. I think Sayori put a gag order on the servants."

"We have to do something. I'm not waiting until they're ready to hang her." Jay rubbed the back of his head. That smell lingered in his throat. Something irritating him like a caught sneeze. Couldn't quite place it.

"There's only so much we can do with the Oshiro pack. Have you spoken to your mother? If you can sway her opinion, she might help us protect Kimiko," Elliot offered.

Jay huffed. "Shit, you're probably right. I'll see what I can do. She seemed pretty set about the whole thing, though."

***

"I thought you'd never come to me," Sara said lightly, sitting at a vanity Jay was pretty sure she had brought from home and applying eyeshadow. "Thought you'd completely forgotten that family comes first, even in our direst times." She dabbed the corner of her eyelid primly.

"Kimiko's family sure doesn't think that," Jay groused.

"Well, look at what the girl did. Honestly, attacking two members of royalty in the middle of the night. So gauche!" She snapped the shadow case closed and plucked up a lining pencil, expertly maneuvering the makeup with one hand while pulling her lid smooth with the other.

"Do you *really* think Kimiko did that?" Jay could hear the exasperation in his own voice. His mother and her damn games. "Set herself up with a bloody rag and everything?"

Sara dropped the pencil and laughed. She almost sounded like a mockingbird. "Good god, *no*, of course she didn't do it. But there's always a scapegoat, isn't there? The question is, what do we gain from a different Oshiro in power?"

Jay felt his jaw pop from dropping too low. "How can you say that? She's my packmate! I'm not letting this happen to her!"

His mom didn't respond at first; too busy carefully applying lipstick a deep shade of garnet. She smacked her lips together and capped the stick, then swiveled on the chair to face him.

"I knew you would feel that way. You've always been a gentle boy, not suited to the politics of werewolves. But it's true: she's your pack, and that counts for something. I'll see what I can do." Her gaze softened a moment, taking him in. "You've grown a lot lately. Strange how I didn't notice." She returned her attention to the mirror to study the work she'd put in. "Oh, you nearly made me forget the mascara." She made a little tutting noise and unscrewed the mascara wand before leaning in close to the mirror and swiping up her lashes.

Jay hmphed and turned to walk out, not entirely satisfied with the conversation, when his mom called out, "Dear, try thinking like a wolf for a change. You might find it helpful among these packs."

Jay opened his mouth to spout something sarcastic, then clicked it shut. "Thanks, Mom," he grumbled.

***

Blake sits beside Kimiko as they speak in hushed tones. He's kept her company for hours, leaving once to fetch her a meal and returning with a plateful of temaki. They snacked together, Kimiko unloading a series of questions on him that all lead to the same conclusion: someone set her up and there are only a handful of people it could have been.

She sighs, one hand tapping an anxious beat on her knee. "It must be Sayori. She's wanted my place as eldest alpha since we were children. *Obaasama* always favored her. I hate to say it, but I think she's betrayed me." Her face goes sour as she admits her thoughts.

"It is pretty convenient for her, huh?" Blake watches Kimiko's fingers—*tap-tap-tap!*—and tries not to grab her hand to make her be still. "She gets all the glory with you gone."

"*Kuso!*" She spits and smacks her palm on the mat beneath her. "I spend all my life working for everyone else's expectations, and my reward is a knife in the back!" Her normally calm eyes blaze.

"I'm starting to think all you alphas get off on dramatic betrayals and court intrigue. It's like I'm in some regency drama."

She barrels on. "She must have had Satou plant that cloth on me. If this is true, there's a good chance she's bound him to her as a personal packmate." She snags his sleeve suddenly, turning the full intensity of her gaze on him. "You should be able to smell him on her. He comes from a fishing family; his whole line smells like the ocean. Unmistakable."

He shakes himself loose and crosses his arms. "Yeah. Okay. That'll go great. 'Pardon me, great alpha, may I smell you? Maybe take a lock of your hair?'"

"Do what you have to do."

He nods, pushing aside his sarcasm to think it over. "All right. Dinner is soon. I'll sneak in. They're all too self-absorbed to even notice me. I'm just another servant. I'll get close and then," he points, "*J'accuse!*"

She nods, lips pulled back from her teeth in a kind of smile-snarl. "Do what you do best, Blake. Tear the damn place down if you have to. Show them their snobby politics don't mean shit to you."

Blake barks out a laugh. "You're not the Kimiko I met in Jay's condo."

"You're right." Her teeth lengthen into points. "I'm pissed off."

***

Jay attended dinner but ate nothing. He had apparently been stricken with a case of lockjaw, because he couldn't seem to loosen up enough to chew anything. Lance and Elliot managed to find seats beside him, avoiding the pointed looks from around the table. They hadn't exactly had the warmest of welcomes. The packs sat around a U-shaped table, Sayori and Akira at the head, Lantish on one side, Servan on the other. Servants dotted the room, topping off glasses and waiting for instructions. Sayori informed them that Kim would join them at the end, to hear her sentencing.

Jay frowned at the other side of the table. Not everyone had joined tonight. No Alina, no Blake. Mikhail must have insisted that they stay behind. Damn, it would have been nice to have Blake backing him up. That meant he was now the only eyewitness present. Maybe Mikhail had planned it that way. He did say he wanted swift justice.

He flipped over the sparse bits of information he'd gleaned in his mind. Satou definitely had something to do with it, and he was also absent from the dining room. Avoiding an accusation, perhaps. Yet another witness left unaccounted for. The odds weren't looking great for Kim. It seemed everyone had already made their minds up about the situation.

Shit. What do I do?

He closed his eyes and took a long breath to quell his thumping heart.

There it was again. That annoying scent he couldn't place. It drifted subtly over the aromas of tea and food and alpha. Something papery, like a book long forgotten on a high shelf. He'd smelled it on the wolf and then again on Satou. He tried to pinpoint it, but there were too many conflicting scents, and it wasn't robust like most personal smells. It was more like a marking, a rubbing of someone's smell on another.

Like a packbond smell.

That was it; he wasn't smelling a personal scent, but rather someone else's scent rubbed on the wolf or Satou. They were the connecting link. The one behind all this.

Jay opened his eyes and squinted around the room.

One of you bastards did this. See if I don't figure you out.

***

Blake watches the packs eat from a position in the back corner of the dining room. He keeps his head down just enough so his bangs fall over his eyes. Not that it matters. He knows these people will never notice a servant; he's seen it every day waiting tables. The lack of eye contact, the vacant responses. He may as well be a fixture on the wall.

He tightens his grip on the water jug he carries. He maneuvered his way here early and took on the duty of refilling everyone's glasses. Even the other servants ignore him. After all, he's nothing but an omega. A foreigner. A stain on the Oshiro estate.

He steps forward to silently refill a water glass of one parliament member. Nearly brushes against the fabric of his dad's *montsuki*. They could smell him, if they wanted to. But he may as well be wallpaper, for all that they care.

That's right, you pompous jerks, I'm just some common servant. Wait 'til I tear this whole thing open.

He sinks back into his corner to stare at the back of Sayori's head.

He's been trying to fill her water glass since the start of dinner, but apparently she only takes sake. He'll have to find the right moment to get close.

Dinner can only last for so long.

***

"It's time to discuss the matter at hand," Sayori announced as the final dishes cleared the table.

Jay felt Elliot tense beside him. This was it, then. The door slid open, and in walked Satou and Kim. Her hair was down, though not tangled, and she kept her head up as she entered to a room of scowls and sank gracefully to her knees in the center space of the U table. Jay tried to catch her eye, but she remained staring straight ahead, almost aggressively at her sister.

Was she trying to tell him something?

Sayori continued, "First, the information my clan has uncovered. It seems that Satou noticed a single camera down while he watched the security system on his shift. He proceeded to alert my sister and follow her to the western hall. There, she dismissed him to check the remaining cameras. Upon reentering the camera room, Satou discovered the entire system hacked." She hesitated briefly before concluding, "The hacker utilized Lantish technology to do this."

A stillness settled over the room as the heads of state processed what she reported.

"What was that?" One of the Servan parliament members growled.

"Impossible," Will Travers said, crossing his arms. "We have nothing to do with this."

Across the table, Mikhail Volkov studied them with a mistrustful glare. "It wouldn't be the first time," he said slowly, "that Atlas has attacked my family."

"How many times do we have to tell you we had no part in your wife running away?" Will made a frustrated gesture with one hand.

"I have another concern," Sayori said, keeping her tone light. "You all know that my grandmother has passed, but what we have not announced are her suspicions that Atlas had something to do with it."

"What do you mean?" Will didn't mask the surprise on his face.

"I mean," she said in a clipped tone. "That on my grandmother's death bed she swore Atlas had poisoned her. And yet my sister was willing to invite you here, into our home, and play host. It would seem odd until you consider her split allegiances." She glared at Kim, who tilted her head up a little higher.

"Sayori-san," Jay's mom said, a gracious smile on her face. "You seem to be implying that we had a responsibility for this attack. I can assure you this is furthest from the truth. We stand to gain nothing by attacking Blake and Alina. Speaking of." She met Mikhail's angry gaze. "Where are they tonight? It seems inappropriate not to have their testimony."

"They've been through enough." Mikhail replied. "I hardly trust any of you at this point. Why should we stay here, if we are among enemies? I move to sentence this woman and abandon all talks of a treaty. I'm taking my son home and out of your Lantish claws."

Jay's stomach dropped. This was getting out of hand. He had to solve this. Clear his head. Figure it out.

He closed his eyes and reached for the wolf inside of himself.

***

Blake swallows. This is not going the way he imagined. His dad looks ready to tear the house down on his way out. That guy, Will Travers, has his face screwed up tight like he might go feral and leap across the table. And Jay... Well, he avoids looking too long at Jay.

He needs to do something. Anything. He's running out of time.

He sidles across the wall until he stands behind Sayori's left side. Just close enough to get one whiff, it's all he needs. He creeps forward.

***

The smell was coming from the head of the table, no doubt in Jay's mind. It hung there like a cloud, so clear to his wolf brain.

He opened his eyes and turned back into the room. The group had devolved into shouting, first Will, then Mikhail, back and forth. At this rate, it would end with someone's throat torn out. He had to make his accusation.

"Sayori—" he started, then a stampede of footsteps burst into the room with a shout.

A blond figure was tossed inside, stumbled, collapsed onto the ground face-first in an undignified heap. A glowering Servan guard stood over him, and several steps behind hovered Alina, face drawn in a tight expression.

Earlier thoughts of a confrontation flew from his mind. "Blake?" He stood to cross the room, but beside him, Elliot snagged his arm.

"Hold on," Elliot whispered. "That isn't Blake."

Sure enough, the cringing heap sat up and revealed an unfamiliar face. The boy, though blond and omega, was clearly not Blake. He sniffed and rubbed his cheek, where a dark bruise was beginning to form.

"What's the meaning of this?" Mikhail demanded in a severe voice. He stood to his full height and pointed at the boy. "Why does he wear my son's clothes?"

"I went to check on Blake," Alina said, stepping forward. "He'd been so quiet this entire time. I thought he might be ill. I found this impostor in his place."

The boy flinched and seemed to try to disappear inside his clothing. He sniffed and coughed and whispered a string of apologies.

Mikhail rounded on the poor kid, teeth bared in a row of impossibly sharp fangs. "Where is my son? Answer me, boy!"

"I'm right here!" The familiar voice came from the opposite side of the room, behind the head of the table. "Now leave him alone!"

Blake stood, clutching a jug of water and positively simmering with anger. He wore the servants' garb from head to toe, complete with bandanna, somehow avoiding everyone's notice until now. He stalked across the room to stick a finger in Mikhail Volkov's face.

"Don't you hurt him!"

"Where have you been this entire time? You were supposed to be safe in your room!"

Blake glowered at his father, looking very much like him for a moment. "I can't believe you! I spend my whole life afraid of you, and when I finally meet you, you act like some victim in all this. Then the moment you can control me, you lock me away and keep me from my *real* family. You're not a father! You're a tyrant!"

Everyone in the room seemed to hold their breath while waiting for Mikhail's response. After all, no one calls out a tyrant to their face.

Then Mikhail deflated. His teeth retracted, and he put a hand to his face. "My son," he started, but Blake would have none of it.

"Nuh-uh. Not buying it. You don't get to terrorize me and my mom for two decades and then play the contrite father. What were you going to do to Mashuu, huh? Hurt him? *Kill* him?"

"I wasn't—"

"You're awful, that's what you are! All of you!" Blake turned his wrath on the group of them. "You're all pompous, arrogant, and completely blind to what people like Mashuu experience every day. Alphas!" He threw his arms up. "What good are any of you?"

The group gaped at him, no one quite certain how to handle Blake's outburst. One of the parliament members muttered, "This is highly untoward."

A little tinkling of laughter interrupted the indignant air. Kimiko's shoulders shook as she laughed in a way Jay wasn't sure he had ever heard before. She sounded slightly mad. This brought everyone back to the matter.

"If the dramatics are over with," Sayori said, clearing her throat. "Kimiko Oshiro, you have been accused—"

"Hang on!" Jay stood this time, uncaring for the series of glares that came his way. "This isn't over."

***

Blake seethes, but some part of him *does* feel a little better. He huffs to catch his breath and remembers what his initial duty had been.

Dammit. Too late now.

He'll have to cause another scene or something and bust Kimiko out of here. Maybe throw the water jug right in Sayori's face...

But Jay is standing now, interrupting the sentencing.

"Kim was set up," Jay says in a clear, courtroom-esque voice. "And I can prove it."

"Oh?" Sayori waves a hand. "I hope you can back that up."

"There's a smell linking everyone involved in this. And if you trace that scent, you find the person responsible. I smelled it on that wolf, and I smell it in this room right now."

"*Really?*" Sayori says in a way that implies she's not buying it. "What smell is that?"

"Like old parchment. I know you can smell it. You probably know exactly who it came from."

Kimiko sucks in a breath and hisses, "*Obaasama.*"

Jay nodded. "Lady Tomoe's smell. It's all over Satou." He points. "He's her lackey."

Sayori sniffs. "So? That doesn't prove he's responsible. How does my grandmother have anything to do with this?"

"The wolf smelled like her. Kimiko doesn't smell anything like Lady Tomoe. You all can tell from here."

"True," Sara pipes up. "Not a whiff of parchment."

A mutter from the group.

"Well, Mr. Reed, it seems this is your word against Satou's," Sayori says. "He says the wolf smelled like my sister. You say it didn't. Who am I to believe?"

Blake snaps at her, "That's just what someone who's covering this up would say!"

She turns a cold eye on him. "I think we've had enough outbursts from you. You are by far the most uncouth, undeserving boy—"

"Speaking with that tone to him is the same as dismissing me," Mikhail growls. "Believe me, I will stand for no further slights."

"What about this kid?" Jay says it loud enough to interrupt their bickering. He points at Mashuu. "He smells like it, too. That paper smell. It's all over him."

"What? No." Blake steps up and wraps an arm around Mashuu. "Leave him out of this." But he smells it, too, so close to the other omega. Parchment paper.

The creeping knowledge in his head only makes him feel angrier and more stubborn. He digs in. "If any of you mess with him, I swear to God—"

"I'm sorry," Mashuu whispers, and it's enough to freeze the words in his throat.

He grips Mashuu tightly and finds his voice. "Don't be like that. Come on. They're bullying you. I... you..." Frustrated, he says, "Aren't we friends?"

Mashuu meets his eyes, and for the first time, Blake notices the flecks of green within the pale blue. "I have kept something terrible from you."

For the first time, Blake can't find words. Mashuu wiggles free of him and stands.

"I would like to make a confession, alpha," he says, a steel to his voice that's never been there before.

The room is silent, but the intensity buzzes as everyone leans in.

"Go on," Sayori says.

Mashuu takes a deep breath and announces, "My mother was a servant in the Volkov house before I was born." Blake wants to see his dad's reaction, but he can't tear his eyes from Mashuu. "She had orders directly from Master Oshiro—Lady Tomoe, as you call her—to infiltrate and take a spot as the queen's handmaid."

Mikhail's sharp voice intercedes. "What was her name?"

Mashuu acknowledges the question without breaking his attention on Sayori. "She went by 'Dinara Lebedev'. She stayed at the queen's side for several years."

Blake blinks, head fuzzy with the idea of his mother ever knowing Mashuu's.

Mikhail hisses out a low breath that sounds like a Servan swear. "Go on."

Mashuu tilts his head up and projects his voice louder than Blake's ever heard it.

"When the queen had a baby, my mother told her the Volkov family wanted them dead. She planted the idea in her mind that Mikhail Volkov planned to kill them to start a war with Atlas. Then she helped arrange passage away from Servos for her and the baby. She did this on Master Oshiro's orders."

Blake suddenly feels like his head is no longer attached to his neck. He sways and sits back heavily on his butt. Little pieces of his life's puzzle rearrange themselves and slip into place, leaving him empty and sick. Still, Mashuu continues.

"After she finished, she returned here and had me. Because of her successful work, Master Oshiro allowed me to stay and made me a servant. Bound me to her by duty. Then as she lay dying, she told me I must follow her orders. That I must do whatever was required to keep power under the Oshiro name and keep Atlas and Servos at war."

"Wait." Sara puts up a hand. "Are you telling us we've been fighting for two decades because of Tomoe Oshiro? Be absolutely clear."

Mashuu takes another deep breath. "I'm sorry." He breaks his gaze with Sayori and looks at Blake. "I can't keep this from you any longer. I wish I hadn't helped Oshiro-sama attack you."

Blake wants to wheeze a response, but his brain has shut down completely. Sara, however, pushes on.

"Which Oshiro? Be clear, I said. Who attacked Blake and Alina?"

Blake watches numbly as Mashuu points across the room to the head of the table.

"Akira Oshiro."

All eyes turn sharply to the front. There, the eldest sibling, the beta, Akira, sits with his fists clenched tightly.

"This is absurd," he starts.

"Is it, brother?" Kimiko speaks up. "Your wolf always looked like mine."

His face flashes darkly, then he insists, "The boy is clearly lying. He's nothing but a foreigner living off our charity. He has no right to dishonor our grandmother."

"Then what about that paper smell?" Jay counters. "You reek of it."

Akira's jaw works for a moment, and he hisses something through his teeth. Sayori reproaches him. "A snake lashes out the hardest when it's cornered. Akira, what have you done?"

"I've done nothing!" he protests. "Kimiko doesn't deserve to be alpha of this house! She's a traitor and a sneak! Packbonding with a foreigner—she shows where her true alliances lie. She worked with them to undermine this treaty summit."

Something clicks in Blake's mind. He stands to ask, "Did you know? About my mom? About the information your family fed her?"

Akira bares his teeth. "I'm not the one on trial. We're here to sentence my sister for what she's done and nothing more."

Blake steps closer. "You've been in the background this whole time. You knew what your grandmother did, and you still followed her orders." He crosses the distance between them and stops inches away. "My mom is in the hospital because of *your* family!" He clenches his fists so tightly he feels the nails cut into his palms. "You go around command- ing people like their lives don't matter, and they can't do anything but follow. You ruined our lives for political bullshit!"

Akira's face contorts. It seems no one has ever spoken that way to him in his life. He snarls at Blake, "Let the alphas talk, pup. You have no place amid greatness."

Blake feels a rush of anger so feral he could shift forms right there. Instead, he pulls his fist back and clocks Akira square in the nose. Akira's head snaps back, and stream of blood splatters over the *tatami* floor.

"I should knock your teeth in!" Blake rounds on the gathering, barely registering the shock and disgust among them. "You *know* he did this! He reeks of it. Let Kimiko go and arrest him instead. Put an end to the bloodshed their grandmother started."

Silence. The sour stench of judgment and disapproval.

He catches the look on Jay's face. Discomfort. He realizes he's stepped way too far out of place. He's out of his depth and utterly alone. Not even his dad will look at him directly.

Then, of all people, Sara Reed stands and backs him up. "Regardless of his actions, he's right. We've all been deceived here. I formally move to dismiss any standing claim of trespass between our packs. Here and now, let us begin a path toward peace."

He gets the distinct feeling that he's just landed a get-out-of-jail-free card. A murmur ripples through the crowd as they all consider the developments, what they stand to gain, stand to lose. Everything is a calculation.

At last, Will Travers stands and says, "Seconded." The Hunt leader follows suit.

Mikhail makes eye contact with Alina, a silent conversation passing between them in a moment. He glances back to Blake with a twist to his mouth, like he's caught between reprimanding him and apologizing for their absolutely screwed up history. Instead, he says, "I, too, wish for peace."

The parliament members mutter between themselves, but one by one step forward and declare support for the movement.

Sayori nods. "It seems we have an accord. That leaves retribution for the attack on the Volkovs. Brother—"

Before she can so much as declare him under arrest, Akira shifts forms. Before them stands the black wolf who attacked Blake and Alina. He snarls at the room, then turns tail and bursts through the paper and wood door that leads to the garden, running at full stride.

The guards in the room take action, shifting form onto all fours and dashing after him in a pack. The remaining people stare after them through a gaping hole that flapped torn paper.

Kimiko takes the moment to stand and announce, "We'll take Satou and Mashuu under arrest while they chase our brother. There are wrongs we need to right."

Blake knows he's pushing his luck by speaking up again, but there's no way he's letting this go. "Not Mashuu," he says. "He didn't do anything wrong."

"He helped in a plot to depose me," Kimiko replies. "He's culpable."

Blake tightens his jaw and steps between her and Mashuu. "No. You want to punish him? You go through me."

"Boy," Sayori warns, "you tread too far. Another step, and not even your father will be able to save you."

His fingertips are numb and his stomach churns, but he crosses his arms and glares at them. It's always been him against the world. This is no different.

"Hold up." Jay steps around the table and comes between them all. "Kim..." He passes Blake without looking at him and leans to say something in her ear too quiet for anyone else to hear. Her face softens. Blake can't tell which Kimiko he's dealing with—the one from Jay's condo or the pissed off one ready to tear the world from its axis. Or is this a different Kimiko entirely? She nods, and Jay straightens up, whatever he had to say to her finished.

She clears her throat and announces, "In light of recent events and the effort you made to assist me while incarcerated, I can pardon him." He exhales heavily, arms dropping his sides in relief. Then she continues, "However, Mashuu can't stay here. I expect him to leave this house and not return."

Blake twitches. His instinct is to fight back, do whatever it takes to spare him, but Jay catches his eye. Shakes his head once, almost imperceptibly. Then, Mikhail speaks up.

"He may come with us."

Blake and Mashuu send matching looks of surprise to him. He adds only, "I extend this offer on behalf of my son."

Mashuu bows. "Thank you. I'll be honored to work for the Volkov name."

Blake isn't sure this is the greatest solution of all, but at least it'll give Mashuu somewhere safe to live out of danger from any Oshiro.

Kimiko snaps her fingers at the remaining guards. "Take Satou. We'll handle his sentencing another day. First we need to complete the summit."

They spend the next few hours ironing out treaty details, signing documents, and finally sharing wine and liquor. Blake finds himself a little dumbfounded, sitting back and watching men and women who spent their entire lives hating one another pour each other drinks. Congratulations all around. He can't shake the feeling he's dodged some bullet.

Jay breaks away from the revelry and sits next to him.

"That was some show." He holds a cup of sake in one hand. "You really shook things up."

"You bailed me out, didn't you? What did you say to Kimiko?"

Jay sips from the cup. "I'll tell you some other time. Just promise me something, okay?" Blake doesn't say anything, but he goes on anyway. "Stop trying to fight the whole world by yourself. You're not the only person who cares about you."

"I..." He looks at his hands. "I guess I'm still getting used to that idea."

"We can work on it together."

"Together..."

"You think you can handle that?"

Blake reaches over and threads his fingers through Jay's. "I can try."

"As long as you don't punch any more people during peace summits." Then he chuckles. "You're kind of badass, though. Will Travers could never."

"I learn from the best."

Jay laughs, and Elliot and Lance notice them from across the room where they're talking to Catalina and walk over.

"Figures the lovebirds would find a quiet spot," Lance greets.

"When did you guys get here?" Blake scoots to one side so they can sit as well.

"Today. Hopped a flight as soon as we heard what was going on."

"You all have a really tight packbond, don't you?" Even he can hear the jealousy in his voice.

"If we don't look out for each other, who will?" Lance reaches across Jay to pass Blake a small cup of clear liquid. It smells like citrus. He takes it and sips. Definitely alcoholic.

"I think Jay might fall to pieces without us," Elliot says with a smile.

"What? Me? What about Kim?"

"She'd be fine. You know her."

Jay looks across the room to Kimiko, who stands, hair still loose to her thighs, discussing something with her sister. He chuckles. "You're probably right."

"I think she needs you guys more than you think," Blake says, sipping again from his startlingly strong liquor. "I think she was glad to see you all here." He thinks about the hours he spent with her, locked in that little room. She told him something then that he says now.

"Pack is everything. Without you guys, she'd be all alone."

It aches a little as he says it.

Lance grins. "I guess that's why she puts up with us." He holds up his cup in a toast. "To pack."

"To pack," they echo. Even Blake. He glances across to Kimiko, who had caught sight of them. She raises her glass as well.

***

They stay another few days in the Oshiro estate, working out details and discussing the future. Blake spends it avoiding the heads of state, especially the ones he's related to, and instead roves the grounds with Jay, Elliot, and Lance. Kimiko uses the time to meet with her sister and see to Satou's imprisonment. Akira was never caught, though they sent out news of his crime to their network of loyalists. She joins the rest of the pack one afternoon by the koi pond while Blake feeds the fish, tired lines under her eyes and a cigarette between her fingers.

"My grandmother made a mess for us all," she intones, voice heavy not with command, but exhaustion.

"What about the claims Atlas assassinated her?" Jay leans on the bridge wall between her and Blake.

Kimiko snorts, very un-Kimiko-like. "Just a dying word from an old woman. A final attempt to sow conflict. I'm dropping the investigation."

"Sorry you've had to deal with it."

"Not for much longer." She drags on the cigarette and blows out a stream of smoke. "I'm abdicating. Let Sayori deal with this; she's so eager to get at the problem anyway. It seems wrong to give her a taste of power and then strip it away. As it is, I have other business to attend to." She brushes her shoulder against Jay's.

"I guess that makes us the burnout pack." Jay chuckles. "Forever disappointing our families."

"Speak for yourself," Lance says with a sniff. "Elliot built a business from scratch, and I get to meet celebrities for my day job. Just because the two of *you* don't do anything substantial—"

Elliot gives him a friendly shove, forcing him back a step to catch his balance. "Big mouth beta."

"I don't see you standing up for yourself. You alphas are ridiculous."

"Speaking of our pack," Kimiko taps a finger on the bridge's red wood. "Are we gaining a new member?"

Eyes fall on Blake now, and he hesitates, handful of fish food halfway in the air. The koi stare at him as expectantly as the pack.

"Let him be," Jay says, coming to his rescue yet again. "We haven't even talked about it yet."

Blake tosses the fish food down and wipes his hand on his yukata, earning him a pointed look from Kimiko. "I can't think about things like that right now. I need to get home to Mom. Whatever happens next..." He feels the exhaustion that's built over the previous weeks weigh on him again. "If she doesn't recover..."

"Hey." Jay brushes a hand against the back of his neck. "We'll be back soon. And we'll do everything we can for her."

Blake nods. "I'm coming to terms with the idea that my life is drastically different forever now."

"Hopefully for the better."

"I guess we'll see."

"No running off again, okay? I nearly died from stress."

Blake makes a face at him. "I'll do what I want." Then he smiles. "But I'll let you in on the shenanigans next time."

"I'm good at shenanigans, you know."

"Don't worry, Cowboy, I know."

Kimiko clears her throat. "Someone's here for you."

Blake leans around Jay to see Mikhail and Alina standing at the base of the bridge, watching them. He nods a greeting.

"We wish to speak with you privately." Mikhail announces.

"Of course." Kimiko motions for the rest to follow, leaving them alone with the fish.

Mikhail steps onto the bridge beside him and instead of his usual perfect posture, leans forward and mimics Blake, forearms resting on the bridge railing. They don't speak for a long moment.

"Sorry," Blake says suddenly. "I blew up back then. I guess you could say I've got some repressed issues."

"You've been strained. You're right when you say I can't imagine what your life has been. But," he glances sideways, "next time avoid physical confrontations. And shouting. And, ah, insults."

"Basically, don't do anything that comes naturally. Got it."

"Do you get in fights in Atlas? Is this normal for you?"

"If you're concerned your firstborn is a ruffian, don't worry about it. The last time I punched someone was in grade school. These days I usually just flip them the bird."

"Ah." Mikhail doesn't seem to know if he's joking or how to take it. "Well. I assume you still wish for passage to Atlas? Home, as you say?"

"Atlas *is* my home. Sure, you're my dad, but that doesn't change where I grew up. Where my heart belongs."

"I'm happy to see you returned there, but I ask you do me a favor."

"I'm not changing my name."

"Keep in touch. I don't expect you to inherit my role, but perhaps you would like to see me once in a while?"

It's said so hopefully that Blake can't help but smile. "Sure. I don't think Mom will like it, but—"

"About your mother." He says it suddenly, throwing off the flow of conversation. "I spoke to my head mage. It seems there is a way to help her after all."

Blake stares, barely able to comprehend. "How?"

Mikhail reaches inside his robe and pulls out a necklace. Blake squints at it. It's the exact match to his own pendant.

"Have you seen this before?"

Blake digs out his own necklace from under his clothes. "This, right? Mom gave it to me. She used to keep it hidden in a box with some old documents from when I was a baby. I found it once, and she got so mad at me." He rubs his thumb over the wolf insignia. "She gave it to me before she went into full time care. Said it would protect me."

"This is the counter to her curse. The farther she is from these pendants, the weaker she becomes, until she wastes away to nothing. It's an archaic method of bonding mates that my family has used since before the Pack Years. If she keeps these two together, then the effects of the curse will recede." He passes the necklace to Blake, closing both hands around his. "She has my blessing to live a free life with you."

Blake stares at the jewelry in his hand. All along his pendant had been the answer.

"That was it this whole time?" He hears himself ask.

"That's it. Servos has some...rather stringent traditions when it comes to choosing mates."

Blake is too busy thinking about healing his mom that he almost misses Mikhail's next words.

"Will you be mating the Reed boy?"

Blake chokes. "Are you serious?"

"As serious as seeing that man naked on your balcony."

"Ah, God, that really wasn't supposed to happen. I'm sorry. He—we—" Blake gropes at the air for the right explanation. "We don't...do weird stuff..."

Mikhail holds up a hand. "Believe me, I neither want nor need to know the details. But if you are considering taking him as your mate, then I need to know. It's my duty to see to the marriage pact." He says it like it's the most normal thing in the world.

"Marriage pact? I'm not wearing some cursed medallion my whole life."

"Nothing like that. But you do understand what your relationship represents, politically speaking? It's the union of our packs, our countries. It's the very essence of the treaty. When you mate the boy—"

"Jay," Blake interrupts, too dazed to say anything else.

"Jay," Mikhail corrects. "When you mate him, it's more than a bond between alpha and omega."

Blake's stomach decides to make a break for it and escape out his mouth. He hiccups and claps a hand over it. "We're not there yet," he settles on saying. "I don't even—" Shakes his head. "Never mind. The only thing I want right now is to get home to Mom."

Mikhail studies him before saying softly, "All right. But be aware I will be part of these proceedings if things continue. Marriage pacts take time to plan. Expect a year at least of negotiations and preparation. And," a little emphasis comes into his voice, "I hope you will consider a ceremony in Moskva. It's only appropriate we host the event."

It's all another reminder that the life he knew, that he expected to live, has flown clear out the window.

"I'll keep it in mind." He tightens his grip around the silver necklaces. "Thank you. For everything. I don't know what I'd do without..." He shakes his head, then, after a brief hesitation, wraps his arms around Mikhail in their first awkward embrace. His dad barely has a chance to raise his hands before he pulls away.

"Thank you," he repeats, dropping both pendants around his neck for safe keeping. "I used to wish I never had a dad at all, but now...well, you're not bad. At least not as bad as I expected."

"And you're not at all the man I expected to meet. It pains me that I never saw you grow up. Or had the chance to keep you out of trouble."

"Sorry, trouble's my middle name."

Mikhail frowns. "Nadine did not dare to name you—"

Blake laughs and waves his hands. "A joke! It's actually worse than that. I'll take it to my grave, though."

Alina steps forward, breaking momentarily into their conversation. "I must thank you again for saving me. You are brave, *syn*."

Blake leans back on the bridge. "And here I thought you didn't like me."

"I don't," she replies flatly. "You're a rude, childish boy. But you're family, like it or not."

Family... That left one question.

"Is Mashuu my brother?" He wishes there were a more elegant way of asking, but he needs to know. "Is that why you're taking him in?"

Mikhail exchanges an uneasy look with Alina before saying, "It's a story for another time. Understand, these things are incredibly complicated."

Yeah, as complicated as a man of power sticking it wherever he wanted.

Blake purses his lips. "Does Mashuu know? Does anyone?"

"Another time," Mikhail insists.

"My family tree is so twisted," Blake mutters, more to the fish than anyone else.

"You must forgive your father," Alina says. "These matters are difficult. There's always another side to every story."

What's he supposed to say to that? He turns around, leaning back on the bridge's rail on his elbows and staring up at the blue sky.

"Damn, and here I thought all I had to worry about was being a son. Now I'm a big brother, too..."

Not to mention there's Mikhail's actual legitimate heir, Kirill, who he has yet to meet. Blake doesn't even know how old he is. Suddenly, his solitary life seems so much larger. He rasps out, "I have cousins, too, don't I? Aunts and Uncles and maybe even a grandparent no one's told me about." He whirls on his dad, a rise of panic in his voice. "What about Mom's family? What happened to them?" She's never mentioned any siblings or parents to him. The two of them have been an island for his whole life. She always reprimanded him when he brought them up as a pup, so he learned to let it go, accept that there would never be anyone but her in his life.

Mikhail's mouth creeps downward. "We'll need to discuss this in the future. Perhaps for now it's in your best interest to put these thoughts away. We'll return to our respective homes in a day or two. I'll be in touch, and we'll make time for the things life has so far stripped from us."

Blake catches his breath and nods. There's nothing he can do right now about extended families or history. One step at a time. First, home to cure Mom. Then he can deal with whatever comes next.

At least he knows that in his search to cure his mom he found a dad as well.

Chapter Twenty-One

Mahler's "Adagietto"

B lake steps into his mom's hospital room hesitantly. She sleeps in bed, stable, quiet, and barely breathing. The steady beat of a monitor accompanies her breaths, and the sound of the nurses' shoes squeaking on the tile echoes outside. He crosses the room and takes a seat beside her. The pendants tinkle against each other underneath his shirt, and he pulls them out.

They don't look like anything special, really, kind of like him. Just another bit of shine in a world that loves to dull. He slips them over her neck and watches them settle into the hollowed-out spot of her clavicle. She's so thin now, barely any muscle left on her. The IV bag beside him drips a clear liquid that he assumes keeps her hydrated enough to live. Her eyes, sunken deep into her face, twitch and open.

"Blake?" It's barely a voice, more like a puff of wind between leaves.

"I'm here, Mom." He puts his hand over hers, afraid any sudden move might break those fragile, bird-like bones.

"I've been dreaming." Her eyes, somewhat cloudy, flick around the room before falling on him. "You were far away. I called to you, but you kept walking. I wanted to chase you, but the ground was like quicksand, and... and..." She heaves a sigh and blinks a few times. Some clarity returns to her gaze. "It's been a long time since we've spoken, hasn't it?"

"Sorry. I was...out of town." Lame, but true.

"You left me." Not an accusation, but a prod for more.

"I wanted to cure you. I had to find out how. So I went—okay, Mom, don't freak out."

Her eyes, still so dark in their sockets, narrow. The look reminds him of her reprimands from when he was a pup. "What happened?"

"I went back. To Servos. To see Mikhail."

For a moment, she says nothing. Then she shifts in her bed, plants an arm underneath herself and props up.

"You did *what*, Blake Legato?"

Ack. The middle name. The embarrassing middle name. Yep, he's in trouble.

"Look, I only did it because I wanted to help. You were getting so bad, and there was nothing any doctor could do—"

She shudders, but manages to sit up fully, swaying slightly. He reaches out to grab her, but she wags a finger at him.

"I'm fine. You see? You worry too much! Tell me you didn't actually go there. Please."

Blake chews his lower lip. "You want the truth or a lie?"

"Blake!" The indignancy in her voice makes her sound so young again, like her old self. He loves her for it.

"I went, but only for a little bit. Then I went to Oceana."

"*What?*"

"I punched the oldest Oshiro son. Don't worry, he deserved it."

"I... *what?*" The clouds in her eyes have evaporated, but she's trembling from the effort of holding herself up. He reaches to help her back to the pillows, but she bats his hands away. "Tell me what happened."

"Well... here's the thing. Everybody knows. About me and you. Atlas, Servos, Oceana, and I guess by now the news is out and it's all over the place. There was a summit at the Oshiro estate, all about us and the war, and, God, there's so much to tell you. But, basically, there's a treaty now. I mean, someone tried to kill us while we were there, but we stopped them, and now there's peace between the countries. That's good, right?"

She gapes open mouthed, reminding him of the koi fish he fed not that long ago. He rushes on.

"Mikhail was never going to kill us. It was all a plot by some old, dead lady. Long story. Anyway, Mikhail is actually kind of nice, in a weird way. He told me how to save you and says he's sorry and—Mom?"

She's fallen back against the pillows, dazed eyes to the ceiling.

"All these years," she mutters. "I protect you all these years, and you go running off the moment I can't watch you anymore. What kind of mother am I?"

"What, no, Mom! You're the best! I needed to do something, but it's okay now, right? You're safe. We're safe."

A knock at the door, and Jay peeks in.

"Am I allowed in?"

"That depends," his mom says with fire under her voice. "Are you that alpha boy who dragged my son all over creation?"

"Yes, come in, and *no*, he didn't. I went by myself. I don't need anyone's permission, you know."

"You should have asked mine."

Blake takes a breath, holds it, and says, "Mom, you weren't in any position to talk. You barely knew where you were or who I was. The fact that you're so lucid now means everything I did was worth it!"

She quiets, retreating to sullen silence like a defense. But it's enough to know she's awake. Alive and maybe even at the start of a recovery.

"Maybe Dr. Dunn should check on you. From what I hear, you've been out for a week." Jay slides up next to Blake and takes a seat. He attempts his charming grin, but she's having none of it. She turns her head away and zones him out.

Blake rubs the back of his head. "At least you're up now. I'm sorry I left, but I had to try. I love you, Mom."

That softened her. She reaches for his head and gives it the tiniest of squeezes. "I love you, too. I'm sorry things have been so hard on you. I only ever wanted..." She blinks rapidly and turns away again.

"It's okay!" Blake leans forward to brush her thinning hair away from her cheek. "You did your best. Better than! We're good now. We don't have to hide anymore."

She lets out a shaky breath and says, "Dear, would you get something for me?"

"Anything."

"There's a nurse here. Ms. Lizzy. If you ask her, she'll get me some chocolate milk. Don't ask any of the other nurses; they'll tell you no. But Lizzy is a nice lady. She'll let me have a sip. Would you, dear?" She blinks her wide blue eyes at him, and he stands up sharply.

"I'm on it!"

"I can—" Jay starts, but Blake is already out the door.

***

Jay frowned. Alone with Blake's mom, and she didn't seem like the frail, dying woman they had left behind. A piercing blue stare beckoned him to meet eyes. As soon as he did, she smiled, suddenly gracious.

"That should give us some time. Lizzy works day shift. He won't find her here."

Oh boy. Buckle up.

Theresa shifted to sit up fully with a small grimace before settling with her thin arms crossed in her lap. "My son loves you."

It was a simple statement, but it knocked the wind out of him.

"Uhh—"

"Hasn't he told you? Hm, maybe he's not hopeless after all. But it's there, even if you're too stupid to see it. If an artist loves you, they'll show you their heart."

The words cut, and he narrowed his eyes. "What's this about?"

"What's your name, alpha?" The word wasn't supplicating, but rather venomous. It contrasted sharply with the easy look on her face.

"Jay. Or Julian. Whichever you prefer." Better to try to win the woman over, at least.

"Well, Jay or Julian, whether or not you know it, my son loves you, and that's not something I'm going to sit idly by and accept."

He held his tongue, asking only, "Meaning?"

"Meaning," and she said it like a teacher berating a dull student, "I will not now nor ever accept you as his mate. Do you understand me, alpha? He's not a toy for you to play with, and I didn't travel across continents to save my son only to see him snatched up again by the likes of you." She jabbed a narrow finger at him.

Speechless, Jay stared at her. At last, he found his words. "I won't take Blake from you. That isn't what I want at all; I know how much he loves you. Maybe one day you can see how much I love him."

Theresa's lips pressed into a thin line. Bony and frail with eyes like blue fire, she reminded him of the old witch tales he'd heard growing up. A veritable Baba Yaga.

The squeaking of the doorknob broke their staring contest. Blake stepped into the room.

"Sorry, Lizzy's not on tonight. I could find you some milk in the cafeteria maybe."

Theresa's expression took a U-turn. Her face blossomed into a smile, and she replied, "Don't worry about it. I was meeting your boyfriend. He's very handsome. What a catch you've landed!"

"Ah, Mom, don't be embarrassing." Blake avoided their eyes and returned to his seat. "Besides, Jay knows he's hot. His ego doesn't need to hear us say it."

"Hey." It certainly was *nice* to hear it said, anyway.

"Why don't you get some rest?" Theresa laid her hand on Blake's cheek. It looked shriveled against his smooth skin. "The bags under your eyes could hold enough clothes to fill a shop."

Blake took her hand in both of his. "A lot's happened. And I found out I don't sleep well on planes."

They had come directly from the airport. Blake wouldn't have it any other way. It was true he looked tired, but jetlag coupled with recent events was reason enough for it. It nagged Jay, though, a feeling like he hadn't done a good enough job making Blake comfortable on the flight back. Or in the days at the Oshiro estate. Or ever, really. Had they ever slept well together? The few nights they'd shared had been filled with triple-X activities.

He chewed the inside of his cheek and blurted out, "You can crash at my place. It's not far, and I'd rather you get a good night's sleep."

Theresa shot him a hawkish glare.

Blake hummed. "Well, I was thinking I'd stay here tonight. Keep Mom company. I can sleep in a chair, no biggie. Then tomorrow I can find out if I still have an apartment." His eyes suddenly shot open, full alert. "Oh my God, I need to call Terri. She's gonna flip on me."

"Not at midnight." Jay put an arm over his shoulders. "You need sleep. You can call her tomorrow."

"Go on, dear," Theresa prodded with a smile. "Get your sleep and come back tomorrow. I don't want you tossing and turning in a chair all night. But, hey," she caught him under the chin and set a parental stare on him. "Sleeping only, got it? No hanky panky."

"Ew, don't call it that. And, yes, sleep only. Got it."

She nodded and waved them out, adding, "I'm so proud of you, Blake. And what a dashing young man you've got!" Her smile could tame a snake.

Jay sucked in a breath as Blake leaned over and kissed her cheek. Theresa glared at him over Blake's shoulder.

Oh God, she's just like Mom.

***

They returned to Jay's condo half an hour later, Charlie greeting them at the door with a pot of herbal tea. They kicked off shoes, abandoned bags at the door, and settled on the couch. It had been replaced with a new cerulean one while they were gone, and the cushions nearly absorbed them. Blake leaned back and stared up at the smooth ceiling, where fan blades rotated lazily.

"What happens now?"

Jay considered it. Now was the aftermath. The treaty announcements, interviews, news articles, and criticisms. Now was the time to shore up defenses while the rest of the world analyzed every little thing they had done.

"Now we sleep. Everything else is tomorrow."

"I need a new phone."

"Tomorrow."

"I need to call my boss and explain why I no-call-no-show'd for two weeks and then beg for my job back."

"Not even tomorrow. Screw that guy."

"I need a job, Jay. Some of us have bills to pay."

"Okay, then. Tomorrow. We'll deal with it all tomorrow." Jay caught Blake around the waist and scooted him close. "You don't have to function on all cylinders constantly. Let yourself be tired, for crying out loud."

Blake leaned his head against Jay's chest and exhaled. The hot puff of breath sent a tingle down his spine. "Sorry, I'm kind of freaking out again. It feels like I've been sleepwalking for two weeks. Living another person's life. And now that I'm back it's all going to fall apart." He put a hand over his eyes. "But I think... Mom's gonna be okay, you know?" His voice trembled as he spoke, suddenly raw. "All this time, and I think she'll finally be okay." He pulled in a sharp breath and coughed. "Shit. Sorry, not my best look." He wiped his cheeks and forced a chuckle. "Thought I couldn't cry anymore. Thought I'd lost that." His face twisted as he fought against the coming tears, and he got out, "I'm just so happy she's alive. You don't know what it's been like. Watching her disappear. Wondering every day if she'd even remember me. She did everything for me, and I couldn't sit around anymore while she suffered. I couldn't—" His throat closed up and he wheezed through some tears, burying his face in Jay's shirt. They sat, silent but for his choked breathing, and Jay soothed the air with relaxing scents as much as he could. A few minutes passed, and Blake recovered himself.

"Thanks." He sniffed and wiped his red nose. "Sorry that kind of came out of nowhere. I feel better now. Tired as hell, but better. You're a good guy, Jay. Thank you."

"I didn't—"

"Do anything. Yeah, you did. But don't worry about it. Can we sleep forever now?"

Blake's hair caught on his damp cheeks. Jay brushed it away. "Sure, Buttercup. Whatever you want."

"Bed, then. As nice as your new couch is, I'd really like to sleep in a giant alpha bed." He stood and proffered a hand. "But you heard my mom. No hanky panky."

Jay took his hand and stood, frowning a little. "You sure? Not even some over-the-clothes groping?"

Blake took on a mock serious tone. "Sir, I ask that you respect my mother's boundaries. She said nothing tonight. She didn't say anything about tomorrow morning."

Jay grinned. "Tomorrow, then."

"Like everything else."

Chapter Twenty-Two

Mozart's "Symphony No. 40, Molto Allegro"

Tomorrow comes, sunlight peeking through the curtains with the heat of Jay's mouth on Blake's neck. Blake mumbles, barely registering the hands that slip beneath his nightshirt and caress his bare skin. He's tired still, half caught in a dream about flying, and not entirely in the mood for heavy petting. He rolls away from Jay onto his stomach.

"Sleep now," he slurs. "Sleeeeeep."

Jay retreats, pausing long enough to plant a chaste kiss on Blake's temple, and Blake feels the weight of the bed shift as his alpha leaves the room.

Time slips away again, distorting his perception, and he awakes sometime later to the smell of frying meat.

His stomach rumbles.

He sits up, rubs gunk from one eye, and glances around. The light through the window is bright enough that it has to be midmorning at least. No Jay, but the smells creeping down the hallway convince him his significant other haunts the kitchen. He clambers out of bed and adjusts his twisted nightclothes with a yawn. Thoughts of his to-do list provoke a nervous flutter in his chest, but he smashes them down and leaves the room to find Jay and hopefully breakfast.

As he rounds the kitchen corner, a sizzling sound cuts through the air, and the smell of smoked meat permeates the condo. Jay stands over the stove, shirtless, hair loose, and tongs in one hand. What Blake hopes is bacon sputters in the pan.

"Oh my god, tell me that's for me."

"I've got good news, then." Jay pokes the meat and motions to the coffee machine. "What would you like to drink? That thing makes lattes, if you want. Heads up: I have no idea how to use it."

"Then why do you have it?"

"It looks nice on the counter."

Blake snorts. "You're kidding."

Jay flips the bacon and says, "Halfway. It's Elliot's. He insists I keep one here for him. I don't bother it, and it doesn't bother me."

"I'll see if I can coax something out of it." Blake crosses to Jay first, though, wrapping arms around him and leaning to the side to peek in the pan. "It smells good."

"Turkey bacon. Less fat, still got all the flavor. Do you like oatmeal? I thought oatmeal would be good."

"Mmm, yes, sounds great." He kisses Jay's shoulder and goes to examine the coffee machine. A contentedness warms him, even as he struggles to make the thing expel liquid. It feels right, being here, even if it won't last. He smiles as the machine sputters and spits out his reward. The mug fills and keeps filling. His smile drops.

"Shit!" Coffee flows over the rim of the cup and down the countertop.

Jay glances over his shoulder. "Something I should worry about?"

"Nope, nope. Nothing!" He hastily snatches up a roll of paper towels and drops a wad on the mess. "Just a miscalculation."

"I'm pretending I don't see anything." Jay eyes the dripping counter.

"Good. Do that." He wipes it all up and switches off the machine before things can escalate.

"Food's done. Tell me it's all clear." Jay arranges the bacon on plates beside their bowls of oatmeal, peeking sideways at Blake.

"A-okay, Captain." Blake tosses the wet towels into the garbage and flashes a thumbs up. "Cleared for takeoff."

Jay smiles at him, and Blake's heart does a little somersault. Sometimes the best moments are the simple ones.

***

After breakfast, Blake borrows Jay's phone to dial up Terri, hoping her new phone has her old number. She answers on the third ring, tone business-like.

"Hello, this is Terri Davis. Who may I ask is calling?"

"Howdy, stranger, just one omega to another."

She drops the unfamiliarity and squeals. "Blake! Finally! Do you know how worried I've been? I called you a million times!"

"Sorry. My phone got stomped. Literally."

"I saw you on TV! That *was* you, right? I haven't stepped into some parallel universe?"

"It's a long story."

"You've been keeping secrets." He can practically see her wagging a finger at him. "Where are you? Can you meet for brunch?"

"I already ate, but I can manage a drink."

"Mimosas?" Excitement in her voice. "My treat. But you owe me a juicy story."

He grins. "Deal. I've got the best you can imagine."

He can feel her energy through the phone, vibrating in her voice. "Meet you at Sundrop? I can be there in fifteen."

"Grab us a table. I'll be right behind."

She drops her tone low, teasing. "Is Jay coming?"

Blake glances across the table, where Jay watches him with a bemused smile. "Maybe next time. I think we can spare him the gossip."

"Okay, but you can't keep him away from me forever! I've heard rumors about you two, you know!"

"Oh God, that's terrifying. I'm not in one of those drama magazines you read, am I?"

"I'm bringing a copy so you can sign it. Guess the headline."

"I'm not playing this game."

"'Runaway Prince's Whirlwind Romance'. It's got a picture of you in your café uniform."

"No. No, it doesn't." He closes his eyes and rubs his temple with his free hand.

"You look good! The ruffles suit you."

"I'm not listening to this. It's insane."

"Meet you at brunch." She blows him a kiss through the phone before hanging up.

Jay takes the phone back and asks, "You want to talk about it?"

"I want to bury my head in the ground and never come out." He rubs his face with both hands.

"One step at a time. Want me to drive you there?"

"No. No chauffeur. I want to take the train like a normal person."

"I think those days might be behind you. The tabloids will be prowling for candid shots. Better to dodge public places as much as possible."

Blake groans and leans back in his chair, tilting it off the front legs. "Life will never be the same, will it?"

"It'll settle down. Give it a few weeks."

He drops the chair, perhaps a little too hard, and asks, "And then what? What happens after everyone forgets I exist?" It almost comes out like an accusation.

Jay shifts, discomforted. "I don't know. What do you want? I'm happy with you here, you know."

An invitation. Blake pauses as he considers it.

"I like it here," he admits. "I like you. A lot." Jay perks up at those words, but Blake counters them. "But I'm not ready for some domestic thing. Sorry. I know you probably want more from me."

Jay reaches across the table and closes a hand over Blake's. "I want you in my life, Blake. In whatever way you feel comfortable. We'll figure it out. I—" He catches himself, then tightens his grip on Blake's hand. "I love you."

Blake freezes. A confession at the dining table. Maybe not the most romantic place, but sincere.

Reciprocate, idiot!

But the memory of his dad discussing marriage pacts and mating ceremonies echoes painfully in his mind. Too much pressure too soon.

"Thanks."

Jay's expression drops.

Great job.

"Look, I appreciate it. And I like you, really. I'm just...still coping with everything. Please don't think I don't care."

Jay plasters on a smile. "I get it. Too much, too soon. We'll take our time. Come on, let's get you to your friend."

They change clothes, and Blake follows Jay to his car, unable to shake the feeling that he messed something up.

***

After dropping Blake off, Jay drove home and tackled his workout routine. His mind spun, barely counting reps.

Blake needed space and time, and that was totally reasonable, but, dammit, he wasn't used to being the one on this side of the relationship. How many men and women had he left in the dust over the years? Surely this was his comeuppance.

Theresa had said Blake loved him. Maybe she'd been messing with his head. A game, like the ones his own mother played. He'd put it out there, and he couldn't help it if Blake's avoidance of the issue stung. He still had his pride, after all.

His muscles ached as he curled the weights, but it was a good feeling, something to revel in. Much better than the ache in his chest.

He'd have to do something to break through Blake's defenses.

He switched to squats, sweat dripping down his lower back, when his phone rang. He sighed, replaced the weights, and toweled off his face before checking his phone.

Mom.

His gut clenched. What could she possibly want now?

"Hello?"

"Good afternoon, sweetheart," she cooed on the other end, a little too syrupy. "Sorry to bother you right after you get home, but I was thinking—"

"No."

"You haven't heard me speak! Manners, Julian."

He rubbed his temples and said, "Fine. What is it?"

"I'm going to throw a party."

Not what he wanted to hear. Her parties could start world wars.

She went on, "To celebrate the treaty. We need you there. You and Blake both."

His jaw tightened, and he rubbed it, trying to ease the stress out. "He wants to stay out of the limelight. So do I, for that matter."

She dropped the saccharine tone and said plainly, "Darling, that ship has sailed. Now you either take control of the tabloids, or they control you." Before he could retort, she spoke over him. "Might I add that appearing together at a formal event like this is a good start. As far as the papers are concerned, right now you two are the reason for the treaty. Miss this chance, and the rumors could turn vicious."

He'd seen it happen. One of the Hunt pack basically went into hiding after a mate scandal erupted over their secret affair. Nothing the people loved more than a good social lynching. He'd avoided it his whole life by ostracizing himself from his family, but now things were too far gone. Blake's story was a tantalizing one, and people weren't likely to drop it.

"I'll talk to him. He probably won't be happy about this."

"In fact, bring him over for dinner. We need a proper conversation, I think. A chance to start again on the right foot."

He almost bit back *darling, that ship has sailed*, but kept his tongue. Instead, he replied, "I'll talk to him. He's with a friend right now. I'll let you know if we decide to show up."

"Seven o'clock. Don't be late." She hung up.

Jay wrinkled his nose as he stared at the phone, half considering tossing it out a window. Instead, he picked the weights up again, adding an extra five pounds to either side. If Blake wasn't ready to run from him, he would be now.

***

At seven o'clock sharp Blake and Jay stand outside the entrance to the Reed family estate, waiting for the mechs to let them in. Somehow, the four stories and sculpted gardens are less impressive now that Blake's seen Moskva and the Oshiro manor. That anxiety from the first time meeting them has dissipated now. After all, his secrets are all out now, and there's no going back.

"You doing okay?" Jay eyes him.

"Hungry. What do you think they'll have?"

"Not pizza, if that's what you were hoping."

"Aw, don't crush my dreams like that. I haven't had good pizza in weeks. Dad gave me pizza in Moskva, and they put mayonnaise on it. Mayo! What is wrong with rich people? I bet if your family served pizza, there'd be some weird balsamic reduction drizzled on it." He sticks his nose up to emphasize his point.

"Preaching to the choir. I like my pizza with red sauce and pepperonis, the way god intended."

"You sure? You don't want to put, like, corn on it or something?"

"A cardinal sin."

"I seem to recall something about pineapple..."

"That's a perfectly acceptable topping."

"Well, you lived on the east coast a while. They must have rubbed off on you. That place is pizza mecca."

Jay grins. "We could go there sometime, if you like. Eat pizza from some hole-in-the-wall joint. There's this awesome place down the road from Times Square, but you'd never know it's there unless someone points it out. They have pizza slices bigger than your head."

Blake grins back at him. "You're talking my language."

"It's a date, then." Jay slips his hand into Blake's, intertwines their fingers and squeezes.

The mechs arrive, and they step into Reed territory to the distant smell of meat and salt and wine. They follow their guides through some rooms opposite the conservatory they first visited, until arriving in a large dining room. An oblong, dark wood table dominates the center, flanked on all sides by high-backed chairs, ten in total. Smaller cocktail tables dot one side, where floor to ceiling windows open out onto a veranda. Rich blood-red drapes adorn them, and—Blake shouldn't be surprised, but is anyway—a full-blown tapestry depicting Sara and Colin Reed's nuptials hangs from the opposite wall. It looks like it could cover Jay's alpha-sized bed and then some.

The family stands clustered around one of the cocktail tables, wine glasses or brandy snifters in hand. They appear to be discussing an investment deal with some national corporation. As Blake and Jay approach, the talk dies down, and Sara beams at them.

"Wonderful to see you both again! So glad you could join us."

Like she gave them a choice.

She steps up, kissing Jay's cheek, and then of all things, pulls Blake into an embrace. "Welcome to the family, sweetheart!"

It would have irritated him if it didn't shock him so much. He figured they'd be cross with him for not revealing himself sooner. He'd prepared for chastisement, not exuberant welcome. All he can manage is a noncommittal grunting sound.

She continues like he responded just as enthusiastically. "We're so pleased to have you. There's much to discuss. Plans need to be made."

Uh-oh. That can't be good.

"Dear, you're hogging him all to yourself." Colin steps up and holds out a hand. "A pleasure to see you again, Blake."

Blake reaches out, preparing himself for a firm shake, but instead the man turns Blake's wrist upward and bends to sniff it lightly. It's an old custom and more polite than Blake ever expected. Any words he might have offered dry up in his throat.

"To think all this time, you were in hiding. It's a pleasure to have you join us. We never expected Julian to do much for the family, but you're quite the catch."

Blake can't help himself but retort, "Yeah, like I'm a salmon, and you're all fishmongers."

Unruffled, Colin replies, "You seem in high spirits. We've just finished the aperitif. Let's sit and take the next course. We can discuss matters pertaining to your mating ceremony."

Whoa, hold up now.

But they usher him to a seat, and immediately a smell erupts from the door leading to the kitchen as a mech in a suit delivers bowls of soup to the table. Beyond the smell of bisque wafts meat and pastry. Saliva fills his mouth. It's been a while since he's been in want for food, but the urge to grab as much as he can while it's available hasn't left him yet.

The mech delicately places a bowl in front of him, soup the color of fall leaves. He sniffs. Pumpkin, undoubtedly. Without waiting for a cue, he snatches up a spoon and sips. Sweet and mellow, the taste of ripe pumpkin and fresh basil fills his mouth. A wine glass beside goes from empty to full, a nearly clear shade of gold. He selects the glass of water instead.

"The chefs do amazing work with the simplest ingredients," Sara muses. "Perhaps soon we can do a meal test with you. Sample some options for your reception."

He almost chokes on the bisque.

"Mom, I don't think we're at that point yet," Jay says, eyes sliding sideways to Blake's expression.

"Oh my, have you two really not discussed it?" She taps her fingers on the tablecloth. "After all you've been through, we assumed—"

"You assumed wrong," Blake says, probably too abruptly.

Her eyebrows knit together, then with all the confidence in the world, she says, "If it's a sexual problem, remember we have two other children who could better meet your needs."

Jay slaps a palm to his forehead. Blake feels his jaw drop, then shuts it with a click.

Sara goes on. "I'm only saying you have options, Blake." She sips some wine, savoring it, before adding, "Isn't that wonderful? Your mother had none whatsoever."

Blake frowns and reaches for his wine glass. If it's going to be *that* kind of dinner, might as well take the edge off. After a long pull from the glass, he sets it down and says, "I'm not rushing into anything. You all might have grown up with political expectations, but the only expectation my mom put on me was to live a free life."

"No one's *trapping* you, darling. In fact, I think you'll find being a part of our family will afford you a number of freedoms you never experienced as a commoner."

The mech returns, sweeping away their bowls and spoons, only to double back a moment later with little plates of mushrooms. Blake sniffs the appetizer, detecting cheese and garlic. He takes a big bite, and is rewarded with a juicy, earthy taste full of savory cheese and the light crunch of breadcrumbs. His momentary beef with Sara is forgotten.

"Damn, I could eat a mountain of these," he mutters.

"We'll put it down for the reception menu," Sara says lightly.

He wrinkles his nose. "Why so eager to get us married? You hated me a few weeks ago."

Sara waves a hand, diamond bracelet swaying. "Bygones. Our misunderstanding was unfortunate, but knowing who you are now, what upstanding character—"

He's caught with a mouthful of wine as she speaks. He swallows quickly enough to interrupt her. "You don't care who I am. You care *what* I am. I was a commoner, and you hated me for it. Now I'm a prince, and you can't wait to sink your teeth into me. No thanks. Not buying."

He feels Jay tense beside him. This is clearly not going the way any of them want. A mech swings by him and refills his wine glass.

Catalina clears her throat. "Maybe we should get through appetizers before talking about mating."

"Tell me," Sara says, ignoring her completely. "What will it take for you to accept this family? There is little we can't provide."

He feels like a hog at the market. He knows he shouldn't drink more wine, but he snatches the glass up anyway and drains half of it.

"Time," he says after dropping the glass to the table. He doesn't let go of the stem. "And space. You might be used to political marriages, but when I mate someone, it'll be because I want them. Forever. Got it?"

Jay looks tense enough that the delicate silver fork in his hand might bend in half.

Blake feels a pang of guilt. He hastily adds for his alpha's benefit, "Not that Jay can't be that person. I just need time. To figure it out."

"I see." Sara polishes off the last mushroom on her plate and dabs her mouth with the crimson napkin. "Well, it wouldn't hurt to at least have one party, would it? Something to introduce you to the world. To celebrate the treaty and all you've done to manifest it."

Around once more comes the mech, carting off their plates and forks and returning with small plates of salad. Blake squints at some of the ingredients, taking a little nibble on a green thing he doesn't recognize. Not particularly tasty.

"Artichoke heart," Jay mutters to him, as though he shares the same feeling towards it. Blake scooches the pieces off to the side of his plate.

Sara clears her throat softly, a reminder that he hasn't answered her. He grimaces. "Can we at least get through dinner without talking world politics? Or is this the usual for you?" He swigs from his glass again, and somehow, it's magically full once more. Those mechs are good.

"Oh no," Catalina pipes up, a little smile on her face. "Sometimes we discuss the trade market and how our investments are maturing. And then sometimes we gossip about which pack leader wore what at the last gathering."

Gabriel sorts and says, "The Hunt pack wouldn't know style if it slapped them in the face. Did you see what Asin wore when he arrived at the Oshiro manor? He must have bought that suit at a thrift store."

Catalina, mirth sparkling in her eyes, winks at Blake. The levity keeps him sane.

"Perhaps over dessert, then," Sara says. "A marriage between our families would behoove all of us, mind you. A perfect match, really. Did you know we have some royal blood ourselves? Our family line traces back to the royal packs of Europe, when it was called that. We'd be proud to have you."

Jay pretends to stretch in order to lean over to Blake's ear and whisper, "Rodriguez." Blake has to silence a chuckle. The wine is going to his head quickly, and Bad Decision Blake is starting to clamor for control. He takes another sip.

Once salads are polished off, in comes the mech once more to deliver the main course, something Blake guesses to be a beef wellington, a dish he's only seen in cooking videos online. It smells so rich he can feel his blood thickening. A fat slice appears on a plate before him, accompanied by an assortment of roasted vegetables. The puff pastry flakes away on his fork as he cuts a bite.

"Holy crap," he says as the salty meat and buttery pastry meld on his tongue. "I can't believe people live like this." Earthy mushrooms and pâté complement the savory tenderloin. He's never in his life eaten something this fancy. It's almost too much for his palate.

"Only the finest for the Reed pack," Colin says smugly.

Bad Decision Blake takes control of his mouth, and out pops a question. "Who were you before you became a Reed?" He knows from the tabloids that Colin had married into the name, and not the other way around.

Colin finishes a mouthful before replying, "Pack Castille. Not quite so prestigious as the Reeds, but Sara deigned to have me nonetheless."

She gives a tight-lipped smile. "The pairing was only natural. Your family ran Hemosynth. We knew it would work even when we were teenagers."

"And then a couple months later, Gabe came alone. What a coincidence." Jay rolls his eyes.

Sara shoots Jay a withering look. Apparently, this is one topic they do *not* discuss at dinner.

Blake motions with his wine glass, liquid teetering precariously close to the lip. "Nice to know you're fallible."

"It's one thing the two of you will not need to concern yourselves with." Sara works to regain control of the conversation. "But making the choice to mate early can have many benefits."

"Such as?" Blake stabs a potato with his fork, wine glass momentarily abandoned. Jay smoothly reaches for it, scooting it closer to his plate than Blake's. Blake ignores the gesture and grabs Jay's glass instead. He knows he's being obnoxious, but his head is mushy, and he can't seem to help himself. Bad Decision Blake is in total control.

Sara speaks as though the two are not silently bickering over a wine glass. "Why, positive media coverage of course. There's nothing the tabloids love more than a Cinderella story. Except a hit piece. If there's one thing you learn, dear, let it be that the media is not to be left to its own devices. You get out ahead of a story and you can shape it into what you want.

"The papers see the two of you together, a mating mark on your neck, and there's nothing but congratulations and speculations on the honeymoon. They see you, a fullblood omega, without an alpha, and suddenly it's suspicions of infidelity and wrongdoing. What would you prefer: an article about your virtues or one about your sins? Or perhaps one about your dear mother's?" She leaves the implication hanging.

Blake drops the wine glass, and it spills the remaining drops onto the tablecloth. He pushes his chair back and stands. "I think I'm full." Head spinning with wine and loathing for himself and the world around him, he adds, "Thanks for the meal, you heartless animals."

He leaves the room without waiting for any of them.

***

Jay stared after his omega as he disappeared from the room. No one made a bid to bring him back.

"Shit, why'd you have to talk to him like that?" He rounded on his mother, teeth bared.

Sara shook her head. "He needs to be prepared. Life isn't easy for us. You've avoided it for so long, but it only gets worse from here on."

Jays stood as well, tossing his napkin on top of the half-finished slice of wellington. "I'm out. This isn't worth it." He followed Blake's trail to the gates.

Outside, Blake stood by the driveway, arms wrapped around himself. Jay took an uneasy step toward him. "Hey," he started, intending to apologize and try to smooth everything over, but Blake cut in.

"It's a good thing you followed me. My epic storm-out doesn't exactly work when I can't drive myself out of here." He didn't turn to face Jay but stared resolutely at the gates.

"It didn't seem worth it to listen to them anymore. Plus, you're way cooler than I've ever been. You practically told my mom to shove it. I've never..." he trailed off with a hum. He'd been so coddled all his life, always thinking himself the family rebel, but he had never really rebelled. Like his siblings, he'd done his duty, even if they'd never given him much of one. "Damn," he muttered.

Blake glanced at him, tilting his head. "Something wrong?"

"Sometimes we're not the people we think we are."

Blake snorted, looking away again. "Sounds about right." Then, softer, "I'm not upset at you. Or really even at your mom. She's awful, but the world made her that way." He squeezed himself. "I don't want to become that."

Jay laid a hand on his shoulder. "You won't. You're, ah, how do I say this? You're violently yourself."

Blake gasped out a wheeze of laughter. He faced Jay with a brilliant smile and said, "You know, that shouldn't make me feel better, but somehow it does."

"Just promise me you'll lay off the wine next time? You'll make yourself sick."

"Sorry. It's just so much. I needed a way to cope. This is why so many rich people are day drinkers, isn't it?"

"I've been known to drink with lunch," Jay admitted. "But let's not make it a habit, okay?"

"Deal."

Jay ran his thumb over Blake's cheek. "Ready to go home?"

"Yeah. And," he huffed a little sigh, "you can tell your mom I'll do the party she wants. I'll even play piano for the crowd. But Mom stays out of it. All of it. I don't want to hear about press or rumors or foreign dignitaries anywhere near my mom, got it?"

"We can go tell her now."

"Nope. Let her stew a while. Give it some time, you know?"

Jay shook his head. "You might be better at this than you think."

"Your mom's a viper," Blake said plainly. "I don't plan on getting bit."

Jay nodded. "Fair. But we have to be a team from now on. Otherwise, she'll use us against each other." He thought briefly of Theresa, glaring at him from her bed, and shook it off. "You and me, okay?"

Blake smiled. "You got it, Cowboy. Now why don't we get back? I got a few ideas for an after-dinner party."

"Oh, like donuts?" Jay forced himself not to grin.

"Shit, now that you mention it..." Jay's shoulders slumped, and Blake laughed. "Kidding! But, I mean, we can get donuts after..."

Jay chuckled and took Blake's hand in his, kissing his fingertips. "Sometimes I think all you care about is food."

"Not true. I think about sex, too."

"I guess that's good enough." He nipped lightly, eliciting a squeak from Blake. "And here I used to think you were some kind of celibate."

Blake rolled his eyes. "Hardly. You don't know what I used to do when I was alone."

"Mm, maybe a demonstration is in order?"

Blake leaned into him, eyes sultry. "That can be arranged."

The sound of the car driving up broke them apart. The color was high in Blake's cheeks, and he laughed a little sheepishly.

"God, we are such dorks."

But Jay was too enamored to feel self-conscious. He followed Blake into the car.

He'd follow Blake anywhere.

Chapter Twenty-Three

Chopin's "Fantaisie-Impromptu"

Blake speaks to Jay's mom again the next day. Doesn't have a choice, really, because a sleek car pulls up to him while he's walking from a visit with his mom, and the door slides open automatically, revealing Sara inside. She curls a finger at him, beckoning him in. It feels like a shakedown. He slips in, astounded for a moment by the champagne bar, and sits across from her.

"Do I need to be worried about my kneecaps?" are the first words out of his mouth.

"Not at all, dear." Sara treats him to her dazzling smile, made all the more predatory by the sunglasses blocking out her eyes. "But it's time we have a private chat. It seems we're not quite seeing eye to eye."

"I'm going to do the party, all right? Don't worry about it."

"Of course you are. That's not what we need to discuss." She pours herself a glass of wine and sips, leaving a red imprint of her lips on the glass rim. Through her dark glasses, Blake feels her eyes bore into him.

"You need to shape up." She says it bluntly. No fake smile in her voice.

"What?"

"This attitude you've grown. Don't think it makes you any more attractive. I rescued you in Oceana, turned the tides in your favor. For the sake of your father, everyone is overlooking your behavior, but it better not happen again. You think the leaders of the world will approve of your mouth? Don't fool yourself into imagining some paradise where everyone just gets along. We're wolves at heart, Blake Fields. Any excuse to rip your throat open, and they'll take it."

Blake's mouth becomes an arid desert. This is not the conversation he expected to have today. Sara goes on.

"You might take my family's and my welcome to you as weakness. As a bargaining chip. It is not. Don't think for one moment I wouldn't do what I felt was necessary to protect my kin."

"What are you talking about?" He barely hears his own words.

She pulls off the sunglasses and stares hard at him, the irises of her eyes a terrifying crimson.

"You endangered my son." A low growl creeps into her voice. "Your thoughtlessness and lies put his life at risk. That's not something I'll forget."

The implication hangs heavy in the air between them. The guilt that's plagued him since the first wolf attack rears its head again.

"I'm sorry. You're right. I should have told him the truth sooner. I shouldn't have tried to go it alone." He sighs hard. "I'll be better. We'll be a team from now on. I didn't mean for things to get out of control like that." Shakes his head. "And, yeah, I lost it in Oceana. I've been on edge for weeks now, and it all came out at once." His hands tighten into fists. "But I'll improve. I'll do your party, and I'll even play piano if you want. Just leave my mom out of it, okay?" He meets her eyes, green versus red. "Please."

"That will do," she says crisply. She replaces her sunglasses. Blake realizes she's been holding her wine glass so tightly her knuckles are white. She sips again. "If you break my son's heart, there will be no more apologies. You won't have any other country to run to, no new identity to hide behind, because I'll hunt you like our ancestors hunted humans. Never forget that some of us are more wolf than man. You can thank me for that lesson later." She taps a button on the door, and it slides smoothly open. "Go. I'm done with this conversation."

Chastised and more than a little freaked, Blake scampers out of the car. It pulls away, and he stands in the parking lot, catching his breath and realizing once again that he's in way over his head.

***

Blake drops his bag on the floor beside the door in Jay's condo and catches his breath. He feels off-kilter since his talk with Sara, head spinning with her threats and accusations.

She's right, though. He had put Jay in danger, and he's been selfish enough not to apologize.

"Shit," he mutters.

"Blake, you home?" Jay calls from the back, the sound of footsteps heading toward the door.

"Here," Blake says. "I'm alive." It's almost impossible to believe.

Jay rounds the corner, all smiles. He stoops to kiss Blake's cheek. "Everything okay? You smell freaked."

"Can we sit for a minute?" He catches Jay's hand and squeezes. "I owe you an apology."

Jay tilts his head to one side. "For what? Did something happen?"

Blake guides Jay to the couch and curls up a little as he parses out his thoughts.

"I'm an idiot."

"What's this about?"

"Seriously. I lied to you and did some stupid shit, and it put you in danger. I'm sorry."

Jay touches under his chin, bringing it up so their eyes meet. "Water under the bridge. I'm just glad it all worked out."

Blake frowns. "Did it? Isn't it all still going on? I mean, what if everything falls apart now? What if I do something stupid again and start a war or get you hurt?" He grabs Jay's hands in both of his and squeezes it, trying to communicate the whirlwind of feelings these months have left in him. "What if you decide you don't want me anymore?"

"Where's this coming from?"

"I'm scared, Jay," Blake forces himself to admit. "Because I've never loved anyone else before. You know what I mean?"

A crease appears between Jay's eyebrows. Blake pushes on.

"And if I love someone that means there's space in my life for another person, and there's only ever been me and my mom. Suddenly, my life is so much bigger. Extended family, pack, in-laws... I don't know if I'm ready for that."

"I'm not asking for you to—" Jay starts, but Blake is on a roll now.

"When I feel like shit you make it better without even trying. When I'm halfway across the world, you're all I'm thinking about. You know, it's really rude to wreck a guy's head like you do. There are days when I can't think straight because all I can see is your smile. It's messed me up. All my decision making has gone to shit. But I know one thing for sure."

Jay doesn't say anything, just seems to hold his breath.

"I don't want to be alone anymore. I'm sick of being a soloist. And the only person I want to accompany is you. I love you, Jay."

Jay breaks out into a grin bright enough to blot out Blake's worries. "Here I thought you'd never say that."

"Yeah, well, I'm not entirely heartless."

"Thank you. I love you, too, you know."

Blake leans forward, bringing their lips together. He lingers, savoring his alpha, eyes closed, hands intertwined, and then pulls away to meet his gaze.

"I think we should celebrate."

"Oh? Any ideas?" A small smirk.

"A few. Most of them involve your bed. One features a blindfold."

The smirk grows. "I have a few toys that might suffice."

Blake kisses him again, then murmurs in a husky voice, "Why don't we see where the night takes us?"

***

Three days later, Blake fidgets with the cuffs of his tuxedo. Jay's mom had it rush tailored for the party, and while it sits perfectly to his measurements, the stiff fabric bothers him. The stiff people here bother him, too, but he's learning to grin and bear it.

They're at the Reed estate after dark, the garden lit up with strings of lights and decked out in linen-covered tables with hors-d'oeuvres and a carving station. He currently hovers around the chocolate fountain, dipping fruit in it with relish. Soft piano music floats through the air from the pop-up stage in the center. They had moved the Bösendorfer outside for the occasion, and now a musician regales the crowd with a smooth rendition of Debussy's "Nocturne". Blake bites into an orange slice as he mentally critiques the musician's choice of rubato.

To his right, at the end of the table, Jay is caught in a long string of meet-and-greets with various dignitaries. He currently speaks to a man with a magnificent bushy beard and bald head. Blake has a vague notion that he's the Raja of Bharata, or some such thing. He's certainly rotund enough to be a head of state. The man glances his way as if overhearing Blake's thoughts. Blake waggles his fingers in hello and eats the rest of the orange slice. It's almost time to play. Sara gave him the schedule of events this afternoon, and he's to play a piece of his choice before the crowd at ten p.m.

Not that he's worried about it. It'll be his first time playing in front of a crowd, but he'd brought his keyboard to his mom's bedside and practiced with her for the last three days, and he feels plenty confident that he knows the piece back to front. In fact, it's kind of exciting, the thought of playing music for so many people. The only other person he's used to sharing this with is Terri, and now he gets the chance to express this love with an entire crowd. Maybe sometimes a dream can come true.

He stretches his fingers. The pianist brings the nocturne to a close and steps away from the piano with a short bow. Sara steps up, and the crowd, who's been murmuring their dignitary conversations at a low tone, falls silent.

"Thank you, everyone, for being here. It's a joy to host a celebration of one of the greatest achievements in modern policy. We're beyond pleased to look into the future with Servos on our side." Polite applause. "At this time, I would like to welcome a new face to the stage. You all may have heard his story, but he's here to share more than that with you. Blake, darling, please join me."

Blake wipes his fingers on his pants and steps forward, the crowd's many eyes burning into him. He walks, head up, one foot in front of the other, to the stage and takes a spot beside Sara, who smiles and addresses the audience again.

"This is Blake Fields, though he was born with a different name. Surname Volkov, son of Mikhail. He's been instrumental in forming the peace between our packs, and, like his father, is a magnificent musician." She steps to the side. "Please tell us about yourself."

Blake licks his lips and takes the spot behind the microphone. He glances around the crowd until his eyes fall on Jay, who flashes him a subtle thumbs up.

"Hi. I'm Blake, and until a few weeks ago, I was a waiter at an omega café."

A murmur at that, like it's a scandal for him to admit it.

"Then I met Jay—Julian—and life changed drastically. I've been keeping a secret for most of my life, something I thought would get me killed. But it landed me here, in front of all of you." He clears his throat. "I'd like to play something now. A piece that was supposed to be a secret, but was released, anyway. Frederic Chopin's 'Fantaisie-Impromptu'. I hope you'll enjoy it."

He abandons the microphone and sits at the piano, its keys gleaming a welcome to him. A small thrill burbles in his chest. He takes a breath and plays the first chord.

***

Jay watched as Blake opened the song with some low rippling notes. He could see flashes of Blake's hands at this angle, as they picked out the keys with spearing accuracy. It amazed him how agile those fingers were, how confident their every stroke. The song, itself, danced through tempos with ease, leaping up and down the piano like an excited pup. He'd heard Blake practicing part of it on his keyboard, but the subtle differences surprised him. Here the sound was robust, even outdoors, and there was something fuller about the tone that he couldn't quite place.

Blake slowed, left hand still working its way back and forth, while the right sang out longer notes. He swayed slightly with the rhythm, eyes closing once in a while as if to better feel the music through his fingertips. Jay had never cared much for classical music, but he could listen to Blake play all day. Could watch him as he transported himself to wherever an artist went when they created. Blake seemed so free, and Jay felt a longing to join him by the piano, to sit beside him and let the music wash over them both until the rest of the world didn't matter.

Suddenly Blake picked up speed again, fingers blasting through an array of chords and spiraling notes, jumping high only to descend in a mad whirl. His hair tousled as a breeze passed through, but he didn't even seem to notice the strands that fell in front of his eyes.

Words from days ago sprang up in Jay's mind.

If an artist loves you, they'll show you their heart.

He watched Blake sway, corralling notes into a repeating pattern with one hand. The other played a few longer notes, everything drawing together to a soft close. He held the final chord, until, head bowed, he removed his hands from the keys.

Damn. I'm one lucky son of a bitch.

Applause broke out as he stood and gave a small bow. He walked to the microphone and said plainly, "That's how I feel about everything right now."

Their eyes met over the crowd. Blake smiled, and Jay felt his heart soar.

****

They make it home from the party before two, which, according to Jay, makes it a success. Blake, not much of a night person, dozes in the car on the way back. After his performance, he was bombarded by well-wishers and compliments, and it was frankly exhausting to be the shiny new toy at the party. He only comes awake when they step into the shower together, hot steam suddenly defogging his mind.

"I don't remember saying we'd shower together." He rubs one eye and leans into the spray.

"Yeah, but you also didn't say *not* to do it." Jay reaches for the soap over his shoulder.

The hot water pelts his skin and erases any stress from the night. He steps in closer to Jay. "Tell me you plan to do more than wash up. I'm only staying here until I find a new place; we should take advantage of it."

"You read my mind." Jay abandons the soap and pulls Blake flush to his body. They kiss under the heat of the shower spray, Blake's mouth opening for Jay. Hands grope, stroking reddened flesh and hardening cocks. A thrill of excitement blurs Blake's mind, a foggy desire that denies all reason.

Jay flips their positions, pressing Blake's chest to the cold tile wall and grinding hips against his backside. Blake arches his back and wishes sorely for some waterproof lube. They'll have to abandon the shower for the bed at this rate. Then the presence behind him disappears, leaving him dripping underneath the shower head. Before he can so much get a word out, Jay reappears, bottle in hand.

"Thought we could use this." He squeezes a dollop of lube onto his fingers.

Blake grins and waggles his hips. "You read my mind."

Jay's fingers are strong but gentle, slipping inside Blake one at a time, stretching and working him with care. Blake focuses on his breathing, head tilted against the wall, hands bunched into fists as strokes of pleasure make his legs shake. It isn't enough. He needs more of Jay, a closeness that only sex can achieve.

"Come on," he pants. "Fuck me already."

"Don't need to tell me twice." That little rumble is in Jay's voice, the deep growl of his arousal. He removes his fingers and aligns their bodies, left hand covering Blake's own on the tile. His cock presses firmly against Blake's ass, larger than his fingers, but not unbearable. Blake presses back, moaning as it slips inside. Jay buries his face in the back of his neck and grunts, right arm wrapping around Blake's waist to hold him in place.

"Shit, that feels good." Blake widens his stance and rolls his hips back. "Come on, alpha, fuck me harder."

No other invitation needed. Jay steadies Blake's body and pulls back halfway before slamming roughly into him, eliciting moans from them both. He repeats the motion, pounding a rhythm into Blake that leaves him breathless underneath the shower, rivulets of hot water splashing away the sweat as it prickles his skin. Blake gasps as Jay's right hand takes a firm grip on his dick, stroking him, sending him another step closer to the edge, where pleasure threatens to drown him. Lips fasten onto his neck, sucking, sharpened teeth grazing the sensitive skin where a mark would go. Such a thin veil keeps them from mating, and his swiftly evaporating self-control wants to tear it down.

"Jay," he moans, voice a needy trill. "I can't...much more..." Heat surrounds him, invades him, steals his breath away. Now the cold tile is a relief from the onslaught of hot pleasure. He presses against it as Jay picks up speed, biting his shoulder hard enough to hurt. Maybe it's the sudden flash of pain to contrast the building pressure, but Blake loses it. He thrusts into Jay's hand, spilling himself over those strong fingers in a series of shaky spurts. His knees nearly give out on him, but Jay grabs his hips and holds him fast. If it were possible, the repeated grinding of Jay's cock inside him would make him come again, but he's too spent. Jay thrusts roughly a few more times, then grunts as he comes inside Blake, pressing as tightly as he can to him. Then, only ragged breathing and the sound of water falling fill the shower.

"Don't," Blake starts to say when Jay steps back, slipping out of him and letting a slick of heat roll down the inside of his thighs. The water splashes it away like everything else. Blake overbalances, nearly taking Jay down with him, but they catch on the soap dish and hold steady.

"I was about to say, 'Don't let go of me'," Blake says wryly. "But you beat me to it."

"My bad. Did I hurt you?"

"I'm fine. Legs are just a little tight. You try angling like that and see where it gets you." He gets his feet under him and pauses before stepping away. "Jay," he starts, feeling unsure of himself for a moment.

Jay catches the change in his tone. "Everything okay?"

Blake nods. "Better than. I don't think I've ever felt this good in my whole life." He rubs an absent-minded circle into Jay's chest with one hand, the hot water spilling off the two of them, somehow making this conversation feel insulated and all the more private. "I've been thinking about everything. And, well, I'm not ready to mate yet, but I thought—" he coughs and shifts his eyes elsewhere, cheeks burning now not from the shower stream. "I thought maybe a promise mark would be nice."

Hands on the sides of his face pull him to meet Jay's eyes. His expression is serious, but excitement flickers there.

"You already know how I feel," he says. "I'm not going to pressure you."

"That's why I thought a promise mark would be good. It's not permanent, but it means something. And it's not because of anyone else," he says sternly. "I'm doing this because I want to, and that's all. Everyone else can suck it."

"Noted." Jay's fingers trail down Blake's side to his thigh and squeeze. "Let's do it in my bed. I want it to smell like you."

Blake shivers despite the hot shower. "That sounds perfect."

The wrap up the shower faster than the sex and tumble into bed together. Blake lays back, damp hair sticking to the pillow, and Jay crouches over him, eyes gleaming gold. Anticipation clings to the air like humidity on a summer day.

"It might hurt a little," Jay warns. His hands brush down Blake's torso, leaving a wake of goosebumps. They settle on Blake's thighs, nudging them open firmly but gently.

Blake's dick overcomes all self-control and stands at full mast. He exhales shakily. "I don't care." His eyes rake over Jay, taking in the man's body—intricate tattoo, firm muscles, cock as hard as Blake's—and lands on Jay face. Tenderness there, a deep affection that makes Blake's brain go fuzzy.

"I hope it does," he adds. He wants to feel every second of Jay's teeth sinking into his skin, marking the scent gland on his inner thigh, bonding them perhaps not for life, but enough so that anyone would smell that they belong to each other. A promise of more to come.

Jay smiles, revealing his sharpened canines. "Let me know if it's too much."

"When it comes to you, I can never get enough."

Jay nods and scoots lower until his lips graze the inside of Blake's right thigh. "You smell amazing," he murmurs.

Their pheromones have shifted to something stronger since arriving in bed. Not lust for sex, but deeper. Mating pheromones. Bake reminds himself this is just a promise mark but can't shake the mental image of Jay's teeth in his skin. He grips Jay's shoulders as gently as he can—his nails have lengthened and he can't seem to make them retract—and manages to say, "I'm ready."

Jay growls a little pleased sound in the back of his throat and sucks at the spot he intends to bite. If he does it right, he'll bite into one of Blake's scent glands and their signature scents would mix. Blake realizes distantly that maybe they'll mess it up, and oh shit, what if he bites the wrong place?

Then Jay's teeth press into him, breaking through the skin and sending a shot of pleasure-pain through his body. He sucks in a sharp breath, hands clenching on Jay's shoulders, and spasms underneath his alpha.

Jay holds him steady, one hand moving to his chest and pressing firmly. Blake's rapid breathing slows, and his head falls back against the pillow, back arching slightly. Jay teeth sink a little deeper.

It hurts, but *fuck*, it feels good.

Jay lingers, letting their aromas mingle in a scent-thickened air, and at last pulls back enough to give the spot a lick.

Blake pants, every molecule of his skin vibrating like a bolt of lightning has struck him. Jay laps at his skin, easing the pain away until all that remains is a pleasurable tingle that permeates to his fingertips and toes.

"Jay," he moans softly, eyes still squeezed shut. "I think I'm gonna lose it."

Jay's attention switches from Blake's thigh to his dick, tongue running roughly up the underside, sucking gently at the tip, until Blake groans and shoots a load down his throat. The tension melts out of Blake's body, and he peeks open his eyes.

Blood streaks Jay's mouth.

His eyes shoot open the rest of the way, and he gasps, "Am I bleeding?"

Jay cocks his head to one side. "Not anymore. Did you...not expect that?"

Blake's hand rushes to his thigh, feeling a toughness under the skin where Jay bit him, but no wound. "I don't know. Nobody ever bleeds in the movies."

"I bit you. Of course you bled. Werewolf saliva heals it up, though." He wipes his mouth.

Blake feels a little silly at that. "Right. Of course." He forces a chuckle. "Guess I should've seen that coming."

Jay leans over him and kisses his forehead. "Everyone will know now."

"Know what?"

Eyes still a deep gold, he answers, "That you're mine."

He kisses Blake deeply, and Blake can taste musk and sex and a hint of copper. They make love again, bodies melding like their scents, giving and taking everything they can, until they collapse, exhausted and utterly intertwined.

Blake can't keep his eyes from closing. Too warm, too relaxed to do anything but doze. Jay curls around him, blocking out the rest of the world.

"I love you," Jay whispers, squeezing lightly.

Blake yawns and nuzzles his alpha. "I love you, too."

Blake yawns and nuzzles his alpha. "I love you, too."

Chapter Twenty-Four

Tchaikovsky's "Waltz of the Flowers"

A few weeks later, the night of the full moon sees Blake gathered with Jay's pack at the condo. He may not officially be one of them yet, but they welcome his presence. The group lounges on the large couch, passing drinks and stories around. After his third glass of wine, Blake feels like his head might float away. Being around them brings a sense of comfort he doesn't think he's ever felt, and he grins sloppily as Lance regales them with a story about his time writing for one of the big movie studios and he met Sophia Lange and—he swears!—she kissed him in her trailer.

"She didn't," Blake says with wide eyes.

"Yeah, she's way hotter than you," Elliot retorts.

"I mean, it was on the cheek, but a kiss is a kiss."

"Whoa." It must be the alcohol because Blake can't imagine a world where Lance is embellishing. "She's super famous. That makes you half-famous."

Jay, who until that moment had some kind of sour look in his eyes that Blake is too tipsy to understand, arches an eyebrow at him. "How much have you had?"

Blake wiggles his half-empty glass. "Not enough."

"Here, let me see." Jay takes the glass and pours its remainder into his own.

"Hey, I was going to finish that!"

Lance snickers. "That's what he's afraid of."

"No vomiting on full moon nights. You've had plenty."

Blake sticks out his lower lip in a pout. "You gave me the drink in the first place."

"He's got you there," Elliot agrees.

"Don't worry." Lance leans over and pats Blake's knee. "Next time we're together, I'll hook you up. Ever tried absinthe?"

"Lance, no!" Kimiko laughs, a tinkling sound that fills Blake with warmth.

Lance pushes on. "In the VU they make a kind they call *La Fée du Sang*. It's strong enough to intoxicate a vampire. It's illegal over here, of course, but I have a trip planned in the fall. We could be travel buddies."

"You'll kill him!" Kimiko must have had a decent amount of wine herself because she laughs again.

"Nope. No way. No vampires." Jay shakes his head. "Don't even joke."

"They'd love him, though! Vampires really aren't bad. Nobody throws a party like a vampire."

"You're going to end up with fangs in your neck one day," Jay says. "They'll thrall you and you'll never come back."

Lance rolls his eyes. "You need to get over it, man. Stop living in the 1500s. You know they all drink synthetic stuff now. You'd think someone who can turn into a wolf would be more open-minded."

"I've never met a vampire," Blake muses. "I've seen pictures, though. They look like porcelain. Are they really pretty in real life?"

"Eh, not all of them. You've only seen the models. Most of them look like regular people. They like to pretend they're really mysterious and powerful, but most of them get along like everyone else. You could have met a vampire and never even known it."

"Oh." Blake considers it. Then his alcohol-addled brain insists he say, "We should go there. To the Vampire Union. I bet it'd be fun."

Jay wrinkles his nose. "I'm chalking that up to the wine. Sober Blake would know better."

Lance winks at him. "We'll talk later."

Blake nods enthusiastically, then immediately stops because it makes his head spin. He closes his eyes and plops back against the cushions. Beside him, Elliot scoots to give him more space.

"I think it might be bedtime," he hears Jay say.

The couch shifts around him as the pack stands. He peels an eye open to see his alpha downing the remains of the wine glass and dropping it to the table. Then the world tilts madly as Jay scoops him up in both arms.

"Let's go, Buttercup."

"I can walk, you know." Despite this, Blake wraps his arms around Jay's neck.

Lance chuckles. "Can you, Drunky McDrunkerson?"

"You're drunk, too!" Blake protests.

He blinks lazily. "What, me? Noooo. I am perfectly in my right mind. My left mind, though, that's another story."

"Come on, both of you." Elliot stretches and waves them to Jay's bedroom. He seems practically sober.

Blake yawns and allows Jay to carry him the rest of the way. His alpha is warmer than usual, and the heat feels nice. Jay's neck is so close, smelling like everything earthy and delightful. He kisses it.

"Hey, now, it's sleep time. No funny business." He can hear the smile in Jay's voice.

"I made that playlist for you," Blake says suddenly.

"Did you now?"

"Feels like ages ago I promised it." Blake wiggles enough to pull a thumb drive out of his pocket. "First song is Mendelssohn. 'Rondo Capriccioso'. Let me know what you think."

"Leave it on my nightstand. I'll listen tomorrow. When we're not all three sheets to the wind."

Blake leans back onto Jay's shoulder. "Made it just for you," he murmurs distantly.

"Thank you, love."

They change clothes in the bedroom and snuggle up under the sheets. He lays between Jay and Elliot, rolling over so Jay can spoon him. He blinks, eyes on Elliot's face.

"You look different without your glasses." Most definitely too drunk to know better, he touches the sides of Elliot's face.

Elliot smiles indulgently. "Good or bad?"

"Just different." He closes his eyes, hands dropping to the pillow. Warm here, surrounded by friends, by pack. "This is nice," he murmurs. "I could get used to this."

Kimiko says something, but he's too far in sleep's embrace to know what.

***

Sun peeks through the bedroom curtains and falls on Blake's face. He grumbles and stirs, scrunching his eyes. An arm snakes over his waist from behind, and he rolls toward it.

"Mornin'," he slurs, cracking an eye open. His head feels like someone stuffed it with cotton.

"Hng," grunts the voice in front of him. "Too early."

Not Jay. He blinks and sits up, bed sheets twisting. Beyond the not-Jay shape currently holding him, another emerges.

"Good morning, Blake, did you sleep well?" Kimiko stretches and shakes out her long hair. She seems unphased by the morning sleepies.

Groggily, Blake pulls the sheets back to reveal the rest of the pack curled around each other. Jay rolled over in the night, and his upper body is currently tangled with Lance, who groans in lackluster protest against the disturbance.

The arm around Blake's waist tugs a little, and he follows it to the source to find Elliot, face obscured in a pillow. He mutters something about alarms and tugs at Blake.

"Uhhh..." Blake looks to Kimiko for assistance.

"He wants you to lay back down," she interprets. "Elliot's something of a late sleeper."

Elliot responds with some kind of sound, but Blake is sure none of it is language. Another tug at his waist.

"Don't mind him," Kimiko says. "Join me for tea?" She steps off the bed without so much as shifting it, and Blake watches the shimmer of her satin nightgown as it clings to her. She leaves the bedroom without looking back.

Another garbled noise from Elliot pulls Blake to attention. He looks to the alpha and smiles. The man's hair is mussed for the first time since they met. No wonder Jay likes sleeping in a pack so much; it's warm and cozy, and everyone smells like home. Blake extricates himself from his spot, careful to place Elliot's arm back on the bed. The arm shifts and wraps around Jay in Blake's absence. He steps out and finds Kimiko sitting on the porch, steeping a pot of tea. A plate of scones sits on the table, ostensibly a morning snack from Charlie.

"It's nice to know one of the boys might be able handle an early morning," she says. He sits across from her. "Jay and Lance are heavy sleepers, but Elliot is the worst. You'd never know it to look at him but getting him out of bed is a Sisyphean task." She chuckles.

"He seems so efficient." Blake reaches for a mug. It has Greek letters on it and invokes the 'Summer of '26!'. Must be some relic from college. Kimiko pours him tea.

"Elliot's an excellent businessman. He's built his own store from the ground up. Unlike Jay or myself, he's not due an inheritance or high station. Everything he has, he's made. I respect him for that." She selects a scone from the dish. "Speaking of, what do you plan to do now? You don't strike me as the type of person to live off Jay's money."

Blake wrinkles his nose. "No thanks." He sips the tea. Jasmine and delicious. "I've got to find a job somewhere. My old place won't have me back, and I don't exactly have credentials for much else."

She hums. "Don't you?"

"What do you mean?"

She fixes him with a steady gaze. "Haven't you ever considered playing music for a living?"

He scoffs. "What? How would I?"

"I heard you at the treaty party. Your playing is excellent. And I know of many people who would gladly pay to listen to a beautiful omega play piano."

He rolls his eyes. "You're buttering me up."

"Not by much. I have a proposition, though." She takes a small bite of her scone and chews, waiting to see if Blake takes the bait.

He does. "What is that?"

She swallows and says, "You're aware that I own the premiere Oceanese health spa on the west coast?"

"Jay mentioned it."

"I could use a pianist like you. To play for clients. Nothing soothes the soul like music."

"Really?" He can hardly believe it. It's one of the only things he's ever dared to dream, and it's dropping right into his lap like some karmic gift.

"Really. You play like there's nothing else in the world. Wouldn't you want to do that every day?"

He jumps on it. "Of course! That would be amazing. You're serious?"

"I wouldn't bring it up otherwise. What do you say?" She watches him over the rim of her mug, not the stern, judgmental gaze she gave him when they first met, but an open, curious look.

Blake feels himself light up. "I'd love to! When can I start?"

She smiles and sips, pleased with herself. "Have Jay drop you off at the spa next Wednesday. I'll have everything ready."

He can't believe his luck. This pack, this life. Things are looking up in ways he never thought possible.

"Thank you, Kimiko. Jay's right. You're pretty amazing."

"I do what I can."

A voice interrupts them. "Is there an invite to this breakfast?" Lance doesn't wait for an answer before he sits down. He reaches across the table and snags a scone.

"Who said those were for you?" Kimiko sips her tea.

"Has anyone ever told you you're beautiful when you exist?" Lance quips. Kimiko cracks a smile. It seems like they play a game and Lance scored a point.

"How are our over-sleepers?"

"Should be up soon." Lance spreads butter over his pastry and grins. "I left my phone alarm on and put it on top of Jay's wardrobe."

Kimiko chortles at that. "Devilish," she compliments.

Sure enough, minutes later the remaining two alphas appear on the porch. Jay drops Lance's phone on the table and declares, "I'm never inviting you over again." He touches the top of Blake's head as way of good morning and takes the final seat. Blake looks to Elliot, who appears to be existing on another plane of reality. The man blinks in the morning sun but doesn't greet any of them. Blake worries he might be sleepwalking.

Charlie comes by with mugs and a coffee press. Blake opts to share tea with Kimiko, but the others take the brew. Blake watches in fascination as a barely cognizant Elliot lifts the mug to his lips and drinks until it's dry. Charlie refills the cup and leaves to grind more beans.

"Don't worry about him," Jay says, reaching for a scone. "Elliot's always like this."

"Yeah, he'll join us mortals after he's finished transcending the ether," Lance says, hand snapping forward like a rattlesnake to snatch the scone out from under Jay's fingers. Jay heaves a long-suffering sigh and changes trajectory to take a different one, only for Kimiko to thwart him with her own speedy grasp. Jay shoots Blake a look that says, *You see this shit?* Blake stifles a laugh.

After his second cup of coffee, Elliot transforms from a dead-eyed mute to a functioning member of society. He runs a hand through his hair to shift it (mostly) back into place and joins them at the table. Blake moves to sit in Jay's lap in order to accommodate the other alpha. "I'm going to have to get another chair," Jay muses.

"And I'll have to get new packmates if someone ever leaves that alarm on again," Elliot says. He reaches for a scone, and Lance makes to take it first. However, Elliot is prepared and counters the beta by grabbing his wrist. Lance chuckles and drops the baked good after a curdling look from Elliot. No one else dares make a move for it. Elliot takes a victory bite.

"Hey," Blake says, changing the topic. "What's that?" He points to Elliot's bare shoulder.

Elliot glances down and swallows his mouthful. "Tattoo," he replies, less than helpful. It seems even coffee is too weak a remedy for his early morning mood.

"He wants to see it, you misanthrope," Lance says while stirring sugar into his cup.

"Right. Of course." Elliot pulls down the tank top strap on his left side to reveal detailed art of a crane arcing over his shoulder. He turns enough for Blake to see the rest. A second crane covers his shoulder blade. It looks like they dance together.

"Wow," Blake admires. "It's beautiful. Did you guys get them together?" he motions to Jay.

"Hm? No, this was with Kimiko." Elliot replaces his clothing and starts on a third cup of coffee.

"We all have one," Lance adds, stretching and standing. He lifts his shirt hem to reveal a koi fish swimming near his hip. "Kimiko picks them out. Says they all suit us."

Blake looks to Jay, "Is that why you have yours?"

"Yeah." Jay extends his arm to look at the tattoo sleeve. "It's how she prefers to pack-bond."

"Tattoos are critical to Oceanese wolf culture," Kimiko explains. "They accompany any bond meant to last a lifetime." She finishes her tea and stands, turning her back to Blake. She shrugs off the straps of her gown, and it puddles on the floor. Down the length of her back grows an intricate tree. The trunk curves toward her left side while branches with red leaves spindle to the right. A nest of roots stretches out at the base of her spine. "I have a branch added for every member of my pack." She replaces her gown and sits. "One day you will have one as well, Blake."

He nods. "I'd like that."

The group settles in for breakfast, cracking jokes and enjoying each other's company. Even Elliot comes around eventually. Blake sighs and leans back against Jay. Everything in the moment is just right. The future can wait, whatever it brings. Jay's family, his own mother, all the drama they entail—none of it matters when he's here with these people. His pack, even if it isn't official. Jay shifts him to one side and kisses his cheek.

All he wants is this moment and the people in it. He leans his head against Jay's neck and feels the steady pulse there. Enjoys the earth smell mingled with his own sweetness.

This is exactly what he needs today.

About the author

Maxwell Kite loves everything bookish, from rom coms to horror. Diagnosed in adulthood with autism, they grew up fascinated by human relationships and interactions. Now, they want to write stories about dynamic, meaningful relationships, especially within the LGBTQ+ space.

For more Max, you can check out their YouTube page, @NormalNotIncluded, or their website, maxwellkite.com

9 798991 276405